WINTER IN TABRIZ

Also by Sheila Llewellyn

Walking Wounded

*

About the Author

Sheila Llewellyn was born in England, of Welsh heritage and now lives in Northern Ireland. She has been shortlisted for the Costa Short Story Award twice, as well as for the Bridport Short Story Prize, the Paul Torday Memorial Prize, the Seán Ó Faoláin Short Story Prize. She completed a PhD in Creative Writing at the Seamus Heaney Centre for Poetry in Belfast in 2016. Her writing has been published in various Irish anthologies of short stories and journals.

Sheila Llewellyn

WINTER IN TABRIZ

SCEPTRE

First published in Great Britain in 2021 by Sceptre
An Imprint of Hodder & Stoughton
An Hachette UK company

1

A CIP catalogue record for this title is available from the British Library

Hardback ISBN 9781473663145
Trade Paperback ISBN 9781473663152
eBook ISBN 9781473663138

Typeset in Sabon MT Std by Palimpsest Book Production Limited,
Falkirk, Stirlingshire

Printed and bound in Great Britain by Clays Ltd, Elcograf S.p.A.

Hodder & Stoughton policy is to use papers that are natural,
renewable and recyclable products and made from wood grown in
sustainable forests. The logging and manufacturing processes are expected
to conform to the environmental regulations of the country of origin.

Hodder & Stoughton Ltd
Carmelite House
50 Victoria Embankment
London EC4Y 0DZ

www.sceptrebooks.co.uk

For David, my brother, and for Liz, Dougie and Maggie

I have become old in grief for him;
but when you name Tabriz, all my youth returns.

Rumi

Hafiz, why art thou ever telling o'er
The tale of absence and of sorrow's night?
Knowest thou not that parting goes before
All meeting, and from darkness comes the light!

Hafez

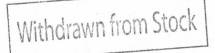

14 September 1978

... The FOREIGN AND COMMONWEALTH SECRETARY said that the situation in Iran was at present very unstable. It was difficult to foresee how events would develop, but he was inclined to believe that the armed forces would remain loyal to the Shah and would restore law and order and that the country, which had been through similar crises in the past, would return to stability. The opposition to the Shah came from a strange coalition of highly reactionary right-wing Muslim forces, groups of intellectuals and elements of the extreme left . . .

Extract from British Government Cabinet Papers

16 January 1979 (124 days later)

SHAH RAFT!

[THE SHAH HAS LEFT!]

Headline, Kayhan *newspaper, Tehran*

Part One

1977

The Problem with *Rose*

Kupfermühle, West Germany, 23 December 1983

The morning after the Winter Solstice, 23 December 1978, Arash the poet left our house in Tabriz and never came back. He was disappeared.

Five years ago to the day.

I raise the glass of schnapps to my reflection in the study window. *Here's to you, Damian. You've done it. Got through another anniversary. Sláinte.*

I've relived that night every Winter Solstice since Tabriz. What the four of us did, didn't do, said, didn't say during those last few weeks. Sifting through the fine detail of it, seeing if, this time, I could spot something I'd missed. Something that would provide some sort of answer. Who took him? Did he know they were coming for him? Did he deliberately go out to meet them in order to protect us, to deter them from coming into the house? Did he know he would not be coming back to us, to me?

We'd all stayed up, Arash and me, Anna and Reza, all of us determined to celebrate Yalda, the rebirth of the sun after the longest night, despite the curfew and the tension thick enough to suffocate you outside in the streets. We followed all the rituals. We ate symbolic Yalda food: chicken and eggplant stew to ward off the winter cold; watermelon slices and pomegranates, both specially chosen for their red flesh to fight off the dark; nuts and dried fruits for new beginnings. We played tapes of traditional *oud* and *tombak* music turned down low. We listened to Arash reciting poetry, mainly Hafez, of course – 'It's always Hafez at Yalda,' he said.

3

I added a ritual of my own – we drank the Stoli I'd acquired earlier from Ali the Vodka, no questions asked. At least, Anna and I drank it. Arash and Reza stuck to the Shiraz wine. All these things we did, we told ourselves, to celebrate the sun beating the tyranny of the dark. What we were really trying to do, if only for a few hours, was to forget what was happening outside. Whatever it was, it was something big, although nobody was admitting it. But at least now all the foreign embassies were saying it was serious. Most likely an attempted coup was the unofficial word on the street, and the latest from the British Council was a short phone message: *We advise you to stay indoors and wait for further instructions.* As if we had a choice.

At about seven in the morning, muffled in parkas, woolly hats and gloves, we went up on the roof and waited for the dawn. There were no signs of Yalda trappings on the flat Tabrizi rooftops – no bright torches, no bonfires, no squealing excited children, like last year: the curfew had put paid to that. Only piles of dirty snow waiting to be cleared. But Arash lit a fat candle, set it in the corner, went back down to the kitchen and fetched up tea glasses of silky-smooth hot chocolate drinks flavoured with cardamom.

We turned our faces to the sun as it lifted itself up through a smear of peach cloud into a pale turquoise wash of winter sky. Then Arash broke with his own tradition, reciting not Hafez but Sa'di, in Persian first, then the English translation I'd been working on with him, his voice cracking a little as the rays broke through:

'With all my pains, there is still the hope of recovery.
Like the eve of Yalda, there will finally be an end.'

I remember the tears stinging my eyes and blurring the sun. I remember the click of Reza's camera in the quiet after Arash's voice had faded.

4

Arash is the word, Reza is the eye. I remember Anna saying that to me once.

We went to our beds soon after, me and Arash staying up in our roof loft, Anna to her room off the living area, Reza making himself comfortable on the floor cushions with a blanket near to the still-warm *bokhari* in the corner.

We all slept till noon, or I thought we had. Then I woke up to find Arash had gone. He'd left a note in the kitchen. *Back at 10, lemons in fridge.* But he never came back.

He was disappeared. I've never spoken that thought out loud, never given it the permanence of the written word until now. It's as if I made a deal with myself, that I'd allow this thought head space but keep it locked in, and if I did, it would stay put, just a thought, unconfirmed, untested, a possibility, not a truth. If I kept it locked up in there long enough, then Arash would reappear. Or, rather, one day they would reappear him, let him go. I'd get the call to say he was alive and living in California, or Canada or somewhere in Europe, or wherever it is the Iranians who escaped ended up.

I've used my Parker pen and a student notepad to record all this, instead of my Olivetti. Maybe I thought handwriting in black ink rather than impersonal typescript would give what I was writing a certain gravitas, as if I was signing some sort of confession, or surrender. But it's come out in a schoolboy scribble with smudges and blots. And there's no relief. All this deliberate act of remembering has accomplished is to leave me fuzzy-headed and finding it hard to get my breath. I need air. I need not to think.

Through my study window, I see it's begun to snow again, a light dusting this time, not the thick blanket covering of this morning, which stuck and froze. It's two thirty in the afternoon, and the light is already beginning to fail. It'll be dark by four. The midwinter days are short up here on the Danish border.

I decide to go and check on the Whoopers. They'll be indulging in their last dabble and dip of the day. I wonder if I

5

should call for Frau Jensen on the way but then remember she's away for Christmas. I get kitted out in my parka and boots, and as I set off, I notice my neighbour's festive candle in her window across the way, and I'm back again to the four of us up on the Tabrizi rooftop, Arash lighting our candle and the taste of cardamom chocolate.

It takes all of five minutes for me to walk through the village. *The house is in Kupfermühle, a village in Germany, just about,* Jesper had said. *It's up in Schleswig-Holstein, right on the German–Danish border. The village is so small, you'll miss it if you blink.*

Great, I'd said. *The smaller, the more isolated, the better.* He was an old friend from my Oxford days, a German with Danish connections, and I'd met up with him by chance back in the October of 1982, when he was in Oxford for a conference. His parents had gone on a 'middle-age-crisis-round-the-world-trip-of-a-lifetime', as he'd put it, and although he was living in Hamburg, he was supposed to check on the house in Kupfermühle, some 160 kilometres further north. But he'd been offered a job in America.

Perfect. I was looking for a place to hole up for the winter; he was looking for a house-sitter. As an added incentive, Jesper said he knew there was a job going in January, teaching English at the teacher-training college in Flensburg, the nearest big town four miles away from Kupfermühle. His ex-girlfriend had had it, until they broke up a few weeks ago, then she'd left the college, and Jesper, at short notice. So they were looking for someone for January. *Your Oxford background should clinch it,* he'd said, and he'd been right.

I arrived in November, over a year ago, thinking I might stay until the summer, but here I am, going through my second winter. Not settled, exactly, but not drifting either, like I had been before I ended up here. It's the longest time I've stayed anywhere in the past five years.

Jesper was right about Kupfermühle, too. I'm not sure it even counts as a village – it's more the size of a hamlet. The eighteenth-century copper mill the village is named after still stands on the main street, though it's long been closed up. It's built in the Danish style, complete with witch's hat clock tower, and has a small courtyard, the Christiangang, at the back, sheltering a group of picturesque *nyborder*, single-storey Danish longhouses, with their distinctive yellow-painted walls. They once housed the mill workers, but now some are empty, or occupied by the older village residents, like Frau Jensen. Her house is on the other side of my hedge at the end of my back garden. She's the closest thing to a friend in the village I've got. It's Frau Jensen who got me interested in the Whoopers – she's passionate about swans.

And that's it, more or less, that's the whole village, except for the horseshoe cul-de-sac where my house is – one of ten, all except mine with immaculate lawns, immaculate cars, immaculate children, out on their bikes in the summer, their sledges in the winter. That smirky reference to my neighbours sounds mean-minded of me. It's just that I'm not used to this small-scale life built around families, children, routine and all the rest. But I've come to respect these hard-working Germans. They are part of the generation that came after the Second World War, Brecht's *nachgeborenen*, the ones who had to pick up the pieces, and God knows, they've learned a thing or two about surviving, rebuilding and leaving the past behind. It's soothing to live among them. Like an outsider looking in, as always, but I'm OK with that.

It's only fifteen minutes or so past the village to the track leading to the lake where the Whoopers are spending the winter. I call it a lake but it's more a stretch of river that widens out just enough for large swans to land and take off without fear of running out of runway. It has enough underwater vegetation to keep them happy too, now the ground is too frozen to forage in the stubble of Herr Becker's barley and turnip fields.

The snow has stopped by the time I get to the turn at the end of the track leading down to the water. I hear them before I see them. The female and the yearling sometimes wander off and the male calls to them to check where they are and the female calls back – a family call, a swimming call, not a flying call, a throaty harmonious *hu-hu*, not the *who-oop* two-note bugle call that sounds like an old-fashioned car horn when they're in flight.

When I get there, the family is together, the two adults either side of their yearling. His whitish-grey plumage has grown paler, and will be true white by spring when it's time to leave. The shadow of pink on his yellowing bill is also slowly fading. In a couple of months, he'll be an elegant young Whooper yellowneb, his bill yellow at the base across his featherline, from eye to eye, then darkening to black from midway to the tip. There is a sense of subtle but constant change about him that never fails to uplift me.

I watch them until they climb onto the bank and start their evening preen before winding themselves in for the night.

The light is ebbing now and I leave them to it. It'll be dark by the time I get home. On my way back, I plan my evening. Time for one of the frozen meals I've stocked up with for the holiday season. Then on to the new bottle of schnapps Frau Jensen left me for Christmas. At some point, I'll open Anna's parcel. She left Italy for a new job in Indonesia last week. Her annual 'Winter Solstice card of remembrance', as she calls it, arrived yesterday. Less solemn than previous years. Definitely more upbeat: *Hard to think it's five years. I've sent you a parcel of odds and ends – they're all from Iran. Could you hang on to them for me, please? Feel free to read what there is of the Tabrizi memoir (abandoned!). Don't be too hard on me, Damian. I think I've moved on: I hope you can too.*

I'm not sure why that last sentence irritates me so much. What does *moving on* mean exactly? That kind of hippie speak isn't the Anna I remember at all. I deliberately left the parcel unopened when it arrived this morning. No doubt my curiosity will get the better of me.

I settle into the desk chair with the schnapps to hand. It could be another long night. I'm surrounded by chaos of my own making. Spilled out on the sofa are the contents of Anna's parcel: her notebook with *Tabriz – A Memoir, 1977–9* scribbled on the front in her loopy writing; a cheap wooden marquetry box, decorated with a typical Persian geometric design, and three manilla envelopes, one thin, two more bulky. She's scrawled *Reza* on the front of them. At some point, I'll get around to opening them and reading her notebook, but not tonight.

Tipped out on my desk is another notebook, this one marbled grey and labelled *Berkeley 1977 to Tabriz 1979*, my own attempt to keep a journal, and a copy of Gertrude Bell's *Hafiz*. Baraheni's book of poems, its violent cover still able to shock me, pokes out from a foolscap folder.

There is a story wrapped up in all this paraphernalia. I need to confront it, to try to make sense of it. If I can tell the story, if only in some disordered, possibly misremembered way, maybe I can learn to live with the gaps, the not knowing.

I stumbled into Arash's life in 1977 and was forced to stumble out of it in 1979.

But I never let him go. Or maybe he never let me go.

I have to start somewhere. I need to go back to Berkeley, 1977.

I need to start with Shamlu and his cockroaches.

*

University of California, Berkeley, March 1977

The Man of Light Who Walked Into Shadow

Two young Iranians stopped me as I came out of the faculty building. They were dressed in the obligatory uniform of most

9

freshmen on campus: denim flares, oversized shirt collars, skinny-fit sweaters to fend off the cool breeze of an early spring day. I'd spotted one in the library earlier in the morning, reading a newspaper in Persian script.

'Great session on later today.' He spoke in good, heavily accented English and handed me a flyer from the bundle he was holding. 'Persian literature. The prof's latest work on Shamlu and his poetry. Caffè Med. Two o'clock.'

He obviously expected me to be well up on Shamlu.

I must have looked suitably blank, because he pointed at the blurry black-and-white photo of the man under the large print heading 'SHAMLU' with the details underneath:

'Ahmad Shamlu. One of Iran's most important contemporary poets.'

'*The* most important,' chipped in his friend.

'Should be good,' the first continued. 'The prof . . .' he paused, searching for the correct English '. . . he tells it like it is.' Pleased with the slang, he grinned at his friend, who grinned back, and they moved off to hand out the next flyer.

I made my way across Sproul Plaza to the Bear's Lair, the main campus café, and over a cup of black coffee, I took a closer look at the photo. It showed a strong face, and a striking head of thick hair. He was looking thoughtfully at an open book, presumably of his poetry.

Shamlu and twentieth-century Iranian poetry were virtually new to me. My Berkeley scholarship was for preliminary research into comparing various translations into English of Sufi poetry. I was working with one of the junior professors in the department, an Iranian ex-student of my Oxford supervisor. I'd been deep into the thirteenth century this past week, reading Arberry's *Mystical Poems of Rumi*, 1968 edition. The prof had suggested I might like to compare Arberry's translations with Nicholson's 1898 versions – 'Exactly seventy years between them, so it would be interesting to note the differences in the context of the translator and its effect on their work.' I wasn't sure I wanted to focus on Rumi: I found his poetry too full of certainties, as if he knew all the answers. Maybe it was me and my own context – I didn't even know the questions.

I'd picked up the Arberry translation from Moe's, a quirky bookshop on Telegraph Avenue, which still had a thriving 'Sufi section' started in the sixties. Rumi, Din Attar – they were all still very much 'in' here. So many of us were still looking East for answers.

The flyer, in English and Persian, gave a short biography of Shamlu, not just on his poetry to date but also his politics. Amazing, the number of times he'd been in prison under various regimes throughout his life for political activities: 1943, aged just sixteen, for distributing anti-occupation leaflets against the British and Americans occupying Iran during the Second World War; 1953, for being a member of the Iranian Communist Party, known in Iran as the Tudeh Party, after a failed coup kept the present Shah in power. Since then, although he'd left the Party by the mid-1950s, and his poetry had moved away from any specific political ideology, he'd been arrested or imprisoned seven more times under the Shah's regime.

He is a man of many labels, says the flyer. *Shamlu the rebel. Shamlu the revolutionary. Shamlu the humanist. Shamlu the poet* engagé. *Shamlu the poet as witness.*

I wasn't sure I liked the idea of my Persian poets so obviously *engagé*. One of my professors at Oxford had given a dazzling series of lectures on poetry and politics, and spoken of poets 'stung into song by some public event'. It had all sounded a bit too muscular to me. But the relationship the blurb suggested between the life Shamlu led and the poetry he wrote intrigued me.

I was finishing off my coffee and pondering whether to go to the session when I noticed a guy sitting in the booth across the aisle from me. He was reading from a small hard-backed book, cradling it in his left hand, his fingers curled around the top edge. I could make out Persian script on the front cover.

He was in side profile too, like the Shamlu photo, and had a similar thick head of hair, although less unruly. His was the dense black I was beginning to associate with Iranians, the kind that, in a certain light, glinted with streaks of gunmetal grey. He looked old enough to be a postgrad, maybe late twenties, like me.

As he read, he would slide his black horn-rims back up his nose when they slipped down, and I noticed how slender his fingers were. On the table next to his coffee cup lay another Shamlu flyer. He looked up suddenly, as if he'd become aware of being closely observed, and turning his head, caught my eye. He smiled slightly, then went back to his reading, those fingers cradling the book edge again.

I decided to go to the lecture. If nothing else, I liked the Caffè Med. Everyone called it the Med, and it was a well-known gathering place for artists and poets off-campus. I had no other plans for the afternoon and I was fed up with my own company. Maybe some muscular poetry was just what I needed.

*

'Cockroaches . . . stare at . . . your corpse . . . with suspicion.'

The prof said the words out loud as he chalked them across the makeshift blackboard propped up on an easel. Then he turned back to us and added, 'This English translation is for the benefit of any non-Persian speakers here with us today.' He had spent the last twenty minutes filling in Shamlu's background and giving us examples of his poetry to date.

'The line is from "Song of the Man of Light Who Walked Into Shadow",' he continued. 'It's not one of his best, or his most recent, it's 1970, but it's interesting. It shows how he deals with the tension of wanting to focus on a political point, but how he also writes poetry that stands up in its own right as innovative and creative in its use of language.'

I was sitting at the back and glanced round at the group

12

crammed into the performance space in the corner of the Med. Half of the audience looked like they could be Iranian, mostly men, a few women dotted around. I spotted my guy from the Bear's Lair, sitting at the end of the third row. The light from the high side window was doing its gunmetal trick on his hair, and I followed the glint on the tiny curls resting along the top of his collar.

The prof spoke with a quiet intensity; he would occasionally pause, and look out to the middle distance, smiling faintly like he was doing now. Then he began to write on the blackboard again. 'And this is the Persian version of the same line, in Latin script.'

As he wrote, he recited the line in Persian, in a flat tone. Then he underlined the first Persian word and said, 'OK, so we have this Persian word *kharkhaki,* and its English translation, "cock-roaches".'

He drew a second line under *kharkhaki.* 'Any comments on this word?'

There was a slight pause, the kind there tends to be when an audience is first asked to speak up. Then someone on the front row said, 'You don't hear that word for "cockroach" in Persian very often.'

I recognised the voice and craned my neck to check. It was my 'tell it like it is' freshman, eager as ever, looking up at the prof. As I sat back, I became aware of the person sitting next to me doodling on his notepad. I sneaked a sideways look at him, and saw that he was an older man, maybe fortyish, Ivy League haircut, neatly dressed in a brown suede jacket. Then I realised he wasn't doodling: he was drawing the layout of the seating. The prof was already marked as a big X at the front of three rows of little boxes representing the seats. The man drew an X in the freshman's box.

'Indeed, you don't hear this word often,' the prof was saying. 'It's a rare beast, this particular cockroach.' He split the word into two: <u>khar</u> and <u>khaki</u>.

'Some of you will notice that this particular word is actually made up of two Persian words, not often used at all – *khar* meaning "donkey" or "ass", and *khaki* meaning "earth". So we have cockroaches who are also donkeys and who are of the earth or earth-coloured.' He was wearing his middle-distance smile again. 'We'll come back to that.'

He pointed to the English word – 'suspicion' – then its Persian translation, *su'-e zann*.

'What about this?'He raised his eyebrows in a question and ranged his gaze round the group. 'Can you think of any connotations for the word *su'-e zann* here?'

There was a longer pause this time. The Iranians in the audience shuffled in their seats.

My note-taker had slipped his pen into the top spring of his notepad, and was watching the room intently. He sat with his hands linked across his notes, the fingers intertwined and continuously making small movements stretching up, feeling the air this way and that, then closing down to fold back into each other.

The prof recited the line in Persian again, with more life and rhythm, then pointed at *kharkhaki*. 'So, we have donkeys who are earth-coloured – wearing earth-coloured clothing, reminding us of khaki uniforms, perhaps? – being *suspicious*,' – he underlined *su'-e zann*, – 'of this corpse.'

He paused, then said, 'So who might these donkeys be?'

I sensed a movement, a sort of ragged unease spreading through the Iranians.

This time it was a woman who spoke, her voice a little quieter, more wavery than the freshman's. She was in the middle of the second row, a bright blue silk scarf around her neck.

'The word "suspicion", I mean the Persian word for it, *su'-e zann*, it reminds me of . . . even the sound of it . . . *su'-e zann* . . . sounds a little like *Sazeman-e* . . .' she gave a small nervous cough '. . . and that reminds me of SAVAK, the police.'

The Iranians shuffled again, some sitting rigidly upright in their seats, others dropping their heads. It was as if the very mention of SAVAK tapped into a shared meaning for most of the audience, a meaning deeply felt that passed around them, like some subliminal anxiety-inducing code.

The prof nodded. 'Good. So we have this seemingly simple sentence, which, by the way, *could* be taken literally, of course – "Is the body really dead? Can the cockroaches, the insects, now go to work?" But in the Iranian context, this sentence really refers to SAVAK. For the sake of non-Iranians, who may not be fully aware, SAVAK are the secret police in Iran. SAVAK is an abbreviation—' He broke off here and scribbled Persian words in Latin script on the board. 'Sazeman-e Ettela'at va Amniyat-e Keshvar – literally translated as Organisation for Intelligence and Security of the Country.'

He underlined Sazeman-e. 'I'd say Shamlu has been quite clever here – the S in SAVAK stands for Sazeman-e, as you just said, and as you also said, the sound of the word has more than an echo of *su'-e zann* – "suspicion".' He was sounding quite animated now. 'So, I'd suggest that this line is actually Shamlu saying that SAVAK are the donkeys, dressed in khaki uniforms, who are suspicious of the corpse, checking to make sure the corpse is really dead, the corpse being, of course, any member of the intelligentsia: our writers, poets, journalists, whom the government consider to be anti-government or anti-Shah, or both.'

The audience seemed to anticipate that he was about to say something even more significant. The tension in the room among the Iranians was palpable.

'By implication, then,' the prof added, 'it's widely assumed that Shamlu has a particular writer in mind in this poem. It's been suggested he's specifically accusing SAVAK of murdering Al-e Ahmad. For those of you who may not know, he was one of Iran's most accomplished intellectuals, a writer and journalist, who met his death in very mysterious circumstances.'

He scanned the room again, then continued, a note of determination in his voice now.

'He wrote a highly influential book in 1962, suggesting that Iran was becoming too influenced by the West, to the detriment of its own economy and its culture, its very soul – a loose translation of what he called this is "Westoxification".' The prof paused, then said quietly, 'He was poisoned, in 1969, by SAVAK, it is said. Hence this poem of Shamlu's in 1970.'

There was a slight tremor in his voice. 'I make that assertion concerning the manner of his death, here, in this room, in this country, and I don't fear for my life. Members of the intelligentsia in my own country are not so fortunate.'

He cleared his throat. 'And that is an example of how Shamlu makes a political point, but he does this in poetry that uses clever metaphor, multiple possible meanings, juxtaposition of unusual words and so on.'

His voice took on a more impersonal lecturing style. 'He does things with the Persian language that none of his contemporaries have done. I'd go so far as to say that no one else since Hafez in the fourteenth century has done it.'

I notice my guy nodding at this. Good, I think. He likes Hafez too.

The prof finished with a flourish. 'Rosenburg wrote in the *Tradition of the New* that the serious enterprise of poetry is using language anew – "The acid of poetry burns each word away from its own links."'

He repeated the quote quietly to himself, as if he were thinking it through for the first time, then carried on: 'I would suggest that Shamlu's serious enterprise is two-fold – to be still *engagé* with politics, that is to be the poet as witness, but first and foremost to be a poet, a poet who uses language anew.'

The note-taker had been scribbling furiously since SAVAK had been mentioned. He finished off by making triple crosses above the prof's box and placing a cross in the box of the woman with the blue scarf.

The prof poured a glass of water from the carafe on the table and sipped slowly, allowing the moment to sit with the group.

Then he began to gather up his notes. 'Thank you, ladies and gentlemen,' he said. 'It has been a privilege to share even just a little of Shamlu with you.' He bowed his head. The applause was soft but prolonged until the prof brought it to a close, and headed for the Med exit, closely followed by the young freshman. There was a quiet buzz as people stood up and slowly moved off.

The note-taker made no move to go. He sat staring at faces as the others made their way out and, in the end, I had to squeeze past him.

I saw my guy sitting at a table in the main bar of the Med, sipping a glass of tea, with a slice of lemon floating in it, and reading his book. Here goes, I thought, and sat down opposite him, smiling as he looked up.

'I saw you at the lecture,' I said, and introduced myself.

'I'm Arash.' He smiled back, took off his glasses and shook my hand.

*

Kupfermühle, 23 December 1983

Meeting Arash was as simple as that. One of those unexpected life-changing sequences of events: a chance encounter on campus with a young Iranian handing out flyers, a cup of coffee in a booth across the aisle from an interesting-looking guy, and an impulsive decision to follow him to a lecture and introduce myself.

I'd convinced myself I was doing OK but, in truth, I was miserable and lonely until I met Arash. I'd been at Berkeley since January, and although I liked the research work, I'd not connected with many people. My fault not theirs: the Americans have this genuinely warm way of welcoming you into their circle, particularly academics. But I'd been at a low ebb when I'd applied for the exchange, back in Oxford, not sure whether academia was right for me – it seemed so mapped out, a life of narrowing in, rather than broadening out. So, as usual, I was putting off making a decision about what I really wanted to do.

I was also pretty disillusioned with the way my personal life was going. Or not going, more like. I'd spent the first couple of years of my Oxford undergraduate life coming to terms with my sexuality. I'd been confused since I was sixteen about what I was beginning to feel for other boys but, like most others of my age going through the same thing, I was guilt-ridden and terrified about trying out my feelings, and even more terrified about being found out. I'd be physically sick some days getting home from school, after listening to some of the boys in the PE changing rooms, sharing jokes about poofters and ponces and queers, although I'd laughed when they laughed. I was instinctively savvy enough to know that at school the best way to survive for someone like me was to be on the edge of groups, seen to be with them, rather than not in them at all.

And I was an academic achiever. That was my saving grace. I went to a direct grant school in Manchester, and schools like mine prided themselves on their pupils excelling at something. To excel was the thing. It didn't matter what in – cricket, rugby, chess, debating society, music or, in my case, intellectual prowess. The pressure was always on, particularly for a scholarship boy like me. So I became known as a swot. A willing swot. I spent most of my life outside school, Saturdays included, in Manchester Central Reference Library – it had a brilliant repertory theatre down in the basement, so while other boys were indulging their adolescent hormones at Saturday all-nighters in the discos in the centre of Manchester, I would spend the day reading in the Central Ref, then get a ticket for whatever play was on in the evening. Arthur Miller, Seán O'Casey, Shakespeare, I soaked them all up. A day in the library reading obscure books brought up from the stacks never felt like studying to me. And it paid off. I took my O levels a year early, nine top grades, and was earmarked for Oxford. Because

I was studious, I got away with not showing much of an interest in girls – in school, it was generally accepted that swots never had much success with them anyway. At home, my mother was positively pleased – girls were a dangerous distraction in her book – while my father could take a quiet pride in casually mentioning my academic success among his engineering colleagues.

So, Oxford in 1968 was a liberal education for me in every sense. It gave me the freedom to find out who I really was, sexually at least. And I took full advantage of it. Sex in all its Oxford variations: first-time sex – furtive in another first year's room, both of us turned on by reading James Baldwin, and Great Tom bonging away in the background – moving on through experimental, rough, pot-enhanced, sometimes satisfying and, very occasionally, tender. But I still had to be cautious. For my first three years as a student, sex with other men for me was still illegal: the 1967 Sexual Offences Act had legalised homosexuality, but only between consenting male adults both aged twenty-one or over and in private. So, technically, several of my fellow postgrad and lecturer partners during my first-degree period at Oxford could have been done for gross indecency, which undoubtedly added a certain risky element to it.

My reaching twenty-one took the risk factor down, but didn't get rid of it entirely. It might now be legal for me and my partners, but the general population, not to mention elements of the police force, could be slow at accepting something they considered at best an unfortunate affliction and at worst disgusting. Being exposed by others as gay wasn't so unusual, after 1967, but the effects could still be catastrophic for your personal and professional life. So, during the five years I took to do the PhD, I was one of the many who still kept a discreet profile among the gay community, in Oxford at least.

Not that I avoided complicated situations. Last year I'd got myself involved with one of the dons at my college, a married man, who was in total denial of his sexuality, and was using me as some sort of experiment, not the first time he'd done that with students, I later found out. It was messy, vindictive in the end, and I was glad to get out of it and away.

The Berkeley post was as good an escape route as any. It was only for six months and I jumped at it. The don had left me wary of encounters, even the quick relief of a one-time-only-pick-up-fuck variety. So I figured a few months of celibacy might not be a bad idea. And that was what I did. I tended to work late on campus, eat a meal on the way home and laze about in the evenings, reading or watching the tiny portable TV my landlady had offered me. Not exactly living the gay Bay life.

*

Kupfermühle, Christmas Day

Came round earlier to squeals outside and the ding-dings of bicycle bells. The cul-de-sac kids are out in force this morning with their Christmas presents, their collective sound effects jangling in my head, just behind my eyes, like a set of malicious tuning forks.

Feeling rough. Not surprising. Once I started to write, a couple of days ago, I didn't stop until about three in the morning. Slept in until after lunchtime, had a shower, wrote some more till about 9 p.m. Rustled up some tinned tuna and potato salad, and successfully avoided the rest of Christmas Eve with another bottle of schnapps. I'm hoping to do the same today.

I decide to leave the kids to it and move into the kitchen – it's at the back of the house, not overlooked and quiet. I make myself a pot of good coffee, and force down a slice of bread and honey to settle my stomach while I read through what I've written so far.

I never realised before how much my life was one of extremes until I met Arash. Extremes of crippling insecurity and anxiety as an adolescent, extremes of application to academic study to the detriment of almost anything else going on around me, extremes of sexual behaviour at Oxford, bouncing from one experimental experience to another, keeping on the move, finding out about my sexuality – OK, that was no bad thing – but not really finding out about what else I was or could be. Then doing the exact opposite at Berkeley. I mean, the Berkeley gay scene was lively, and San Francisco, the gay centre of the world, was only half an hour away. So, that whole self-imposed celibacy bit – what the fuck was that about? Underneath all my dismissive bravado about 'the gay Bay life', I was pathetically lonely: that was what it was about. So I think I can rightly say I was a mess until I met Arash, and what I've just read about that time proves it.

When I started this, I hadn't meant to go back so far. I'd meant to stick with life after meeting Arash, with the road to Tabriz, and what happened when I got there. That's the problem meddling with memory: it's like being on an archaeological dig. There's always another layer underneath the one you think you're excavating. It's left me feeling disoriented. But at least the hangover has gone.

I fix myself a frozen-chicken dinner, about the nearest I'll get to turkey and all the trimmings, then ring my parents to wish them Merry Christmas and half wished I hadn't. I tell a white lie to my mother, so she won't fret, saying I'd been across to my neighbour's for Christmas lunch. Then my father succeeds in choking me up, by ending the call with 'Look after yourself, son. We've transferred some money to your account. Your mother says to buy yourself one of those Scandinavian duvets to keep you warm over there, but I said a bottle or two of Bushmills would do the same thing and still leave you enough for a good supply of books to read while you're downing it.'

It isn't the cheque, or the chuckle as he passes on my mother's instructions that gets to me, it's the way he says 'son' – sort of gruff but still managing to sound caring. Not for the first time, as I put the phone down, I wonder if I'm a disappointment to him, but if I am, I know he'd never show it. When I was really bad, after I got home from Tabriz in 1979 and fell to pieces, he was there in his quiet way, not asking any questions. He's always been there.

I don't want to go back to that time, the time immediately after Tabriz, not tonight, that's for sure, maybe not ever. In fact, I've had enough for tonight of my own memories about anything.

I need to take a break from myself.

Over the first schnapps of the evening, I start to read the introductory section of Anna's memoir/journal, whatever it is. I've got over my irritation with her 'I've moved on, I hope you can too' comment. I've worked out that the reason it annoyed me so much is nothing to do with the hippie style. It's because I'm envious. If she means she's managed to come to terms with what happened, then I believe her and I wish I could, but I can't. Not yet.

She didn't get to Tabriz until March 1978, six months or so after me, but her reasons for finding herself there have a surprising resonance with mine. Strange, both of us starting off in Oxford at roughly the same time, Anna two years before me, and then the two of us ending up in Tabriz sharing the same house. Not exactly the Oxford glittering-prize career path expected of either of us. And by the sound of it, it was a similar random set of choices to mine that led her there.

It's good to read her words, hear her voice. Just let her speak for herself. See things from inside her head, rather than from inside mine.

*

Anna

Oxford, June 1976–June 1977

One to treasure

I spent the last half of 1976 in free-fall. My father came home from Zambia to visit in late April, staying longer this time to celebrate my graduation. He loved Zambia and he loved his job. He was a good doctor and mentor of newly qualified Zambian doctors, so was even more in demand since the country's independence. He said he'd like to see out the rest of his days there, if they'd let him. But he always 'came home' to Oxford on leave in the spring. He was brought up here, went to university here, it was the place he knew best, although he'd never really lived here since his early thirties.

We rented our usual cottage in Rhossili in mid-June. It was already revving up to be one of the hottest summers on record, although we didn't know it then. We walked along the cliffs, had days out motoring round the Gower, ate at local pubs, where he introduced me to anyone who'd listen as 'my daughter, just got her doctorate from Oxford'.

Being in Rhossili again reminded me of the years at boarding school back in England, my father coming home on long leave and taking me away for our Gower summer holidays. It was just the two of us by then – my mother had died when I was thirteen. He never remarried, although there was a steady flow of women friends, kept at a discreet distance, and they never came on holiday with us.

So we had this wonderful holiday – 'One to treasure,' he said.

The last week of June, a fortnight before he was due to go back to Zambia, he had a massive coronary, sitting in the back garden. I was out doing the shopping, and when I got back, I found him. He'd set up his easel under the shade of the clematis arch and there was the beginnings of a watercolour of a branch of the clematis. He'd rejuvenated the plant on his last home leave, and it had rewarded him this year with a glorious constellation of starry lilac flowers. It was his favourite place.

He was slumped slightly forward on the kitchen chair, his chin on his chest, his brush on the floor at his side. I shook him gently, knowing something was wrong, but willing him to be asleep. He was dead. He had his battered cream Panama on, the sort you could roll up and pack. I couldn't bear thinking he'd died alone.

The next few months were a blur. The funeral, the distant relatives from America, the colleagues from Zambia, who came later, the tying up of loose ends. He'd left me the house, which meant I didn't have to worry for money or rush to get a job. The irony of it. A twenty-eight-year-old woman with a PhD from Oxford, reasonably well off, no family commitments, free to go anywhere, do anything within reason, and all I wanted to do was crawl into bed and stay there. Which I did, on and off, for the rest of the year.

I missed the hottest summer on record. Missed the great drought. Stumbled through autumn. Stayed with Charlie over Christmas and New Year. As usual, he was there when I needed a shoulder to cry on, which was often. We've achieved the near impossible, Charlie and I – long term ex-lovers who've managed to stay friends. Had first-time sex together, helped each other work out how to survive in the Oxford hothouse, stayed as a couple for three years. But we were too comfortable with life, with each other – even the sex ended up feeling too comfortable. I had no idea what kind of life I wanted, but what I had with Charlie wasn't it. As it happens, he felt the same about us. We slowly drifted apart. He was three years older than me, studying medicine, so we graduated the same year, and Charlie went off travelling. I stayed in Oxford, taking what turned out to be a slow route to a PhD, but I got there in the end. I was lucky, more than lucky, when I was a postgrad student, as I lived in the family house, so didn't have accommodation costs, and took on casual English teaching work to get by. Charlie would come back from time to time, stressed out, stay a while with me, on a strictly platonic basis, then wander off again.

We've both had other relationships, none permanent. He's an only child too, so I think maybe we've ended up with a sister–brother thing. I could have hidden myself away longer with him, that Christmas, but he was getting ready to go to Tanzania to work with UNICEF in mid-February, and I didn't want to drag him down with my misery. So he went off to Africa, and I moved back home and got through the rest of February and March. That's the best you could say. I got through it, day by day, week by week. It still felt like I was carrying a small block of concrete, immovable in the pit of my stomach, and I would occasionally dissolve into tears without knowing why, or be gripped by a terrible rage, which was worse than the tears.

The house was full of my father. I'd gone through a phase of sensing him being there, a presence who had just left the room I went into, like the kitchen or the sitting room. Or the feeling that he'd just turned the corner on the landing as I started up from the bottom of the stairs. Most upsetting of all, I'd actually experienced a full-figure sighting of him in the garden on a chilly spring day in March, incongruously dressed in the summer garb I'd last seen him alive in, complete with Panama, enjoying the early daffodils. I knew that was just wishful conjuring up on my part. The spirits may be there, but it's you who make them visible by your sheer wanting them to come back to you. That phase passed, but the house still hung on to him – the smell of peppermints on the shelf near his reading chair, its stuffing hanging out of the bottom, his walking shoes on the boot rack in the back kitchen, with traces of Rhossili sand from our last holiday still visible round the rims and patterned perforations of the broguing.

I knew this wasn't healthy, living with a spirit mainly of my own making, but wasn't sure what to do about it. I thought of trying to make a move, maybe leave Oxford altogether, just for a while, go travelling, like Charlie. But I couldn't do it. Whenever I thought seriously about it, I'd get that awful bereft feeling, the weight of loss that pulls you down. I thought, in the distorted, unfathomable way grief takes you, that if I left, I'd be leaving my father behind. I couldn't acknowledge to myself that he was the one who'd left me, by dying. So I'd put off making any decisions.

Then, by late April, I slowly began to get a little of my energy back. Maybe it was the realisation that it had been a year since my father had come home for the last time. Maybe I was just so weary of the paralysing grief that the choice was to sink down and not come up again or to do something about it. Whatever it was, I began to make small moves, each one wrung out of me. His Panama was still hanging on the coat-stand in the hallway, so I put it out of sight in his wardrobe and felt guilty but forced myself to leave it there. I shifted his books and papers off the desk in the front room so there was now plenty of room for mine, and I packed up all his clothes and shoes, including the brogues, and carted them off to Oxfam. All the usual heartbreaking things you do when you feel strong enough.

Then I moved on to bigger changes, and once I got going it was like I couldn't stop. I had someone in to redecorate the sitting room, and got rid of the reading chair, which my father had been meaning to do but never got round to – doing that reduced me to tears, but I did it. I replaced the fifties sofa and chairs with some good second-hand stuff, including a reuphol-stered chesterfield and two colonial-style wood and rattan chairs. It looked like a totally new sitting room, and at first I felt as if I'd betrayed my father, but I found myself gravitating to the chesterfield more and more. I'd made the room my space and that eventually felt OK. I realised my father was still there, but not so much as an actual bodily presence, more as part of the weft and weave of the house's history, its memories, and that was a little easier.

I still felt rudderless, wondering what to do with the rest of my life. Then, in mid-May, my old professor in the Education Department rang me and asked me to call in. She'd supervised my PhD in curriculum design for Teaching English as a Foreign Language, and we'd survived the experience to become friends. She'd got funding for some research and was looking for research fellows. It was a specific project to look at a new series of textbooks to teach English for Medical Science to overseas student doctors. English for Specific Purposes, or ESP, such as English for Medical Science, English for Engineering and so on, was the in-thing, the new approach. It was an attractive concept, as it focused on the type of English supposedly found in various fields of academic study. But did it really exist? Or was it little more than a marketing ploy to attract would-be students who thought they'd be getting targeted language teaching that would help them in their specific subjects? And if such specific English did exist, how could you evaluate the effectiveness of textbooks based on the approach?

One of the research posts was mine if I wanted it. The initial ground work would take place in Oxford, start in June and last for six months, but there would be the possibility later of working in other centres of research dotted around the world, using the ESP textbooks. The professor suggested I take a week or so to think about it.

In the meantime, there was also a temporary job going, teaching on the English for overseas students summer school starting in July. I guess my professor could sense I was still struggling personally, because she also broached the subject of my taking in student lodgers for the various summer schools coming up. It would be extra income, she suggested, only for three months or so, but more importantly, it would be company and fun. I needed a bit of fun, she said. I told her I'd think about that, too.

I wasn't keen at first. I'd never had to share a house or accommodation before, apart from when my father was home, of course; Charlie and I had lived more separately than together. But the more I thought about it, the more sharing the house seemed a good idea. I liked the changes I'd made around the place, but I was still rattling around in it like a pea in a bucket.

So I agreed to the lodger idea. It wasn't until I was in the student accommodation office filling in the forms that I realised I'd taken a major decision about my life, and about the house, which I still thought of as my father's, rather than mine, without discussing it with him first. It was slowly dawning on me that I was technically an orphan, with no immediate family around me. It sounded so Dickensian, and slightly ridiculous at my age, seeing myself as an orphan, but I sometimes did feel as abandoned as a child must do when it finds itself adrift from its parent in a supermarket.

I went on a bit of a downer towards the end of June, struggling with the first anniversary of last year's holiday in Wales, and of finding my father dead in the garden. Not that it took anniversaries to send me off track. I could be emotionally ambushed any time, any place, by the most surprising things, even after the house change-round. But this time I didn't fight the sadness. I told myself it would pass. And it did. And I began to look forward to July and teaching on the summer school, although it still felt strange to think of myself as an Oxford landlady. Then again, it was an improvement on thinking of myself as an orphan.

*

Kupfermühle, Boxing Day

Anna never said much about why she had come to be in Tabriz. She would always answer the usual Tabrizi question that everyone asked everyone else in the prerequisite ironic tone, 'How did you end up here?' with a dry 'Just lucky, I guess', but there was sadness too, if you listened carefully. She had a double photo frame on her bedside table, one side with her father, at least I assumed it was him, mid-fiftyish, slight build, wearing a Panama hat that had seen better days and sipping a beer, sitting in a garden chair somewhere tropical, next to a bed of white canna lilies. But she rarely spoke of him. The other side was a young guy, rangy-looking, dark-haired, in jeans and a T-shirt with a faded yellow smiley face on it, standing outside a simple white-painted chalet bungalow, with a queue of African women, babies wrapped in *kangas* on their backs. This must have been Charlie, although Anna never mentioned him either. The two men looked similar to each other, but a generation apart. Not so much a physical resemblance, although they were roughly the same build, it was more the looks on their faces, the way they held themselves, the sense of them being in harmony with their environment and comfortable with themselves, doing what they wanted to do.

I wondered if Anna realised this about them too, and if part of her restlessness had to do with her wanting to feel like that. If so, that wasn't too dissimilar to what I was going through at roughly the same time. Each of us was edging our way towards Tabriz without knowing it, Anna in Oxford, grappling with grief, and me with Arash in Berkeley, trying to work out how to handle the first grown-up relationship of my life that actually meant something to me.

*

Berkeley, March–June 1977

Kind of Blue

I had a room on Chilton Street, about five blocks away from campus, so I could walk to college every day through Sather Gate. The landlady, Mrs Miller, was a Berkeley graduate, like her father before her, and the house had been handed down through three generations. It was a lovely old street, with comfortable sprawling houses, most of them still family homes, some letting student rooms. The Miller house had three student rooms, two of them the bedrooms of children long flown the nest. The other was mine, the attic floor, up a couple of stairs from the top landing. It was done out in white and had a small skylight. I would lie on the bed and feel like I was drifting along, cocooned in a cloud, observed by a square blue eye that misted over from time to time with February rain.

The top landing had two more small rooms off it – one a bathroom with a shower, so it was like having my own miniature split-level apartment, the other a box room, converted to a guest room. Mrs Miller had done that out too, and squeezed in a single bed, somewhere for family or friends of her lodgers to stay. The 'overnighter', she called it, and charged a nominal amount for it, which she often forgot to ask for.

She might be a bit soft with money, but she was shrewd with people, Mrs Miller.

I liked her, and I sensed she took to me. She'd sussed out right away that I was gay. I think certain older women must have gay radar and, if they don't have a problem with it, I've always found them reassuring. Not too difficult to see they were mother substitutes, my landladies. There was no way I'd ever come out to my parents: my mother would have headed for the chapel with her rosaries and wallowed ever after in a miasma of guilt, my father would pretend he hadn't heard me so he wouldn't have to deal with it.

Mrs Miller would sometimes invite me for coffee when I got back in the evening and we'd sit at her kitchen table. She'd tell me about the riots and demos on the Berkeley campus in the sixties. The student freedom-of-speech riots, the anti-Vietnam demos – 'My daughter was tear-gassed from a helicopter,' she'd said, and sounded proud of it.

After I met Arash, I mentioned him to her on one of our coffee get-togethers. 'He's a student friend of mine, Persian, he's helping me with my research, but he's in a grim place on

Telegraph Avenue. I wondered if he could come and stay in the overnighter on the odd occasion.'

She gave me a long look, but all she said was 'Fine – it's pretty private up there.'

A week after the Shamlu lecture, Arash stayed over on the Friday, supposedly in the 'overnighter', but actually in my bed. The sex was surprisingly hesitant, for me at least. Sex and not much else was all I'd wanted out of relationships, and all I'd got. I knew from the start, though, that I wanted something more with Arash. But I didn't want to come across as needy, so I found myself holding back and I sensed he did the same, for whatever reason.

On that first Saturday morning, we lazed in bed, listening to Miles Davis, both of us lost in *Kind of Blue*. Then more sex – less hesitant – followed by coffee, a wander round the campus while it was still quiet, and brunch at the Med. Back to my room. More Miles Davis. More bed, but by this time feeling easy enough with each other just to lie close, skin to skin. One thing was for sure, for me at least, this was more than just sex.

Gradually, he told me a little about his life. He was from Tabriz, the capital city of Azerbaijan province in the north-west of Iran. Once, he brought me a map and pointed out where Tabriz was. 'Azerbaijan is this province up here, shaped like a cat's head,' he said, tracing his finger round the border outline of the area. 'See its pointed ears sticking up? This one here, to the west, next to Turkey, and the other here on the eastern side, near to Russia and the Caspian Sea.'

Tabriz, he said, pointing to the name on the map, lay between two mountain ranges in a fertile valley. He and his brother Reza had been brought up by an uncle, after first their mother, then their father had died. He'd done Persian literature at university in Tabriz, then one semester in Tehran, on library services, then back to Tabriz to a part-time job as a librarian in the university library. He had another part-time job in the small library at the American Consulate, which helped him improve his English, so he was able to get a postgrad study place at Berkeley in library information services.

He choked up when he spoke of home. At first I thought it was homesickness, and it was, partly at least, but it wasn't till later I found out there was more behind the emotion than he let on.

I told him a little about me, an edited version of my Oxford years of flailing around, in and out of unsuitable relationships. He told me he'd had two encounters with women – 'Not the kind you were expected to marry,' he'd said matter-of-factly, but chose not to elaborate and I didn't ask. The sex with them had been disastrous, except that the experiences confirmed his sexuality, something he'd been aware of since adolescence, but had fought. After that, he'd had only one serious relationship, with a university friend in Tehran, but had had to keep it secret, it being Iran and totally illegal. It had ended when the man got married. Seems like something else we have in common, I said, and told him about my Oxford don.

He'd noticed my accent, but couldn't place it, and asked me whereabouts in England I came from. As usual, like most foreigners I'd met, he knew about Manchester from the ubiquitous fame of Manchester United. I explained he could probably hear a mixture of Mancunian vowels, Northern Irish rhythms and Oxford drawl, depending on what mood I was in. I told him I had Irish parents, Northern Irish to be precise, although we'd moved across to Manchester when I was eight, for my father's job. The Northern Irish accent was of the faint residual kind that children in families who move from their homeland seem to hang on to because it's what they still hear at home. It had been hijacked by the Mancunian vowels when I'd gone to grammar school, then further polished away at Oxford, but sometimes there was still a trace, and I hadn't tried to mask it in Berkeley. I'd noticed that an Irish accent with a Catholic Christian name went down well here, with the Troubles in full flow.

I talked about my parents' 'mixed marriage', which intrigued him, and surprised me, it was something I'd never spoken of with anyone before. My mother was a Catholic, and my father technically a Protestant, but had never gone near a church for his own spiritual purposes that I knew of. And I also told him that, although they'd never said so directly, I thought they'd had a rough time of it back in late forties Northern Ireland when they'd got together. It had led to a split in their families, which was never talked about. There were no trips home for family reunions, apart from one in 1973, for my grandmother's funeral, but that was just my mother, as it was her mother, and my parents thought it would be best for everybody if she went on her own. My mother was wobbly about what had happened there since 1968, when the Troubles started up, and tended to go to chapel more often to pray for peace. My father's way of coping with it was to say, 'A plague on both their houses,' and refuse to discuss it.

We learned all that about each other, touching knee to knee under the table in various coffee shops, or lying close in my bed, Friday nights and Saturday mornings, watching the sky as the Berkeley spring rain gradually gave way to brilliant summer sunshine.

Bed got better. It could be tender, passionate, fun even, or just plain old lust. Whatever it was, it worked. Once, just after we'd had sex, we were lying face to face, taking each other in with long lazy looks. I was resting my elbow on the pillow, my hand cradling the side of my head. He reached across and began to stroke me from just under my chin, down my breast bone, then across my lower rib, back to the slight curve in at my waist, then down over my hip. His hand came to rest on my thigh.

I tensed – I'd always been so self-conscious of my skinny frame and wasn't used to someone taking their time to gaze at it like he was.

He seemed to know what was going on in my head, because

he said, so softly I could hardly hear him, 'I love this line of you . . . *Cypress slender*, that's what you are.' And then he looked more than a little sheepish and smiled and confessed that those words weren't his, they were Hafez. 'I couldn't be that original,' he said, 'but that's what I was thinking of, seeing you lying there.'

Having someone take their finger for a walk over my body, then describe it with such tenderness was a new sensation, and it took my breath away.

God bless you, Mrs Miller, for the 'overnighter' that was never slept in.

*

Kupfermühle, 27 December
I lay in bed last night and thought about him. Wished him next to me, skin to skin again, whispering *cypress slender* in my ear. That first year without him, 1979, I often thought about him like that. I could feel his actual physical presence, the warmth of him, taste the saltiness of his sweat. I would sometimes find myself aroused by the memories – not something I did deliberately, it just happened naturally, but when it did, I felt incredibly guilty afterwards. It was as if the very act of experiencing him as an erotic memory was exploiting him.

Five years on, I've found increasingly that whenever I think of him now, in a physical way, which is still often, there is little arousal. I'm beginning to forget what his face looks like. His features and contours are slowly fading. The gunmetal-flecked black hair is still there, but the expression lines around his mouth, the slight indentation across the bridge of his nose from his glasses, the shadow on his chin when he needed a shave, they are becoming stock items in my memory, as if I have to retrieve them from storage and fill them in on an identikit outline of his face each time I see it. I can fetch up his body, but I've lost the essence of him. This happened last night. It left me indescribably sad. It always does.

28 December

Impossible to do more writing yesterday. Five days in total isolation digging up painful memories left me feeling low. So I schnapped the day away. I should know better. I do know better. I need to look after myself more. But then again, for what?

Frau Jensen gets back from visiting her sister in Hamburg tomorrow. She usually visits twice a year, once in July and once during Christmas week. It'll be good to meet up with her again. I find it comforting to see her outside light on from my kitchen window, signalling the presence of another human being, particularly one I have come to like. I've probably shared more with her than I should. For some reason I haven't fathomed yet, I trust her, although I still use code when I mention Arash – *He's 'a close friend' I once knew in Iran.* She sometimes gives me Mrs Miller's long look when I say that, so I guess she's another of my women of a certain age who's worked things out. I've missed her to talk to.

In the meantime, another hour or two with Anna will have to do. Her second entry for 1977 reminds me of another strange coincidence: that she should meet Firuzeh and Farzad in Oxford and then I should meet all three of them back in Tabriz. I can just imagine her listening to them talk, getting them to tell her about themselves, Iran and Tabriz. She was the sort of person who did that. She listened, she asked questions, she recorded the stories people told her. If she didn't know something, she'd try to find out about it. If Arash was the word, and Reza was the eye, as Anna once said they were, then she was the chronicler.

*

35

Anna

Oxford, June–July 1977

Kings and Poets

They were my first lodgers, Firuzeh and Farzad, cousins from Tabriz University in Iran who wanted to be in the same house together, and who arrived in late June. I liked them on sight. They'd both graduated from London University, Firuzeh with an MA in Teaching English as a Foreign Language, Farzad a newly qualified doctor. Their English was excellent, Firuzeh's better than Farzad's, not surprisingly. They were doubly pleased when I told them I was also teaching English classes at the university. A language teacher for them at home was definitely seen as a bonus. They would only be in Oxford for three months. They'd managed to extend their stay in the UK by signing up for Oxford summer school short courses until the end of September, one month on the advanced English course, then two months on short specialist courses in their own disciplines. I suspected what they really wanted to do was to experience living in Oxford for as long as possible and the summer schools were an easy and cheap way of doing that.

They were more like brother and sister than cousins. The same fine-boned features and high, arched brows. Firuzeh had beautiful shoulder-length hair, dark and lustrous but with subtle tones of rich caramel streaked through it. She told me when I got to know her better that she put a henna rinse on it. 'Queen Farah does it too. It's fashionable in Iran.'

I brought them coffee in bed on their first morning, knocking on Farzad's door, getting no reply, then saying loudly that there was coffee on the landing table if he wanted it. It didn't seem right to go into his room. Firuzeh was awake, though, and called, 'Come in,' so I went in and picked up a glossy book from her bedside table to make space for the coffee cup.

'This is a first-morning welcome,' I said, smiling, as she sat up, 'so if you'd like an early morning coffee, it's self-service from now on. Feel free to use the kitchen any time. Just wash up any dishes you use and leave them to drain.' It seemed odd to hear myself in landlady mode, spelling out house rules. I'd never been good at following my own house rules, unless my father was around, and then they tended to be his, rather than mine.

I went back to looking at the book. It was an art exhibition catalogue and the cover was a full-colour miniature of an ancient eastern-style palace, full of musicians, exotically dressed princes and courtiers, all painted in jewel colours.

'This is so beautiful.' I flipped through the pages and handed it back to her.

'It's from our *Shahnameh, The Persian Book of Kings*.' She smiled. 'Persia's greatest epic poem, like Homer and the *Iliad* to us. It was written in the late tenth and early eleventh centuries by Ferdowsi, one of our most revered poets.' She put it back on the bedside table and stroked it. 'I brought it with me because it reminds me of my father.'

'Ah, I see.' I nodded and smiled, and hoped she didn't pick up the catch in my voice.

'Many famous Persian court miniaturists and other artists down the centuries have illustrated the poem. The Met Museum got hold of a sixteenth-century copy with illustrations, and held a big exhibition of it. My father took me to New York to see it, back in 1972. My first real trip out of Iran – so exciting.'

'It looks very Persian,' I said, swallowing hard, trying not to think of my father and our trips. 'I mean, it looks like you expect ancient Persia to be.'

'It's part history, part myth and legend. It's how our ancient shahs saw themselves, or how they wanted themselves to be seen – shahs do battle, heads roll, heroes slay lots of demons.'

She came down later to breakfast with a small print in a clip frame. 'Is it OK to put this on the bedroom wall?' she said, holding it up.

Farzad was knocking the top off his boiled egg. He pointed his knife at the print, and shook his head. 'My cousin is art mad. Spends all her allowance, and more if she can, on paintings or prints.'

'Not this one. I could only afford a cheap copy from the catalogue.'

It was another *Shahnameh* miniature, but only in a black-and-white print this time. A Persian military camp, with soldiers in ornate uniforms charging round on horseback, and carousel-shaped tents decorated with intricate mosaic patterns, pennants flying from their pointed tops. It reminded me of *The Field of the Cloth of Gold* painting, celebrating Henry VIII's attempt to out-dazzle the King of France.

'It's a satire on battle,' Firuzeh said, handing it to me for a closer look. 'See how fat and lumpy the Persian warriors are – they're supposed to be the elite, defending the camp, but they're drunk and it's chaos.'

I pointed to the Persian calligraphy along the top. 'What does it mean?'

'It's Ferdowsi's poetry,' she said. 'We're still trying to work out what it means.'

*

They weren't in my classes for the summer school, which I was pleased about. It would have felt awkward living with them and teaching them formally. I went on a few trips with them, though, the usual student visits to Stratford-upon-Avon, Warwick Castle, Blenheim.

Stratford in July turned out to be revealing. We had tickets for *Henry V*. The brilliant Alan Howard played Henry, once the irresponsible Prince Hal, now an introspective king, brooding on the conflicting qualities of kingship. Henry, the charismatic leader, motivating his men with rousing patriotic speeches, winning the battle of Agincourt with the odds stacked against them. But also Henry the ruthless king, creating and condoning violence to get what he wanted and keep his crown, putting to death friends who had once served him well.

Farzad and Firuzeh were buzzing about the play all the way back to Oxford on the coach. Although they couldn't follow some of the language, there was plenty of action on stage for them to get the gist. And they were both surprisingly well up on Shakespeare.

When I remarked on this, Firuzeh said, 'We've had some of his plays in Iran since the 1900s, translated into Persian, but they were translated from the French, or from Arabic, rather than from English.'

'Why was that?' It seemed amazing to me to go from English to Arabic or French to Persian, and I wondered how much would have been lost linguistically in a double translation, not to mention three different cultural contexts, interacting with each other.

'Because back then, in our country, French was a much more predominant language than English. And because of our history and geographical position, Arabic was too, so there were several Arabic scholars who translated the plays into Arabic from English.'

Farzad chipped in: 'Then Reza Shah – he was our present shah's father and was shah from 1926 until 1941 – he wanted to encourage Western culture, and make Persia appear more open to the West. He was the one who changed the name of our country from Persia to Iran. Sometime in the 1930s, he allowed a performance of *Hamlet*, in Persian, to be put on in Tehran.' He raised his eyes to Heaven as he said this and paused for breath.

I wasn't sure what he was being disparaging about – Reza Shah in general, or his idea in particular of putting on a Persian version of *Hamlet* in Tehran.

Firuzeh nipped into the gap. 'I would have loved to see it. It must have been a bit strange. The lead actor couldn't speak

Persian so his *Hamlet* spoke French while all the other actors spoke Persian.'

Farzad interrupted again, a distinct note of mockery in his voice now: 'But Reza Shah had no idea about the storyline. He didn't know it was about weak princes who couldn't make up their minds, or kings being murdered or their kingdoms being stolen from them, or their queens being unfaithful. It wasn't the kind of royal behaviour Reza Shah wanted Persians to think about. Probably because it might remind them that he was a lowly Persian Cossack officer, who rose to become shah in 1925 by deposing the then ruling shah of the Qajar dynasty. So he banned any more performances.'

He glanced at Firuzeh, who seemed to have given up for the moment, then carried on. 'His son, our present shah, Mohammad Reza, obviously thinks the same as his father – *Hamlet* has never been put on since he came to power, either. Probably for similar reasons too, given his own questionable route to the throne. In 1941, during the Second World War, the British, Americans and Soviets invaded Iran. They needed a base to help defeat Hitler's advance into the Soviet Union. Reza Shah had made no secret of his admiration for Hitler. The Allies 'persuaded' him to abdicate, and Mohammad Reza took over. So you could say he came to power as a result of a coup against his own father, manipulated by outsiders.'

Firuzeh gave him a sharp look, then said she knew Shakespeare had written plays about Henry IV, too, Henry V's father. 'I'd like to see those plays. See what Shakespeare says about fathers and sons and handing on power from one to the other.'

'If what Farzad has just said is true,' I said, '*Henry IV* probably wouldn't be performed in Tehran either. One of its main themes is whether Henry IV had a legitimate claim to the throne or not, or whether the crown really belonged to Richard II and Henry took it by force. And Shakespeare's King Henry IV was prone to be a bit melancholy about being a king: "Uneasy lies the head that wears a crown,"' I quoted, which was the only thing I could ever remember from the play.

Firuzeh got her notebook out and wrote down the quote in English.

Farzad chipped in again: 'He didn't give it up, though, did he? It didn't lie that uneasy. However they get it, once they've got it, they hang on to it.'

Firuzeh frowned at him. 'Every country has its version of the *Shahnameh*, and what its kings get up to. Every king has his poet. Shakespeare wrote the English version. Ferdowsi wrote ours. They were writing beautiful works of art, but they knew they would have to write what the shah they were serving wanted to hear. That was how it was then, if they wanted to stay in favour.'

'That's how it is now, too,' Farzad whipped back.

As I listened to them bickering, I remembered what Firuzeh had said, that first morning after they'd moved in. *It's how our ancient shahs saw themselves, or how they wanted themselves to be seen – shahs do battle, heads roll, heroes slay lots of demons.* There'd been no political point-making in what she'd said, no irony in her tone, it was just meant as an amusing simplification of a work of 'great literature'. But I was beginning to wonder if Farzad's remarks were always as simple as they seemed.

We had different lecture hours at the university and I was usually out when they were at home but when we could meet up, we'd eat together, and they'd tell me about Iran. We'd take turns to cook or, rather, I'd buy takeaway, Firuzeh would make wonderful soups and salads, and Farzad would manage something on toast. He loved the idea of toast. The whole notion of putting a whole light meal on it amused him – he worked his way through poached eggs, cheese, beans, was polite about sardines, and drew the line at Marmite.

One evening, it was his turn, so it was beans on toast. We

were just finishing off when Firuzeh said, 'You should come to Iran. There's so much to see. We've got everything: art, poetry, music, archaeology—'

'Poverty, illiteracy, poor health care.' Farzad ticked the words off on his fingers.

'Our health care is better than it was,' Firuzeh countered sharply. 'And the Shah has pushed for more doctors to be trained overseas. And more teachers are being trained.' She was now also counting off points on her fingers. 'And,' she said, 'I notice you forgot to mention that we had the first woman Minister for Education in 1968, and we've had a woman as the Minister for Women's Affairs since 1975. The first two women in our government ever. All down to the Shah.' She seemed well practised in defending these criticisms from Farzad.

'Both women are connected to Queen Farah, or the Shah himself,' Farzad said, 'and both rich.' He sounded a little peevish.

'So? At least they are doing something worthwhile with their lives.'

She turned to me. 'My dear cousin here thinks all rich people are – how do you say it? – "the idle rich". He wants to be a hero doctor, maybe specialise in heart disease at our hospital in Tabriz, then help the poor in his spare time,' she said, smiling, trying to keep it light, and managing to sound like an indulgent mother.

'The rich can help themselves, and they do – they help themselves to everything, at home at least,' Farzad said, obviously not going to back down.

She shook her head at him, and her tone changed to serious. 'Come on, Farzad, that's enough now. It's not OK to talk like that. I hope you're more careful outside.'

He nodded. 'Sorry.'

'Why? Why do you need to be more careful outside?' I said.

'SAVAK,' said Farzad. 'Our secret police.'

'Iranian secret police? In Oxford?' I could hear the squeak of surprise in my voice.

'Did you not see the protests here in Oxford, in June last year, when Princess Ashraf, the Shah's twin sister, came to visit Wadham College?' Farzad asked.

'No, I must have missed it.' My throat constricted at the memory of my father and June last year, and I squeezed the words out, but neither of them noticed.

'Princess Ashraf came to inspect the plans for the new college library – she donated funds for its construction.' Again, there was that eyebrow-raising gesture of disapproval from him that I was beginning to associate with his references to the Shah and his family.

'Anna doesn't want to hear about all this, Farzad,' Firuzeh said, cranking up the warning tone.

'No, it's OK,' I said, conscious that I might be disturbing the waters between them even more, but I really wanted to know. 'I haven't heard much about the Wadham-Iran connection at all. Sounds interesting.'

Farzad readily jumped in again. 'There'd already been a big protest in London a few days earlier, at the Iranian Embassy, when Ashraf came there for an official reception. We'd just arrived back from a trip to Paris, do you remember, Firuzeh?'

'I remember being very embarrassed that Iranians who were guests of another country could behave like that.' Firuzeh's tart tone was lost on him.

'Some of the protesters threw eggs at the car, and there were chants, some of them very strong, like "The Shah is an American puppet! . . . Ashraf out! The Shah is a murderer!"'

He looked straight across at me. 'There's been trouble in Iran since last year because of reports that SAVAK uses torture in our country, and that the Shah knows about it.'

'Farzad, you really shouldn't be repeating that sort of thing . . .' Firuzeh was looking distinctly uncomfortable now, but he just smiled innocently at her and batted on.

'So, when Ashraf came to Oxford, there were rumours about possible demonstrations here, and they made arrangements to

43

smuggle her in through the back gates of Wadham. But the students were there too. They say there were about a hundred of them, and they blocked the way with cars parked across the road. Eventually the police arrived and the princess was escorted into the warden's lodge to look at the plans there. But the chants carried on outside. They were more or less the same as the ones in London.'

He sat back then, still smiling, as if he'd really enjoyed telling the tale. Firuzeh was looking daggers at him.

'Goodness me! And to think I missed all that,' I said, to break the awkward silence between them.

'The students were taking a chance,' Farzad nodded, a more serious look on his face now. 'There must have been SAVAK secret police there among the protesters, keeping a pretty close watch on those marching down the High and around the back alleys of the college. Someone would be held accountable, for sure, here or back home. SAVAK are ruthless.'

'How do you know that SAVAK were here?' I asked.

'Wherever there are Iranian students overseas, there'll always be one who's there to watch the others,' Farzad said. 'It's the Iranian way – at least, at the moment it is.'

'Farzad, that really is enough.' Firuzeh sounded icy calm now, as if she was trying a different tack to get him to shut up. 'Things can be misunderstood. Better not to say anything that can be misunderstood.'

The notion of secret police lurking among students along the High or Catte Street, or Broad Street, or round the back alleys to get to Wadham was something I couldn't get straight in my head.

Farzad patted Firuzeh's shoulder, saying, 'Sorry,' but didn't sound as though he meant it, then said, 'It's a good honest meal, beans on toast.'

I'd long forgotten we'd just finished eating. It felt like a clumsy attempt to change the topic of conversation.

Firuzeh began to clear away the dishes. 'Tomorrow, I'll make *ash-e-jo.*' She smiled at me, obviously relieved to be on safe ground again. 'That's also a good honest meal, Iranian style – also with beans. Bean and barley soup. But we serve the bread on the side.'

Farzad smiled at me too, but there was a hint of self-satisfaction on his face. He'd been polite, but he'd managed to say what he needed to, and maybe what he wanted me to hear. He knew exactly what he was suggesting, regarding the present Shah in Iran. The political edge to him was there all right.

*

Kupfermühle, 29 December

Like Anna, I missed the protests around Princess Ashraf's visit in 1976. There was always some kind of demo on somewhere in Oxford, so I tended not to take much notice. Another coincidence: Anna finding out about the existence of SAVAK around the same time as I did, only mine was through the prof's lecture on Shamlu whereas hers was from Farzad telling her what they might have got up to in Oxford. I never realised until much later in Tabriz that she'd picked up on Farzad's critical stance of the Shah's regime. She never let on. But then, she never let on about a lot of things.

Frau Jensen calls by this afternoon and asks if I fancy a walk up to the lake. I'm so pleased to see her, I almost give her a hug, but she wouldn't like that, she isn't the hugging type.

'You look terrible,' she says, direct as ever. Her English is good, as it tends to be with so many people who live on borders, but hers also reflects a natural tendency I suspect she has to get to the point in any language.

'It's been a long week.' I sound as weary as I know I look.

'For me, too.' She shakes her head. 'Christmas!' She sighs as she says the word, as if that explains everything.

It's a grey day, and the snow on the ground is two days old, rutted and grimy. But as soon as we reach the lake, the Whoopers work their magic. Both of us break into huge smiles as we watch them dabbling and dipping as a threesome, like some slightly off-kilter synchronised swimming team. Then they glide in a line, a flotilla of white, then grey, then white, the yearling content to dander along in between, dabbling here and there, while the adults hold their long pointed wings close to their sides, like soft white cushions, hiding their tails, their long necks stiffly erect.

'Other swans are regal,' Frau Jensen once said to me, wafting her hand towards the Whoopers, 'but the *Singschwäne* are imperious.' That was the first time I'd met her, up at the lake, the November I'd arrived. I'd only just moved into the village that morning and had gone for a walk to get my bearings. I found the lake and there Frau Jensen was, with the Whoopers. We began to meet up there occasionally. There was only an adult pair last year, no yearlings. Towards the end of that month, she took me up to Herr Becker's field, a kilometre away, to see the main flock foraging among the stubble.

It was about half an hour before sunset. 'Just watch,' she whispered. The birds slowly stopped beaking about in the stubble, and some began head-bobbing and wing-flapping, calling to each other with soft bugling noises. 'They're getting ready to fly off and return to their roosts for the night,' she whispered again. 'They bob and flap and call to each other to gather their families together.'

A few groups took off with a short run, heads and necks thrust forward, clapping their wings, then up they went. We drove back quickly to the lake, just in time to see our own pair arrive back in the last of the light. We heard them first, a low clamouring in flight as they planed down, their wings angled, their black feet spread to act as brakes as they hit the water and glided to a stop. It was a heart-lifting moment, that little expedition to Herr Becker's stubble fields and back, watching those beautiful creatures at their winter work.

That was the beginning of our friendship. She was a fund of knowledge about swans and passed some on to me, using hand gestures in a mime show when her English wasn't up to technical descriptions, which made us both laugh, and German names for different types of swan: Whoopers obviously differ from the *Höckerschwan* (Mute), *which has a big black knob on its upper bill* (hand gesture of blob on nose), *but even if the Mute didn't have this, the Whoopers carry their necks in a stiffer, straighter manner* (stretching up her neck, holding up her chin with the back of her hand), *and also, the Whooper bill is more yellow than black, while the Zwergschwan* (Bewick – lucky guess on my part: it was the only other swan name I could think of) *which the Whooper is most confused with, has a bill more black than yellow.* This much I know about swans, in English and German, thanks to Frau Jensen. She is an acute observer, not just of wildlife, I've come to realise.

I am reminded of all that as we stand here together, observing this year's family. But we don't stay long, it's nose-numbingly cold without the sun, and will be dark soon. As we reach the village, she invites me in, as usual, for hot chocolate and Danish cookies.

We take off our boots and outer gear in the small alcove inside her back door and she tells me to go through and warm myself by the stove while she makes our hot drinks. I love her longhouse, especially in the winter. It's very un-German, with its comfortable chaos and shabby furniture that has seen better days. The long, narrow room is naturally divided into two, with the kitchen at one end, sitting area at the other. Mismatched white-painted chairs with cushion seats in cheery red gingham surround a scrubbed pine table in the kitchen area.

A low bookcase stretches along the whole of one long wall from kitchen to living area, crammed with books, a jumble of old black-and-white photos in various frames vying for space on the top shelf.

The sitting-room end has a wood-burning stove, faced by

two comfy chairs, their arms draped with folksy hand-knitted covers to hide the threadbare patches. An incongruous modern-style aluminium-stemmed reading lamp with a flexi-head and a bright yellow metal shade stands beside one of the chairs. The kitchen is cheerful all year round, catching whatever light there is from the window looking onto the courtyard, but the stove end of the room is definitely for short winter days and long winter nights.

She sets the tray on the low table between us, and lights the candle on it. Then she busies herself with pouring the chocolate from a white swirly patterned pot into two mugs with swans flying round them, and puts it down on its own terracotta tea-light stand. We sit back, cradling the mugs in our hands, sniffing up the sweet-smelling steam. She pushes the plate of cookies towards me. 'Home-baked,' she says. 'My sister always sends me back with a basket full of goodies.'

I take one shaped like a knot that melts into a delicate buttery treat in my mouth.

'Mmm. This is delicious!' I laugh. 'God! I sound like a TV advert, but it really is good.'

'Lise has definitely got the baking blessing.' She offers me another. 'I usually buy my Danish cookies in a tin.'

'Oh, well, you've definitely got the birdy blessing,' I say, and she smiles at me, and I can see around her eyes how tired she is. 'So how is your sister? Is she well?'

'As difficult as ever. Christmas is always a bit tricky. Christmas 1943, in the middle of the war, she was due to get married, but in the May before, her fiancé was killed. He served on the *U-Boote*, the submarines.' She paused for a moment, then said, 'She was never the same after that. Something in her died with him.'

She took a sip of her chocolate. 'So every Christmas is a reminder of what might have been.'

I know that feeling, and I almost say so, but Frau Jensen carries on, which is unusual for her.

'We get through it. We eat too much. And we walk. It's good to walk round the city – it reminds us of the happy times before the war, when we were young. Going to Hamburg to see relatives used to be the high point of our year. Not that I like all these modern buildings and concrete. But it's a great city. It took all that the war threw at it and survived. I keep telling Lise that we did the same, took all the war threw at us and survived. That should be enough. But she seems to be slipping back to her war memories more and more. It's not good.' She shrugged and went back to staring into the fire.

She'd told me a little about her family and her sister on one of our lake walks this past July when she'd come back from her visit to Hamburg. I remember there were only a few homely mallard ducks fussing about in the reeds for company, and for once, she'd seemed distracted and hadn't taken much notice of them.

I'd made the mistake of asking her if she'd had a good time.

'I don't really go there to have a good time,' she'd said tartly, then apologised. 'I'm sorry. My visits to my sister are always a little difficult.' And that was when, by way of penance, or so it seemed to me, she'd shared a little of the family history, although she'd never mentioned her sister's loss. She'd hardly mentioned the war at all.

Lise, her sister, was fifty-nine, the older by four years. Both had been born in Flensburg and then the family had moved to the Kupfermühle *nyborder* house just before the beginning of the Second World War. They'd gone through the whole war here, then Lise had moved to Hamburg to find work. Frau Jensen had stayed to look after their parents, their mother dying in 1964, their father in 1965. Lise had wanted her to move to Hamburg, but Frau Jensen knew she'd never move. Kupfermühle was her home.

She'd clammed up after telling me that, as if she'd said too much. Listening to her now, talking about Lise's wartime tragedy, I've gained the impression that the two sisters had clung to each

49

other throughout their lives in a sort of shared resigned spinsterhood, one never able to get over her first love, the other becoming the dutiful daughter, staying at home to look after the parents. I have the feeling Frau Jensen has adapted to her fate better than her sister – she seems at ease with living alone.

I look across at her. Her eyes are closed and I think she's fallen asleep. But she must sense my gaze because she stirs and shuffles up in her seat.

'Too much remembering going on. It's not good for the soul.' She says it as much to herself as to me.

She picks up the pot. 'It's still warm.' She pours the last of the chocolate for me, and offers me another cookie. Then she sits back and eyes me in that beady way she has. 'So what have you been up to?'

'Revisiting the past. Like you.' I sound rueful.

'Ah! That explains it. You also seem sad.'

'As you say, too much remembering.'

She nods. 'I said to Lise, it's OK to revisit the past – after all, it's part of you – but you shouldn't stay there too long. It can get a grip and drag you down.'

'Christmas,' I say, shaking my head like she did earlier on our way to the lake, and we smile across at each other. There's solidarity now in our shared acknowledgement of our misery over the festive season.

We fall into a companionable silence. What with the comforting glow of the chocolate inside me and the crooning and whispering of the wood fire, I feel the tension in my body ease away. I hadn't realised how wired up I've been. It's good, sitting here with her, being outside my own thoughts for a couple of hours. I feel I never have to explain anything to her. She makes room for me, and seems willing just to be there and share the quiet. She makes me feel safe.

I sit there for a bit longer. If I don't move now, I think, I'll doze off completely. 'I should go home, go back to bed for an hour or two, catch up on some sleep,' I say.

She allows herself a yawn. 'Me too.'

As we stand at the kitchen door, she says, 'Come round for Sylvester, if you're not busy. We'll do the same as last year. I'm only going to make lentil soup again, nothing special – I've had enough fancy food for one year – but you're welcome to share. I'd be glad of the company.'

'Thanks, Frau Jensen. That would be great. I'll bring the whiskey.' She waggles a cautionary finger at me, but she was thrilled last New Year's Eve when I brought the Bushmills round. I'd bought it duty-free in November, but since moving in here, I'd got stuck into the schnapps, so it had survived until New Year. This year, a friend from college had gone over to Dublin in early December and brought me a bottle of Jameson as a thank-you for some small favour I'd done for him. By some miracle, I hadn't broken into it yet.

By the time I get back to my place, her outdoor light has gone off. I have a pang of guilt – she must have been tired out, but sensed I was quite melancholy and didn't like to say. But then I think, no, she would have said. She doesn't stand on ceremony. It sounded like Hamburg was a tough few days for her too.

I decide to go straight to bed, make the most of an alcohol-free evening, and aim for some decent sleep. I'll get back to Arash in the morning. I'd like to stop at *cypress slender*. Freeze the memories right there. But I'm too far in to stop now.

Kupfermühle, 30 December
Woke up at six this morning, tired but clear-headed, feeling brighter than I have for a while at that time in the morning. I've just realised what I've written there – *woke up*. As opposed to *came round* in an alcoholic fug. I'd forgotten how different that feels. I make myself a proper breakfast, rescue a grapefruit lurking in the bottom of the fridge, poach a couple of eggs, pop them on a slice of Gouda. Percolate the coffee.

I'm feeling stronger than I have for ages and don't want to

break the mood, so I think about not writing today, but I know what has to come next, so I might as well get it over with.

I didn't know it at the time, back in Berkeley, but those first three months with Arash turned out to be the most uncomplicated time we ever had together. We eased into each other's lives and found we fitted like a Chinese puzzle. Maybe it was because we were both outsiders in America. Maybe it was because it was the first time for both of us to get close to someone from another culture. Maybe it was just the right time, right place for us. Whatever it was, it felt different from anything I'd experienced before. It felt right.

And then, early June, his brother Reza pitched up. And everything changed. Or, rather, he changed everything.

*

Berkeley, June 1977

Reza

He arrived two days ago. He was meant to come in two weeks' time, but changed his plans at short notice, and came early without telling Arash, ringing him from the airport. It was fucking inconvenient – Arash had to leave yesterday, for a departmental trip to New York for a conference on library information services. He was to be away for a week, the longest we've been apart since we met, and we wanted to spend Wednesday together. Reza's arrival put paid to that, so we had only a hurried hour or so on our own yesterday morning at the airport. The last thing Arash said to me as we hugged goodbye was, 'Look after Reza for me.'

'Of course I will,' I said. Not that Reza came across as someone who needed any looking after. The three of us had spent the day he'd arrived together, off and on, and I'd noticed how quietly confident he was. A man who was used to doing things his own way.

We'd arranged to meet on campus in the Bear's Lair, when I got back from the airport. I'd planned to do some work – I'd got things to finish off in the department – but Arash obviously hero-worshipped his big brother so I decided to try to get to know him a bit more.

'I'll just wander around Berkeley for a couple of days,' he said, as we sat outside, eyeing each other over a pitcher of beer. I was surprised he drank beer. Arash wasn't much of a drinker, but when he did, he stuck to wine. But that was something I slowly came to realise about Reza, how easily he adapted to wherever he was.

He pointed to his camera bag, with the Nikon lens poking out of it. 'I'll try out my new toy, take a few happy snaps and some photos of the architecture around here, then fly to New York, spend a day with Arash, then on to Toronto, and finally back to London. Couldn't have worked out better.'

For him, maybe, but not for me. I was lumbered with him.

We spent the afternoon 'doing' the campus – Hilgard Hall with its bull-head frieze and its paean to rural life carved in stone; the Campanile; Ludwig's Fountain. I found myself boring him rigid with the story of Ludwig, the legendary pooch of the 1960s, who took over the fountain during the major student riots, providing unconditional doggy love to all, so they decided to name the fountain after him. All the usual tourist stuff, which Reza listened to politely in between snapping away.

I soon ran out of fun facts and as we walked along in not exactly easy silence, he began to fill me in with some of the family history, particularly the life he and Arash had led in Tabriz. There was only a two years gap between them, and from the little Arash had told me so far, they didn't have much family left, at least in Tabriz. The uncle Arash had mentioned was their father's brother, who'd worked for the government in Tehran, but had been transferred to Tabriz the year before the boys' father died. He had two sons of his own, and he'd left them in Tehran, with his wife, on the assumption that the job would be

53

temporary. He worked in Tabriz during the week, then went home on Thursday nights and came back early on Saturdays. In the event, it was five years before he was transferred back to Tehran.

'So many Iranian families have found themselves on the move these past few years,' Reza said, 'from the country to the city, from city to city – wherever the jobs are, what with the oil boom, the economy boom, then the slacking off. You have to go where the work is, and just because you have qualifications, it doesn't mean you're guaranteed a job.' His face hardened as he said this. 'And if you do get one, you don't know how long the work is going to last. Better to come and go. But it's a strain on family life, that's for sure. And in our case, it was an extra strain for my uncle, having to take on two nephews.'

He was quiet for a moment, as if thinking how much more to reveal. 'My father had left more than enough money to see us both through a good education, but we were left in no doubt that what my uncle did for us was out of duty, not affection, for either us or my father.'

This chimed with the way Arash had talked about his uncle – he hadn't said much, but I got the impression that while he respected him, and was grateful to him for taking the brothers in, he didn't like him very much. Neither did Reza from the sound of it, although he was more direct.

'Tabriz was too provincial for him,' he said. 'He preferred the capital, where the better jobs and influence were. He thought Tabriz was full of . . . what do the Americans say? . . . "country hicks", and he didn't like the Tabrizi Azerbaijanis much. He said they wanted to cling to their ethnic identity as Azerbaijanis when they should have seen themselves as Iranians, part of the new Iran, under the Shah.'

His tone became harsher. 'He got especially annoyed with them if they refused to speak Persian in the shops and deliberately spoke Azeri – he didn't even like them calling their own language Azeri – he thought they should call it Turki, that's what the central government called it. When they did something he found particularly annoying, he'd curse them under his breath, "*Turk-e-Khar*" – Turk donkeys. It's an old Persian saying that all Azerbaijanis are *Turk-e-Khar*.' He paused. 'Our mother was Azerbaijani. But she was quite happy to adapt to being Iranian. She actively encouraged us to do so as we grew up, and made sure we spoke and read Persian as our first language. But my father's family always thought he married beneath him.'

He looked at me, a frown creasing his forehead. 'I think that was why my uncle was so disparaging of Tabriz and the Tabrizis. He viewed the job as a demotion, although it was specially created, a sort of checking-up job on the local government employees to see they were implementing national policy as they should.'

I was beginning to see why Arash had never said much about his uncle.

'I'm sorry, you don't want to hear all that. But he was a truly bigoted man. It shames me to say it, but he was. Anyway, he was transferred back to Tehran and it all worked out OK.'

'What did you and Arash do then?'

'That same year, I went back to Tehran to go to university to study psychology. It was a new go-ahead department, a new subject for the university to be offering, with important contacts in European universities, and psychology intrigued me. I finished my degree and got the opportunity to do postgrad work in London.'

'Arash told me he stayed in Tabriz. He didn't want to go to Tehran.'

Reza smiled. 'He didn't want to leave Tabriz even then. He said the noise and the pollution and the crowds in Tehran made him ill. He just about lasted the semester to do his library stuff, then scurried back to Tabriz, like a mouse down his hole. Not like me – I couldn't wait to get away. It suited me to escape to Tehran.' He added, 'And it suited me even better to get away to Europe.'

He fell silent abruptly, as if mentioning his own feelings had been a mistake, and made a show of stopping and checking his camera again. Then we moved on.

'When he got the part-time job at the American Consulate, he was thrilled. He wanted to improve his English and they wanted a local face to work for peanuts, so everyone was happy.'

I'd noticed a shade of cynicism in his voice whenever he spoke of either his own government or its allies, especially the Americans. So different from the way Arash saw it: he always sounded so grateful for what he felt he'd been given.

'The best thing was, he had time for his poetry and his reading.' His expression brightened again. 'He's a good poet,' he nodded, 'but he seems to enjoy working on translations too, especially modern translations of the Sufis.'

'I know.' A memory drifted into my head of being with Arash in my room, in Chilton Street, me stretched out on the bed, reading, him working away at the desk under the skylight, absorbed in some poetry collection.

I felt a little pulse of sadness. 'I could do with a coffee,' I said, needing to break the mood. We'd ended up near the Bear's Lair again so I steered him inside. When I explained it was named after the college football team, he raised his eyebrows and smirked. It was still shiny new, they'd renovated it only last year, although the jury was out as to whether it was an improvement or not. It was in here where I'd first seen Arash in the corner reading, the day of the Shamlu seminar. The pulse of sadness turned into a definite twinge.

We bought coffee and doughnuts and went back outside to sit on the terrace. Reza was in happy-snaps mode again, focusing on passers-by, mostly pretty girls in shorts, as far as I could tell. Then he took one of me, holding the cup in one hand, the doughnut with a big chunk bitten out of it in the other, a deliberately exaggerated grin on my face.

'All-American Boy.' He smiled, setting down the camera.

'More like Irish boy making a prat of himself,' I said. Then I had to explain 'prat'. He laughed, a genuine open laugh, and just for a moment, I saw Arash in his face.

We sat for a while, not saying much, me people-watching, Reza back to taking shots of the comings and goings across the plaza. He was a careful photographer of people, I noticed, sizing up his shots, taking his time to focus, running off two or three of what to me seemed like the same shot.

'How's the new camera shaping up?' I decided I'd take advantage of the friendlier vibes around the doughnut moment and show an interest in what he was doing.

'It's fantastic. Nothing on the market to beat the Nikon F2, even Leica. It's the one they all used in Vietnam.'

A bit over the top, then, for happy snaps, I thought, but I kept this to myself. I wasn't sure how far I could stretch this new lightness of mood.

As if he'd read my thoughts, he put the camera down and said, 'It's not so much the expensive camera, it's what you do with it, the shots you choose to take, and why.'

Suddenly he seemed to see something in the distance he wanted to shoot, so he picked the camera up again, focused quickly, clicked, then carried on. 'But you can take a shot of someone, thinking you're saying one thing, but the person who sees the photo might view it totally differently. That's what really interests me, the psychology of photography – why a photographer takes a particular picture and why a viewer might see that image in a particular way.'

'Do you feel the same about photographing architecture? You seemed to take enough shots of the campus buildings this morning.'

'They're all part of a historic American campus, I suppose, but I've seen more interesting buildings. I went to Paris earlier this year to visit the new Pompidou Centre. One of my friends from Tehran is in London studying architecture so we went over for the weekend. It's an extraordinary building.'

He was genuinely animated now, talking quickly, using his hands to emphasise a point. 'Buildings, bridges, towers, whatever, tell you a lot about people – about how they want to be seen or remembered. But the same principle applies – how people want themselves to be remembered by a work of architecture and how they are actually remembered can be two very different things. It depends on the experiences of the people doing the seeing. I've shown photos of certain buildings to people and got very different reactions.'

He looked at me, and seemed a little awkward again, like he'd been earlier when he'd mentioned getting away from Tabriz to Europe, as if he'd let his guard down and allowed me to see an aspect of him he usually kept well hidden. He looked away, adjusted his lens and panned across the terrace, taking more shots, then put the camera in his bag.

Two young men walked towards us and one waved. Reza stood up, shook his hand warmly, and started chatting in Persian. They both looked quite serious. The other man strolled over and I recognised him as the 'tell it like it is' freshman, the one the note-taker at the Shamlu lecture had ticked. He said something quietly to Reza, who smiled and patted his camera bag. The other two nodded, smiled back and walked away.

Reza sat down. 'I met them this morning when I was waiting for you to come back from the airport.'

'I met one too, way back,' I said. 'He was handing out flyers for a seminar on Shamlu. That was the day I met Arash.'

He ignored this last reference to Arash and me, which irked me a little.

'He's in the Confederation of Iranian Students, the CIS.' He gave me that look again, the one in which he seems to be sizing up what he might say next. 'Did you know they have a group here on campus?' He added, 'It's a political group, not a social club.'

It hadn't taken him long to annoy me again, the way he was telling me about my own campus, as if I was the stranger here.

'I don't think Arash is in it. There are so many political student groups, I lose count.' I heard the airy tone in my voice, ringing false to me, as I'm sure it was to him, but I went on. 'He seems to make a point of avoiding political groups, particularly when it's his own people.'

He shrugged. 'That's Arash for you – don't get involved, keep your own counsel, it'll all come right.'

It irked me again when he said that, perhaps because he was right, that was just what Arash would say, but it sounded to me as though he was belittling it. He may have sensed my irritation, because he fell silent until we'd finished our coffees and I wasn't inclined to pick up where we'd left off. Then he suggested we go our separate ways for the rest of the day. 'I want to wander round downtown Berkeley, take a few more photos, probably catch something to eat later, then have an early night. The travelling is catching up on me.'

'And I need to get back to the faculty. I have a final seminar paper to plan.'

The white lies on both sides came easily. We arranged to meet up in the morning.

Back in my room in the faculty, I sat at my desk, unable to concentrate, fiddling with some stray paperclips, thinking about what Reza had said. I was getting more and more annoyed with myself and not sure exactly why. I looked down. I'd straightened out the clips, and lined them up like a row of question marks. *You think you know my brother? How I looked after him? You think you know about our country, our province, our town? About our life over the last ten years?*

It began to dawn on me how well he'd manipulated the situation – a friendly enough first meeting, a relaxed wander around campus, seemingly happy to make like a tourist. And then, a gradual takeover of the conversation. There were things he'd planned to say, to let me know about. Several times as I'd been listening to him, I'd found myself thinking, *No, I didn't know that. How come Arash never mentioned it?*

It had felt like he was deliberately pointing out how little I knew about Arash's background and how different it was from mine. But most of all it had seemed like he was claiming Arash back for himself. He was saying one thing, but what he really meant was *I've spent a lifetime with my brother. You've spent three months.*

I didn't know what to make of him. He needed to be in control, that was for sure. But then, he was a psychologist. For a short while in Oxford I'd had a boyfriend who was doing psychology, and I'd hung out with his crowd until we'd got bored with each other. They were all pretty good at coming across as being very together, the psychologists. It took me a while to realise they were probably as fucked-up as the rest of us, just hid it better. I wondered if that applied to Reza as well.

I couldn't say I was looking forward to another walk-and-talk session.

As it turned out, I was right to be apprehensive.

*

Happy Snaps

The day started off well enough. I was determined to keep it light, away from politics on the campus. Going on what he'd said yesterday about boring campus buildings, I thought we'd do The Ark, a place Arash and I loved that couldn't fail to impress him.

We sat on a bench under a tree in the red-brick terrace court-yard of North Gate Hall. While Reza reloaded his Nikon, I read out the notes from *A Guide to Berkeley Architecture*, which Arash had borrowed from one of his student friends. *Built in the early 1900s, as the School of Architecture, and known then as The Ark, as it was meant to be a temporary wooden building, it is one of Berkeley's most treasured old buildings.*

Reza laughed at this bit. 'Treasured old building? Just over

60

seventy years old? Call that old? We've got an old building in Tabriz – we call it the *Arg*. Hey, come to think of it, it's sometimes translated as The Ark too,' he said, 'but ours is early fourteenth century, brick-built. Started off as a mosque, ended up as a military citadel. Or rather, we did have it, there's not much left of it, just a remnant of the old wall, although it's still impressive. But now it's surrounded by a twentieth-century park, courtesy of our Pahlavi dynasty.'

He snorted. 'Mellat Park. "The Park of the People". That's the name they've given it.'

There was that sarcasm in his voice again. 'Not enough work in Tabriz but at least there's a bit of green space to pass the time in when people don't have jobs to go to.'

Seeing this harsh side of him again unsettled me. Arash only talked of what he missed about home. I didn't know how to respond to this constant criticism from his brother, so I just kept quiet. Anyway, I was determined nothing would stop me lying back against the bench and lifting my face to enjoy the heat of the sun glimmering through the June leaves, now in their rich midsummer green.

He sighed and wandered off towards the block of old architecture-drafting rooms facing onto the terrace. He spent a while taking photos of the banks of windows, with their square-paned wooden casements. When Arash had first brought me here, I found the simplicity of those windows strangely calming. They obviously had the same effect on Reza, because when he wandered back and sat down, he seemed less abrasive. 'Such beautiful wood,' he said.

'Well, if it's wood you like, I know where we should go,' I said. We walked back across the campus from the North Gate to Sather Gate onto Bancroft Way, in the direction of the First Unitarian Church. It was a little gem Arash had shown me on that first weekend we'd spent together in Chilton Street. It was his favourite building on the campus, and had become special to us, but by the time Reza and I got there, I could have kicked myself for suggesting it. I was about to let his brother into an intimate corner of our lives. The place wouldn't be exclusive to me and Arash any more.

'Wow!' Reza stood there, looking at the church, taking it in. It was only about sixty feet by eighty and built in wood. *1890s Simple Home style, a fine example of building with nature,* according to the guidebook. No longer a church, it had been converted into a dance studio for the university now, but nothing had changed on the outside. The age-darkened red cedar shingles lipped each other on the side walls and took on a dull sheen of brown shot silk as the sunlight played on their textures. I could hear Arash's voice: 'Warm and woodsy.' The east wall was completely hidden by an overgrown wisteria, its lilac blue flowers long gone, leaving in their place a tangle of feathery green leaves in new growth. The west wall was shaded by overhanging redwoods.

'I need to get some close-ups,' Reza said. All I could hear as he wandered round was 'Wow!' as he snapped away. He spent ages framing arty shots of the half-conical roof over the apse, with its parasol-like skylight in its centre. Then he was down on his knees taking angled shots of the curved wood-shingled buttresses shoring up the sides. Arash reckoned the architect was injecting a touch of early twentieth-century sly humour here – 'They're just for show, you don't need wooden buttresses for a wood-frame building.'

I closed my eyes as his voice came back to me. God, I was beginning to miss him.

'Wow!' Reza had disappeared round the corner. I followed him and found him staring at the west gable, balanced with its two redwood logs at either end, holding up rough roof beams, both logs at least three feet in width and with the textured bark left on. The wall consisted of a low relief wooden cross hung above a large circular window, divided with small amber panes in metal sashes. Arash had called it a study in grace and symmetry.

Reza took a close-up of the redwood bark of the logs. 'It reminds me of a dried-up riverbed,' he said, running his hands down the wooden rivulets naturally carved from top to bottom, and I followed his fingers over their roughness and thought of Arash again.

I felt a pull in my stomach. I heard myself saying, 'I hope you don't mind, but I should maybe make my way back – I still have my paper to finish. Why don't you come round to my place later and we could go for something to eat?'

It sounded a bit weak, but that first Saturday morning with Miles Davis and Arash was fresh in my mind and I didn't feel like sharing him with anyone. That's not quite true – in particular, I didn't feel like sharing him with his brother.

He gave me a side-smile and said that was fine, he'd had a great time. Yes, he'd come round about six. Then he nodded and turned away and headed off up Bancroft Way, towards Sather Gate. I had a feeling he'd sussed me out, but I didn't care. I needed time out from him.

*

He arrived at Chilton Street bang on six. 'Change of plan,' he said. 'I brought food. Thought maybe we could stay in and get to know each other a bit better.' He put a paper bag on the low table between us, and took out cartons of barbecued chicken and salad, then a bottle of wine from his camera case which doubled as a shoulder bag.

After we'd eaten, he lounged in the wicker chair, his leg over the arm, drinking the California red. 'It's good,' he grinned, 'although not quite as good as our Shiraz.' You could tell he was Arash's brother – the same thick hair, although Reza kept his longer, and the same full lips. But he was more self-assured than Arash. Maybe it came from being the older brother, and their parents dying: he'd had to grow up quickly and accept responsibility for both of them. Arash was so open to other people and their ideas; he took people at face value. Reza was more cautious, more on his guard. More streetwise.

I still wasn't sure what to make of him. There was an easy charm about him, I had to admit, and the way he was always looking out for Arash touched me. He seemed OK with the thought of the two of us being together, although he was constantly looking at me, in that cool appraising way he had.

'My little brother is obviously enjoying being here, especially now he's met you.' It was uncanny, the way he could tune in to what I was thinking. He raised his glass and toasted me, before taking a sip. Then he unhooked his body from the chair, put the glass on the table and leaned back, resting his wrists on the chair arms so that his hands dangled over the edges. His face was suddenly serious.

'But what will happen when he returns home to Iran?' He flexed his fingers. 'It's difficult enough over here, in America or Europe, although everyone says how free they all are to be what they are, and all that – but in Iran? I mean for men like you and Arash.'

His tone was neutral, but I could feel myself bridle at men like you and Arash.

He was probing me, and I didn't like it. He'd sensed an area of weakness, my insecurity about Arash, and was determined to worry away at it.

'Maybe he won't go back.' I surprised myself. I'd done quite a bit of thinking about what might happen next for Arash and me, and his deciding not to go back had certainly seemed to be an option. But it was the first time I'd said it out loud to anyone.

'Oh, he'll go back all right. This year has been good for him, it's widened his horizons, in all sorts of ways, but Iran . . . No, not just Iran, Tabriz, to be more exact, that's where his soul lies.' He sat forward now, and took up his wine again, looking at me over the glass. There was sadness in his eyes and I wasn't sure if it was for me, anticipating how hurt I would be to lose Arash, or for Arash, knowing about the life he would have to lead back home to keep himself safe.

'Well, then, maybe I could go with him,' I said, and immediately wished I hadn't. That had been the second option I'd been considering, for me and Arash to stay together, and now, in an attempt to appear unfazed at Reza's snuffling around like a truffle hound, I'd blurted it out. I wasn't sure he'd keep it to himself before I'd had time to talk to Arash about it.

As far back as April, only a month or so after meeting Arash, I had this germ of an idea that I could find work in Iran. A university post, research or teaching – my Oxford credentials would help. Not that I was interested in furthering an academic career, it was just a means of being able to follow Arash back to Iran to see how things went. I'd put out feelers in Oxford, and my tutor had got back to me to say that a few exchange posts had come up for September. I hadn't mentioned anything to Arash, mainly because he might tell me what I didn't want to hear: that what we had was good, special even, but only temporary.

'Go to Tabriz?' Reza's voice cut in, a sharp edge to it now. 'You? You'd be willing to go back with him?'

'If he wanted me to. We haven't discussed it. We haven't really talked about what happens next.' I sounded defensive.

He sat up straight in the chair again. 'I hadn't anticipated you going back with him. I thought he might decide to stay here with you, or you might persuade him to go back to Oxford with you or somewhere.' He stared at me intently. 'Have you any idea what you'd be letting yourself in for?'

'Like I said, we stay away from the Iranian student groups on campus, but we pick up stuff from the papers.' It gave me a tiny burst of satisfaction, playing the 'we' card.

'Iran's not exactly what you'd call a liberal place, and I don't just mean about sexual preferences. There's censorship and persecution – it's supposed to have got better since last year, but that's only window-dressing.' He looked across at me now and there was a new toughness about him when he spoke. 'In fact, it's going to get a whole lot worse – the Shah pretends to listen to the people, occasionally makes a small gesture here or there, but those who disagree with him or the regime – and let's face it, he is the regime – he's utterly ruthless. Any sign of protest or resistance and back comes the repression.'

'I learned a little about that from the lecture I went to here on Shamlu. But Arash says you can respect the dissidents and the critics and what they're saying, but you have to make sure you don't get involved. You have to be careful.'

He stared hard at me for a moment, then bent down and fumbled at the side of his chair for his camera bag. He took a book out, and held it up. I could just about make out a striking graphic in red and black on the front. He laid it on the table and picked up his glass again.

'Do you know Baraheni's work?' He gestured towards the book.

'No, I've never heard of him.'

'He's one of our most prominent literary figures – a poet, playwright, writer, critic, and a founder of the Writers' Association of Iran. Some of its members have built up a reputation as dissidents, critics of the regime, the Shah, the government, and they use their writing to voice their criticism. Baraheni was one of the key critics. Still is.'

He finished his wine. 'He was arrested in 1973, by SAVAK, and spent a hundred and two days in prison. They tortured him.'

I thought of the Iranian woman and her wavery voice – *Su'-e zann . . . suspicion. Sazeman-e . . .* SAVAK. And I remembered the tangible fear in the room as the prof had worked through Shamlu's SAVAK cockroach metaphors.

Reza carried on: 'The American literati – Joseph Heller among others – caused such an outcry about it. They got together with PEN, and Amnesty International, and other influential players.

Even got our own Committee for Artistic and Intellectual Freedom in Iran involved. They all played their part to get him released. Then he escaped to America.'

He put down his glass and picked up the book. 'This is his first collection, *God's Shadow*, published in English last year. It means God's Messenger, or Representative, on earth – a term most of our shahs, including the present one, like to use to give themselves a sort of ultimate religious legitimacy. It's how they see themselves, or how they want themselves to be seen. Needless to say, it being Baraheni, the title is ironical.'

He offered it to me. 'You should read it. Get a sense of what it's like to be a free thinker in Iran, and what can happen to you if the regime doesn't like it. At least then you'll know what you're really letting yourself in for.'

I took it from him. 'Has Arash seen this?'

'I got a copy to him when it came out. He's never mentioned it to me, though.'

'He never mentioned it to me either.' I felt annoyed with Arash for keeping the book from me.

He carried on, unaware of the effect of what he was saying. Or very much aware of it and enjoying it. It was impossible to tell with him.

I stretched over and put the book back on the table. It felt like some sort of chess game between us, moving the book around like a pawn.

He leaned forward and rested his hand on it as he spoke. 'I got this copy from one of the student groups on campus – the CIS, the group I mentioned before. They've got a well-organised underground distribution of material going on, not that it needs to be underground – they're on free American soil – but you never know who may turn out to be SAVAK, even here.'

I remembered the short conversation between Reza and the two Iranians in the Bear's Lair coffee bar, and Reza tapping his camera bag. Then I remembered the note-taker beside me in the

Shamlu lecture marking a cross in the boxes where those who'd made comments had been sitting.

It felt like Reza was making crosses in boxes too, only this time it was against my name. There was certainly some sort of assessment of me going on, but I wasn't sure what. Was it to see if I was capable of protecting Arash? Or even whether Arash could trust me? And what had he meant by that last remark of not knowing who might be SAVAK? I didn't like it. Big brother was beginning to irritate the hell out of me.

'Like I said before, Arash makes a point of not getting involved, even though he sympathises with some of what they do.'

He seemed to sense my annoyance as I said this, and it felt as though he suddenly wanted to bring the conversation to an end. He pushed the book across the table, saying, 'I'll leave it with you. It's tough to read. But I'd be interested in hearing what you think.' He paused. 'And you could check out what Arash thinks about it too.' He slouched back in the chair, watching for my reaction, his face expressionless.

Checkmate. I sighed as I picked up the book again. I told myself I was sick of playing this game anyway, and it wouldn't cost much to take a closer look at it. It was beginning to nag at me that Arash might have read it and not shared it with me, if it was as significant a modern collection as Reza was implying.

The dust jacket was a cross between an anarchical Ralph Steadman illustration and Picasso's *Guernica*. In the background lay a bird, a raptor of some sort, spread-eagled, sharp-beaked, crazily cross-hatched in black and shades of grey. Overlying its sinister outline was a blast of grotesque imagery in red and black, drawn in a disturbing childlike scrawl. A skull, complete with cartoon macabre grin and gobstopper eyeballs, resting atop a spinal column of exposed vertebrae. A single forearm dangling upside down at the end of hair's-breadth wires. Disembodied heads, blood-red. A hand gripping prison bars, the fingers only just visible under a thick daub of scarlet. And over these images were handwritten lines of poetry, in tiny script and seemingly scribbled at random, like the manic outpourings of a half-mad prisoner on his cell wall.

Reza watched my face as I took all this in, his mouth now settled in a hint of a hard smile. 'That's just the outside. Wait till you read what's inside.'

Then he got up to go. Mission accomplished. I was glad to see him out, but agreed to meet up the next day when he suggested it. Not something I was looking forward to. Based on what I'd seen so far, I wasn't sure I was looking forward to reading Baraheni either.

*

Kupfermühle, 30 December

I don't want to write about the *God's Shadow* episode yet. Don't feel I can stomach it. But thinking about Reza reminds me of the envelopes with his name on them in Anna's parcel.

I decide to open one. I know it's a displacement activity, I should be writing about *God's Shadow*, but still. It's the thinnest envelope of the three. Inside, there's a sheet of foolscap with the date written in Persian script ۱۹۷۷, 1977. Anna has scribbled underneath: *from Reza, 1980. Paris postmark. No return address.* The paper is folded around some photographs.

It's a bit of a disappointment at first. Reza's happy snaps tumble out, from his visit to see me in Berkeley. It gives me quite a jolt to see the campus again, and the places I took him to. All the architecture shots are there, from the Hilgard to The Ark and the Unitarian Church, from the boring to the wow! Plus the doughnut picture of me, looking so young and such an idiot. And the pretty girls with their tanned legs and easy California style.

At the back of the bunch, shots of the two Iranians, my freshman and his friend, caught walking towards us. And last of all, shots of a man sitting at a table at the edge of the Bear's

Lair terrace. I know the face, but can't place it. It is an older face, not that of a student. Then I recognise the haircut, and my stomach lurches. It's the note-taker. The man I sat next to in the Shamlu lecture. The man who ticked boxes on his seating plan and wrote down names.

Reza had taken a clear, detailed close-up of his face. I wonder why he'd picked him out of the crowd on the plaza terrace, and taken a close-up photo of him. Was it just coincidence? Or was he SAVAK, and Reza had known he was? And how did he know? I remember the two freshmen coming over to Reza and having a quick conversation, him tapping his camera case. Even after all this time, it makes me feel uneasy. Maybe a bit of SAVAK agent-spotting was what some politically minded students did, if they travelled round Europe and the US. I wonder if copies of that photo had found their way to various Confederation of Iranian Students groups on US and European campuses. It wouldn't surprise me. There was so much I never knew about Reza. I was never entirely sure of his motives for anything he did.

Which brings me back to *God's Shadow*. I guess I can't put it off any longer.

*

Berkeley, June

God's Shadow

After Reza had gone, I poured myself the last of the Shiraz and settled down at my desk with *God's Shadow*. I wasn't settled for long. Now I understood the dust jacket.

It wasn't like any poetry I'd ever read before. I didn't even know if it was poetry. There was no poet 'stung into song' here, there was no song at all, just words screaming out in pain. Page after page. Visceral and shocking, but then it was meant to be – every nail-pulling, tooth-cracking, feet-whipping, shoulder-breaking detail of it. Like a medieval tract on torture.

70

And as if that wasn't enough, he'd added annotated explanatory notes to the poems – *bastinado* – *whipping the soles of the feet . . . application of electric shocks . . . boiling water . . . hot irons through cheeks.* And rape, as a deliberate tool of torture – *male rape, female rape, threats of raping wives, daughters, sons.*

I would start a poem, then be unable to finish because of its content, move on to the next and hope it would be different. But it was sometimes worse. Most shocking of all was the portrait of Dr Azudi, the torturer. I had to keep reminding myself: this man wasn't a fiendish fictional character in a book. He existed. Third in command in a chain leading directly to the Shah, if Baraheni was to be believed.

I reached my limit with 'Barbecue'. Baraheni speaks in his introduction of how bunk beds and a makeshift electric grill device are improvised as instruments of torture. The prisoner is fastened to the bare metal framework of a top bunk bed. A guard then works in the space between it and the lower bed, and casually applies the grill to the man's buttocks. He sometimes moves it up towards his spine – 'If it touches the spine . . .' Baraheni adds, in his annotations '. . . paralysis nearly always follows.' A wave of revulsion overcame me and I couldn't read on.

It was four in the morning but my mind wouldn't rest. It was as though I was consumed with a high fever, my skin paper-thin and so sensitive, I felt that if I touched it, it would burn. There was no point in trying to sleep: my whole body felt spring-loaded. I put Baraheni's book in my bedside drawer, conscious I was hiding it but I didn't want to be reminded of it. I lay down on my bed, my head buzzing. I tossed and turned for the next two hours, wary of closing my eyes in case the images came back.

I hadn't pulled the blind down, and was slowly aware of the sky beginning to lighten. The bedside clock said six a.m. Then I heard Tony, one of the students on the floor below, banging doors and moving around, getting kitted out for his morning run. I decided to get up, too, and take a shower. I stood for a good while under water as hot as I could bear it, hoping it would sluice away the torment, but it didn't help much. I thought about going downstairs to make proper coffee, but couldn't face meeting anyone, so got dressed in my sweats, made a cup of instant and sat at my desk, trying not to think.

The shock of what I'd read was giving way to anger. At Reza, mainly. I wondered yet again what he was trying to do in exposing me to Baraheni's work. Was it to frighten me, or revolt me so that I'd reject Arash and decide I wouldn't go to Tabriz? Or maybe he was just 'telling me like it is', to quote my young Iranian freshman friend. Well, he'd succeeded in frightening and revolting me, for sure. But whatever his motives, I was not going to let him get away with his hit-and-run tactics.

Seven a.m. sharp, he arrived with his luggage to go straight to the airport. He had the grace to look apprehensive when he saw my face.

We sat down facing each other across the low table. I didn't even offer him coffee, just dived straight in. 'What the fuck are you playing at, Reza?'

'I don't know what you mean.'

'Why did you make a point of leaving Baraheni's work with me? Did you think you'd frighten me? That it would make me give up on Arash?'

He shook his head. 'I wanted you to see our country at its worst. What it's capable of.' He passed his fingers through his hair, lifting his face slightly, and I noticed the dark shadows under his eyes. I don't think he'd slept well either.

'Who's to say it's true?'

'Are you seriously suggesting he made it all up?'

'I'm asking you a straight question. Do you believe him?'

'Why shouldn't I? He's not the only one to have been tortured in prison. Most prisoners are too terrified to talk when they're released but stories leak out all the time.'

'But how do you know for sure? All those things Baraheni

said they did to him? And all the things he said were done to others? I mean, grilling someone's buttocks and spine? Dear God! It's barbaric. Medieval.' I could feel my gorge rise again at the thought of what I'd read.

'Torture is medieval, whatever century it takes place in.' He shrugged his shoulders. 'The principle of it never dates. Those with power can apply pain, physical or mental, to those who are powerless in order to get what they want from them. Confession, conversion, betrayal of others, recanting. How it's done is almost incidental.'

'Not to those on the receiving end it's not. All those horrible things.' I had to swallow before I asked him again, 'So, do you think it's true, what he says?'

'He's a respected literary figure. Why would he lie?'

'He might be exaggerating – if he was taken up by PEN, like you say . . . they got him out. Maybe he felt . . . I don't know . . . as if he had to paint things as bad as possible.'

'You mean he might feel obliged to exaggerate, as a way of justifying PEN's support?'

I could hear exasperation creeping into his voice. 'Something like that,' I stumbled. I was challenging him, yes, but in my own mind I was challenging what I'd read just as much.

He opened his mouth to say something, then clamped it shut and reached down into his shoulder bag. He pulled out a folder and drew a slim, official-looking pamphlet out of it. As he thumbed through it, I noticed a large map of Iran on the front, similar to the one Arash had shown me the first time he'd told me about Tabriz. *Cat's head. Cat's ears.* God, I thought, I wish Arash was here now. I'm not sure I can cope with another emotional scourging. It's like fucking *bastinado* for the conscience.

He found the pages he was looking for and bent them open. 'Here,' he said, sounding weary, as he passed it to me. 'Don't take my word, or even Baraheni's, for that matter. Read this. It's your own Amnesty International, an up-to-date briefing from last year on what's going on in Iran, some of it from the Shah's own mouth.'

He'd put an asterisk against a paragraph midway down:

When questioned about the use of torture in his country, the Shah has never denied that it occurs. In a recent interview reported in Le Monde on 1 October 1976, the Shah replied to a question about the use of torture by saying: 'Why should we not employ the same methods as you Europeans? We have learned sophisticated methods of torture from you. You use psychological methods to extract the truth: we do the same.'

There was another asterisked paragraph on the opposite page summarising the testimony of other prisoners, who repeated some of Baraheni's claims and provided even more horrific details of physical rather than psychological torture.

I suddenly felt even more weighed down than I had last night with the ugliness of what I'd been reading. Why was Reza so intent on shocking me?

I passed the pamphlet back to him, and slumped in my seat.

I half expected a smirk from him as he took it, but there was sadness about him as he said: 'So, you see, it's not just Baraheni's account, it's others as well, and the Shah himself admits it goes on.'

'Assuming it's all true,' I said, 'why do you think I need to read that stuff? It's almost like you're determined to turn me against your country.'

He looked at me directly then, and spoke in a quiet, determined voice: 'That's the point, Damian. I want you to see our country at its worst. What it's capable of. Then you can make your choice. And, more importantly, there's Arash and you to consider. At the moment, in Tehran at least, there's a thin layer of pseudo-liberalism regarding homosexuality in certain circles. There are rumours about what goes on at the Shah's court, about what is tolerated there – "turning a blind eye", isn't that the English saying? But what goes on in elite circles in Tehran doesn't reflect the more conservative views of Tabriz, or the rest of Iran for that matter. If you come back to live with my brother, it doesn't matter how discreet you are, someone will get to know about you. And it's the sort of information they'll store up to use when they need it.'

He hesitated, still staring hard at me, as if to assess my reaction to him referring to my relationship with his brother as homosexual. It felt better than his reference to us last night as 'men like you and Arash', which I'd taken on trust to be non-judgemental, but couldn't be sure. At least today he'd said the word, and I acknowledged this with a nod.

Then he continued, 'And it's illegal – you can get three to ten years. And if that tolerance should ever change, for whatever reason, it won't be you they go for. You're a Westerner, and they like to keep Westerners sweet, so they'll find a way of allowing you to leave the country. It'll be Arash they'll go for. Are you sure that's a risk you're willing to take, not just for you but for him?'

I was overwhelmed by what he was saying, but I believed him. I think he was genuinely marking out the implications for Arash. We weren't dissidents, but we'd be considered deviants, and if someone wanted to make trouble, it would be worse for him.

We fell silent, Reza sitting upright in his chair, me on the edge of mine, arms folded.

He broke the silence first. 'I need to be on my way.' He stood up. 'I know you're good for Arash – I've never seen him so happy. But he's my brother. He has no one else to look out for him. I've done it all my life and I'm not going to stop now, just because you've come along.' He held out his hand to me. 'But I want us to part friends. Arash would want that, too.'

We shook hands, a weak gesture on my part, not much more than a fleeting touch. He sighed and made a move to gather up his suitcase and camera bag. He'd get a bus to the airport, he said. There was no need for me to come to the front door with him. So we said our goodbyes and I watched him go down the stairs. He didn't look up.

After he'd gone, I pulled down the skylight blind to keep out the morning sun and crawled into bed. I fell into a sort of semi-stupor, my eyes closed. And in burst Baraheni's 'Barbecue'. I forced my eyes open, but the same images floated across the blind above me, like some grotesque silent movie, and a small sharp pain began to nip inside my right temple. I lay there trying not to move in case it made the headache worse, then a wave of nausea came from nowhere and I just about made it to the bathroom before I was violently sick.

Back in my room, I opened the skylight window. I needed fresh air, but I kept the blind down, and sat at my desk, feeling wrung out, stinking of sweat, the sour aftertaste of vomit in my mouth. I put my head into my hands and wept.

*

Kupfermühle, 30 December

Ten questions for Dr Azudi

I have *God's Shadow* here, in my foolscap folder. I haven't looked at it for six years, and still its cover shocks me, and still the memory of its contents fills me with anxiety, just like it did that night back in Berkeley.

I remember sitting there, weeping at my desk and thinking I needed to sort out my thoughts, make some sense of what Baraheni had said about torture and his torturer.

I remember hearing inside my head, over and over, one line from the poems:

Dr Azudi has shattered the mouths of twenty poets today.

76

I remember reaching for my pen, my hand shaking slightly when I began to write.

I lost all sense of time and wrote till my hand seized up. What tumbled out onto the page was mostly questions. Then I folded the page without looking at what I'd written, and slipped it into the back of *God's Shadow*, deliberately wanting to hide the questions, knowing I'd never look at them again or the terrifying poems they lay next to.

But here they are, in the book just where I hid them. I slip them out of their hiding place. The handwriting is shaky, the student notepaper slightly sallow with age, the crease marks fragile in the folds. It wouldn't take much for it to split and disintegrate.

Ten questions for Dr Azudi

1. What made you become a torturer, Dr A? Was the urge to inflict pain always there, only needing the right conjunction of circumstances? *Torturers are born, not made. Discuss.*

2. Do you even see yourself as a torturer, Dr A? Or, in your mind, are you just a specialist interrogator? You only ask the questions, others apply the pain? *I'm the interrogator, they're the torturers.* Is that how you distance yourself from what you do?

3. How do you see your prisoners, Dr A? Do you say to yourself: 'If only the dumb bastards would confess, recant, inform on the others!'? But, no, they won't, at least in the beginning, so any guilt you might be inclined to feel in torturing them is subsumed by righteous anger – if they would just do as they were told, you wouldn't have to do these things. But they don't, so it's they who are making you do these things to them.

4. And what about when you see them crawling round the cell floor, in their own shit, Dr A, or even eating their own shit, when you force them to? Do you say to yourself: 'Why do

they degrade themselves like that? Behave like non-humans, sub-humans, dogs? No wonder I feel disgusted by them.' So, once again, you convince yourself. It's their fault. They deserve to be punished. That sleight of thinking, Dr A – it must make it so much easier for you.

5. Why do you always insist on a hood or a blindfold for your prisoners, Dr A? I can see how it would disorient them, ramp up the fear – they can't see what's coming, can't anticipate what's coming, can't prepare their bodies for the blow, the whip, the heat. Most important of all, they can't see you. I get all that – but does the blindfold work for you, as well, Dr A? If you blot out their faces, their eyes, does that make them look less human, less like an individual human being? Does that make it easier for you to do what you do?

6. Let's talk about feet for a moment, Dr A. By all accounts, you've become quite the expert on feet. On the whipping of feet. *Bastinado*. You've even had a special room set aside for the purpose, *Otagh-e Tamshiyat* – 'the room in which you make people walk', the prisoners call it. You know how the nerve endings congregate in the soles of the feet, as do many small bones and tendons. So the trick there is to know just when to stop, so these nerve endings don't die – if that should happen, the prisoner doesn't feel the pain any more. So it's important that you stop the whipping and they think the worst is over. Then you make them walk, on the spot, or round the cell, so that the blood courses to the nerve cells. Walking on swollen feet is a new pain, so they're grateful when you tell them to stop. Then the whipping starts again and whipping swollen feet inflicts a pain worse than the first whipping.

7. But all this whipping and walking is so time-consuming, Dr A. What do you do about the hard-liners? Those proving difficult to crack? You could take it up a notch. Electric wires attached to this part or that part. Specially designed cuffs so

78

prisoners dangle from the ceiling at a certain angle that dislocates their shoulders. But these methods, too, can be slow and labour-intensive. So, do you lie there at night, Dr A, next to your wife, with your children safely asleep in the next room, mulling over the efficiency of one method over another? Was it you who had the light-bulb moment about the grill, Dr A? Is the grill a cutting-edge technical solution to a manpower and productivity problem, Dr A? Quick results guaranteed?

8. Why do you call yourself *Doctor*, Dr A? Is it your ironic little joke? You aren't a doctor. Or do you see yourself as doctor-like, someone who takes on misguided, deluded patients and gets them well? Or maybe you call yourself a doctor to show these smart arses from the intelligentsia whom you torture that you are at least their equal, or their superior. Maybe, Dr A, your mastery of technique implies a certain doctoral level of knowledge in order to take another human being to the very edge of physical or psychological collapse, while ensuring that they don't actually die. Judging the moment just before that's likely to happen might well need a level of skill worthy of a heart surgeon.

9. Are all of these questions part of an ethical dilemma you've solved for yourself, Dr A? Do you tell yourself that what you do is a vital job in a security organisation? Torture for terrorists, you say, is a necessary evil, for the good of the state, for the safety of the people, because terrorists are willing to carry out despicable acts, to kill and maim. We need to know what they are planning next, or who they know, and anything we do to get that information, to minimise that threat, is OK.

Many would agree with the-ends-justify-the-means argument, Dr A. But who exactly do you define as a terrorist? That's another problem. Are all dissidents terrorists? A dissident poet, a critical journalist, a typesetter who typeset *Long Live the Shah* every day of his working life, until, on one day only, he typeset *Long Live Liberty* – at what point do they become terrorists/enemies of the people? When they take up words and use them as weapons?

10. What happens when you are no longer a torturer, Dr A? Tricky one, this. Maybe something you've never really considered. But there will come a time when one day you will be stripped naked, maybe literally, maybe metaphorically. You will be standing there, degraded and dehumanised, and it will slowly dawn on you that you are, in fact, no different from the prisoner you have been torturing. The same degradation and dehumanisation you inflicted on your victims, you inflicted on yourself by doing what you did. There is no 'you' and 'them'. You share the state of being human; you share a common humanity. Only you lost yours long ago. What then, Dr A? Will you be able to live with the man you see in the mirror?

So many questions, Dr A, so many questions.

White on White

It's strange reading through the Ten Questions again. It's as if a different person had written them. The hysteria in the writing is almost embarrassing, but the feelings of confusion and revulsion they convey are still surprisingly live, even now. I remember sitting there, faintly aware of the morning soundtrack of Chilton Street coming through the open skylight, and struggling to come to terms with what I'd just experienced.

The effects of the poetry eventually faded a little, but I couldn't get rid of my thoughts about Reza. It had been a clever move on his part. Cruel and calculated, but clever. The poems certainly concentrated my mind, that's for sure, which was exactly the effect he'd planned. He'd said as much. And he'd come prepared today. He'd pre-empted all my possible objections and presented me with supporting evidence, as if he was some barrister for the prosecution. I began to feel angry with him for manipulating me in this way, and angry with myself for letting him. Under the anger, though, was fear. For the first time, he'd forced me to consider not just that I wanted to be together with Arash, and how I might bring that about, but the reality of us being together in a place like Iran. I feared for myself, but I feared for Arash too. In a crisis, I had a way out. He didn't. Reza was right about that.

The image of 'Barbecue' haunted me for months, and I never forgot the savagery in the lines: *When I see cooked meat /I say that's me/roasted/barbecued.* Confronting Baraheni's poetry again now, and all the barbarity contained within it, I find myself asking the same question: how could one human being do that to another?

I look out at my opposite neighbour's garden and take in the cold purity of the snow blanketing her front hedge. Suddenly I need to get out, to feel that same cold purity on my face, breathe it in, allow it to numb me and cleanse me from the inside out.

I grab my parka, shove on my boots, and almost run out of the house, heading towards the lake. It's late afternoon, with a pale lemon sun already low in the sky. It didn't snow yesterday, but it never rose above freezing so the path is trampled by glittering ice-rimmed footprints. It doesn't take long for the cold to set my sinuses throbbing. But breathing in the sharp air slowly does what I want it to do, each breath helping to dissolve the half-formed hellish images hovering at the edge of my memory. I blow into my gloved hands and inhale slightly less icy air, and exhale, concentrating on clearing my mind. Slowly I'm able to bring myself back to the moment I'm in.

I tell myself I'm in the here and now on a beautiful midwinter's afternoon in Kupfermülhe, looking across at the white on white of the Whooper family, already asleep on the far snow-covered bank. Gradually I'm able to focus. They huddle together, the yearling in the middle, their necks curled along their backs and draped between their wings, faces to the rear, tucked beneath their scapulars, their bills buried up to the eyes in feathers. Not for the first time, I marvel at the soft-edged sculpture of curves and lines they've created, folding their bodies in on themselves to fend off the overnight cold, but still allowing them to open their eyes without having to move anything but their eyelids. Which they do, as they sense me standing on the opposite bank. 'The Angels of Winter', the Japanese call them. Another detail supplied by Frau Jensen.

Thinking of her reminds me that I'm going round to her place tomorrow for Sylvester. As I walk home, I consider cancelling. I'm in no fit state to be sociable. But she won't expect me to be sociable, she'll just expect me to turn up and she'll take it from there. It will be something to look forward to, something to stop me sinking down again, which I'm in danger of doing after revisiting Baraheni's poetry today.

When I get back to the house, I can't face the study and the memories, so I turn up the heating in the living area, and spend time in the kitchen warming up a homemade vegetable soup, the last of the supply I cooked three days ago. I take it with some black bread and a mug of coffee on a tray to the corner-sofa living space, which feels warm and safe. I suddenly feel drained. It's only six o'clock, but all I want to do is hide, so I go to bed. I'm not sure I want to fall asleep, 'Barbecue' might come back – but I do, and don't wake up until well after midnight. I'm disoriented at first and think I'm in Berkeley, waiting for Arash to come back from New York. Then I realise I'm in Kupfermühle, but I lie there and think about Berkeley and Arash anyway.

That week after Arash got back from New York turned out to be the crunch point.

*

Berkeley, June

The Little Black Fish

The first thing he said when he hugged me at the airport was 'I spent the day with Reza yesterday, before he went on to Toronto – he said how well you looked after him.'

I bet he did, I thought, but I heard myself say, 'Yes, he's an interesting guy, your brother,' and I left it at that. All my firm intentions to 'sort things out' faded away when I saw him. All I really wanted to do right then, apart from go to bed with him, of course, was to be with him, share simple things with him again, spend a quiet day wandering round Berkeley, or reading under a tree somewhere, anywhere as long as we were together. I needed his calmness. The heavy stuff could wait.

We spent the night together in Chilton Street. Mrs Miller was away visiting her daughter, and the other two students were on field trips. We had the house to ourselves, the first time that had happened. It felt easy between us to wander about downstairs in the kitchen, as if we owned the place. We'd bought poppy-seed rolls and goat's cheese from the deli on the way home. Arash didn't feel like much after the flight, and we sat near the window at the kitchen table to eat, taking in the view of the jacaranda. It was Mrs Miller's pride and joy, and was still in full bloom, its ghostly purple flowers, the shade of grape-sherbet, lighting up the backyard. We sat out on the veranda steps, me with a beer, Arash sipping wine, until the sun went down, comfortable in the silence. Then we went upstairs, squeezed into the tiny shower, and had soapy sex.

I don't know who fell asleep first when we stumbled into bed, but the sunlight woke me up first the following morning.

I lay stretched out along the length of his back, my splayed fingers resting lightly on his right shoulder-blade – I could feel the weight of him lift and fall as he breathed. I'd missed his body, missed its strength and solidity. *The expression of a well-made man ... appears not only in his face ... You linger to see his back and the back of his neck and shoulder-side ...* The words drifted in from somewhere. When was the last time I'd heard that poem? I dozed off, trying to remember. Arash must have stirred because when I woke up again he was facing me, stretching and reaching out for me.

'You were muttering in your sleep,' he said, smiling, looking baggy-eyed, but relaxed.

'Walt Whitman,' I said. 'I was dreaming about Walt Whitman.'

'You were dreaming of Walt Whitman? Should I be jealous?'

'Not unduly. I was admiring your back and something he wrote about a well-made man came into my mind.' I repeated the lines. 'It's from "The Body Electric",' I said. 'I haven't thought about it since I was a first-year undergrad. It's a sort of rites-of-passage poem for me – the first time I read something that said lust for a man was OK, sex with a man was OK, that I could have sex without guilt, without shame. I read it and believed it. Well, I half believed it.'

'It's beautiful.'

'Up there with *cypress slender*, I reckon.' My voice had got huskier. He slipped his hand down and across my thigh. The body electric, for sure.

Afterwards, he got up, made coffee for us both, saying he was going round to his place to drop off his bags and check his mail. I was dozing off again when I heard the key in the lock and he was back. He'd only been gone about fifteen minutes.

'That was quick,' I said, rolling over. 'Come on back to bed. I'm still in need of a well-made man.'

Then I caught the look on his face. He was holding a letter and waved it at me feebly.

I scrambled up and put on my shorts as he made his way over and sat down heavily at the end of the bed. I bent down and touched his cheek. 'Bad news?' I asked. Unnecessary

84

question. Close up, I could see his face had taken on a peculiar olive pallor.

'Terrible.'

I went across to the corner sink, poured a glass of water and brought it over to him. He took it and sipped it slowly as I sat down next to him.

He lifted the letter up, then let his hand drop, as if the envelope weighed a ton. 'It's from Amir, a friend of mine in Tehran, telling me about a mutual friend of ours, Mirza, a lecturer on our course.' He looked down at the letter. 'It says here he's been arrested. SAVAK came for him in the middle of the night. Mirza in prison – I can't believe it. He's a good man, a gentle soul. He'd never do anyone any harm.' We sat quiet for a while, while he struggled to gather himself together. Then he started to tell me more about Mirza, about how he'd lectured mainly in Persian literature and specialised in Hafez's poetry.

'He was so proud of reminding us he came from Shiraz, like Hafez did. And he also had a bookshop, not much more than one smallish room at the back of the house he shared with his brother and family, near the university. He called it The Book Room. It was an easy meeting place for students, and it was full of treasures. You'd have to dig around for them but that was half the pleasure.'

He put the letter on the bed and took another sip of water. His hands were trembling, I noticed. 'The censorship restrictions toughened up, way back in 1971, when there was an increase in opposition to the Shah from both armed and peaceful activists. It wasn't just writers like Shamlu and others who suffered. It was a tricky time to have a job of any kind involving books. Publishers, booksellers, even school libraries had lists of banned books they had to get rid of, or refuse to stock.'

His body tensed as he remembered. 'They'd carry out spot checks – SAVAK, I mean. They were the ones who enforced the rules. They removed any books they considered to be misleading, and arrested over sixty publishers and booksellers. They held some of them for over a year, without formal charges, but Mirza escaped that initial trawl – he shifted books he thought might fall foul of censorship laws out of The Book Room to sympathetic friends, until the initial surge in reinforcement died down.'

His body relaxed a little. 'Then last year, just before I left to come here, the Shah had come in for overseas criticism about SAVAK, civil-rights abuses and his treatment of prisoners. Jimmy Carter made it part of his presidential election campaign to speak out about countries with a poor human-rights record and hinted America might not be so keen to do business with them. Then Amnesty International came out with a report on world-wide abuses and specifically mentioned Iran.'

It was on the tip of my tongue to say, *I know. Reza made sure he filled me in on some of the gruesome details on that*, but I held back: he needed to talk, he was obviously in shock.

'Whatever the Shah thought about the accusations, he obviously decided he'd better show he was willing to make some changes. He gave orders to ease up on censorship a little, and he let some dissident writers out of prison. I thought things were getting better.'

He picked up the letter and tapped it on the tips of his fingers. 'But it looks like there's been another purge. It says here that Mirza has been in prison for the past month.'

'I thought you said he'd got rid of any books that might incriminate him.'

'He must have forgotten this particular book was there. It's quite old now – it's been out for nearly ten years. It's a children's book.'

'They arrested him for having one book on the censorship list? A children's book?'

'Well, I guess it's a bit more than a children's book.' His eyes filled with tears. 'It's *The Little Black Fish*. It's a book that has special meaning for anyone from Tabriz, or has an Azerbaijani background. The author, Samad Berhangi, was from Tabriz – everyone from there knows his work and loves him. He was an Azerbaijani, a short-story writer, and a teacher, and he wrote in Azeri. The authorities tried to discourage that sort of thing, and he had to translate his work into Persian in order to be published.'

'But if it's a children's book, what did they find to censor?'

He shrugged. 'Little Black Fish is a young fish who leaves home because he longs to break away, to see what might be beyond the stream. He asks questions, difficult questions, of all the people he meets on his journey. He meets up with creatures like the Big Bad Pelican – who scoops up shoals of tiny helpless fish into his dark pouch-prison and eats them.'

He stopped for a moment, then managed a half-smile as he said, 'Reza used to read it to our next-door neighbour's children with a torch under his chin. He'd do a gobbling kind of sound for the Big Bad Pelican and grab them.'

I remembered the feeling I'd had when Reza had been checking me out, protecting his younger brother. I could imagine him scaring the shit out of next door's children.

'Anyway, Little Black Fish fights against dangerous creatures and outwits them by getting small creatures to work together. They all get swallowed by the Pelican, but Little Black Fish just happens to have a knife given to him by a friendly frog he met earlier on his adventures, so he slits the Pelican's pouch, and they all swim free.'

'Is that it? It sounds pretty innocuous to me.'

He shook his head and said sadly, 'This is Iran, Damian. Nothing is how it seems. It's an allegory, of course. Berhangi was a leftist sympathiser. When the tiny fish are first swallowed, they plead for their lives, and address the Big Bad Pelican as "Your Highness, Sir Pelican, so great and good and kind", so it's pretty obvious who that's meant to be. And Little Black Fish himself eventually dies, rescuing another little fish from a wicked seabird, another symbol of authority and danger. So Little Black Fish sacrifices his life and dies a hero.'

He added, 'But he did what he set out to do. He saw the stream through to the end.' He managed another small smile. 'It's always interpreted as being about the danger of daring to be politically different, and about the right to freedom and outwitting those with power, whatever the cost.'

He fell silent for a long moment, then said, 'They found Berhangi drowned in the Aras River, on the Iran-Azerbaijani border. The rumour has always been it was SAVAK police who killed him, although it's never been proven. A year after his death, in 1968, *The Little Black Fish* was published, but then the Shah's authorities banned it, and it's still banned.'

He shrugged. 'So, yes, in truth, it's not just an innocent children's book – everyone knows that. But to kill someone for writing it, or to imprison others for reading or circulating it . . .' His voice tailed off, and then he couldn't hold out any longer: he began to weep softly. I rested my hand on his arm until the tears subsided.

He straightened, moving quickly, almost in a panic, and put the letter into his shirt's breast pocket. 'I can't stand it in here. Let's go out for some air,' he muttered, and headed for the door, me trailing after him.

We drifted down to Telegraph Avenue, gravitating as usual towards Moe's Books.

Arash didn't say much, but he seemed to calm down as he rummaged around the second-hand section, picking out books, reading the title pages, then putting them back. Suddenly, he gave a little yelp of excitement. He'd found a 1928 second edition of Hafez poems, translated by Gertrude Bell, published originally in 1897. *Poems from the Divan of Hafiz*. There was a certain charm about Bell's use of *Hafiz*, the earlier spelling of the poet's name, something about it that spoke of the respectful correctness of her scholarly work.

It looked well travelled. It still had its dust jacket, a faded buff colour, nicked and worn at the corners, but intact. The spine was slightly slumped and there was a good deal of foxing, scattered like faint brown age spots, around the Heinemann windmill logo on the title page.

But the scars of time were all things that gave Arash pleasure. 'It's got its own hard-earned personality over nearly fifty years, this little artefact,' he said. 'Just think of the story it could tell in its own right – who might have read it and where it might have been, and now here it is, ending up with me, on the very day I hear about Mirza.'

It was expensive, but he bought it, and his face lost a little of its sadness.

We went across to the Med. While we were sipping our tea, he inscribed the book and pushed it across to me. 'For you. And thank you,' he said.

'For what?'

'For listening.'

'Not one of my strong suits.'

'You're getting better at it.'

He'd written: *To Damian. Berkeley, June 1977.* The rest was in Persian script.

'It says: *Remember the Little Black Fish who dared to be different and saw the stream to the end.'* He reached across and stroked my hand.

He didn't come back to Chilton Street with me. He just wanted some time on his own, to think some more about Mirza. I sat in the wicker chair in my room, going over the day. In the space of less than an hour, we'd gone from indulging ourselves in the sensuousness of Whitman and Hafez and early morning sex, to the reality of the Iranian security services imprisoning one man and probably murdering another over a children's book.

The choice was suddenly very real. Should I take a chance and go back with Arash, or should I walk away, given what I now knew? Maybe *should* I walk away was the wrong question.

Maybe it was more like *could* I walk away. This was no allegory I found myself in, and I was no brave and bold little black fish. The Tabriz question had suddenly got a whole lot more urgent and even more complicated.

*

Kupfermühle, 31 December (Sylvester)

I have decided not to write today. I need to take a break, or it will break me. I'm going to have a leisurely lunch, my last frozen meal, then read the next part of Anna's journal, clean the place up, listen to some music. Ordinary things. I need to remind myself of ordinary things.

Anna's last entry for 1977 ends in September. We made the same decision about Tabriz around the same time, then, but it took her another four months to get herself there.

*

Anna

Oxford, July–September 1977

The *Shahnameh* summer. That's how I remember the summer of 1977. The three of us sitting outside on warm evenings, round the table near the clematis arch. The first time I did that, I found myself panicking. Farzad had led the way out into the garden and naturally headed for the table, but the thought of spending an evening sitting near to the spot where I'd found my father was so unsettling I almost bolted. I wanted to shout, *No, not there, the bench up nearer the house would be better*, but by the time I'd got myself together, Farzad was already sitting down and pouring the wine. It was difficult, and I knew I was overly quiet, but I stayed put. And that was the spot we ended up in every evening we sat out. I surprised myself, because it got easier to be there although I always sat with my back to the arch.

On the evenings it rained, we'd stay in the sitting room, with the French windows open. Firuzeh would use a magnifying glass on the *Shahnameh* catalogue illustrations to show me details, such as a minuscule whisker in a prince's beard.

Farzad would chip in, as usual. 'Make sure you show her the corners.' He said it teasingly, but his comments were as pointed as ever. 'Take a close-up look at the servants, the peasants in the corners, not the princes. The real story is in the faces of the little people.' But after a few glasses of wine, he'd also end up telling stories of princes and shahs, good and bad. When he began a *Shahnameh* tale he'd deliberately parody what he said was the Persian storyteller style, all rolling eyes and extravagant hand gestures, but almost despite himself, he'd finish off reciting Ferdowsi couplets from memory with quiet respect. One of his favourites was the story of Prince Rostam choosing his wonder horse Rakhsh, a stallion with a 'red coat', which I eventually realised probably meant a 'bay', a word that seemed to delight Farzad, for some reason.

'A bay stallion with the strength of an elephant, the speed of a racing camel, the courage of a mountain lion,' he'd say, 'and beautiful, of course – *black-eyed, iron hoofs . . . his body a wonder to behold . . . like saffron petals, mottled red and gold.*' He'd recite in Persian, and Firuzeh would help me, translating some lines into English as best she could, which delighted her as well. I didn't mind not understanding the actual language. I preferred to listen and go with the Persian rhythms, sounds and cadences. Farzad's dramatic gestures would give me enough of a clue as to the storyline and the emotions. It was a good time, the *Shahnameh* summer.

The first week in August, we went to London. It was my birthday and Firuzeh had arranged a surprise for me. She'd contacted a friend of her father's in the Middle East Department at the British Museum, and set up a special viewing for us of a *Shahnameh* miniature they had in their collection. It just so happened it illustrated Farzad's favourite story, of Rakhsh, of course, who kills a lion while Prince Rostam sleeps.

'It's an early sixteenth-century miniature, a very fine example, from the Tabriz School, when Persia was ruled from Tabriz by the Safavid dynasty.' The young curator chatted to us as we followed her through huge oak doors to the Middle East Collections room. 'The experts say it was meant for a new illustrated version of the *Shahnameh* and was probably painted by Sultan Mohammad, a brilliant court miniaturist in a Tabriz atelier at the time.'

She ushered us over to the long table in the middle of the room and pointed to a painting, no more than twelve inches by eight, placed on a small table easel in front of us.

The miniature glowed with colour and energy, its old gold borders still gleaming, down through more than four and a half centuries.

'So here we have Rostam lying down,' the curator pointed at the exotically clothed prince, 'and falling asleep on his carpet, in a forest – that's not strictly true, by the way. The actual *Shahnameh* story has Rostam falling asleep in a pasture, but I guess a menacing forest with rocky outcrops was more interesting for the artist to paint. Anyway, forest or pasture, it turns out to be the lair of a lion who returns and attacks Rakhsh, but he kills the lion, and saves the sleeping Rostam.'

Rostam's sleeves, leggings and quiver glimmered jewel-like in lapis lazuli – 'Only the most expensive paint colour for the prince, of course,' whispered Farzad.

The depiction of the two animals in mortal combat was so well observed – the lion's wide nose, flattened as he latches onto the horse just above his fetlock, and Rakhsh's nostrils flaring as he sinks his teeth into the back of the lion's lower neck.

But for me, it was the forest itself that was mesmerising. The more you looked, the more alive you realised it was. 'Phantasmagoric vegetation and rocks,' the curator said, passing us her magnifying glass so we could see the exquisite detail and textures hardly observable to the naked eye. Individual fronds with long thin necks tipped by snarling feline heads. Rocky outcrops with grotesque faces, possibly human, or big cats, or monkeys. Leaves of flat matte green, flowers in violet, cobalt, spiky red. A tree, its bark the colour of eau-de-Nil, like shot brocade.

The curator guided us to Rostam's clutch of arrows. 'This is one of my favourite details,' she said, with a little self-conscious smile. 'Look closely with the glass and you'll see tiny, tiny strokes or, at most, just the hint of a stroke, for each individual arrow. Stunning.'

How did they create them? I wondered. Even the glass struggled to magnify the strokes for each individual arrow.

As if reading my thoughts, the curator said, 'Hairs from a squirrel's tail were the most sought after for their brushes, and sometimes single long hairs of Persian cats. They separated the hairs into exactly the same length, then threaded them through a quill, pulling them out at the narrow end, varying them from extremely fine to thick.'

My eyes suddenly filled with tears. That's just the sort of detail my father would have loved to hear. Ambushed again. No one noticed, they were all too absorbed in the miniature.

We had lunch at a little café near the museum, all of us moved in different ways by what we'd seen. Even Farzad had mislaid his cynicism, which surprised me.

'For me,' he said, 'it's the way Ferdowsi's poetry is woven into the picture. Did you notice the leaves of the tree in the top right corner? They are Ferdowsi's words written in calligraphy. Each leaf is a word. His poetry becomes the leaves in the trees.'

I hadn't seen that at all.

When we got back to Oxford that evening, they gave me a present. It was a copy of the *Shahnameh,* a prose translation in English by Reuben Levy.

'We got it in a second-hand shop in town,' said Firuzeh. 'It's the only version in English we could find.'

Farzad had written on the title page, in painstakingly neat

English: *To Anna, from Firuzeh and Farzad, 1977. Poetry written as leaves in the trees.*

They left for Tabriz in mid-September, with promises to keep in touch.

I missed them. The feeling of restlessness came back when I was at home alone, but I was no longer so susceptible to such deep sadness. The house seemed to have acquired a new set of memories, which had nothing to do with my father. I'd be stretched out reading on the chesterfield and I'd look across to his corner, expecting to see him there, but sometimes it would be Farzad, sitting in the rattan chair, wine glass in hand, reciting Ferdowsi. Or I'd be at the kitchen table, and rather than seeing my father eating toast and reading the Sunday papers, I would have a sudden memory of Firuzeh leaning over her *Shahnameh* catalogue with her magnifying glass, zoning in on some Persian courtier's jewelled turban.

One late September day, I looked out into the garden down to the clematis arch, its leaves beginning to drop, and the first image that came into my head was not the day I found my father there. It was of Firuzeh and Farzad sitting at the table on a summer evening, the three of us laughing as Farzad hammered up the tale of Rostam and Rakhsh.

I was shocked at first by the idea of these new memories usurping the old. The image of my father dead in that spot in the garden was burned into my mind. To think I could now associate a new memory with such a highly emotive space was unsettling, as if I was forgetting what had happened to him there. But of course I never would forget. And the more I thought about it, the more convinced I became that my father would not like his beloved clematis to be associated with death. He'd nursed it back to health and new life and was overjoyed when it flowered so well that last time. He would like the idea of it being associated with laughter and wine and Persian poetry. So that was how I needed to remember it, too.

I slowly began to realise I'd turned the corner. I was accepting his death and letting him go. Something Charlie had said when I'd stayed with him last Christmas came to mind. I was having a particularly bad day, spending most of it in bed, weeping on and off. He'd sat beside me and held my hand in the kindly way I suspect he uses for his patients.

He hesitated, then said, 'It must be so painful for you, Anna. I know you were close to your father. But, remember, you are his legacy. He played his part in giving you life, and from what I knew of him, he'd want you to get on and live it.'

I bridled at that – what could he really know of how painful it was? His parents were still living. But he carried on speaking, choosing his words carefully. 'He wouldn't want you to be miserable and unfulfilled and lonely.' He stroked my cheek. 'I don't want you to be miserable and unfulfilled and lonely.' He kissed my fingertips. 'Just remember you won't always feel like this. Grieve for him, yes, that's natural, but at some point, you'll realise you need to move on. And don't feel guilty about that. He'd want that too.'

Quite a speech for Charlie, but I was still too engulfed in grief to appreciate what he was saying. Deep down, I knew he was right. I just hadn't quite got to that point.

Then, at the end of October, everything fell into place. The early groundwork for the research was going well, and the project had been extended. The field work was now spread out over three locations, worldwide. The prof rang to say they were in the process of arranging two new project field centres at Iranian universities, one in Tehran, the other in Tabriz. If it got the go-ahead, it would be around March next year. Was I interested? This is it, I thought. This is the push I need. I thought of Firuzeh and Farzad. It would help that I knew people in Tabriz. So I accepted the post and this time I knew I'd keep to it. It was time to move on.

*

Damian

Kupfermühle, 31 December (Sylvester)

Now I understand. Moving on for Anna wasn't dated hippie-speak. It was a genuine hard-earned change in her way of thinking. Allowing her father to be dead. That's what moving on meant for her. Christ, I envy her. But how can I allow Arash to be dead when I don't even know for sure that he *is*? That's the worst, the not knowing.

I'm in danger of spiralling down again, so I force myself to get ready for Sylvester with Frau Jensen. I take a slow hot shower, dress in my neatest jeans and the cashmere sweater my mother sent me for Christmas last year, and go round to the Christiangang courtyard about eight p.m. She has also made an effort, which for her means casting off her ubiquitous double-thick cardigan for a slightly less bulky Aran sweater, her prize possession from a birdwatching trip to Ireland. Ever practical, she's still in her comfortable tracksuit bottoms and woolly slipper socks with their Scandinavian patterns. The long room is bright and cosy as ever, and there is a wonderful smell of spicy soup.

We sit at the kitchen table. 'No point moving to the other end,' she says. 'The soup is nearly ready.' The table is set with cheerful crockery, none of it matching.

I hand over the Jameson and also a bottle of Franken wine, which Jesper had left in the house and had told me to drink. 'What luxury!' she says, her eyes widening as she holds up the green Bocksbeutel by its short neck to admire its flattened ellipsoid shape.

'I wasn't sure it would go with lentil soup, but I brought it anyway.'

'We'll drink it now, so we don't have to see whether it goes or not. It'll already have gone,' she says, and gets two wine glasses out of a nearby cupboard.

'*Prost!*' I say, and raise my glass.

'*Sláinte!*' she says. She learned that on her Irish birdwatching holiday.

The wine is wonderful, earthy and dry, glowing a pale metallic yellow in the glass.

We don't say anything, just sip and enjoy it. Frau Jensen tops up our glasses. 'A little more, then we'll have the soup.'

She sits back in her chair. 'It doesn't seem a year since you moved into the village.'

'I didn't think I'd be staying this long.'

'Couldn't stand the excitement?' She laughs.

'Something like that.'

'We had enough excitement in the war. Not the good kind of excitement either.'

'I can imagine.' I'm surprised she mentioned the war again and wonder if it's a leftover from visiting her sister. No one talked about the Second World War here, at least not the people I'd met, even though there was a strong, proud naval tradition around the Flensburg area. It had deep historical connections to the German Navy during both world wars, but particularly the Second. I'd noticed though, that sometimes the students at the college were starting to ask questions about what had gone on in the Third Reich, which was not encouraged by the education authorities.

I take my cue from her having brought it up. 'They were saying at college that at the end of the war, what was left of the Third Reich moved up here from Berlin to form the government, the Flensburg government, after Hitler committed suicide in April 1945.'

I realise I might be on delicate territory, mentioning the Third Reich, Hitler, and the 1945 Flensburg government in the same sentence.

Frau Jensen takes another sip of wine. 'That's right. Flensburg was teeming with German officers. Admiral Dönitz was Hitler's successor and, being a Navy man, he thought Flensburg was one of the safest places to be. Albert Speer and Jodl were here, too.'

She continues thoughtfully, 'They all eventually ended up at the Nuremberg trials in 1946, of course. Jodl was hanged for war crimes. Speer got twenty years in prison. Donitz got ten years. When he came out, he lived in a pretty little village quite near where Lise lives, outside Hamburg. He only died three years ago. Christmas Eve, it was. Huge funeral. Over two and a half thousand mourners, and a forest of Iron Crosses.' She sighed.

This is the first time I've heard a German mention any Nazis by name, apart from the students mentioning Hitler. I wonder if it's the wine, but I think not. Maybe a week with her sister, reliving the traumas of the war, has made her more open to talking about it.

She hesitates, then says, 'Did your students tell you about Lord Haw-Haw?'

'Lord Haw-Haw?' I'm so surprised, I sound like a donkey when I say his name.

'You know, William Joyce. The British called him Lord Haw-Haw. He was British, although apparently he had a claim to being Irish and American too, but he broadcast propaganda from Hamburg for the Third Reich during the war.'

'Yes, I know who he was. He'd put on an affected upper-class English drawl when he made his broadcasts – that was why the British press nicknamed him Lord Haw-Haw.'

What on earth has made her think of him? I ask myself.

'He was hanged for treason in your Wandsworth prison, thirty-eight years ago this coming Tuesday.'

Her face has a slight flush to it. I wonder what her special interest is in Haw-Haw. She's well up on the detail. I remember his story had been all over the news in 1976. The authorities back in 1946 had buried him in an unmarked grave within Wandsworth Prison grounds, but his daughter, backed by a group of influential campaigners, succeeded in getting his remains taken back to Galway and buried in Bohermore Cemetery. At the time, there'd been re-runs of his infamous broadcasts, with that fake upper class accent of his: 'Jairmany calling! Jairmany calling!'

The reason the story had caught my attention back then was not so much because of what he'd done – to me the Second World War was very much my parents' war – but because his father was Irish and Joyce had lived in Galway for some years as a child, and that was where my mother's family was from originally.

But why would Frau Jensen mention Lord Haw-Haw? I am about to ask when she beats me to it.

'He lived next door for over a month.'

'What do you mean, he lived next door?'

'Here. He lived here, next door, with the Asmussens. Joyce and his wife moved in with Frau Asmussen – she was English – and her husband Fred, in early May 1945. I remember it was beautiful weather, full of May blossom, and it was the first year we had the bunting up for *Pfingsten* – your "Whitsun" – since before the war.

'I think they'd been trying to escape over the border into Denmark, hoping to go on to Sweden and across to Ireland if they could get a passage, but they had to come back. They were frightened of getting captured by the Danish resistance, who were on the border, looking for escapees. They called themselves the Hansens. He was Fritz, and he always spoke English, and she was Margaret. I was seventeen, then. I thought she was very sophisticated – she had a wonderful fur coat, which she wore when she first arrived in the village, even in the warm May weather. Lise used to chat to her. Said she was very nice to talk to, very sympathetic when Lise told her about her fiancé. There were rumours the couple drank a lot, though. Gin, mostly. And quarrelled a lot too.'

She pauses for breath and grins at me. 'You look shocked.'

'I am. I had no idea Kupfermühle had such a colourful past.'

'It's not something we talk about. It was not so good after

the war to be known as the village that harboured a British traitor.'

'I seem to remember two British soldiers caught him in some woods somewhere. I always thought the woods were near Hamburg, but it must have been here.'

'That's right, just along the road there. He'd gone to collect firewood for Frau Asmussen. One of the British soldiers shot and wounded him in the backside – they thought he was going for a gun in his pocket, but he wasn't. The one who shot him was a German Jew, who'd gone to your country before the war, and then joined the army.' She drains her glass. 'God's little joke,' she says.

'What happened to the Asmussens?'

'The British arrested them, but let them go. They always said they had no idea who the Hansens really were. I do remember being scared.' She looks thoughtful again. 'The British came right up to our houses here. They had two armoured cars with guns on them, and a group of soldiers surrounded the house and went in. They searched it and took Margaret away. She was wearing her fur coat. They questioned everyone in the village, everyone in our row of houses here. But no one in the village knew anything about them.'

'What did you think about Joyce?'

'He was a Nazi sympathiser. I hated the Nazis and everything they stood for. But all of us just felt helpless and terrified. So, I suppose we should have hated Joyce – after all, he worked for Goebbels and his propaganda machine. But Lise thought he had a certain charm. And he always managed to get food brought out from Flensburg for us – things were scarce then. But he put us all in danger. Lise said we were lucky. If it had been the Russians, rather than the British, who'd caught him, they would probably have shot the lot of us for collaborating with the enemy. Thank God the Russians never got to Flensburg.'

She shudders, then refills our glasses and raises hers. 'To no more wars.'

'No more wars.'

'Time for the soup, I think.'

The rest of the evening is taken up with eating the coppery-coloured lentil soup, which is delicious, then chatting about swans. She gets out a beautiful book about them. It's not just about the swans themselves, but about the folklore, art and literature associated with them.

'"On they fly,"' she reads, '"to Valhalla and the Moon."'

She says I can borrow it. We sit in front of the stove, drinking coffee, having finished the Franken wine between us. It seems to get to midnight quickly and she brings out two small sherry glasses for the Jameson. We hear fireworks go off somewhere in the distance and toast the New Year. 1984. George Orwell territory.

I leave soon after. She makes me take the Jameson home. I must admit, I don't argue too hard. 'One last tot before I go,' I say, so she fills the sherry glasses again.

'To Lise and you,' I say. '"To Valhalla and the Moon".' We clink glasses.

Her eyes fill with tears. 'To all of us. "To Valhalla and the Moon".'

I give her a hug, and her bony shoulders underneath the bulky Aran wool remind me of the Whooper scapulars.

It's a cold, clear night with no fresh snow. I walk round to my place and check her outside light from my kitchen window. It's still on. I can imagine her sitting in front of the stove, watching the last of the embers dying down, probably thinking about Lise.

Tonight, for the first time since I met her, I've had a sense of her as a young girl. To me, she's always been a feisty middle-aged woman. But once, she was seventeen. Surrounded by May blossom and Whitsun bunting. Watching a sophisticated Englishwoman wafting around the *nyborder* houses in the Christiangang courtyard in a glamorous fur coat in the middle of May. Something about that image touches me and warms me through.

It suddenly occurs to me that this will be the last Sylvester I'll be here. My contract with the college finished in December. And I didn't extend it. Jesper's parents are back in April, so I have to be out of the house. I have no idea what I'll do next. No idea at all.

It's a new year, a new month, a new day. And I haven't thought about Arash for the past three hours. But I'll be back to the Berkeley journal later today for one last time.

*

Berkeley, June

The problem with '*rose*'

Things came to a head this week, and it was Arash, not me, who triggered things off. He'd seemed a little distant, but I put it down to tiredness from his trip and the news about Mirza. He didn't talk about that, and I didn't push him, but I was beginning to panic inside. A space was opening between us and I couldn't reach him.

Then, on the Friday, I had an invitation to an end-of-semester faculty drinks party, in the early evening, and Arash was invited with me. We had the afternoon free and he wanted to go for a walk – anywhere, he said, where there weren't any skyscrapers. I think he'd found New York quite stressful. He wasn't a big-city man, that was for sure. So we decided to visit the Rose Gardens. It was a half-hour trek uphill on Euclid Avenue, north of the campus, through a pleasant residential area. It felt good to leave the student buzz behind us, but we walked slightly apart, the distance between us palpable.

The gardens weren't exactly a cool place for students to hang out, but Arash had a thing about roses. We'd already been there in the second week of May, when most of the first blooms had made their appearance. '*In the city of Tabriz, roses, roses scent the breeze,*' he'd quoted, his smile as wide as I'd ever seen it when we stopped to take them in. They were planted in tiered rows down the side of a hill, creating a living amphitheatre of at least fifteen hundred bushes. Brilliant rainbow rows curving around the hillside, from velvety purples, through reds and pinks, yellows and oranges to purest white.

Mrs Miller had told me that on a clear day, there was a spectacular view of the Bay and the Golden Gate Bridge, looking out to the west from the top of the rose terraces.

'You don't get to see that unique colour in all its glory, that iconic international orange,' she said, 'it's toned down by the distance. But you do see the very bones of the bridge, connecting with the hills and the sea and the sky, like it belongs. It's wonderful.'

But that first May morning we visited, it was the early summer fog rolling in from the sea that stunned us most. It funnelled through the metal structures, slowly ghosting upwards over the vertical rows of steel suspension ropes and the convex curves made by the two main cables, leaving only the saddles of the two towers poking through the mist. Its eerie beauty was mesmerising. Then the south tower foghorn sounded. A short note, deep and low, a pause and it sounded again, a longer note this time, as though it had breathed in, then breathed out harder to make sure it was heard.

Arash had rested his hand on my shoulder and stroked my upper arm.

'This is one of those times I'll remember for ever,' I said. 'The two of us here, that view, that sound, the scent of the roses.'

This afternoon, it was a hot June day, and we ended up sitting on a bench in the shade. The Golden Gate shimmered in the distance, stripped bare to its fundamentals, just as Mrs Miller had said, its curves and perpendiculars silhouetted against green hills, blue sky and even deeper blue sea. The view was sharp and clear, no fog to befuddle the mind.

This is it, I thought. Now is the time to talk. But just as I was about to say something, a young mum with a toddler and a baby in a pushchair came and sat down on the next bench along and pandemonium broke out around manoeuvring straws into drink cartons and sun cream onto noses, and the moment had gone.

Fuck.

We stayed a few minutes longer, then walked back down to the campus, talking about the mundane things we had to do for the rest of the day. As we went through the North Gate entrance I had a sudden memory of watching Reza taking photos of the casement windows in the courtyard of North Gate Hall. Six months ago, I thought, I didn't know either of these two brothers. Now my life was inextricably tangled up with them.

The drinks party was in full swing when we got there. I'd been doing the social rounds more since I'd had Arash with me. His quiet charm went down well with the faculty academics. We were standing in a little circle of students gathered round one of the younger profs. He was bemoaning the fact that the seventies had turned out to be the decade when it seemed nothing had happened on campus, give or take the odd demonstration, all a bit feeble compared to the sixties, when everything had happened. That turned the conversation round to the sixties' Freedom of Speech Movement when students had insisted that the university administration lift the ban on campus-based political activities and acknowledge their right to free speech and academic freedom. That had led to the daily protests on campus in 1964–5.

'Reckoned to be the first mass act of civil disobedience on an American college campus,' said the young prof, a note of wistful pride in his voice.

Those were the riots Mrs Miller had mentioned, when her daughter was tear-gassed.

A group of earnest Californian academics soon gathered round the prof, debating the philosophical tenets of freedom of speech. The discussion got pretty heated towards the end of the party. Arash listened but didn't join in the conversation and I could feel him slowly growing tense as he stood beside me.

When we got back to Chilton Street, we just about made it to my room before he exploded. It was the first time I'd seen him like that: he was ordinarily so even-handed, he'd drive me mad sometimes. I'd be fizzing about something, and he'd just sit there, Zen-like.

'Freedom of speech? Freedom of speech?' He sat down heavily in the chair under the skylight and banged the wicker arm with the palm of his hand.

'They live in a country where it's an intellectual game to discuss the pros and cons of freedom of speech. In Iran, you could be arrested for having the conversation they had this evening. That lecture the prof gave on Shamlu, he'd have been imprisoned or worse if he'd done that back home.'

The mention of Shamlu's lecture brought Reza to mind, when I'd told him about how Arash had said you could respect the dissidents, but not get involved, and how that had probably triggered Reza's decision to educate me with a dose of Baraheni's poems. This is my chance, I thought. I could use Reza and the Baraheni poems to start the conversation about Tabriz and what it was like, and that might lead on to what we were going to do. But this time I needed to be the one who stayed cool. For once, I needed to do the listening first, rather than the jabbering on.

'So tell me about it,' I said, my voice slow and quiet. 'Tell me what Iran is really like.'

'I haven't been honest with you, Damian. I haven't been honest with myself. It's only now, when I'm beginning to think about going back that I realise I have to face it.'

He ran his fingers through his hair, making the same gesture of exasperation as Reza had when I was challenging him about Baraheni.

'It's even worse than I told you, what's going on. Writers in my country end up in prison if they use the wrong word! One single word!'

He said it in a tone not of sadness and despair, like when he'd had the letter about Mirza, but more a tone of quiet fury, alien to the Arash I knew.

'Individual words are banned. Can you believe that? *Night* is banned. *Winter* is banned. *Forest* is banned.' He ticked them off on his fingers.

'The censorship authorities say writers could subvert these words, use them as secret metaphors to criticise the Shah and the government. There's some truth in that, like the Shamlu poem about the cockroaches. Poets come up with double metaphors, writing for two sets of readers: to open up the ideas of repression to the people, and to conceal those ideas from the censors. So *night* and *winter* can be read as meaning a time when things are uncertain, even dangerous, or where things die or lie dormant rather than grow and flourish. They don't fit with the image of the vibrant, dynamic new Iran. As for *forest* – they say it can be associated with the guerrillas fighting the government forces up in the northern forests of Iran.'

His face was now more anguished than angry. 'Even *rose* is banned.'

'*Rose?*' I said, disbelief in my voice. 'How can you ban *rose* from Persian poetry? From any poetry?'

He looked at me, shaking his head. 'The problem with *rose* is that the censors think it would remind people of one of our most extreme dissidents – a writer called Golesorkhi. The word *rose* in Persian is *gol* and a red rose is *gol-e sorkh*. So using the actual word for rose, or red rose, is near to using his name – Golesorkhi – so that would make people think of him and what he stood for. He was a journalist and poet, but he was also a committed Communist and activist, a member of the Tudeh Party. A hero to some. People compared him to Che Guevara.'

His voice had become quite flat now, the emotion pushed down, as he recounted the details. 'Our military put him on trial in 1973, accusing him of planning to kidnap the Shah's son and assassinate him. It was never proven and he always denied it. But it shocked people that anyone could even think of doing such a thing. They tried him in a military court, so there was no defence, and it was televised live. He said at his trial that he was being tried for being a Communist, not for conspiracy.'

His shoulders sagged, as if the burden of remembering was too much. Then he said, 'It was unbearable to watch on the TV. He was defiant to the last, disobeying the judge, delivering fiery speeches about the exploitation of the masses, and against tyranny, criticising what was going on in the name of the Shah. Whatever you thought of him and his views, there was bravery about him, the way he stood up and said what he said. And poignancy, really. It was obvious what the outcome would be. And he knew it.'

'What happened to him?'

'They executed him in 1974, with his comrade, Daneshian. They took them to a field outside Tehran, and shot them both at dawn. They showed that live on TV too.'

Then he hunched forward. 'So, that's why *rose* is banned. And all the other words. The security powers see writers using words not just to express themselves but as weapons against the state. Writers themselves say words are their only weapons. And the state sees words as more dangerous than guns.'

'*Night. Winter. Forest. Rose.*' He listed the words again, like some sad litany. 'One word could get you six months in prison, or worse, and everything that goes with that. And then . . . what they do to people in there.' He raised his hands in a gesture of despair.

Now was the moment. I settled my breathing. 'I know,' I said. 'Reza lent me the Baraheni poems.' I kept my voice as neutral as I could. 'I didn't know what to make of them. Do you think it's true, then, what he wrote?'

No need to mention the torment I'd gone through reading them, I thought, or tell him his brother was a manipulative

arsehole. And no need to tell him I knew he'd had a copy of
God's Shadow for some time, and wish he'd shared it with me
earlier, so Reza wouldn't have ambushed me. None of that
mattered.

'Why would he lie?' he said, echoing Reza's argument. 'He'd
be betraying every other writer who's been imprisoned, making
all that up.'

He rubbed his forehead with the side of his hand, and it
reminded me of myself, trying to massage out the Baraheni
images. 'Even if I didn't believe him, the fact that it's a possibility
– the thought that maybe they could take you and torture you,
like I'm sure they've done with Mirza . . . The fear of that. Fear.
That's SAVAK's biggest weapon.'

He looked straight at me. 'I've been wondering whether to
ask you to come to Tabriz to visit me, stay a while, see how
things go.' He shrugged. 'But how can I? You don't have to be
an activist to get into trouble, you don't have to be involved at
all – you might not even agree with all the things the dissidents
say or write. I certainly don't. I don't see things in such extreme
terms as they do. I benefitted a lot from the opportunities in
Tabriz for a good education – I kept my head down, worked
hard, got a university place. A generation ago, that would have
been nothing but a dream for someone like me. Then I got to
do extra training for my librarianship qualification, then
Berkeley, all paid for by the government. I would never have got
any of that if it hadn't been for the Shah's determination to
improve education and literacy in our country. I have to believe
in a better future for all of us. Yes, there are huge problems – on
censorship and intimidation – and we should be allowed to
comment and criticise, as long as we do it constructively. But I
can't be like the dissidents. I'd like to be fearless and outspoken,
but I'm not. I don't have that kind of courage within me to fight
openly for those things. I'm just an ordinary person, trying to
live a peaceful life. I want to go back. I *need* to go back to
Tabriz, maybe I can help to change things by encouraging

students in their university studies so they can secure good jobs in our country, without getting involved in demos and dissident groups and all the rest of it.'

All this came out in one long rush, a year's worth of pent-up anger and tight self-control to avoid the open expression of any opinion about what was going on in Iran to either his fellow academics or Iranians on campus. But underneath the anger I sensed despair.

'But I'm not deluding myself.' He sounded weary. 'The reality in Iran right now is that you might be just an ordinary person who gets caught up in something by accident. The fear is always there, the tension – you breathe it in.' He let out a deep sigh. 'That's my country, Damian, that's Iran. One side of it anyway. How can I ask you to live somewhere like that?'

He'd thought of asking me to go to Tabriz with him. So he felt the same about us as I did. Now I could say it.

'Because you live there,' I said quietly. 'And I've thought about it for months and I haven't a clue how it will work out. All I know is I want to be with you and see where it takes us.' I reached across for his hand.

And that was the starting point. That was when we really began to talk about us. I surprised him when I told him how long I'd thought about coming to Tabriz and how far forward I was with fixing up a job at the university. And for the first time, we said we loved each other. However bad it might get, we said, we couldn't face not being together.

We talked a little about practicalities. He said we'd have to live separately in Tabriz, definitely not in the same house. He said he knew a woman from Tabriz University who rented rooms to Western teachers. We didn't come to any more firm decisions, not then, but the more we talked, the more it all seemed possible.

We fell into bed, exhausted. Neither of us slept very well, but there was a new closeness, as if we'd put ourselves through a test and passed it. The next morning, I made coffee and told him I needed a morning to myself – the first time I'd ever said that, I always fitted in with him. He smiled, said, 'OK,' hugged me and left.

I wandered over to a small café I'd always ignored, near Sather Gate, and treated myself to waffles and maple syrup and ate them slowly, going over what we'd talked about last night. I ran a list of names through my head – Shamlu, Golesorkhi, Baraheni, Berhangi and all the others I'd learned about in the past six months. How many more writers and poets and activists were there out there suffering, because the only weapons they had were words, and they were prepared to use them? To risk being persecuted, imprisoned, tortured, and possibly killed because of something they'd written. Not to mention the people who printed the books, sold the books, read the books, or passed the books on, ending up the same way.

Could I really live with that? I told myself that if Arash could, then so could I.

*

A week later, I'd signed up to teach summer school at Berkeley, for some extra cash, and then fitted in a quick trip to Oxford, to get the paperwork sorted for the job in Tabriz. I'd have to go back to the UK briefly again for the visa and to see my parents, but if all went according to plan, I'd finish teaching summer school, then follow Arash back to Tabriz sometime in late September.

When I got back to Berkeley from Oxford, it was different in those last few weeks we had together. I felt more of an equal partner. We'd been honest with each other. I'd made a decision. It felt right.

He left at the end of July. I buried myself in teaching summer school and lived off his letters, which came weekly. We'd arranged to send them through the American Consulate in Tabriz, as Arash, having been the part-time librarian, had American contacts there who would act as posties for us. It was quicker that way, and more secure, Arash said, as mail was prone to go astray between Tehran and Tabriz by ordinary Iranian services. I made it a ritual to take myself off to the Med, drink tea with lemon, read his letter and try to conjure him up.

The first was mainly about how glad he was to be back in Tabriz, but also how much he missed Berkeley, which I knew was code for how much he missed me. The second was more of the same. The third was to tell me he'd fixed up a room in a house for me. He hoped it would be OK. 'I'm still glad to be back,' he wrote, 'but so much has changed. Or maybe I have changed,' he added.

That sent me into a panic. Was that code to say he was having second thoughts about us? There followed a three-week wobble, reflected in letters to-ing and fro-ing, like demented carrier pigeons. Well, I was the demented one, Arash his usual cautious self. But was he cautious because he'd changed his mind, or because he was wary of prying eyes?

What do you mean, things have changed? Is it still OK for me to come?

I wish it more than anything. I just don't want you to be disappointed when you get here. The mood in Iran has become quite tense. I can't say too much in a letter.

Whatever it's like, I'm coming. I've booked my flight.

His next letters were more relaxed, telling me about the things he wanted to show me when I got there. We'll be all right, I told myself. Once I'm there, it'll be like it was.

But it unsettled me, his reference to things being tense and the change in mood. So, I invited my faculty professor to lunch at the Bear's Lair, He was from Tehran originally but had been in the US for six years and was well respected in academia, fast making a name for himself in comparative linguistics. We'd got on well, and it was he who'd made a point of inviting Arash to come with me to the end-of-semester drinks in July. I thought I'd sound him out about how things were back home.

We made small-talk about Oxford and the summer he'd spent there in 1973, how much he'd enjoyed it, and I said I was looking forward to going to Iran. 'I've heard from Arash that it's changed a lot in the year he's been away.'

The prof nodded. 'I've heard that too.'

'I guess I should find out more. I've really been concentrating on the poetry, and on Arash, if I'm honest, rather than the politics of the place.'

'You're going at a time of great change.' He sat back in his chair. 'Some of it is exciting, some of it maybe too fast for people.' His voice sounded very even, as if he were formulating an academic proposition – *The pros and cons of great political change: discuss.* He seemed distinctly wary of expressing a personal political opinion.

He gave me a look, the kind I recognised from Reza – a sizing-me-up sort of look.

Do all Iranians have that look in their repertoire? I found myself thinking.

He seemed to come to a decision, because he went on to say, 'One of my Iranian undergraduate students is involved in an interesting project. He's just finished part one of it for his first year end-of-year paper. It could possibly be of help to you.'

'What's it about?'

'He's thinking of going on to do a master's here in journalism, and he's begun to look into how the Western press has been writing about Iran, the Shah in particular, over the decade from 1970 to the present day. You know, publications like the *Washington Post, New York Times, Time Magazine,* plus a few European contributions – mainstream middlebrow journalism for the most part. If he does stay on to do research, he'll be around until the end of the decade to provide an overview of the whole period. It should be a fascinating piece of work – he's a bright spark. It's highly selective, and a bit rough and ready at the moment, in terms of his thinking, but even as it stands, it's an easy way to learn something about what's been going on, at least from a Western perspective. You might like to take a look at it.'

He raised his eyebrows speculatively, his tone still very much that of a neutral academic recommending useful background material.

I played along. 'Sounds good. Is he still on campus?'

The prof nodded. 'I'll get him to contact you.'

The next day, a message had been left in my faculty pigeon-hole from a Massoud Amini, with a sheaf of typed notes and an expensive-looking full-colour-Xeroxed front page from *Time* magazine, dated 4 November 1974.

> *The prof asked me to pass these on to you. They're the notes I used for my informal presentation on the paper I submitted. It's actually a tapescript, as I recorded my presentation in English to begin with, with the help of the prof, to practise and make sure my English was good enough, before I 'went live'! I'd be pleased to know what you think. Happy reading!*

I spent an interesting morning at the Med going through the tapescript. It might have been selective, and his bias was obvious, but if even half of what was said was true, it made more sense of Arash's comments about how things were.

Massoud Amini. Tapescript of Seminar Notes, June 1977

The Shah of Iran. Myth and Reality.

I'd like to spend time looking at the way in which the Shah of Iran has been presented in the American main-stream media over the past three years or so, and I'll be using specific examples to illustrate the points I'm going to make.

Example 1. 1974. I have here a slide showing the *Time*

magazine cover for 4 November 1974. As you can see, the Shah of Iran is on it – Mohammad Reza Shah, to be precise, our current shah. They've presented his cover image as a soft pencil sketch, not a photo – head and shoulders, three-quarter profile, emphasising a determined face, some would say hard.

He's wearing his favourite white dress uniform with elaborate gold embroidery on his raised collar. This image implies imperious, military, resolute.

'Emperor of Oil'. This caption accompanies the image, and two articles on the inside pages continue this emphasis on the Shah's exotic titles, most of which he has given himself. He is referred to as: the Shadow of God; His Imperial Majesty; Aryamehr (Light of the Aryans); Shahanshah (King of Kings).

A note on being 'the Shadow of God' and the significance of the *farr.* Whoever becomes Shah of Iran is deemed to be God's Messenger on earth, 'the Shadow of God', and rules by virtue of the *farr* – a divine power bestowed on kings by God, a power that validates their rule. But for the king to keep the *farr*, he must hold on to the trust and consent of the people. If he makes mistakes, commits unjust acts, loses their trust, then he loses the *farr*, that Divine Power, and is deemed unfit to rule.

The main thrust of the accompanying articles focuses on the Shah's achievements – the emphasis is on portraying Iran as an international force to be reckoned with, and the Shah as the impressive leader of that force, likening him to Cyrus the Great of ancient Persia. We must, of course, see this positive take on the Shah in the context of certain world events of the previous year, 1973. In October of that year, the Arab-Israeli war took place, resulting in a victory for Israel. Arab oil-producing nations then imposed an oil embargo on the US and other Western countries because they perceived that they had supported Israel. In December, the Shah seized the opportunity to negotiate a quadrupling of oil prices, which brought Iran an estimated $23 billion in oil money for 1974 alone. This, in turn, gave the Shah a sense of real power and influence over Western economies, and he was more than willing to demonstrate this to the West. Fast forward to 1974 and to the articles accompanying the image of the Shah in the copy of *Time* we are looking at here, and you can see how much he enjoys this power.

1. He lectures the West on its inability to control inflation, and on how there can be freedom of speech, but only if it's not influenced by Communists – he is a virulent anti-Communist.
2. He defends SAVAK, saying it is an effective force in dealing with Communism.
3. He comments on Iran's military build-up, and on his five-year plan to be among the top armies of the world, although he maintains that Iran 'will not go nuclear'.
4. The articles describe him as a visionary, and as energetic, international in outlook, urbane, a speaker of three languages. His people revere him as he brings them prosperity and national prestige. His courtiers and aides kiss his hand; his peasants kiss his feet.
5. The articles outline his plans for projects ranging from dams to schools to hospitals. He states his five-year plan, dating from 1973, will culminate in 1978 in the creation of 2.1 million jobs, but there will be only 1.4 million Iranians to fill them, so there are plans for foreign workers at all levels. And, of course, he has his huge army, air force and navy, and plans to increase his military investment even more. If the Shah buys eighty F-14 fighter planes from the US, then sales beckon of up to $ 1. 5 billion for this one item alone.

So, we can see that the *Time* articles portray the Shah as a strategic player in the power balance in the Middle East, a head of state who sees Iran as the bulwark against Soviet invasion and ambitions in the area. There is some slight acknowledgement of social problems – a passing reference is made to some social inequality, to food having to be imported where once Iran was self sufficient, to the reputation of SAVAK, to corruption, and to suggestions that his monarchy is absolute. But throughout, the emphasis is on the Shah's commitment to social reforms and his ambitions for what he calls his 'Great Civilisation'.

By the way, there is a rumour that the Shah bought the space for part of these articles in *Time* – but I guess we'll never know for sure.

Why are these articles so interesting, from a journalism point of view?

Shaping and framing – the power and constraints of journalism

I think the *Time* articles demonstrate two points of interest. First, how journalism can deliberately shape and frame the content and angle of reportage, not just by degree of emphasis, but by what it *doesn't* cover, as much as by what it does. Another important aspect of that question is whether journalists are ever *influenced* to shape or frame the content one particular way or another. For example, the articles mention the possibility of lucrative arms deals worth billions of dollars. Would that bring political pressure to bear on what and how journalists write about a head of state who draws up a substantial military shopping list?

Second, in this particular example of the portrayal of the Shah and Iran, these articles provide a baseline for our assessment of the Shah and what comes next – they were written in 1974, remember, and today, in 1977, the situation is already much changed in Iran.

Example 2. 1975. I'd like to give you another example to compare with the *Time* articles we've just looked at. Just over six months later, in 1975, on 24 June, an article appeared in the *Washington Post*, covering rioting in Qom, a key religious city eighty miles or so from Tehran. Earlier in the month, on 6 June, Muslim traditionalists had been out on the streets, commemorating the twelfth anniversary of a bloodbath in Qom in 1963, when over a hundred religious traditionalists had been killed during demonstrations against the Shah's reforms. He had recently introduced these as part of his 'White Revolution'. Among other policies, they had included redistributing land by taking it from the clergy; and also laws promising the establishment of women's rights. Such policies were seen in traditional Muslim circles as an attack on religion and an attempt to secularise the state.

The 1975 commemorative riots covered by the *Post* also noted an anti-American tone to some of the unrest. An American culture centre in another religious city, Mashad, was bombed. Two US Air Force officers were gunned down in Tehran. There were protests against the Westernisation of Iran's major cities, again one of the Shah's key policies lauded in the 1974 *Time* articles, when he spoke of recruiting foreign workers. Muslim traditionalists maintained that Iran had become 'like a harlot running after the evil ways of the West'.

So, my point here is that just six months or so after the glowing *Time* articles, the *Post* paints a totally different picture of the Shah, Iran and its problems, and the relationship of Iran with the West.

The article also suggests confusion as to who organised the Qom riots. The government claimed that red flags were waved, communist leaflets distributed, Marxist slogans chanted. It tried to explain the riots and unrest as the work of the Red (Marxists) or the Black (Islamist traditionalists), or even as a combination of the two working together, the Red and the Black. This fits with the Shah's personal conviction that there is a 'Red and Black' conspiracy at work in the country, the Islamist Marxists, as he calls them.

To the present day, he continues to suggest that these two groups sometimes work together to achieve their aims. There may well be some legitimacy in this, but it is typical of the Shah and his approach that his personal conviction limits the consideration of any other interpretation of what might be the causes of unrest.

A note on Ayatollah Khomeini.

I'd like to bring in one more feature, linked to the 1975 riots, which I think illustrates an aspect of the opposition to the Shah's policies that has been played down to date.

The *Post* article focuses on religious clerical unrest, but doesn't mention the name of one particular cleric, Ayatollah Khomeini. In case you are not familiar with this word, *ayatollah* is a Persian word for a high-ranking leader of the Shi'a religion, the official state religion of Iran. Khomeini was highly influential in both the 1963 and 1975 riots. Maybe the *Post* journalist didn't know his name, but it's far more likely that he did, but decided not to use it, for understandable reasons. Speaking Khomeini's name out loud has been banned in Iran since 1963, so it certainly wouldn't have been allowed in print. But he's been around for a long time.

He's an elderly cleric from Qom, pious and a scholar, who came to prominence in 1963, when he was already sixty-one years old. He emerged as a leader, coordinating and fronting opposition to the Shah's 'White Revolution'. He spoke out then, saying that the recent elections, which had created the government to push through the Shah's reforms, had been rigged. Khomeini opposed the 'White Revolution' vehemently. SAVAK stormed the divinity school in Qom where he was preaching, killed some students, arrested Khomeini, who was imprisoned until 1964, when he received a rapturous welcome back to Qom on his release. It wasn't long before he was back in action.

In 1964, the Shah passed a law providing legal immunity from prosecution in Iran for all American military personnel, their families and household staff. This caused outrage, such special privileges for foreigners smacking of colonialism. Khomeini wrote that by implementing this law, the Shah was treating his own people worse than dogs, saying, in the clear, inflammatory language for which he has a reputation: 'If an Iranian ran over a pet dog, he could be prosecuted, but if an American ran over an Iranian, he couldn't.'

In typical Khomeini fashion, he issued a call to arms to all Iranians. It goes without saying that he was rearrested, and this time he was deported to exile, first in Turkey, and then in Iraq, where he is now. He is still very active in promoting dissent in Iran and his influence in the 1975 riots was considerable, if unofficial reports are true. As I noted earlier, his name still dare not be mentioned in Iran.

You can see that we have two different viewpoints as to what was going on in Iran within a six-month period, reflected in two very different shaping and framing approaches. I would suggest that the *Time* articles reflect the myth, the *Washington Post* the reality.

One final personal observation brings us up to date with how the Shah's image is being 'framed' in present-day journalism. Over the past few months, there has been a recent series of articles, again in the *Washington Post*, by an American journalist, Richard Sale, who has actually travelled round Iran recently, and has excellent contacts, from the sound of things. He is, to my knowledge, one of the few journalists to comment critically on the Shah's policies from first-hand experience of having seen some of the results. In my opinion, he is a journalist who, as my American friends say, 'tells it like it is'.

I'll leave you with three further examples from Sale's work to illustrate this.

Three major mistakes the Shah has made.

1975. The Shah abolished the two-party political system and replaced it with a one-party state, the Rastakhiz (Resurgence Party). Anyone who didn't like this new way of doing things was, said the Shah, either a supporter of the Tudeh (Communist) Party, and should be in jail, or was a traitor, and should leave the country permanently. Sale suggests that this now makes Iran a 'dynastic dictatorship', rather than a constitutional monarchy.

1976. The Shah abolished the Islamic calendar, which took the year of Muhammad's flight from Mecca as year 1, and replaced it with the Persian Imperial calendar, which dated back to the accession of Cyrus the Great in 599 BC. Iranians went to bed one night in 1355 and woke up in 2535. Sale points out that this triggered the most serious riots for more than thirteen years, led by religious leaders who called the Shah 'the enemy of Islam'.

1977. Sale visited a village outside Tehran which he suggests is typical, noting that there are 61,000 of such villages in Iran, with no piped water, no sanitation or electricity and no doctors. The villagers live on an average of four to five grams of protein a week, and scavenge for undigested oats in horse droppings. The 'White Revolution', comments Sale, is skin deep for this section of the Shah's people.

We have come a long way in three years from the portrayal

of the Shah as the 'Emperor of Oil', to the Shah who has made serious mistakes and blames others for the results. I hope Sale's article will be one of an increasing number of journalistic pieces that provide alternative viewpoints of the Shah, examining the myth and the reality. I have given examples of *what* kind of subject matter is now being presented. The questions of *how* and *why* subject matter in journalism is 'framed' in such ways invites further research.

Massoud Amini, Berkeley, June 1977

*

It was clever, the way he'd focused on the journalism and used it as a way of delivering a critique of the Shah, his personality and his policies. From what Reza and Arash had said, Massoud's notes meant he wouldn't be going home any time soon. He wouldn't be safe.

I arranged to meet up with the prof again at the Med, for one last coffee and chat. He brought Massoud along with him. I should have guessed: it was my 'tell it like it is' freshman, as bright and earnest as ever.

'I saw you at Shamlu's lecture,' I said.

'And I saw you with Reza, at the Bear's Lair.' He grinned back. 'Great guy!'

'He'd have liked your work.'

'He's already seen it. He came to my presentation that same evening.'

'He certainly made the most of his time here.' I forced a smile that I hoped was benign, while I dealt with a flash memory of that day when Massoud and his friend had come over to speak to Reza at the Bear's Lair. They must have invited him then. So much for Reza's spur-of-the-moment decision to have a bit of time on his own to take happy snaps of downtown Berkeley. The devious fuck.

We chatted a while longer, then Massoud excused himself: he was off to some meeting or other. 'Good luck,' he said, 'I hope it all works out for you.'

The prof and I watched him walking across the street, his step almost jaunty.

'God, he makes me feel old!' the prof said. 'To think I was like that once, six years or so ago, first time away from home, fresh-faced and fearless.' He was smiling, but I thought I detected a hint of sadness.

'So when are you thinking of going back?' I said.

'Not for some time.' He gave me a direct look. 'My research is nowhere near finished. My official funding will run out soon, but I have an uncle and my sister over here – they came last year and seem to have settled in Los Angeles. He has an import-export business, and has decided to remain here and build up this end of it. So I can stay with them. Then we'll see.'

I was getting used to cracking the Iranian code. *I'm not going back because I don't feel safe in my own country. My relatives have got our money out through their business. So we'll camp out in Los Angeles until we see what's what.*

He was still wary of saying too much that could be construed as criticism of his country and the Shah – any even slightly negative comment was tempered with a subsequent positive gloss. The most he was prepared to do was use Massoud's work to give me a possible viewpoint on some of what was going on. He couldn't know for certain how either Arash or I felt about events in Iran. And Arash might be SAVAK for all he knew.

We finished our coffee, and I walked back with him across campus. We stopped on the faculty steps and he turned to me, his face serious now.

'I hope Iran turns out well for you. One thing to remember, we're great survivors, we Iranians. We've been invaded so many times over the centuries, and ended up with so many different regimes – they all come and go, but the people stay strong. Our strength has never come from one man, one system, one style of government, although it might seem as though it does from time to time. It comes from the sum total of what we are, what we've absorbed over the centuries from other civilisations, what we've endured, what we have created.'

Then he patted my arm and gave me a bright smile. 'And if all that homespun philosophy fails to impress you, and things get tricky, then get the hell out of Dodge, my friend, and make sure you bring Arash with you.'

He turned on his heel and headed towards the faculty doors.

Around the third week in September I was packing my things, all set to go. I was dithering over what books and notes I should take with me. I decided to keep Massoud's tapescript and the *Time* cover of the Shah and put them in a package to send to Oxford with my 'Berkeley 1977' journal, the 'Ten Questions for Dr A', and the Baraheni poems. A friend there was going to store stuff for me. After some heart-searching, I decided to send Gertrude Bell's *Hafiz* into storage too. The reference to *Little Black Fish*, in Arash's handwriting inside the front cover, might cause problems if I took it with me, and it was still a banned book. I was no Little Black Fish, and there were too many Big Bad Pelicans where I was going. I needed to be careful, not just for me but for Arash.

Being careful about what I said. Making sure there was nothing controversial in my personal belongings. Protecting not just myself but those close to me. I realised I was beginning to think like an Iranian. It'll be all right, I said to myself. We'll be all right. I found myself repeating it like a mantra.

Part Two

1977–9

Caravanserai

Kupfermühle, 6 January 1984

Today is Epiphany, Three Kings Day, and the window opposite now displays three new Epiphany candles. It's a Christmas festival that had passed me by until I came to live here. All the Christmas trees will be chucked out by tomorrow. Or, rather, all laid out neatly at the end of the cul-de-sac, a forlorn pile of naked has-beens, so Herr Becker can come along with his trailer and take them away to his farm to be chopped up and disposed of.

Frau Jensen comes round this morning on her way out for the day to visit a friend in Flensburg. She hands me a *Dreikönigskuchen*, a Three Kings Cake, for Epiphany, in the shape of a round crown, five large fingers of cake encircling another central round. We eventually establish, in a mixture of German and English, that it's made of currants, raisins, candied peel, brandy.

'The last of Lise's baking,' she says. 'It's too rich for me.'

Later, I have a slice with my morning coffee. It's delicious, a cross between the fruity taste of my mother's barmbrack and the texture of Italian *panettone*. Even better, you can dunk it.

Mid-afternoon I go up to the lake to clear my head. I don't expect to see the Whoopers, it's a little early for them to be back from the fields, but they're there. There's a serious flurry of preening going on, as if they're also having a post-holiday tidy-up. It looks like they've not moved off to the fields at all. It's bitterly cold and misty, and sometimes they decide to stay put on days like this. Frau Jensen's book says they may decide that flying to their fields in low temperatures would waste too much energy, so they'd rather stay at home, conserve it, and dabble for their dinner.

I leave them to it, and walk back slowly. I've successfully filled the day so far with trivial displacement activities. I haven't done any writing since New Year's Day, mainly because there's nothing left to write about now except Tabriz. I've said all I want to say about getting there. Now it has to be about being there. And that means going right back to why I started writing in the first place, the need to face it, to examine what happened head on.

So here goes.

I arrived in Iran on 23 September 1977, my mantra at the ready. We'd be all right.

As it turned out, of course, everything wasn't all right. Tabriz proved to be both better than I thought it would be, and much worse than I feared. Better in the beginning because Arash and I were together again. Worse because, as time went on, nothing could have prepared me for what happened.

I've said Anna and her romanticised *Shahnameh* summer idea of Iran was naive. Well, if she was naive, I was deluded. All the angst back in Berkeley, in the aftermath of what Reza had told me, all the procrastination after the *Little Black Fish* moment, all the perfunctory efforts to find out more about the politics by reading Massoud's work – all of it was just one long exercise in self-delusion. I wanted to be with Arash. Nothing would be so bad that we couldn't get through it together. Nothing would keep me from going to Tabriz.

*

Tabriz, 23 September 1977

Kucheh Mulla

I caught my first sight of Tabriz as we came in to land. We circled down over a wide plain collared by mountains, their slopes barren and rounded, tinted a harsh Martian red by the late-afternoon sun. Seen from above, the city was an untidy mass of flat-roofed buildings, low and dusty brown, spreading out from both sides of a river. A couple of medium-rise modern-style tower blocks dotted here and there punctuated the flatness. Small areas of parkland broke up the drabness, the treetops forming a sparse fretwork of early autumn leaves on the turn.

A shiny new oil refinery, studded with grey-white storage tanks, stood aloof and incongruous some distance away from the outskirts of the town. And that was it.

One thing in its favour, it looked nothing like Tehran. I'd stopped over in the capital for just one night en route to Tabriz, but that was enough. The crazy traffic, the pollution, the crowds, the ugly half-finished concrete high-rises scarring the skyline were all such an assault on the senses that I couldn't wait to get out of it. I'd not come to Iran for the brash urban sprawl, so I was glad Tabriz wasn't like that.

It had an exotic history. I knew that because, back in Chilton Street, Arash had spent many a summer night telling me about the invasions down the centuries by Mongol rulers, then Tamerlane, Arabs and Turks, among others. Tabriz stood at the crossroads of different empires and kingdoms, so had found itself caught up in all their conflicts. 'It was once the capital of Persia,' Arash said, 'under the Safavid Empire, from the sixteenth century to the early eighteenth. Then the crown princes of Persia, during the Qajar dynasty, made it their official residence until the early twentieth century, when the power shifted south.'

He was especially proud of the city's historical link with the Silk Road. It was in a central position along the route, so merchants from east and west met there to trade with each other. 'Our bazaar dates back to ancient times,' he said, 'it even earned Marco Polo's seal of approval. It's one of my favourite buildings in the whole of Tabriz. Dynasties have come and gone, earthquakes have flattened it from time to time, but it's survived and regenerated itself. All our Tabrizi history is built into its walls.'

For him, this wasn't just an exotic chronicle of warlords, empires and dynasties, or a fact of geography, it was where he'd been born and where he'd always lived. It was all part of his identity. I think he saw himself as a product of Tabrizi history combined with Azerbaijani and Persian culture, and was quietly proud of that. He didn't seem to have the hang-ups Reza had about perceived Azerbaijani inferiority. 'To be enriched by two cultures is no bad thing,' he'd say, 'as long as you remember to take the best of both.'

I had to admit, though, as I looked down now on its unprepossessing present, it was hard to imagine its vibrant, ancient past. Maybe I was being unfair, I told myself, as I waited for my baggage. Tabriz might turn out to be one of those cities you had to walk around in, absorb the bones of the place and work a little to get it to reveal itself.

And then Arash had been at the airport to meet me, and I couldn't have cared where I was. He looked thinner, but the blue-black hair was still the same and the slow smile hadn't changed. The room he'd found for me was in a house not too far away, in an old part of the town, on the edge of the Armenian quarter, down an alleyway he called a *kucheh*. It was too narrow for a car to fit down, about twelve feet at most, so we had to leave the taxi and walk. 'Remember the name – Kucheh Mulla,' he said. 'There are no name signs on the *kucheh*s, but you only have to ask. Everyone knows where they all are.'

I was feeling a little light-headed, partly through exhaustion, but more because I was finding it hard to believe I was actually there with him in Tabriz. So I can't really remember much about that first walk down Kucheh Mulla. I know we went through a dilapidated archway, left the shops behind and the *kucheh* became even narrower, with old wooden doors in deep shadow set at irregular intervals into the walls. It felt like we were venturing deeper and deeper into a labyrinth, the walls closing in behind us.

As if he was reading my thoughts, Arash said, 'There's an old Tabrizi joke about the *kucheh*s – they say they built them this narrow to keep the sun out in summer, the worst of the cold out in winter, and the invaders out all year round.'

We eventually stopped at a door with an old-fashioned keyhole and a white plastic doorbell. Arash produced a key from his pocket and let us in. It was a surprise to see a small two-storey house directly in front of us, set back about ten feet from the *kucheh* wall. It was built of smooth-textured brick, a sort of dirty ochre colour, with an ordinary-looking front door painted green, and a modern mortice lock, nothing fancy.

Arash unlocked the green door and went ahead of me up the staircase leading to the first-floor landing. He talked me through where everything was. Living area directly opposite the stairwell, two bedrooms off to the left of the living area, shower room to the right. The living area was surprisingly large. A window with a simple muslin curtain looked out across the top of the wall to the *kucheh* we'd just walked down. A sizeable corner of the room had been partitioned off as a kitchen, with a small table and four chairs shoehorned in.

The main room had a blend of east and west about it – sparsely furnished with a *bokhari* stove puttering away in the corner, huge floor cushions next to it set against the wall, low table in front of them, and a hessian lampshade for the suspended light above the table. A large desk and chair took up another corner.

It reminded me of a typical student house in Oxford, but with no junk and a whole lot cleaner. Not exactly a cosy living space, but functional.

'I called in earlier to light the stove,' Arash said. 'It can get cool at night now, even though it's still warm during the day. You're lucky – your room gets the heat.'

He steered me out of the living area and I was about to ask which of the two bedrooms was mine when he said, 'We keep going,' and headed towards a narrower flight of stairs, leading to a tiny landing with two doors opposite each other. One had a handwritten notice, '*Roof*', Sellotaped to it.

'You go first.' He opened the door opposite the one that led to the roof and stepped back to let me squeeze past him. This was also sparsely furnished. There was no bed as such, just a large thick wool rug of some kind, with a thin double mattress on it that looked new, as did the white sheet and Western-style green quilt. But I hardly noticed any of this. All I could take in was the skylight, a square of darkening pink-purple. I heard Arash laugh as he caught the look on my face.

'This is terrific!' I threw my shoulder bag on the bed and lay down next to it, put my hands behind my head, and stared upwards at the sky.

He stood there smiling, his arms folded and an I'm-pleased-you're-pleased expression on his face. 'I think it used to be a junk room, but I told Firuzeh, whose family owns the house, "My friend Damian has a thing about being able to see the sky. Whatever else the room is like, it has to have a view of the sky, preferably through a roof window," so she did it out specially.' He looked at me as he said 'my friend Damian' and frowned a little, as if it didn't sound right.

'Now all we need is Miles Davis,' I said, as I pulled myself up and rested my back on the pillow against the wall. My voice sounded slightly brittle. There was nervousness between us, like you get when you haven't been physically close to the person you've been longing to be with for such a long while, and then there you both are, occupying the same small space again, but suddenly aware that so much past time has been unshared.

He went over to the chest of drawers, took out a cassette player and brought it over. It looked new. 'I know you can't do without your music.' He sat on the edge of the mattress and handed it to me.

'That's terrific, thank you. I was hoping someone would have one I could borrow, I didn't have room for one in my own packing.' I could hear myself gabbling. And why was everything suddenly 'terrific'? It's not a word I use, ever.

I fumbled in my bag, fished out a cassette and slipped it into the player. The first smoky notes from *Kind of Blue* smoothed in, slow and tentative, and I could feel the tension in my body begin to drain away. Arash reached over and stroked my face. Slowly stroked away the nervousness.

Then he lay down next to me and we pulled the quilt up over us and stayed like that, fully clothed, close but not yet moulded into our old familiar shape, until the music finished.

I looked up at the Tabrizi sky, inky blue now, with a scattering of stars. In Berkeley, when we'd lie in bed at night, I'd sometimes insist on keeping the blind up.

Why do you do that?

So I can see the stars.

But you can't see anything. The city lights bleach them all out.

Yes, but I know they're there.

There's no bleaching out of these stars.

I'm here, we're here, and everything is going to be all right.

6 October

Ten Nights at the Goethe

We're fine if we stick with Rumi or Din Attar, or any of the Sufis, and Hafez is always OK, but Arash and I have decided to try to avoid any discussion concerning contemporary Iranian poetry. I was so agitated after the shock of reading *God's Shadow* and what it had stirred up for me that I've engineered a sort of unspoken agreement with him not to discuss poetry and politics here in Iran. The theory goes that if we don't talk about what's going on around us, we can fool ourselves that the problems don't exist, or if they do, they'll just fade away, not touch us. Either way, we won't have to face them.

So when I spotted the small flyer on the British Council

notice-board about the poetry readings to be put on at the Goethe Institute in Tehran, I was in two minds as to whether or not to tell Arash about it. It was completely overshadowed by a huge poster advertising the great British Cultural Festival, on at the same time in Tehran, involving the Prospect Theatre Company, the Royal Ballet, the Aeolian String Quartet, even British military brass bands 'in full uniform' playing in various parks.

It was billed as the greatest British festival ever mounted overseas, and Princess Fatemeh, the Shah's youngest half-sister, had given it her personal support, so no expense had been spared. I thought for a moment we'd be better going to that, it would be less controversial, but then I reasoned that Arash would hear about the Goethe event anyway, on some grapevine or other, and I knew he wouldn't want to miss it. So I asked one of the secretaries at the Council for a copy of the flyer and brought it home for him to look at.

'Ten Nights at the Goethe, the tenth to the nineteenth of October.' I handed the flyer to him. 'A bit of a marathon – ten consecutive evenings, and over sixty writers, speakers and poets.'

'It looks good, so many poets—' He stopped scanning the details and looked up. 'My God! Soltanpur will be there!' He was more animated than I'd seen him for ages.

Saeed Soltanpur was yet another dissident writer, militant poet and playwright, a firebrand considered particularly extreme because he openly supported the politics of a Marxist guerrilla organisation in Iran, the Fedayin, which advocated armed struggle against the Shah's regime. He'd been imprisoned several times.

On the few occasions since I've been here that Arash and I had ventured into the tricky territory of contemporary political poets in Iran, before we agreed our truce, he would always bring up Soltanpur as an example of a 'political versifier' and dismiss him as a 'guerrilla poet'. He'd maintain his verse was the worse for it, compared to, say, the subtlety of Shamlu.

'One of our critics here wrote that Shamlu shines the light

on injustice, while Soltanpur merely mans the barricades and tries to drag you along with him,' he said to me once, 'and I must say, I agree with him.'

He could be quite lofty, sometimes, Arash, when he got on his high horse about poetry.

It was one of the things I loved him for, back in Berkeley. We'd argue about the merits or not of political poetry, usually after a few glasses of wine. I'd say something like 'Mayakovsky wrote, "I want the pen to be on a par with the bayonet,"' and Arash would say 'But then he also wrote, not long before his suicide, if you remember, "I subdued myself/setting my heel/on the throat/of my own song."' It had been fun, back then, jousting over poetry, because it really didn't matter – it was just an intellectual to-and-fro. It had also been a great aphrodisiac: we usually ended up in bed, teasing each other about who had sounded the most pretentious. Here in Iran, I was beginning to understand that the conflict between literary ideals and political reality was played out every day, and discussing it was no fun at all.

He looked up from reading the flyer with an expression that told me he was struggling not to appear too eager. I couldn't resist a dig. 'You said once Soltanpur was little more than a sloganeer.'

'Yes, but I have to admit, he's exciting to listen to.'

'I take it we're going, then.' I grinned at him.

'It's too good to miss,' he said, smiling back. 'That's if he turns up, of course. He's more than a bit unpredictable. But in any case, it's a chance to hear other poets read their stuff.'

It was the first time we'd managed to have a light-hearted exchange about any contemporary poetry and I was amazed by how much it lifted my mood.

So it was settled, we were going. At least, we thought we were. There were some doubts at first as to whether the event would take place at all. The Goethe Institute had established a reputation for literary evenings and prided themselves on such cultural exchanges. But it had always been in conjunction with the Literary Society of Tehran, made up of artists officially approved of by the government, and therefore ridiculed by the more radical intellectuals as 'Pseudo Artists'.

The ten-day Goethe event would be different. The Iranian Writers' Association, with its dissidents and anti-Shah, anti-government group of writers and poets – the kind Reza had told me about back in Berkeley – had somehow managed to persuade the powers that be that they would behave themselves and not be political. So, we decided we'd wait until the event was up and running and see how it went.

Then Arash came home on Monday, the day the Goethe event started. He had the *Kayhan* Sunday newspaper with him. 'There was trouble in Tehran on the university campus yesterday. Made the headlines last night.'

'What kind of trouble?'

'Some sort of attack on students in the cafeteria. Some of our students here in Tabriz got phone calls on Sunday, right after it happened, from their friends in Tehran.'

It appeared that a group of men had set fire to student buses in the campus car park, then run into the cafeteria, forcibly separated male students from the women, and beaten up anyone who resisted.

Arash shook his head as he told me the details, and took out a crumpled leaflet from his pocket. 'The attackers left this, apparently. It's addressed to the female students.'

He read it out to me:

Warning to the Elements of Corruption.

Don't ever come to the self-service restaurant in the boys' section of the dormitory . . . in no way may you ride the boys' bus. Demand a separate dormitory and a separate bus. If you violate the guideline, your lives will have no guarantee of safety.

He shook his head again. 'I've no idea where our Tabrizi students got this leaflet from so quickly. There were rumbles on our campus today, but nothing violent. We'll have to wait and see.'

'Wait and see about what?'

'If it gets worse in Tehran. The Goethe event might be cancelled.'

My heart sank. I'd been in Tabriz just over two weeks and was coming to the conclusion that Massoud had been right: there was so much unspoken anger in Iran. You could be fooled into thinking everything was OK, things could seem pretty normal in a subdued sort of way, and Tabriz struck me as the sort of place where the everyday normal was subdued anyway, not frantic like Tehran. But discontent was always there, just under the surface, and I'd soon learned that what happened in one part of the country was relayed to others and set off more trouble there. A quick telephone call from one city to the next was all it took, sometimes backed up by copies of leaflets, which mysteriously appeared during or shortly after the event in cities that were far apart. Rumour and counter-rumour were the common currency of unrest.

The Tabriz campus always seemed to be in the know about what was going on elsewhere. I'd picked up right away on the sense of distrust and disconnection on campus with the Shah and his government. You didn't hear it straight out – people were too wary to speak openly and criticise, and I'm sure not everyone was critical of what was going on. But those who may have had different views from the dissenters kept quiet.

Maybe here in Tabriz, it was also the added Azerbaijani factor that Reza had mentioned, the sense of frustration and injustice around those who wanted autonomy, or even those who didn't want to go that far but needed their different culture and languages to be recognised and given equal respect. In the ordinary streets, off campus, if you spoke Persian in the small hole-in-the-wall shops on Kucheh Mulla, you would be served, but if you spoke a few words of Azeri, you might also get a smile. Or maybe Tabriz was just like any other place, reflecting the general mood of discontent and dissent in other parts of the country. Whatever it was, the tension seemed to hang over the city like a toxic cloud, trapped within the bowl of the mountains, with no means of escape.

And we were trapped in it too. At least, that was the way I was beginning to feel. I wasn't sure how Arash thought about the situation, I'd avoided talking to him about how I was feeling because I needed to give myself time to settle in. But that sense of being trapped had been with me on and off since I first arrived. I couldn't seem to shake it off. So, I was secretly pleased at the prospect of getting out of the place for a while, then desperate to think we might not go.

On Wednesday, the English-language newspaper, *Kayhan International*, had the government version of the story, so I could read it for myself: *Revolting attempt to revive medieval horrors. Women on campus will fight bigotry. University students later staged a sit-in, protesting against the attack and the sentiments of the attackers.*

On Thursday, another leaflet came out on the Tabriz campus: *The whole event was staged by SAVAK, trying to discredit Muslim activists, portraying them as 'women-hating zealots'.*

Rumours. Secret phone calls. Leaflets. Counter-rumours. Counter-leaflets.

'Welcome to Iran,' Arash said to me. 'It's the way things are done here.'

The Goethe event had been running for two nights. We heard that the first night went off OK – well, more than OK: five thousand people, most of them young students, had turned up to listen. Even more on the second night, ten thousand, some said, so they'd moved the event out into the Institute courtyard and gardens. No trouble, just large crowds. Arash had found out that Soltanpur would be appearing on the fifth night so we decided to treat ourselves to an airline ticket: we'd be going for one night and didn't want to spend the time we were there recovering from the long bus journey and not in a fit state to enjoy the readings.

'We can meet up with Mirza,' Arash said. 'It'll be good to see him again.' He'd heard from their mutual friend Amir that Mirza was out of prison. 'God knows what state he's in.'

The day we set off, I was as excited as a schoolboy allowed out on a school trip.

*

15 October

Mirza

Arash asked the airport taxi driver to drop us off at Tehran bus station. Mirza lived about a mile away but Arash didn't want to arrive in a taxi, he felt it would draw too much attention.

'We just need to be careful, for his sake as well as ours,' he said.

We made our way through a rundown area of the city at the back of the station, a cold breeze swirling rubbish and paper round our feet, the rain wet on our faces.

We reached a corner, and Arash stopped to get his bearings. We were standing outside a shuttered shop. 'Down here, I think,' he said, and we turned left into a short side street, wider than our *kucheh* in Tabriz but going nowhere. A few nondescript buildings faced each other, and the street petered out.

'It's five doors down from the shop, according to the directions I have,' Arash said. He shook his head as he looked around. 'His house near the university was a lovely old place. I wonder how he's ended up here.'

We stopped outside a house with a bleached wooden door. Arash examined the three nameplates and rang the grubby top doorbell. He dropped his voice to a whisper. 'He's only been free for the past six weeks, and I heard from Amir he's not too good, but he won't talk about what happened to him. None of the ex-prisoners will.'

'It's no wonder he's in a bad way, then.' I felt a flutter of nerves as we waited for the door to be answered. He'd be the first torture victim I'd ever met. Reading about it in Bahareni's poetry and arguing over it with Reza had been bad enough, but meeting someone who'd actually gone through it felt much worse, and I wasn't sure how I'd handle it.

We waited a while longer, then heard the locks being drawn, and the door cracked open. A face slowly edged itself into the gap, the eyes flitting quickly from Arash to me to beyond us to check who might be behind. Then the face broke into a warm smile, the door opened wide and a wisp of a man with thinning grey hair beckoned us in.

He and Arash embraced each other, and he offered me his hand as Arash introduced me. 'Welcome, you are most welcome, come, follow me. I'm at the back along the passage here,' he said, in precise English. We followed him down the corridor under the light of a single unshaded bulb. I noticed he had a limp and used his hand to steady himself against the wall.

We reached a battered door, opening into a larger than average room. There was one long thin window on the back wall, the iron security bars on the outside casting a dark vertical outline against the glass.

Books were crammed in everywhere, stacked high on shelves around the walls, some almost to ceiling height. An old Anglepoise lamp shed a pool of light on a tower of hardbacks on a desk in a corner. Paperbacks, some in English, I noticed, were scattered across a low table and spilled over onto the floor cushions near the *bokhari* in another corner.

There were touches of a former, more comfortable life, probably the most treasured possessions that Mirza had clung to – a small worn Shirazi rug, with its angular nightingales in a traditional coarse wool design, hung on the wall behind the table, and an oversized brass lamp created a delicate openwork star pattern of central light.

He hugged Arash again and I could feel the warmth between them. 'It is so good to see you, my friend. How long has it been? More than a year or so, surely.' He seemed vague, as if he had trouble remembering.

'I called in to see you on my way to America. So it must have been July 'seventy-six.'

'And when did you get back from your studies?'

'End of August, just gone.' Arash hesitated. 'I phoned your old house, but . . . no one could tell me where you'd gone . . .' He didn't finish his sentence, and I could tell he felt awkward about mentioning Mirza's family.

'Ah, yes. That would be just after they released me.' He nodded more to himself than to us, then gave a small smile. 'As you can see, I have had to make changes. I used to share my old house with my brother and his family, but now it's safer for them if I live separately. I miss them, especially my nieces and nephews.' He looked away for a moment, then waved his hand over the books scattered round the room. 'But I still have my old friends with me to keep me company.'

He ushered us towards the floor cushions. 'You must excuse me . . . Sit, sit. I'll go and make some tea for us.'

As he turned and walked towards the beaded curtain leading into what must have been the kitchen, I noticed that the limp had become more pronounced. It was more of a shuffle, as if he had stones in his shoes and it was difficult to put any weight on either foot.

Bastinado. Flagellation of the feet. At the very least he'd suffered *bastinado*, I thought, and my mind jumped back to *God's Shadow*. Punishment, so you see the error of your ways. Persuasion, so you tell them about others who have transgressed. *Whipping and walking*. I felt the bile rising in the back of my throat.

He hobbled back with glasses of tea and small brown sugar

lumps. As he bent down to put the tray on the table, I got a close-up of his face.

Whatever they had done to him, or made him do, you could see the experience etched in the premature lines across his forehead and the creases in his cheeks. It was the face of a middle-aged man, yet he could have been no more than thirty-five years old. His eyes held a deep sadness, the sadness of a man who has seen too much. Whatever he had been through, it might not have broken him, but it had surely bent him out of shape.

He brought the desk chair across to the *bokhari* corner. 'I find it a little problematic to get up and down off the floor, these days,' he said.

There was a knock at the door. Arash and I started. Mirza smiled and said it would be his upstairs neighbour. As he opened the door, the aroma of cooked lamb wafted in and there was the rattle of dishes. A cheerful-sounding female voice spoke quite rapidly, and there was much thanking her on Mirza's part. Then the door closed again. He came back to the table carrying a tray with a platter of *chelow kabab*, a dish of cucumber and yoghurt dressing, and a round of fresh-baked flatbread.

'My neighbour insisted on cooking for us when I told her I would have guests staying with me,' he told us. 'I help her son with his homework from time to time. It's no hardship, he's bright and hard-working, and our sessions break up the early evening for me. I do a lot of private teaching now,' he added, 'since I lost my job at the university.' He said it matter-of-factly, but it left me thinking of how much he'd lost after his imprisonment. His house, less contact with his family, a job he loved, his income – all for hanging on to a book the authorities didn't like.

'It's simple food,' he said, as he went into the kitchen, 'but my neighbour is a good cook and, most importantly, it spares you my efforts.'

He came back with plates, forks, spoons and napkins. 'I'm not sure if this is a late lunch or an early dinner, but it will still taste good,' he said, handing out the cutlery. I was almost drooling as he told us to help ourselves, the juicy lamb and slightly singed tomatoes resting on the gleaming buttered rice reminding me of how hungry I was. We hadn't eaten since an early breakfast.

At first, the chat as we ate was about Arash's family. *How is Reza? Is he still studying? Still want to be a photographer? Is he back from London?* Then he turned to me. *When did I arrive in Iran? What did I teach? What did I think of Tabriz? How did I find the climate there?* I gave him the standard tourist replies, and he told me a Tabrizi joke about the climate – 'In Tabriz, six months of the year it is winter, the other six months is a nuisance.'

I smiled and said I hadn't heard that before, which was true – I'd not heard the Tabrizis joke much about anything, but I kept that observation to myself. He smiled and said the students were lucky to get a native speaker of English as their teacher.

The three of us sank into silence, concentrating on the food.

Arash set down his fork, and sighed in appreciation. 'That was wonderful,' he said. He reached for his overnight bag next to him on the floor and dug around in it. He drew out a thick woollen sock and, like a magician pulling a rabbit out of a top hat, fished a bottle of Shiraz wine out of it. He must have got it in Tabriz and risked bringing it on the plane. For the first time, Mirza's face showed genuine delight as he held the bottle, lightly caressing it, then read the label out loud, and professed it to be a touch of home. There was much 'Don't open it now, keep it for yourself' from Arash, and 'I couldn't possibly,' and 'A good wine needs good friends to share it' from Mirza, until finally they agreed that as it was getting on for six o'clock we should leave it until we got back from our evening out.

He said we could freshen up in the bathroom, which was through the kitchen. 'I pay extra for my own bathroom, but it's worth it,' he said. It was tiny, but spotless.

He never asked for details of the poetry readings. In fact, he avoided mentioning the event at all, except as we made ready to go. 'I hear there have been big crowds at the Goethe,' he said, 'and it is well policed.' He shuffled over to the corner, and fished out an oversized, black business-style umbrella. 'Here, take this. It's bound to rain.'

We left him at about five thirty, which gave us time to get to the Goethe Institute. Arash was quiet as we walked along. On cue, it began to rain, and I gave his arm a squeeze as we organised ourselves under the umbrella. It was big enough to cover both of us with ease, down to the shoulders, which made it awkward to see where we were going, but when we stood still, our faces wouldn't be seen.

I felt Arash tense and looked at him. There were tears in his eyes. 'What did they do to him? He's an empty husk of himself. What on earth did they do to him?'

*

Soltanpur

We got to the Goethe Institute just before six. The rain had set in and there were fewer people than there had been on the previous nights, but still in their thousands. There was also a heavy showing of government security outside the Institute boundary wall. Armoured cars. Police in khaki uniforms, which made me think of the prof and his *kharkhaki* cockroaches. And a smattering of SAVAK agents, in over-long belted raincoats and trilby hats, as conspicuous as any military uniform, looking like something out of an American B-movie.

There was a certain arrogance about the SAVAK men, standing there openly, scanning the faces of everyone going through the gateway, their own faces impassive, but sharp-eyed.

The Institute grounds were protected by diplomatic immunity, so government forces had to keep out, but their very presence was enough to intimidate, and they knew it. We made our way past them, huddled together under Mirza's umbrella.

The ground was wet, but we hadn't brought anything water-proof to sit on, so we found a spot to stand near the back of some of the crowd who were sitting on plastic bags and various makeshift ground coverings they'd brought with them. I looked out over a sprawling mass of umbrellas, their arched spokes and stretched skins of red, blue and multi patterns, bobbing like a bright flock of tropical birds. From time to time, an umbrella popped up above the others, setting off a nervous ripple as if the whole lot were preparing to take off, until they settled down again.

We'd placed ourselves at an angle to the armoured cars and the police to the left of us, and Arash tipped the umbrella down so that we blocked their side view of us. The most they could see of us was from our waists down.

'Why are SAVAK here?' I whispered to Arash. 'Is it so they can see who takes part and hear what they say?'

'Partly. Many of the speakers are known sympathisers of our old Tudeh Party, the Communists, so they're probably out to see how far they can go, criticising the Shah's regime in such a public arena. But that can't be the only reason SAVAK are here – they already know the speakers. They've arrested some in the past, taken them in for questioning, imprisoned them.'

He nodded to himself. 'So it's not so much the speakers, more the audience that SAVAK are interested in. Look at them – thousands! They all seem to be young, probably students, come to hear their heroes, writers and poets they admire for fighting the good fight against censorship and for freedom. No wonder SAVAK are taking an interest.'

He gestured over the umbrellas. 'There's probably some SAVAK in front of us, under the umbrellas, listening in.'

He hesitated, then said slowly, as if he was clarifying things for himself: 'Most of the students here are new to what it means to oppose something so openly and in such numbers. I guess it'll show them that if you can get like-minded people together it gives them a kind of power. They'll realise they can gather in large numbers, demonstrate and express their opposition.'

He pointed to the left, in the direction of the police, taking care to keep the umbrella down, so no one could see his face. 'That lot over there – this kind of thing must be new to them too, a supposedly cultural event that could end up fronting a highly political message. I reckon they're here to observe, then they'll go away and work out how to deal with it, next time out.' He shook his head. 'It'll probably be OK tonight – but how they'll react to something like this happening again could be very different.'

A sudden smattering of applause interrupted him, as Hans Meyer, the urbane Director of the Institute, stepped up to the stage. According to Arash, he was well liked among the Tehran intelligentsia. He adjusted the microphone and began to speak, slowly, and in German, his voice sounding warm through the impressive number of loudspeakers the Institute had rigged up in the trees. He welcomed us to the fifth night of the poetry-reading event, saying with no hint of irony that he'd had no idea it would be so popular. The event, he said, was already becoming known informally as the 'Ten Nights', *Dah Shab* – his Persian pronunciation raising a good-natured hum of approval.

But for all his quiet authority, he looked slightly weary. The anxiety of the last four nights had obviously begun to take its toll. On the one hand, it was something of a coup for the German Embassy to be seen to be encouraging such cultural events, there was more than a touch of one-upmanship over the Brits and the Americans, for sure, not to mention the French. On the other, it was a minefield, inviting some of Iran's most vocal political poets and speakers to read, and expecting them to keep it non-political.

And now, with the increased security, he was anxious that the government might close down the Institute altogether, if things got out of hand. So far, he'd attended and watched from a distance, helped along, it was rumoured, by occasional disappearances back into the Institute though the French windows to a small ground-floor office, where a bottle of Irish whiskey was waiting for him. It was slowly emptying as the Ten Nights went on.

Every night, he delivered the same welcoming speech, short but carefully worded, stressing the cultural nature of the events and minimising the political. He was proud to remind the audience of the Irano-German Cultural Society in Tehran, represented by the Institute, and its tradition of sponsoring poetry-reading events. 'After all,' he said, a respectful tone creeping in, 'we are the homeland of Goethe.'

He then made another request with just the right nuance: 'Would those about to perform please not use the word *censorship*.' He repeated this quietly, respectfully, in Persian. Arash had told me before we got there that on the third night in particular one of the speakers had agreed at first that he would not use the word. Then he'd said that he'd meant he would not use the Persian word for *censorship*, but instead he would speak of *momayezi,* a more neutral Persian word of Arabic derivation, denoting 'evaluating'. This bending of the rules had prompted the government to send in the military and the police last night and tonight.

The crowd listened to Herr Meyer's request in polite silence.

Arash jinked his head to the row of performers seated at the side of the low stage. 'That's Soltanpur second from the left. He's just been released from prison.'

'What did he do?'

Arash shook his head. 'Anything and everything to aggravate the Shah and his government. His writing, his Marxist-Leninist politics, his refusal to keep quiet – they're all more than enough to have him jailed. But one thing's for sure – there's no way he'll keep quiet tonight.'

Herr Meyer moved smoothly on, wishing us an enjoyable evening, and handed over to one of his Iranian cultural assistants, who would be introducing the participants. Then he left the stage, mopping his brow with a white handkerchief and heading for the Institute building. I imagined him nipping out of sight, up the corridor, making thankfully for an overstuffed wing-back chair and a small side table bearing a whiskey bottle and a crystal glass.

We listened to the speeches and the poetry, each reader staying more or less within Herr Meyer's literary rather than political guidelines, although a good deal of innuendo was creeping in. The patter of steady rain on a thousand umbrellas created a soft but insistent drumbeat in the gaps as the speakers and poets changed over.

The crowd became increasingly quiet in the silences between the speeches and the poems, even between the lines of the poems, and between the words, as if the men at the microphone were transmitting a subliminal message – 'Listen to what we're saying, but listen more to what we're not saying. Listen to the silences. Listen to what we're not allowed to say.' I've noticed since I've been here that Iranians seem to have perfected the art of transmitting and interpreting silences so that what is not said becomes more meaningful than what is.

The umbrellas seemed to have morphed into a giant carapace of a single spiny-backed creature, rippling in response to what it was hearing. I began to think that being under umbrellas created a sense of security, that you could react to the poetry without being seen, and I wondered if that was what Mirza had had in mind when he insisted we bring his with us.

About an hour in, an almost palpable sense of unease had built up, and nothing Herr Meyer could have said would have contained it. Then, as if on cue, at the point of a poet change-over at the mike, a man just in front of us got up, handed his umbrella to the woman sitting on the ground next to him, and shouted something. He looked like a young student and was wearing a long red scarf, so he stood out from the crowd. Heads turned to see who it was.

I couldn't catch the Persian, and Arash translated in a low, shocked whisper for me: 'He's asking for a minute's silence for all the writers from the last half-century who've fought against censorship and oppression.'

The student continued, his voice clear.

'My God!' murmured Arash. 'Now he's asking for a minute's silence for all those who've died "prematurely".'

Someone else from the crowd shouted, then more shouts joined in, before the silence settled over us as the student began to read out the names. The only name I recognised was Behrangi. For an instant, my mind slipped back to Berkeley, and Arash weeping over Mirza and telling me the story of *The Little Black Fish*, and his fingertips touching mine in the Med.

The whole audience seemed numbed by what they'd heard. As the student with the red scarf sat down, Soltanpur made his way to the microphone. The umbrellas tipped backwards so that people could take in the full effect of his presence. He cut a striking figure, with his unruly mop of hair and the way he moved, drawing himself up, looking straight out over the crowd at Arash and me, at every individual there, or so it seemed, then stretching his gaze beyond us to the railings and the police and the SAVAK agents. Then he raised his hand to the crowd as if he were blessing them. His voice, deep and trembling with emotion, rang out: 'Greetings to you, broken by those black years, thirsters after freedom.'

The audience gasped. There was a smattering of applause.

He began with Hafez.

'That was mild enough,' Arash said. 'What's he up to?'

Then he let rip with the next poem, one of his own. I could understand only a little of what he was saying, and Arash tried to translate simultaneously for me.

> *On this shore of fear*
> *Upon this plain of blood roses and iron stalks*
> *I will not stay silent . . .*
> *I chose defiance . . .*

I asked Arash to stop translating, I preferred to listen and sense the feelings transmitted from Soltanpur to us. It was electric. The very air we breathed seemed to thicken as he stood there, first rocking back and forth, drawing us in close to him with his words, then he was still, then jolted himself into motion again, his agitation plain to see.

It was an onslaught of poem after poem.

'They're all inspired by explosions, guerrilla warfare, hand grenades,' said Arash.

And after each one, growing applause from the crowd.

At the end of a particularly tense reading, Arash muttered, 'My God! His whole appearance here is one huge hand grenade.'

Finally Soltanpur finished, stood stock still for a moment, head bowed. Then he left the stage and headed back towards the French windows of the Institute, where Herr Meyer stood listening, with a resigned expression. He placed his hand on Soltanpur's shoulder and they disappeared inside, quickly followed by the other speakers and poets.

The tension dissipated a little as the crowd began to mill about, quietly chatting among themselves, beginning to make their way slowly to the boundary gate. But the nearer people got to it, the more the tension coiled around us again.

A different kind of silence descended, almost sullen. It was as if people seemed to realise that the ideas the poets had shared with them, the possibility you could voice what you wanted and needed to say in the open, that sense of freedom, was just an illusion that would vanish once you went through the gates.

Arash put a hand on my arm and held me back. 'We'll make sure we're in the middle of the crowd going out,' he said. It had begun to rain again, more lightly than before, but we kept our hoods up and our umbrella low as we shuffled through the gates past the police and SAVAK. We were about fifty yards down the avenue, when there was shouting and commotion behind us. We looked back. The student with the red scarf was being bundled into a dark car, his girlfriend screaming after him as the vehicle slid away.

We quickened our step, huddling together under the umbrella, and made our way slowly back to Mirza's, Soltanpur's explosions ringing in our ears.

Dagger in the Dish

We got back to Mirza's about ten. The street, with its oily pools of rain, looked even drearier in the dark but it was cosy enough inside his room. The bottle of wine was still on the table, and he brought in glasses of tea first to warm us up, then hobbled out to the kitchen again to fetch a corkscrew and three glasses.

This time, he sat on the floor cushions with us, levering himself down gingerly. He opened and poured the wine, taking his time, passed our glasses to us, then raised his own to admire the dark ruby colour. I had the impression he hadn't enjoyed sharing a glass of wine with friends for a long time.

He tipped his glass to us both. *'Leave the tavern, Hafez, you are too old!'* He smiled as we laughed at his joke, a smile of uninhibited pleasure, and for an instant there was a flash of the open-faced, open-hearted man Arash had described to me in Berkeley.

He finished his glass and the smile was now all but gone. He leaned back against the wall and seemed to sink deep inside himself, his chin drooping onto his chest. I wasn't sure if he'd fallen asleep, but he suddenly jerked his head up, eyeing us blearily. 'My apologies, my friends, I'm not used to company.'

'It's been a long day for us too,' said Arash, gently. 'We have to be up early tomorrow.'

Mirza seemed relieved, and stood up, his face pinched in pain as his feet touched the ground and he had to transfer his weight onto them. 'I'll fetch your beds.'

He went through to his bedroom, and returned with coarse

woollen rugs, blankets and pillows. He laid the rugs side by side, and placed the blankets on top.

'You should be warm enough.' He pointed to the *bokhari* in the corner. 'The stove is low, but it keeps the chill off the room through the night.'

He lifted the Anglepoise lamp off the desk and put it on the floor next to the bedding. 'In case you need a light during the night. I hope you sleep well.' He raised his hand in a slight wave, then went back into his bedroom.

We woke to the smell of fresh bread. Mirza's neighbour had left it for us. He'd got hold of two eggs, a costly item for him, I was sure, and probably a kind gesture towards me rather than Arash. He served us boiled eggs and tea and we ate the bread, making awkward small talk about this and that. As we were gathering up our bags to leave, he disappeared into his room and came back with something wrapped in newspaper.

'To remind you of your visit,' he said, offering it to Arash. 'Wrap it in your smuggler's sock and open it when you get home.'

*

We were both quiet on the journey back to Tabriz. Arash seemed to doze off and on for the whole flight, while I spent the time mulling over the Ten Nights experience, all of it, from seeing Mirza, with his injured feet and even more injured soul, to listening to Soltanpur in all his glorious defiance, surrounded by an electrified crowd.

We sat in the kitchen when we got back to Kucheh Mulla. I made tea for Arash and poured myself some vodka, while he opened his newspaper parcel. It was the latest collection by Shamlu, published earlier this year after he'd already left Iran. Sick of the artistic repression, he'd chosen to live in exile, first in America, then in London.

Arash's copy was a first edition and it had sold out within a month. He translated the title for me: *Dagger in the Dish*.

Mirza had written something on the title page in beautiful Persian handwriting, so I asked Arash to translate that too.

> *Oh, if liberty sang a song*
> *small*
> *as a bird's throat,*
> *not a single wall would stay crumbled.*

Arash sat with his hand resting on the writing, his face sad and drawn. I sat across the table from him, sensing he wanted to say something, but was finding it difficult. I wanted to talk to him, too, about the trip, but I held myself in check to give him the space to speak first.

It felt to me that the relationship between us had been changed by our going through the Ten Nights experience together. Back in Berkeley, the 'problem with rose', and the 'subversive little black fish' had been poetic metaphors for dissent, which Arash had had to explain to me. But now we'd shared that moment of reality at the Goethe event, and for the first time, I could look him in the eye and say, 'Now I really know what you mean about being a dissident in Iran.' That was what I wanted to say to him.

He looked at me. It was as if he knew what I was thinking.

'This is Iran, Damian. This is what it's really like to live here now. Are you sure you made the right decision?'

I reached across the table and put my hand over his. 'Yes. We'll see it through.'

I expected him to relax, to smile, to say he was pleased to hear me say that. But he just looked down at Shamlu's words on the page, and left me feeling unsure as to whether or not he believed me. Or whether the question was really one he was addressing to himself, rather than to me: had he made the right decision in encouraging me to come to Tabriz to be with him? It saddened me that I didn't know for sure the answer he would give.

*

Kupfermühle, 6 January

Less than a month after the Ten Nights event, in mid-November, Soltanpur was due to speak and recite his poems again to students at the Institute of Technology in Tehran.

There was trouble – the police were at the gate, as they'd been for the Ten Nights, but this time the students challenged them and SAVAK agents were called in. The rumour was that at least one student was killed and many were seriously injured. Just like Arash had said, the students had learned the power of protest, and SAVAK had learned how to counter them.

Things on the streets and the campuses were never the same after that. Tabriz continued to rumble on, like a distant arrhythmic drumbeat, low and slow, but persistent.

*

Tabriz, 17 October

Good session with the prof today on translation. I'm still mapping out a specific area of research. I like him – he has an other-worldly charm about him and wears his erudition lightly. We got on to the question of form in poetry and how to treat it in translation.

'Bonnefoy has some interesting things to say about form,' he said. 'I was at a seminar of his in Paris last year . . . He suggests that you can "relive the act" behind the original poem, and discover in a new language the original intention or the intuition, even if in doing so, you strip away the form of the original – after all, he says, the form is only a poem's footprint.'

The form is only a poem's footprint. Thought for the day. I told him I'd have to think about that, then mentioned I might look at translations of Hafez.

He beamed. 'A lifetime's work ahead of you, then, but what better companion through life than Hafez?'

I think we're going to get on.

24 October

News hit the campus yesterday of the suspicious death of Ayatollah Khomeini's son, Mostafa.

Khomeini? Where had I heard that name before? Not here in Iran, but I'd heard it somewhere. Then I remembered Massoud's seminar back in Berkeley and how he'd mentioned the name at the end of his presentation and stressed the man's importance as an anti-Shah religious cleric. Mostafa had been found dead at his home in Najaf, Iraq, where he'd been living in exile near his father. The official story was he'd had a heart attack. The rumour was he'd been visited by two unidentified Iranians the previous evening, thought to be SAVAK agents, who'd poisoned him. This was more than enough to set off a reaction on the Tabrizi campus – how do they find out about things so quickly? Many students didn't pitch up for lectures today, and there was tension in the centre of the city too, although on the surface everything carried on as usual.

I'm looking forward to getting away again at the end of the week, if only for a couple of days. Arash has permission to attend a seminar at Pahlavi University in Shiraz, on the history and services of the libraries of Shiraz. There's a good research group based down there in the Department of Library Science, according to Arash, and they've just had a paper published in the *International Library Review*, London.

'It's quite an achievement.' He sounded proud of his fellow librarians – they tend to be a forgotten minority in academic circles. 'The university there is more than willing to organise the seminar – it's a bit of one-upmanship as much as anything else. All the universities compete for funding, especially from Western institutions, so it doesn't do any harm to have a paper published by Western academia.'

There was trouble in Shiraz earlier in the year, with strikes, but they'd managed to keep the university open for most of the spring semester, unlike Tehran and Isfahan. Little sign of much overt student trouble there so far in the first weeks of this semester, so everything is going ahead as planned. I've cleared it with the prof for me to go, saying I'd change my schedule and take someone else's tutorial when I get back, if they'd cover for me. It would be good, I suggested, to visit Hafez's birthplace.

'Indeed you must go,' he said, '*All hail, Shiraz, hail! O site without peer!* and all that. There's a splendid little Tomb of Hafez Library – it has a good collection of translations of Hafez's poetry in different languages. Worth taking a look at.'

He was so enthusiastic I thought he might invite himself along, which would have put a dampener on things, but he didn't, just gave me the name of the head librarian there and said I should introduce myself.

At the time, we were walking across the campus to the main gate, towards a group of glowering students standing just inside. 'Yes, indeed,' the prof said, more to himself than to me. 'A day or two with Hafez in Shiraz would put the world to rights.'

He sounded quite wistful and I noticed he'd lowered his voice a little as we went past.

30 October
We got back from Shiraz tonight. We flew down yesterday morning via Tehran, attended the seminar, stayed overnight, and got the early morning flight back, as we couldn't spare the time or the money for a longer stay. Two trips in one month, both including flights, has squeezed the finances more than a little.

But it was worth it. The Shiraz group introduced the paper, had the seminar discussion, then took us on a tour of the libraries in Shiraz, both private and public. I've never seen Arash so animated – he was gabbling away to the Shirazi research group and wandered round the libraries wearing a permanent smile. We got access to religious collections with priceless copies of the Qoran, and a wonderful private library, with a special section of old books on medicine.

We finished off at the Tomb of Hafez Library, with its

collection of translations of Hafez's poetry. The head librarian wasn't there, but I left my name and the prof's regards with the assistant, and said I hoped to be able to come again. I was pleased in a way that I didn't have to spend more time there, as it meant Arash and I could be together, looking around.

The library is built as part of Hafezieh, the site of Hafez's tomb, with its soothing pools, streams and gardens, so after the official library tour was over we wandered across to the tomb. It's raised about three feet above the ground, covered with a marble slab and a copper-domed roof, shaped like a dervish's hat, supported by eight tall columns. The underside of the roof is lined with an intricate arabesque mosaic of enamelled tiles. It's an airy, graceful place for Hafez to rest.

Two of his poems are inscribed in calligraphy on the marble. Arash studied them, and smiled. 'I have a surprise for you.' He rested his hand on my shoulder as he translated one of the poems.

My soul, like a homing bird, yearning for Paradise,
Shall arise and soar, from the snares of the world set free.

It was Gertrude Bell's translation of the last *gazhal*, number 43, in her *Hafiz* collection. I choked up. 'Did you know her translation was on his tomb when you bought me the collection back in Berkeley?'

'Yes. Ever since that day in Moe's Books, I've had this fantasy of you being with me and the two of us here like this, and my translating it for you and seeing the look on your face when you realised it was her work.'

He brushed his fingers over the calligraphy. 'And now here we are.'

I bent to touch the tomb too. The calligraphy seemed to merge with a memory of Arash's own handwriting on the title page of my copy: *Remember the Little Black Fish who dared to be different and saw the stream to the end.*

It felt as though all the anxiety of my first five weeks in Tabriz had just melted away.

31 October

Reza turned up this morning.

Fuck.

He's been home from London since August, and is back for a year. He's fixed himself up with some private teaching and some translation work, and is staying with a friend in Tehran. After Arash returned in July, they saw a lot of each other, Reza coming and going between Tehran and Tabriz, although he's not been up here since I arrived on the scene.

Arash was pleased to see him today. It's the first time the three of us have spent more than a day together, so it'll be interesting to see how that works. Or not.

He filled us in with the latest news around the death of Mostafa. We'd sensed some tension on the campus in Shiraz, which one of the library group said was to do with his death, but no one was keen to talk about it. Everyone seemed as eager as we were to forget the world outside for a day. Needless to say, Reza was in the know about what was going on. The Shah had given Khomeini's representatives in Iran permission to hold the traditional forty-day mourning rituals for Mostafa in the mosques, even though he'd been *persona non grata* in Iran, like his father.

'Big mistake. They've used the mourning so far to whip up support for Khomeini,' said Reza. 'The forty-day memorial rituals are going on in all the main cities – Qom, Yazd, Shiraz, and here in Tabriz.'

We knew none of this. Very little was ever mentioned in the papers about what the clerics were up to.

He obviously wanted a bit of time with Arash on his own, so I left them to it. I had to go into the university anyway to cover my swapped tutorial.

The tension on the campus had definitely gone up a notch.

I had to sign in at the faculty office, then go to the classroom, but there were still no students to teach. They'd come onto the campus but didn't attend lectures. They either stood about in groups in corridors, muttering to each other and looking surly, or took off to the mosque to join in the mourning rituals. A few tried to carry on as normal, pitching up in the lecture halls, or spending time in the library – mostly in the medical section. Medical students seemed the most diligent and least militant of all. I wondered how many students weren't in favour of the disturbance on campus but were too fearful to say or do anything against the most vociferous.

I had to sit in the empty classroom until the hour was up, which I did, reading Hafez, then sign out and go home. Pretty pointless, but all part of the everything's normal charade I'm slowly getting to understand.

Reza had been out and came back with the next rumour to do the rounds. He'd heard on the Tabriz grapevine that the clerics in the mourning rituals at the central mosque in Tehran had offered prayers for 'our one and only leader, Grand Ayatollah Khomeini'.

'What's so important about that?' I said. 'After all, he was Mostafa's father.'

'It's the name! They mentioned him by name,' Reza said. 'I was wondering how they'd get through the forty days without doing that, but they obviously didn't.'

I suddenly remembered Massoud again, back in Berkeley, saying that mentioning Khomeini's name in Iran had been banned. The significance of that at the time hadn't registered.

'That's the first time his actual name, Khomeini, has been spoken in public in Iran for fourteen years,' said Reza. 'The Shah banned anyone speaking or writing about him by name. Definitely a big mistake now to give them a platform.'

'I thought you were anti-Shah,' I said.

'I'm anti this Shah, but I'm even more anti the ayatollahs, all of them.'

Arash looked uncomfortable, but he always did when there was talk of politics.

Reza shipped out later to Arash's flat for the evening, he'd got some photos he wanted to develop and he could set up Arash's tiny windowless bathroom as a makeshift darkroom. He'd got a stock of developer and other stuff he stored in Arash's bedroom. I found it irritating to think of him staying over in Arash's house, it's something I've not done yet. But I'd rather have him out of the way over there than between us here at Kucheh Mulla.

*

6 November

Yesterday, a bomb was defused in a Tehran cinema reportedly showing 'porn'. That's the first bomb incident, or at least the first to have found its way into a newspaper. Reza was right about the forty days' mourning for Mostafa leading to an increase in dissident incidents. There have been demands from the mosques, in several cities, for Khomeini to return to Iran, and repeat accusations that SAVAK murdered Mostafa. Tabriz still feels tense, although nothing untoward has happened that we know of.

I've been here six weeks now, and for the second time, I've seen how quickly the atmosphere can change from something that passes for normal to a sense of threat. The Ten Nights with Soltanpur and his explosive poetry was the first time, and now this, the reaction to the death of the son of a man whose name no one is allowed to speak.

It seems to come in waves, this strange collective turn of mood in the city, and all you can do is sit it out until it ebbs away again.

It's not just Mostafa's murder that's led to the latest unrest. Social and economic problems have been building for some time. It wasn't until I actually got here that I grasped how difficult this year must have been for Iran, with the downturn in the economy. Obviously there'd been some chat among the Iranians on the Berkeley campus about the Saudis flooding the oil market with cheap oil at the beginning of the year, and the adverse effects it had had on Iran's revenues. The students were worried about their college funding. But I'd been much too preoccupied with what might be happening with Arash to pay it much attention.

I realise now that by the time Arash got back in the summer, Iran was trying to cope with price inflation, manual workers being laid off, loss in industrial production and so on. Social conditions were already dire in some of the poor areas, and got worse. But people like engineers, professionals, businessmen – the new middle classes the Shah's policies had created – were suffering too.

It's surprising sometimes how one huge issue affects all of the people at the same time and gives them a shared focus for their discontent. Arash had told me about this past summer in Iran, when the main problem affecting everyone had been the electricity cuts, particularly in Tehran. Stories had made the daily papers of workers climbing eight storeys to their offices in 100 degrees and no air-conditioning, and people in poor areas going without power for up to ten hours. It was something everyone had to put up with, except the very rich, who had their own generators, and it showed up the weakness in the Shah's plans for modernising Iran's public works too quickly.

It's only as I got to know all this that I understood the reason for the change in tone in Arash's letters during the summer. Once he'd got back in July, and seen how bad things were, he'd begun to wonder if he should tell me not to come because he might lose his job, or I might get here and lose mine, or there might be trouble on the streets and he didn't want me to get caught up in that. When I asked him about this, he said, yes, that was what he'd been struggling with when he wrote to me.

'I didn't want you to take the risk,' he said.

So that's the atmosphere I found myself in right from the start, a sense of slow-burn discontent. It looked as though the Shah's great push for economic growth and social development was going to founder, although no one was saying that – in public at least.

It's not stopped him going on a shopping spree, though. The rumour is, says Reza, he's off to America mid-November to spend billions on arms, and get a pat on the head from Jimmy Carter for cleaning up his human-rights record.

In the meantime, the country keeps ticking on, but the social and economic problems haven't gone away. They're the background to everything that's going on here now. It just seems to be that different groups have different complaints, and different ways of voicing them. Arash said that the most recent public criticism had begun in August, during Ramadan. Religious leaders had warned a crowd of twenty thousand in Tehran 'not to worship two gods, the one in Heaven and the one in the palace'.

But it isn't just the religious leaders. We get copies of out-of-date foreign newspapers sometimes, like the *Guardian* or the *Washington Post,* that's how we find out more about what's going on here. Apparently, middle-of-the-road Iranian lawyers, judges, writers, professors and the like have published letters calling for the disbanding of SAVAK, free elections, and greater freedom of political expression, although they've not called for the abolition of the monarchy. None of these letters has been made public in the Iranian press, but if these things really are going on, it suggests the need to protest is spreading, and exposes more fault lines in the system.

Strange how I've been sucked into the politics here, when all I really want to do is bury myself in Hafez. Maybe it's impossible to be here and not get sucked in.

8 November

Reza picked up an old *Guardian* in Tehran, dated 26 October, and brought it back with him for us to read. There's a few lines in an article suggesting that the human-rights issue in Iran had improved, after it had been highlighted in 1976 by the US and other sources, such as Amnesty International. The number of political prisoners had dropped by 1500 since 1976, from 3,700, and there'd been no reports of any torture.

I exchanged a deep and meaningful look with Reza while Arash was reading this out. I'm sure we were both back in my room in Berkeley, Reza patronisingly pointing out paragraphs for me to read from the Amnesty report, me seconds away from throttling him.

I shuddered as a flash memory of Baraheni's 'Barbecue' came in from nowhere.

Reza and I smiled thinly at each other as Arash laid down the paper.

'That's a start, releasing fifteen hundred prisoners,' Arash said. 'We can only hope they're right about the torture.' I had a strong feeling he was thinking of Mirza and what they'd put him through just over a year ago.

'Doesn't mean the ill-treatment isn't going on any more,' Reza said. 'They've just got better at covering it up. They've been doing a bit of housekeeping in time for the Shah's visit to the US next week. It suits both sides to say there's been progress – the US wants to keep its influence and show it can wield power when it needs to, and the Shah wants to buy arms as part of his plan to make the military one of the most powerful in the world. That's what the visit is about. All his minor attempts to show less repression are to create a good impression for the arms trip.'

Once I would have dismissed comments like this, especially coming from him. Now I find I'm listening more, wondering where the truth lies.

17 November
We sat round the kitchen table, gawping at Tuesday's front page of the *New York Times*, with its picture of the Shah standing in front of the White House, his face buried in a large white

hanky. Queen Farah, next to him, is also seemingly in tears. Jimmy Carter's face is strained, but he's staring straight ahead, looking as though he's in the middle of giving a speech.

'Wow!' Reza shook his head in amazement. 'These pictures have gone all round the world and landed right back here at home. Iran's great military leader, the Emperor of Oil, crying like a baby.'

It's an extraordinary image, certainly not what the Shah would have wanted – he'd gone to buy fighter planes, navy boats, army tanks. It should have been the Shah and Jimmy Carter, two leaders as equals in front of the White House, standing on the world stage, sealing an arms deal worth billions to America. Instead, the world has been treated to reports and pictures of anti-Shah demonstrators on the south side of the White House, holding placards saying, 'SHAH, FASCIST MURDERER!' and 'SHAH, US PUPPET!' and 'CIA OUT OF IRAN!' while pro-Shah supporters stand on the north side, holding placards saying, 'WELCOME SHAH!'

According to the *New York Times*, the anti-Shah crowd broke through a police barrier and began attacking the pro-Shah crowd. The police couldn't bring the fracas under control, so they used tear gas. Unfortunately, the wind was blowing in the wrong direction. The Shah got the tear gas full in the face, as did Queen Farah and Jimmy Carter. Hence the image of the Shah, seemingly crying into his hanky.

The world's press also published rumours that the pro-Shah supporters had been flown into Washington from all over the US, fares and hotels paid, and given a hundred dollars each.

I wondered if Massoud had been in Washington. He'd have added the articles to his research, that was for sure. His theme 'The Shah –Myth and Reality' suddenly had an extra dimension to it, with the tear-gas image and coverage of the fracas on American soil.

I felt a sudden pang of longing to be sitting in Caffè Med with him, drinking tea with lemon, and arguing with him about the 'fact versus "framing" in mainstream journalism', both of us knowing we could express an opinion without being thrown into jail or worse.

'The word on the street,' Reza said, when he came in later that day, 'is that America allowed the tear-gassing on purpose, to show the Shah that their support for him was on the wane.' He shook his head, as if he despaired of how gullible people could be. 'It doesn't matter whether that's true or not, it's crazy what some Iranians will believe.'

'It doesn't look good for the Shah, whatever the truth is,' said Arash. 'It proves he's not invincible, and he's always depended on the people believing he is.' He was so different from his brother with respect to the Shah – Reza seemed to take a grim pleasure in seeing the Shah embarrassed, or shown to be weak, while Arash just looked despondent.

I have to say, though, Reza has proven to have his uses. He always seems to know what's happening. The way he uses 'the rumour is' and 'the word on the street' has become a standing joke with us – he starts so many sentences with one or the other. He has all sorts of contacts, including journalists in Tehran working for the *Kayhan International*, the *KH* he calls it. I read it when I could get my hands on it, but it was usually two days out of date.

He took great delight in telling me not to believe all I read in it. 'It operates under censorship, but then, there's no censor-free journalism in Iran. You have to read between the lines and work out what's not being said rather than what is.'

Then he added, rather slyly, I thought: 'But at least it's in English, so you don't have to rely on Arash to translate.'

Reza was right about the Mostafa mourning rituals, too. Since the beginning of November, the demonstrations as part of the mourning have continued, and seem to have taken on a more violent tone. There's been rioting in Shiraz and other cities. In Tehran, there have been telephone calls from men threatening to blow up the family welfare centres that were set up so women could meet and take their children there. These centres, according to Reza, are important to the poorer women of the slum districts in the south of Tehran. They get health-care advice, post-natal and family-planning information, and can learn to read and write if they want to. It's one of Queen Farah's initiatives and has a good team of dedicated, qualified women social workers. Intimidation of these centres has been happening in other major cities too. In Tehran, after such a threat, they would be evacuated. Once they were up and running again, the threats would start once more.

'The men behind these threats are not only anti-Shah, they're anti-women,' Arash said. He seems to be getting increasingly exasperated with what he thinks is backward-looking dissident behaviour.

It's as if the opposition to the Shah, whoever is leading it, has re-energised itself under the cloak of mourning and has become something more threatening. It's drip, drip, drip, small-scale action, but it's making a statement that such opposition to the Shah will not go away.

31 December

11 p.m. We've just been sitting here, listening to the live broadcast on the radio of Jimmy Carter's New Year's Eve banquet speech from the Shah's palace in Tehran. The tear-gas visit to Washington is still very much in people's memories, and there has been more trouble in Qom, Khomeini's Iranian stronghold, so the level of unrest all over the country has risen. There's a real sense of dread hanging over the main cities. Carter is here for just one night, so Arash was wondering if he'd deliver some sort of coded rebuke, tell the Shah to get his act together, and make a sharp exit in the morning.

So what did Carter say?

'Iran, because of the great leadership of the Shah, is *an island of stability* in one of the more troubled areas of the world. This is a great tribute to you, Your Majesty, and to your leadership and to the respect and admiration and love your people give to you.'

'An island of stability?' Arash looks at me in astonishment.

3 a.m. Arash has gone to bed, deeply depressed. I've stayed up to finish the second bottle of wine.

Some thoughts on President Carter's speech.

On this island of stability, we've had certain men in Tehran and some other major cities threatening to bomb centres set up to improve the lives of women and children.

On this island of stability, trouble has broken out through most of December, all over the country, like a rash that subsides, then reappears, slightly more virulent, and the country as a whole gets imperceptibly more sick. And the focus of the protests is the Shah and/or his government. We had major rioting in the streets of Qom, on 2 December, marking the last day of the forty days' mourning for Mostafa, twenty-nine days before President Carter's New Year's Eve visit to Iran, so the Americans would have known full well what was happening.

On this island of stability, where the Shah 'enjoys the respect and admiration and love of his people', rioters made speeches demanding Khomeini's return from exile, freedom of speech, and shouted: 'Death to the Shah!'

But from where I'm standing, on this *island of stability*, three hours into the New Year of 1978, no one cares what is really going on. The Shah is still as invincible as his ancient hero, Cyrus the Great. Invincible, with his army of half a million men and his cohorts of highly paid generals and his elite 'Immortals' – his Imperial Guard, sworn to defend him to the death. And there's not just his army, but his air force, his police, his SAVAK, and his friends, like the US, we British and all the other Western interests who have sold him arms and tanks and equipped his air force, and need him in power for the oil and for the strategic bulwark against the Soviets, not to mention as a counterbalance to the Israelis and the Arab states surrounding Iran.

I suppose, the way President Carter and the Shah see it, stability is contingent on invincibility. And invincibility can be bought by the exchange of oil for arms.

*

Kupfermülhe, 9 January

I was in a full *New Year's Day 1978, Tabriz – how could Jimmy Carter have been so deluded?* frame of mind this afternoon, when Dieter called round and interrupted me. He's just back from a Christmas holiday in Cyprus. He's the one who brought me the Jameson from Dublin. I was so pleased to see him that I only realised, when we were sitting chatting, that he's the first person under fifty I've spoken to since the Winter Solstice on 23 December.

He teaches at the local Gymnasium and was in his final year of training when I began tutoring at the college.

He broke up with his girlfriend just before Christmas. 'Her move,' he said, 'but I felt it coming. She was never as committed as I am to the Greens.'

His whole life seems built around Green politics. I wouldn't be surprised if he had a pin-up poster of Petra Kelly on his bedroom wall.

He's interesting, Dieter. His family came across to West Germany in 1959, two years before the Wall went up, and never went back. He's never met one side of his family, who live in Dresden. He's convinced that Germany will reunite some day, 'maybe not in my lifetime, but in my children's, for sure'.

He brought a poem to one of my sessions once, by an East German poet, Uwe Kolbe. He told me later he'd been to a Green Party rally and got talking to a girl whose uncle was a university lecturer in the DDR. She'd given him a photocopy of the poem, handwritten on a piece of squared notepaper. The opening is brilliant:

We are living with cracks in the wall,
have you noticed?

'Where did you get that copy?' asked a girl in the class.
'It was given to me.'
'When?'
'By whom?'
He shrugged off the questions.

They were fascinated that he'd got a piece of subversive literature from East Germany and was actually showing it around. It was a good poem, ostensibly about a decrepit Berlin apartment, but obviously a metaphor for a decrepit system and the Berlin Wall as a decrepit symbol of it. I was amazed the students talked so much about East and West – what they feared about the East, and how much of what was said about it might be true, but how odd they felt it was to have a country divided for more than twenty years. It was the same as the couple of impromptu sessions we'd had on the Third Reich. They really wanted to talk about the past, these young Germans, I think they were beginning to see it was the only way they could understand what was going on now.

A week later, I was called into the head of department's room. He was an officious little prat, and I'd never got on with him. He'd heard about the poem and the session. How? I wondered, but didn't ask.

'We tend to avoid political literature, particularly from the *ossies*,' he said. 'In fact, we tend to avoid all politics in terms of East and West . . . and also, I've been meaning to say to you, we definitely avoid discussions about the Third Reich.'

How had he heard about the discussions on the Third Reich, which, by the way, the students had always instigated, not me? I didn't ask him that, either.

I could have fought my corner about Uwe Kolbe, but it wouldn't be me getting into trouble if I annoyed him, it would be Dieter, and he was due to graduate. It wasn't worth jeopardising that:

the department head was the sort to give a damaging reference. So I was humble.

'It was my fault. I'm so sorry. I encouraged the reading of it. I just liked it as a poem.'

'No problem,' he said, giving me the full force of his fat, self-satisfied smile. Then, as I was going out, he asked casually, 'You don't know where he got the poem from, do you?'

I said no, and left, thinking about SAVAK and Shamlu's cockroaches.

That was how I ended up with the Jameson I'd shared with Frau Jensen for Sylvester.

This time, Dieter brought me some ouzo, which went down well with both of us. He talked about his plans for next year, the highlights being the protests and demos he'd got lined up with the Green Party. After filling me in on the Greens, he rambled on about the vigilance still needed for the nuclear arms race. He used to wear a smiling sun sticker – '*Atomkraft nein danke*' – on his anorak, but he'd removed it. He'd been involved in the demonstrations against the siting of the Pershing missiles here in West Germany last October. Over a million turned out in the cities for an anti-Pershing rally. Human chains linking Stuttgart with an American missile site at least ninety kilometres away. Protests against East and West governments. Banners. Chants: *No to Bonn! No to East Berlin! No to Washington! Yes to Peace!*

It must be the way my mind has been working this past while because as I was listening to Dieter I was thinking, here we go, another generation, another cause, another march by millions on the streets, to fight against another wrong.

I suddenly felt very old.

'Have you thought of where you go next?' Dieter said.

It wasn't till he asked me that I was reminded I'm leaving at the end of March. I'd completely forgotten. My head has been in the past for the last eighteen days, or whatever it is. The future hasn't had a look-in.

'Haven't a clue. Maybe somewhere warm for a change.'

After he'd gone, the more I thought about it, the more I thought: yes, I need to break this habit of deep winter hibernation. But not yet. There's still a way to go.

*

I've just reread my 1978 Tabriz New Year's Day rant again, to get back on track.

All the signs were there, whatever Carter said, that something was slowly being set in motion that would take on its own shape, move at its own pace, and once it got started, would be difficult to stop. But no one thought that the discontent with the Shah and his government, as bitter as it was, would take on its own momentum in the way it did in 1978.

I really did try to understand the different opposition groups, but there was a bewildering array of them, all coming from different ideological positions. The National Movement, wanting constitutional reform, and the Liberation Movement, wanting constitutional reform but also a place for Islam in the governmental process. Then there were what Reza contemptuously called 'the Shah's step-by-step colour-coded guide to dissident groups': 'the Red and the Black', the same groups that Massoud had mentioned in Berkeley (how much Massoud must have known, but didn't let on). I'd heard a lot more about them since I'd been in Iran: they were the first reason the Shah always gave for any trouble: 'It's the Reds!' (Marxists); 'It's the Blacks! (the Islamists); 'It's the Reds and the Blacks!' (the Islamist Marxists).

'Islamist Marxists'? I remember Massoud saying that was the Shah's term for the two groups that he perceived were working together as one against him. It was constantly used in the newspapers. It confused the hell out of me. How could you be a Marxist, opposed to any form of organised religion, and also a follower of Islam? Reza said not to waste my energy trying to follow the Shah's simplistic approach to what was really going on in his country. It was too late for that.

I've made the political situation sound quite lucid. But it was far more complex than I've suggested here. I couldn't make head or tail of what was happening. All I knew was that it wasn't about to go away. And it was going to get so much worse.

*

Tabriz, 11 January

Qom

There was trouble in Qom again on Monday.

Just rumours in the Tabriz bazaar, at the moment, about what's gone on, but if only half of it is true, it sounds bad: a clash of some sort between the police and a group of religious clerics with their students. There's been no official news in the papers here but official news travels slowly. Reza is up from Tehran tomorrow – he'll have the latest.

So much unrest seems to centre around Qom, these days. Not surprising, I suppose, it's Khomeini's stronghold, even though he's not lived there since his exile in 1964. Whenever I hear his name mentioned now, I think of Massoud's presentation in Berkeley. I didn't fully appreciate what he was saying back then, but it looks like Khomeini has been a powerful presence here all along, a constant bass note in the drumbeat of dissent and opposition to the Shah, with Qom as its source.

The city is only eighty miles or so from Tehran, but it couldn't be more different. When I first started to hear about it, I asked Arash why it was so important. He told me it's one of the most religiously conservative cities in Iran. The Holy City of Qom, they call it, where many of the leading clerics of the day, including Khomeini, went as boys or young men to study in the schools attached to the seminaries, and then stayed on to involve themselves in Shi'a scholarship.

'It's like Iran having two capitals,' Arash said, 'Tehran, the secular one, which I think the clerics in Qom see as Sin City, and Qom, the religious centre, which prides itself on being as conservative as Mecca.'

'Why is there always such anti-Shah feeling there, though? Just because it's a religious centre, it doesn't have to be anti-Shah.'

'The clerics think he's taken a lot of their power away. And I guess he did, with his White Revolution land reforms in 1963. They've never really forgiven him for grabbing so much land from the clergy and redistributing it. They don't trust him. They certainly don't see him as their leader. In Qom, there are no standard portraits of him in the shops like you see everywhere else. They display a stylised representation of the Twelfth Imam instead.'

We tend to notice what goes on in Qom more than some of the other cities, mainly because there is a strong link between it and Tabriz, particularly at the moment, courtesy of the Grand Ayatollah Shariatmadari, the most important of the ayatollahs. He has strong personal connections with Tabriz. He's immensely influential, according to Arash, and is known as a moderate, cautious thinker, who doesn't like Khomeini and his extremist views.

So what happens in Qom, even though it's around 350 miles away from us, always gets a reaction in Tabriz. Which means we could be in for trouble too.

*

12 January
QOM: 6 KILLED AS MOB TURNS VIOLENT. Reza set the KH on the table. 'Six killed? The word on the street in Qom is twenty killed and three hundred injured.' His face is pinched with anger. 'I know who I'd rather believe.'

'What happened?' Arash sounded really shocked.

According to Reza, no one knows for sure what caused the people to demonstrate, but it must have been something serious because they were saying in Tehran that thousands took to the streets in Qom, and they were incensed. They rampaged through the centre of town, wrecking buildings and setting them alight. Then they ended up outside the main police station and tried to force their way in. The police went on the roof and fired down on them. There was a stampede to avoid the bullets, and a thirteen-year-old boy was crushed. The army was brought in and now they are under martial law and curfew.

Reza went out later to the bazaar to see what else he could pick up. The Tabriz bazaar is next to the Friday mosque, the main mosque, the Masjed-e Jameh, and news travelled faster from mosque to mosque and bazaar to bazaar than from any formal news outlet. He looked quite shaken when he came back.

'It was something to do with the government insulting Khomeini. No one knows the exact details. But it's serious all right – serious enough for even Shariatmadari to speak out. He seems to have lost patience with the government – he's actually calling for Khomeini's return from exile, too.'

Arash sighed. 'Shariatmadari is always the moderate one, and there's no great respect between him and Khomeini, but if even he is pushing for action . . .' He shook his head.

14 January

The Letter

'Take a look at that.' Reza passed the newspaper to Arash.

It was the *Ettela'at*, a national newspaper reckoned to be the government's mouthpiece, even more so than the *Kayhan*.

Arash frowned as he scanned the page. 'What am I supposed to be looking at?'

Reza leaned over and pointed. It could easily have been missed: it was in small type, with a small-size headline, and swamped by the large advert for machinery it was placed next to. It was almost as if the editor hoped people wouldn't spot it. At first glance, it looked like an anonymous letter to the editor. Arash translated it for me.

Iran and the Red Black Colonialism. It was actually a thinly disguised, virulent attack on Khomeini. He was a fraud. He had lived in India and had ties with British imperialism. He opposed the White Revolution and was plotting to replace it with a Red (Marxist) and Black (Islamist) imperialism. He would repeal the laws on land reforms (give back land to the clergy) and women's rights, so Iranian Muslims must beware this imposter dressed as a clergyman. He did not have the support of other senior clerics in his opposition to the monarchy. He might not even be Iranian.

As a final flourish, it implied he might well be homosexual.

'My God!' Arash's voice trailed off and he put down the paper.

Reza filled us in on what had happened. The newspaper article had appeared in Qom the same evening it was published. So that's what had got people out on the streets and provoked such outrage. The *Ettela'at*, the voice of the Shah, had done the unthinkable. It had attacked a *marja* – a Grand Ayatollah.

Arash shook his head. 'It's unheard of, to target and slander a *marja* like that. Even the Shah wouldn't do it.'

'Well, someone on behalf of the Shah obviously did.' Reza looked shocked too.

'No wonder they went crazy in Qom.'

The buildings they had attacked and burned tended to be symbols of the government, like the hated Rasakhitz Party offices, schools and banks. And there was that chant again: *Marg bar Shah!* Death to the Shah! Even though he wasn't physically there, Khomeini was front, back and centre stage in provoking the trouble. The day after the main riots had subsided, on 10 January, he praised the demonstrators for their courage and called for them to go out on further demonstrations.

So, it all sparked off in Qom, with the publication of that letter in *Ettela'at*.

Also on 10 January, the same day that Khomeini called for more demonstrations, Ayatollah Shariatmadari called for forty days of mourning for those killed in the Qom riots.

The fortieth day of that mourning ritual is 18 February.

'Emotions are always at their highest on the fortieth day,' Arash said. 'If there's going to be trouble in Tabriz, that's when it will be.'

2 February

The leaflet

Arash spotted the leaflet in the dirty slush in front of the university library, its handwritten message already beginning to run. Translated, it read: CLOSE THE BAZAAR, 18 FEBRUARY. IN SOLIDARITY WITH THE MARTYRS OF QOM.

'They were all over the campus,' he said, dropping it onto the kitchen table when he got back to Kucheh Mulla. 'This is the strongest message so far.' He slumped wearily in a chair.

We've noticed more leaflets than usual this past week, declaring solidarity with the Qom rioters, but nothing specific about taking any action. They've been tucked behind the windscreen wipers of cars parked on the university boulevard or left in empty classrooms, daily reminders adding to the grim mood on campus. The university was officially open, but the students hadn't been turning up for lectures since the rumours had started about what had happened at Qom. Small groups of restless young men would mill around, then disappear.

The leaflet was unsigned. Whoever it is, they've focused on 18 February as the fortieth day of the mourning cycle already in progress for those killed in Qom.

'Who do you think is trying to organise this?' I said. 'It says they want the bazaar to be closed – that's a huge demand to make. Is it just students or some other group in the city? I wouldn't have thought students had that much influence.'

'They might not have much influence, but they're good at

organising themselves. When you think about it, a university campus is a great place to set up protest groups. They're the very places students are supposed to gather to discuss things – who's to know what they're actually talking about? And even SAVAK couldn't check every single student to see what they're getting up to.'

He ran his fingers through his hair, as if trying to straighten out his thoughts. 'It looks as though they're definitely planning something for Tabriz.'

He drank the last of the tea and spooned out the soggy lemon into the small dish he always used for that. 'I'll go and talk to Ervand, see what he knows.' He sounded thoroughly miserable. The possibility of real trouble coming so close to home was beginning to drag him down.

'I'll come with you. It's a while since we've both been to the bazaar.' I didn't say that I'd not been with him since Reza had been coming to Tabriz, because Reza made sure I got the message that if they went to see Ervand, it would be a family-only outing that didn't include me. So, it would be good to go with Arash again. And I like the bazaar. I've missed going there with him. It's the first place he took me to when I arrived in Tabriz.

*

Kupfermühle, 18 January
I've not thought about the bazaar for years. It's true what I've written, though, it was one of the few places Arash and I went to together openly in Tabriz. We were just two men in a crowd there, and I loved it. Like most foreigners, I used to think a bazaar would be a quaint collection of shops selling typically exotic eastern products, a kind of superior covered street market. Even when Arash had tried to describe it back in Berkeley, I hadn't appreciated its scale and beauty. He was right, there was a real sense of place, of it being the centre of centuries of the city's history, played out within and outside its walls.

It doesn't have quite the level of business it once supported – Arash says the Shah's reforms have meant new businesses and investment opportunities have grown up outside the bazaar, a real bone of contention with the merchants, the *bazaaris*. But all levels of business are still done there, from multi-million-dollar investments to the one-man activities of the artisans, not to mention the middlemen who oil the wheels of commerce and keep it going.

The Friday mosque, the Masjed-e Jameh, being next door is no accident – the main bazaars and Friday mosques in the cities are usually side by side, and there's a complex relationship between the two. The Tabriz bazaar is connected directly to the mosque through an entrance from within the bazaar, so going to pray, then doing business, or the other way round, can be seamless. Most of the Tabrizi bazaar merchants are Muslims, and the bazaar handles much of the clergy's investments and banking needs, to the mutual benefit of both. Its network of contacts is deep and wide, throughout the city, which is helpful if the mosque wants to get a particular message out to all the people, not necessarily just to those who attend regularly. So, the clergy and the *bazaaris* working together can be a powerful combination.

The first time Arash took me there, I wandered around open-mouthed. It was rebuilt after the earthquake in 1780, and is a beautiful, deceptively simple building, its series of elegant arch-ways framing the *raasteh*s, the shopping rows, with their angled-brick walls, and its occasional domed ceilings with their polygon ribs of intricate brickwork. Arash pointed the roofs out to me, with quiet pride, saying that whoever had built and rebuilt the bazaar over the centuries was mindful of the cold and snowy climate of Tabriz. There are fewer domes and they tend to be smaller than other main Iranian bazaars. The roofs are flatter, allowing more of the surface to catch the sunlight and warm the brick, providing some natural heating down to the *raasteh*s below.

Each *raasteh* tends to specialise in certain items, like food-stuffs, and, in Tabriz's case, of course, beautiful carpets of all sizes. Arash took me to his favourite place, the most prestigious *raasteh*, specialising in carpets. I could see right away why he likes it so much. The dome there is elegant and understated, with a round skylight in the brick ceiling, casting a soft light onto the *raasteh* below. The carpet shops along its sides are two-storey, the carpets on the ground floor, the offices above. The buildings have clean lines, businesslike but stylish. The brickwork here is more complex, too, herringbone, and jack-on-jack patterns, meticulously laid in the arched ceilings.

We wandered up and down, drifting into the shops with their restrained displays of the most exquisite carpets, works of art in their own right.

'This gives me the same feeling as being in an art gallery,' I said to Arash. 'I mean a really good one, where you can lose yourself in the ambience of the place and what you're looking at. This whole experience is so seductive.'

He laughed when I said this. 'It's intended to be, but not in the way you mean. People come here with a limit to what they can spend, but somehow end up spending double, and leave thinking it was worth it. The cool, elegant ambience is part of the trick.'

I can see him now, standing in the soft light falling from the dome, laughing at me, and my heart aches.

*

Tabriz, 3 February

The mice have ears

Ervand, the spice-seller, has one of the most popular sites in the bazaar. There are other spice stalls nearby, but Ervand's is known to be the best quality at the best price. It's in a prime position, under the last arch of the foodstuff *raasteh* before you turn into the carpet area, where he also holds a part-share in one of the smaller emporiums. If anyone would know what was going on in the bazaar, it would be Ervand. The Tabrizis can't live without their spices however bad things get, and Ervand has a constant daily flow of customers who would tell him the latest news. I'd been there a few times with Arash, before I realised that Ervand was at the centre of a complex network of business and family contacts, through brothers, uncles, second cousins and other assorted relatives, all part of the intermarriages between powerful *bazaari* families, and all providing a super-efficient conduit for rumour.

He was the family friend Arash had stayed with when Reza had gone to Tehran, and Arash stayed on at Tabriz University. Apparently, their mother, who was distantly related to Ervand's wife's cousin, had persuaded their father to do him a favour, something regarding another of his lucrative investments, his almond orchard outside Tabriz. Arash was not sure of the details – the boys were quite young when this had taken place – but Ervand had obviously been very grateful, which was partly why he'd looked after Arash.

The first time we visited him and Arash introduced me, his shrewd eyes flickered over me lightning fast, assessing me through to my very bones, or so it seemed to me. It felt as though he'd gleaned everything there was to know about me, about us, there and then. He was always polite with me, although a little reserved. But Arash told me he was secretly impressed that I was an Oxford graduate. His eldest daughter, his favourite, was at university in London, and the one topic of conversation he never tired of was how well she was doing in her medical studies and how he couldn't wait for her to come back and take up a position at the local hospital.

I could imagine him saying, beaming, to anyone who would listen 'my daughter, the doctor'. He had three daughters, 'the lights of my life', he always said, hand on his heart, 'and all three are beautiful. They take after their mother, and all will marry well.' But I always thought he was a little sad not to have had a son, and wondered whether that was also why he'd been so willing to look out for Reza and Arash, that and the fact that he felt he owed their father a favour.

He was rich, like many of the merchants in the bazaar, although you'd never know it. Modestly dressed, neatly tailored jacket and trousers, nothing flashy, although he had a penchant for handmade shoes, softest leather, made by the best shoe-maker in the shoes *raasteh*, who, of course, was another distant relative. As well as his bazaar holdings, he owned several properties in Tabriz, small houses he rented out. When Arash got his job as the university assistant librarian, he'd offered him one at a very low rent. 'You'd be doing me a favour,' Ervand had said. 'It's where I keep old furniture and things for the other houses I rent out, so it's good to have someone in it.' There were three rooms to live in upstairs, and two rooms downstairs, full of stored furniture. Basic, but in a quiet, ordinary neighbourhood, the sort where teachers and lower-level government officials lived, quite near the American Consulate. I'd visited, but only with Arash's colleagues from the library, and never stayed overnight: it was a little too local for us to take risks.

When Arash moved in, Ervand sent round a beautiful carved bookcase. 'Can't have a librarian with nowhere to put his books,' he'd said, when Arash had called in to thank him.

I got the impression he was fond of Reza, he recognised and admired his worldliness, but he loved Arash for his gentleness and learning. He would hug him and smile, when they greeted each other, and say, 'How's the poet?'

We got to the bazaar mid-afternoon, just in time to hear Ervand berating a lanky lad for not keeping the display of spices neat enough, although it seemed perfect to me, with its wonderful warm palette of cinnabar reds and ochre yellows. We went through the greeting, the hugging and smiling, then the handshake for me, while the lanky lad served us tea and sweets on a brass tray. We sat on high stools at either side of the drop-leaf counter leading to the back of the shop. Ervand asked about Reza, about what it was like up at the university, and shook his head when Arash told him it was open, but no students came.

'Such a waste,' he said. 'They should finish their studies. They are so fortunate and don't know it.' He has some English, although he speaks Persian to Arash, who translates some of what he says, while I struggle to make sense of the rest.

Arash showed him the leaflet. 'This was floating round the university today.'

He nodded as he read it. 'There are many of these round the bazaar too.' He reached under the counter and brought out a handful, all single-line messages, handwritten.

'It's the students up at your university. They are a new group, so I've heard, with links to the mosque here and to Qom. The Patriotic Muslim Students of Tabriz University, they call them-selves. They are very well organised. Some say they get funding from other groups, but I don't know. I just think they've become very religious – they feel a strong link with Qom, and have lost patience with the way things are.'

He was careful not to mention the Shah or Khomeini. 'The way things are' was about as pointed a comment on the situation as we'd get. But we knew he was no friend of the Shah and his policies. Back in 1975, one of the first actions of the Shah's new much-despised Rastakhitz Party, the only party now allowed in Iran's politics, was to send badly trained inspectors into the bazaars to uncover what the government called 'profiteering'. They suggested that the *bazaaris* were inflating prices as the oil boom of 1973 took hold.

Ervand wasn't one of the profiteers, but several of his friends and associates were judged to be so and were arrested and fined.

The rumour was that informants in the bazaar helped the inspectors. This was never proven, but it was enough for the *bazaaris* to choose even more carefully whom they shared gossip with. 'The walls have mice, and the mice have ears,' Ervand would say, when he felt the conversation was straying into risky territory. And that would be that.

'Do you think the bazaar will close?' Arash fingered the leaflets. 'It seems such a strong gesture.'

I fully expected the wall-and-mice warning but, to my surprise, Ervand nodded.

'Yes, the bazaar will definitely close. They want the shops on Pahlavi Avenue to close too. In fact, they want the whole city to close down for the day, in solidarity with the Qom martyrs.'

'Martyrs! Why do they use such emotive words?' Arash sounded exasperated. 'They're victims, yes, but martyrs?'

Ervand shrugged, but didn't venture an opinion.

Arash frowned. 'Well, I just hope we don't end up with any Tabrizi "martyrs".'

'It's supposed to be a peaceful demonstration. That's what Ayatollah Shariatmadari has told them – if they demonstrate, it must be peaceful and orderly. That's the best way to commemorate the dead.'

I marvelled once again at Ervand. He missed nothing, either by eye or ear. Shariatmadari would have been in touch from Qom with the mosque next door, but somehow Ervand had got to know about it.

'Still,' he said, patting Arash on the shoulder, 'it's maybe best you stay away from the city centre on February the eighteenth. Leave them to their little demonstration. Then we can all get on with earning a living.'

18 February

Chasing Shadows

One minute the university entrance gate was clear, the next a police Land Rover rolled up and parked in front of it. Two policemen jumped out of the back, one with a walkie-talkie. They stood there, stamping their feet in the slush, the one with his hands free flapping his arms round his body. It hadn't snowed for a couple of days and there was a bright morning sun, but a bitterly cold wind blew down off the mountains.

We slowed our pace, unsure whether to go on or turn back and return across the campus to the library. Arash had been determined to come up to the university early this morning, even though it was officially closed. The librarian had gone off sick two days ago, on Thursday afternoon, when Arash wasn't there. He'd rung Arash at his house, and by some miracle, he'd got through on the notoriously unreliable Tabriz local line to tell him he wouldn't be in for a few days and that he'd locked everything up. But Arash was nervous about leaving the library unchecked for two days. He had this nightmare about students getting carried away, breaking into the library and burning all the books in English, as some kind of act of aggression against all things American and/or Western.

'It's just the kind of pointless act of bravado some hothead might think was a good idea,' he said.

The police at the gate were eyeing us as we got nearer. 'Keep walking,' I said, 'I'll show them my Council ID and they'll see we're staff and let us pass.' My 'Council ID' was a scruffy letter with the Council logo and Tabriz address on it, saying I worked for them at the university, but at least it looked official, and I'd been carrying it with me for some time, on the off-chance it would come in handy.

We were within about twenty yards of the gates when the two policemen turned away from us and stared into the distance down the road running parallel to the gates. The one with the walkie-talkie rested it on the Land Rover bonnet. Both men stood up straight, bodies tensed. A group of students shuffled into view outside the gate and slowly came to a stop a few yards in front of the police. There were about a hundred of them, most with their parka hoods up against the cold, or possibly to hide their faces from the police.

'Where did they come from?' I asked Arash.

'God knows, but it's obviously planned, not impromptu – they've brought their pre-prepared placards with them.'

The students were slanting the placards down, so you couldn't see what was written on them. They were quiet, except for the occasional exchange with each other as they organised themselves into a column about five students wide. Then they curved away from the police to face the boulevard leading into town. A tall man, standing centre front, wearing a dark woollen traditional Tabrizi hat with its rimless crown, shouted something I didn't understand in a clear, strong voice, and they set off slowly, still keeping their placards facing downwards.

'What did he shout?'

'I think he said: "Let's go! Keep it peaceful!"' said Arash.

We reached the gates and I showed my 'ID', both of us shaking our heads as if we disapproved of the group heading off. The police waved us on, their faces impassive, and one closed the gates behind us. That left us no choice: we couldn't go back onto campus if we wanted to, so we had to follow the group – there was no other way into town. I wondered if anyone was still on campus, although we hadn't seen anybody while we'd been there. It looked like we were the only ones who'd disregarded the advice about staying clear, 'just in case there's trouble'. The leaflets distributed over the past week had achieved their desired effect.

We walked along the pavement on the right, not down the middle of the road as the students were doing, and we kept the gap between them and us as constant as we could. There was a sudden stutter of movement from the middle of the group, and the same voice that had called before shouted something that sounded like 'Keep it peaceful!' again, followed by something else I had to check with Arash.

'He said, "Keep it peaceful. Don't react."'

'Don't react to what?' Then I saw that we were approaching the first intersection, and that over to the left, a black police truck was parked across one half of the road, engine off.

Two policemen were standing beside it, one holding a walkie-talkie – it must have been their latest bit of kit.

The students began to reshuffle, having to narrow the rows to three abreast, so they could walk on the pavement and get through the remaining gap. This meant they had to slow down, so the police could get a good look at them.

I was beginning to feel uneasy. Arash was at a disadvantage being with me – I hoped that, with my beanie pulled down over my ears and my scarf muffling my face, no one would notice I was a Westerner. But the policeman at the gate with the walkie-talkie could quite easily have let this pair know I was obviously a foreigner.

We kept our distance from the students as we went past the police truck, hoping we were signalling to the police that we weren't part of the demonstration. But they took little notice of us: they were much more interested in scanning student faces as they passed through the gap. The black tarpaulin above the tailgate of the truck was down, so we couldn't see in, and there was no noise coming from it, but I had the strong sense that other human beings were in there, policemen probably. It wasn't only the students who had planned for the day.

We'd only gone another twenty yards or so when we heard a low rumble behind us. The police truck had turned onto the boulevard, and passed us slowly, catching up with the students, who'd re-formed into a wide column. The truck now blocked any means of escape from the back of the group. It reminded me of a border collie, driving a herd of sheep towards an enclosure.

We could see another intersection coming up, in about thirty yards, and another police Land Rover parked on it to the left.

'Before we get to the intersection, there's a narrow street on the right,' whispered Arash. 'We'd better turn down it, get away from whatever's going on here. We can always double back and head for home.'

We came level with the street on the right and strolled

casually round the corner. After a few yards, we increased our pace, then broke into a run, Arash leading the way, me squinting into the sun, chasing his shadow, my coat streaming behind me. I thought my ears would burst, I was listening so hard for the footsteps of police chasing us, or the engine noise of a Land Rover driving into the street. I could see my short hot breaths puffing out in front of me and feel them clammy on my face as I ran through them.

I was vaguely aware of running past small shops, all closed and shuttered. Arash eased up a little so I could draw level with him, and tugged my elbow to guide me as he veered right into an even smaller street, not quite as narrow as a *kucheh*. We slowed to walking pace to catch our breath. A scrawny dog with its stringy tail curled tightly between its back legs scuttled across the end of the street in front of us. Otherwise there wasn't a movement or a sound.

'This should lead us back to the boulevard and the police will have gone past by now, so we can cross over and head for home,' Arash said. We took another right turn into another narrow street, and I could see the boulevard in the distance. We walked on without speaking, the sun on our backs now, cold sweat running down between my shoulder blades.

The boulevard was empty both ways, so we crossed.

Kucheh Mulla was about a mile away, taking a labyrinthine route Arash knew through yet more narrow streets. We walked at an even pace this time, we didn't want to look like we were running away from anything, not that there was anyone to see us, the streets were deserted. That was unusual for a Saturday morning, an ordinary working day. The leaflets had obviously done their work here, too. We didn't speak – we didn't want our voices to carry in the quiet – but as we walked, I began to hear chanting, loud and rhythmic. I couldn't distinguish what the chant was, but then it stopped abruptly and was followed by a distant bell ringing, strident and getting louder. I looked at Arash and frowned.

'Sounds like a fire engine,' he said. It clamoured on, then stopped.

It was just after 10 a.m. when we turned into Kucheh Mulla, through an entrance I didn't know about, at the opposite end to the one we usually used. It was disorienting, approaching our house from another direction. But, then, the whole morning had been disorienting. While Arash was unlocking our door in the wall, I looked towards the archway and saw a plume of smoke rising above it, inky black against the blue sky, in the direction of the city centre.

We went straight up onto the roof to check out where it was coming from. By the time we got there, two more smoke columns, all three very near to each other, were beginning to reshape and spread into a single oily cloud drifting slowly towards us.

Arash was trying to locate what was on fire. 'I think it's near the bazaar,' he said.

'I hope Ervand took his own advice and stayed clear.' His voice was strained.

Kucheh Mulla was less than a mile from the bazaar, if you could have walked straight there, but the *kucheh*s stopped you going straight to anywhere. Like Arash had said, only half joking, they were built to keep invaders out, with their unexpected dead ends and their twists and turns leading into and out of each other. So, I reasoned that we'd be safe enough in our house. Even if it got a bit tricky for the demonstrators in town, and they decided to make a run for it, hopefully they'd be put off running into the *kucheh*s, in case they were chased, made mistakes and found themselves lost or trapped.

Then the chanting started again. The wind was blowing in our direction so we could hear it, faintly at first, but it was still impossible to make out the words. It was a strong rhythmic sound, made by many voices.

'So much for "Keep it peaceful. Don't react",' I said to Arash, remembering the tall, imposing student in the Tabrizi hat, leading the column up the boulevard, and suddenly feeling fearful for him. The chant floated nearer, and became loud enough for us to make out the words.

'*Marg bar Shah!*' Death to the Shah! We looked at each other in astonishment.

Hearing it with my own ears for the first time, chanted by so many voices sounding so determined and with such anger, made my stomach lurch.

Strident fire-engine alarms drowned the sound.

'Thank goodness,' said Arash. 'That should sort the fires out. I hope they haven't spread to the bazaar.'

He'd hardly finished speaking before there was a faint whump and a fat ball of smoke and flames ballooned into the sky a little way off from the others.

'Christ!' I said. 'That sounded like a proper explosion. It'll have done some damage.'

'I'm not sure,' Arash said, looking intently at the fireball in the sky, 'but I think that was over near the banks.'

I thought I could hear screaming, but couldn't tell if they were screams of pain or anger. I shuddered. 'I think we'd better go in, Arash. That smoke's drifting our way.' I suddenly felt as though I wanted to be inside, away from it all. It felt surreal to be watching and listening as if it was a Hollywood movie. It was really happening and people were probably getting hurt.

We went back inside to the blare of more sirens.

I felt a bit calmer in the kitchen, watching Arash making the tea.

'All we can do is sit it out,' he said, passing me my mug. 'It'll probably be over in a few hours. The protesters have made their point so they'll go home.' He didn't look convinced.

It all went quiet around lunchtime. I went up on the roof again, praying it was all over. Arash stayed behind, he'd had enough. A dense pall of smoke hung over the city centre, the edges thinning and drifting our way. I didn't stay long. The acrid smell of burning rubber caught the back of my throat, so I went down to the kitchen.

'It looks bad over there,' I said. 'But at least it's quiet now. Maybe that's it.'

The gunfire started at about two o'clock. I didn't realise it was gunfire until Arash said, 'My God! They've started shooting at each other!'

I'd never heard live gunfire before. You expect it to go rat-a-tat-tat, like a film soundtrack, but this sounded like single handclaps, randomly spaced and hollow.

Then the sound changed. The handclap was obliterated by a rapid *crack-crack-crack*, evenly spaced this time.

We ran up to the roof again and crouched against the wall, protecting ourselves, which was a silly thing to do – the gunfire was nowhere near us – but we felt so exposed standing up. Then the firing stopped. It's strange the way you use certain senses in new ways when you feel under threat. I had the same sensation in my ears that I'd had when we were running down the side-streets earlier, when my eardrums had felt fit to split, they were stretched so thin, trying to pick up the tiniest sound.

The gunfire started again, the *crack-crack-crack* more continuous, the sound echoing round for what seemed an age.

'I can't stand this,' Arash said. 'We're listening to people getting shot. It's madness, madness!' Tears were sliding down his face. He clutched my arm. 'Come on, Damian, come away!'

I was just about to move when a loud *wokka-wokka-wokka* sound came from nowhere above our heads, and a helicopter cruised over. It happened so quickly, and the noise was so deafening, we both fell over and landed in a tangle together in the slush. It would have been funny if we hadn't been so terrified. We scrambled up, and this time, we didn't bother going downstairs, we scuttled to our roof loft. We stripped off our wet jackets and jeans, put our sweats on and got under the quilt, lying there, side by side, trembling with shock.

After about an hour, we crept down to the kitchen. We were

still fearful, but we decided maybe it would be quieter down-stairs, spasmodic gunfire was still going on and the helicopter was still circling overhead. The phone rang. It was Julia Greenwood, the director's assistant at the Council. I was not to go out in any circumstances. The same went for anyone else who might be in the house. The army was being called in. I was to await further instructions.

We camped on the floor cushions with some bread and sheep's cheese, not that we could eat anything. The window began to rattle and I heard a faint growl, slowly growing louder. I couldn't place it at all. Then I realised it was tank engines. They must have been heading down the boulevard from the Tabriz barracks towards the city centre. My head was full of sounds I'd never heard before and felt like it would explode.

Julia rang again. In all probability, the army would impose martial law. The city would be under curfew. I was to await further instructions, she repeated.

We went back up to bed and spent the next couple of hours watching the smoky light fading above us through the window, listening to the soundscape of a riot and wondering what the world would be like tomorrow.

20 February

Where are we?

No gunfire this morning. I thought maybe it was all over. I opened the window for some fresh air, but closed it again, quickly. The smoke must have drifted our way and settled, I could taste it. Arash was in the kitchen, making us something to eat, so I decided to try to concentrate on my translation work. I needed to do something to centre myself.

The prof had suggested some time ago that I take a look at a contemporary translation of a complex pun in a Rumi poem. 'As I'm sure you know, such puns are common in Rumi,' he said, 'they're part of the pleasure.'

He forgot to add that translating them is nearly always impossible, the result can be so clumsy.

'See what you think of how the translator has tackled it,' the prof said. 'He's an ex-student of mine, an American, living in Paris now, the lucky chap. He's hoping to get it published, so I said we'd both have a look.'

The poem has the pun built around the sound of a word. *Ma ku*, with the space, means 'Where are we?' in Persian, but *maku*, without the space, means 'a weaver's shuttle'.

A bright weaver's shuttle flashes back and forth,
east–west, *Where-are-we? Ma ku? Maku.*
Like the sun saying *Where are we?*
as it weaves with the asking.

I tried to focus on puns and the difficulty in translating them, but I was unable to concentrate fully for long. I had one ear on the sound of the pun, while the other listened for gunfire. I should be a little more used to it, after our experience of the last two days. I've driven myself half mad wondering where the gunfire might be, if it was getting closer or more distant – was it a stray sniper, or an army squad? When it stopped, that was just as bad. Its absence was almost as disturbing as its presence, and I filled the silence with anxiety. And the anxiety filled the space in my chest, like a flexing iron fist.

Yesterday was the worst. The silence. Then more gunfire. No more single clapping hands. Just the rapid even *cracks* of sound. Then the *wokka-wokka-wokka* of more helicopters. Then the rumble of the tanks.

I've started to listen out for the shopkeepers' shutters. Gunfire and shutters. Yesterday one followed the other – the shopkeepers in the *kucheh* did their best to keep open, but when the gunfire started, down came the shutters. Ali the Baker was the last to give in – everyone needs bread and he needs to sell it – but even he couldn't take the risk, so down came his shutters. They always stick halfway, and as I heard them rasping to a halt, I automatically thought: *There go Ali's shutters.*

Then back to the silence. Then more gunfire.

I don't think either of us could have stood another day like that.

It seemed to have gone quiet for the moment, so I tried one more time with the Rumi pun. I liked what the American poet had done with it. The prof might think he's avoided the issue, importing the Persian words into the target language, but I liked the way he captures the sense of the original pun, unpicks the meaning, the trick of the pun, then reweaves it to create something similar but new.

Ma ku?
Where are we?

Arash came in with some vegetable soup for lunch, so I cleared a space at the end of the desk for us to eat.

'What's that you're working on?' he asked.

'I know you'll find this hard to believe, but it's Rumi,' I said.

He smiled. 'Have you changed your mind about him, then?'

'Not really. But since I've been working with the prof, I've grown to appreciate his dexterity, his cleverness with puns. That's as far as it goes, though. I just don't seem to be able to engage with his work on an emotional level. I find his connection with Shams far more intriguing than his actual poetry.'

Arash frowned. 'There's a great deal of mystery about the relationship between Rumi and Shams. But it really irritates me, the way western scholars misinterpret it. We'll never really know, and anyway, it's not important to the poetry.'

That put me in my place, but I knew what he meant. In the thirteenth century, the wandering dervish, Shams of Tabriz, met up with Rumi in Konya, Turkey, where Rumi was head of the dervish learning community. The two became inseparable. Rumi called his collection of odes and quatrains *The Works of Shams of Tabriz*. The modern Western academic take on Rumi's work is that it contains much homoerotic poetry, with Shams at its centre.

It doesn't escape me that my ex-psychology boyfriend in Oxford would have a field day with the resonances to be found in my own life trajectory so far.

'Can I take a look?' Arash pointed to my papers.

He read the American poet's translation slowly, nodding as he did so.

'It's strange that you should decide to work on Rumi today. When I got up this morning, I was still so agitated by what we witnessed yesterday, I did a Rumi-esque bit of work, too. Maybe we both needed something well inside our comfort zone.' He laughed.

'So, I guess it's my turn. Can I read it?'

He pulled a face. 'It's not a poem. I'm not sure what it is, but it's definitely not a poem. I thought I'd set down on paper my thoughts about the violence, just to get it out of my system. But I found myself writing not so much about violence but about Rumi, and a story of how he found a way to draw from his inner strength. It came out in a torrent – I just scribbled it down as fast as I could. More cathartic than creative, I suspect.'

After a little more persuasion, he went into the kitchen and brought out his notepad.

'We could work on an English translation of it together,' I said. So we settled down at the desk together, me with a pot of coffee, Arash with his lemon tea.

It was so soothing to talk about poets and poetry with him. When was the last time we'd done that? So long ago.

He read the piece in Persian so I could get a feel for it and enjoy it in the original. We translated it roughly into English, then worked on a version reflecting its rhythm and energy.

I've stuck his original Persian version here in my journal, on the opposite page to this translation. It's the first piece of work we've done together in Tabriz.

Rumi and the Dance of the Dervish

The Shah's army from the Tabrizi barracks brought the tanks onto the streets yesterday and turned their guns towards the people. I lay there, with Damian, listening, rigid with fear.

And then, this morning, still agitated, from nowhere I found myself thinking of Rumi and how he came to imagine the dance of the dervish and how that helped him find inner strength.

The story goes like this.

One day, Rumi was walking in the city of Konya, through the goldsmiths' quarter, and was intoxicated by the sights and sounds. The furnaces exhaling smoke from holes in their tops, the bellows boys squeezing the slightest of breaths over the coals to feed the fire, the iron anvils with softened gold laid upon them to be stretched and pulled and formed with tongs and hammer. And all the tools laid out: the rasps and files, the scorpers and dividers, the sharp chisel for engraving, the touchstone for testing, the hare's foot for smoothing and polishing. But what moved Rumi most was the sound of the hammers – the metallic echo of the peen heads, the chink of their chisel edges against the gold rims of bowls, the rapid tip-tip-tipping of more delicate hammers working with gold sheet.

He closed his eyes and could hear music in the hammering, and as he listened, he began to turn to its rhythm. The more he turned, the more in harmony with it he felt. The more harmony he felt, the more he surrendered to a kind of madness, a liberating, healthy madness, a sense of freedom, ecstatic freedom, but still held fast at the centre. Turning, he discovered, took him to the dervish, the doorway, an empty space, a place where the human and the divine come face to face and can become one.

Arash, 20 February 1978

We worked intensely for a couple of hours, side by side, arms and heads sometimes touching. It was a vibrant, evocative imagining and the process calmed us. And, briefly, we forgot the mayhem outside and the powerlessness we'd felt at having to witness it.

23 February

40/40

Here is what we know about 18 February. The police closed the mosque, on the orders of the Governor, so the mourners couldn't take part in the fortieth-day mourning ritual for the martyrs of Qom. The mourners were enraged and protested outside the mosque. A policeman shot a student in the leg. The protesters went on the rampage.

Those are the only indisputable facts about what sparked off the riots. The rest is claim, counter-claim, rumour, lies and unverifiable possibilities.

Reza read from the paper: *'Twelve dead, 125 injured.'* He snorted. 'Try a hundred dead. Hundreds injured.' He was up from Tehran again, almost a week after the riots, with copies of the *KH,* 20 and 21 February.

'How do you know which is true?' Arash sounded weary. He hadn't been sleeping well since the riots.

'This is a government newspaper, Arash. And look at the headline: *Tabriz after the Mob.* The Mob. That tells you what side they're on.'

There was no shortage of facts and figures for the damage.

Seventy-three banks gutted, including branches of the Saderat Bank, owned by a Baha'i – taken as a warning to others of the Baha'i faith, whose followers Islam deems to be heretics. Destruction of bank files and accounts. Rumours of clients' banking details floating around the streets.

Cinemas showing Western films, liquor stores, most of the shops along Pahlavi Avenue all destroyed. Coca-Cola truck set on fire. Iran-America Society building set ablaze.

The Tabriz Justice Department smashed.

Childcare and welfare centres attacked. Small local hospitals attacked.

Rastakhiz Party headquarters set on fire and gutted.

Commemorative tiled panels celebrating the Shah's White Revolution smashed.

A twelve-storey hotel for foreign workers set on fire.

Broken windows alone cost nearly a hundred thousand dollars.

Damage overall – millions of dollars.

More disturbing were the rumours about attacks on women. A witness in the French community in Tabriz happened to see a woman dragged out of her car. She disappeared and was rumoured to have been burned. At the Parvin girls' school, which had a reputation for being progressive, a group of pupils were said to have been severely beaten, and their parents contacted to pick them up, with a warning to make sure they brought with them their daughters' chadors – the full length veils which covered their heads and wrapped round their bodies. We'd begun to see more women wearing them around Tabriz these last few days. Women in jeans or whose heads were uncovered were chased down and assaulted. One of the Americans who teaches science at the university is supposed to have told an American journalist that women in Western clothes were dragged out of taxis and beaten up.

'Did he actually see that?' said Arash. 'Or has he just heard about it?'

'Who cares?' said Reza. 'It makes good copy in Western papers. It's what the West thinks we get up to.' It reminded me again of Massoud and his theory of 'framing' the news.

More bizarre rumours flourish. Twenty dogs, with white towels wrapped round them, each with a name of a member of the royal family scrawled on them, were supposed to have been set free to roam around the city centre as a symbol of how the royal family could be got rid of and ridiculed.

A policeman whose job was to guard the American Consulate was sent home, but on the way he went to join the protesters, who were destroying the Rastakhiz Party headquarters. Then he joined in the looting, stole a chair and was arrested. He was later released after a word on his behalf from the American consul himself.

Rumours went round about the police. They hadn't bothered to use water hoses or tear gas. They'd gone straight to live ammunition. No, they hadn't: they'd fired over people's heads but no one took any notice. No, they hadn't: they'd refused to fire at all at the people – maybe they knew some of them. Then when the army had moved in towards the evening, they'd also been reluctant to fire on the crowd. They were from the local barracks, so they must have known people too.

'Well,' said Reza, when he read this, 'someone must have fired at the people, because at least a hundred, probably more, ended up dead.'

Twelve policemen were also injured and government officials killed, possibly pre-targeted. So the protesters must either have had arms, or got hold of them as the skirmishes progressed. Rumours about how well prepared and well armed the protesters had been flew around, encouraged by reports in the *KH* about 'imported incendiary bombs'. Witnesses described protesters throwing 'things that looked like balls' into buildings and the balls then exploding into flames. They seemed to know what they were targeting and even had basic tactics, like breaking up into small groups. At one point, it was rumoured, the protesters had controlled 7.5 miles from the university to the railway station.

'Whatever this was,' I said to Arash, 'it was no little local riot.'

The three of us went to the bazaar to check on Ervand. We'd tried to ring him, but local phones are notoriously bad at the best of times so there had been no chance during a riot. We were shocked by the damage to Pahlavi Avenue, which was wrecked all the way down, but already they were clearing the debris, putting in new windows. They wouldn't let us near the bank area, but as we walked into the city centre, paper was lying everywhere, on the street, even in the branches of trees. Reza stopped and picked a sheet up and saw it was the bank details of a business client. It was true, then, what people had been saying. There must have been hundreds of bank-customer details blowing in the wind.

Ervand was OK. Angry but OK. For once, his usual mice-have-ears tactic of saying little had deserted him. He obviously needed to let off steam. *The demonstrators were stupid to lose their tempers with the police. The police were stupid to shut the mosque doors. The Governor was stupid to order the police to close the mosque in the first place.*

Tanks in the middle of Tabriz! Our own tanks!

But Tabriz would survive. The bazaar would survive. The mosque would survive.

Let's hope that's the last of it, and we can all get on with earning a living.

I noticed he was unusually gentle with the lanky lad. Reza told me afterwards that the boy's older brother had been badly injured in the riots and the lad was distraught.

The word on the street, says Reza, is that this sequence of events is deliberate. They're calling it the 40/40. The victims of Qom had been killed on the fortieth day of mourning for the supposed murder of Mostafa Khomeini. The riots in Tabriz happened on the fortieth day of mourning for the victims of Qom. There are now forty days of mourning for the victims of Tabriz. Whose turn will it be in forty days' time?

*

Kupfermühle, 27 February

Looking back, I realise that this was the point at which everything began to change, although we didn't know it at the time. Tabriz recovered, like it always did, after the chaos and upheaval of the February riots. Ervand was right about that. The city had been invaded so many times, ancient and modern, that it must be embedded in the psyche of all Tabrizis that they can pick themselves up and get on with surviving, whatever is thrown at them. But the city was never the same, to me at least. Perhaps, as an outsider, I saw things differently. We took to sitting round in the evening, discussing what had gone on and seeing if we could make any sense of it. At least, Reza and I did. Arash tended to listen. He was finding it really hard to cope with 'seeing and hearing Tabriz in such agony', as he put it.

There were so many unanswered questions about the riots. The organisers, whoever they were, had persuaded the *bazaaris* to close. That takes power. I couldn't imagine Ervand doing anything he thought would be bad for business and that he wouldn't get any benefit from, so they must have closed voluntarily. Reza thought that showed a depth of desperation, anger, and a determination to change things, together with a belief that this time they actually could.

But there were other questions. If you're facing a tank, and all you've got are stones to throw at it, what keeps you standing there? Why doesn't the fear take over and make you run? Maybe it's when despair becomes a greater force than fear – that's when you stand your ground: when you think you have nothing to lose.

Why did the Shah feel it necessary to bring out the big guns – literally bring out his British Chieftain tanks?

'Because he could,' said Reza. 'He wanted to show his power, what he was capable of doing, if necessary, even to his own people. He labelled the protesters the Red and the Black, remember – Marxists or Islamists, or a combination of both. As soon as you label your own people as something else, not part of the normal fabric of your own society, it becomes easier to see them as the enemy.'

Why did the rioters choose those specific targets?

'Because,' said Reza, 'many of them were symbols of Westernisation – cinemas, liquor stores, overseas banks, even hairdressing salons frequented by Iranian women wanting Western styles – opposition to the Westernisation of women was a strong theme.'

What he said made sense to me. But then, a lot of what he said was beginning to make sense to me, much to my surprise.

Soldiers were shot. Who shot them? And where did they get the arms? This wasn't some ramshackle student outfit carrying stones in their pockets and waving a few placards. Someone had had arms: wounded police and dead government officials were evidence of that.

One thing was for sure: those riots weren't a spontaneous expression of discontent from a bunch of student hotheads. There had been serious, well-planned insurrection.

It was amazing how soon we all got used to the changes after the riots. Fundamental changes, like not being able to choose when you could go out because of the curfew. If you were caught outdoors under curfew, you risked being shot. And changes like building extra time into your travel schedule to get somewhere because you knew you'd get stuck in road-blocks, traffic diversions, checkpoints, all manned by soldiers with weapons.

You don't notice how quickly you learn to live with tanks and armoured cars in your life. You start off by seeing a tank in front of the university gate and stop dead. After a day or two, you hardly notice it: it's just there, a blot on the landscape. After a week, you might actually stop and have a look at it – maybe you've never seen a tank up close in real life, so it's a rare opportunity to see a piece of unusual equipment. You check out the tracks, the turret, the cupola, the length of the gun, and it becomes an object of interest, not a weapon.

Then, one day, it isn't there any more, and you miss seeing it. You realise that the tank in that space had become normal, an artefact, just something that was there every time you passed that spot. A car might come and park in the same space, but maybe you'll always remember that a tank once stood there: it has changed your memory of the old normal.

I opened one of Anna's manilla envelopes this morning, the slim one of the three, postmark Paris, 1980, addressed to Anna, in Reza's untidy English hand. A few yellowing leaflets tumbled out. I remember Reza coming home to Kucheh Mulla with leaflets that were on the streets after the February riots. He'd found them stuck to the beautiful Tabrizi trees on the boulevard, fixed with an ugly splurge of glue, or tied round a railing.

He wrote out a translation for me, and must have kept it because it's here, with the leaflets. The Patriotic Muslim Students of Tabriz again. Theirs was the first leaflet to appear: *Down with the anti-God and anti-people Pahlavi regime!* Later in June, the same group produced a leaflet quoting Khomeini: *The righteous person should be armed . . . Victory to the armed struggle of the Muslims in Iran and all over the world!*

I still felt the anger rise, even after all this time. There was no room for compromise with that lot. Their fanaticism burned through.

After the riots, I became increasingly worried about Arash. He was withdrawing into himself. He wept at night. 'All this cruelty, this lack of compassion,' he would say, 'where will it all end?'

Then, into this chaos and upheaval, came Anna. I couldn't believe the Council had sent her out at that time, a month after the riots and the university a hotbed of dissent. She hadn't a clue what she was letting herself in for. Not a clue.

Firuzeh came round to let us know she'd be staying with us. 'You'll like her,' she said. 'She's lovely. Very sensible. She went to Oxford, same time as you, Damian.'

That's no guarantee, I thought.

As it turned out, she fitted well into the Kucheh Mulla set-up. She was sensible, although not boringly so. Common sense was in short supply, what with me flapping around and Arash falling apart.

Underneath all that pragmatism, though, she was a bit of a romantic. Weren't we all, back then?

*

Anna

Tabriz, 13 March 1978

Archways

I caught the lunchtime flight today to Tabriz, bone-weary. The hotel in Tehran last night was a nightmare. The receptionist warned me not to open my door, he'd ring if I had visitors.

'It's safe in the hotel, madam,' he said, 'but we advise you to take the usual precautions.'

I'd spent the night hovering on the edge of sleep, eventually dropping off, only to be startled awake by footsteps thumping along the corridor, then stopping at my door. Soft tapping, then silence. More insistent knocks, more thumping footsteps heading away. Other doors getting the same treatment. Around four in the morning I gave in and got up.

I sat on the stool in front of the dressing-table, wrapped the bedspread round me, and looked at myself in the mirror. Had a full-on 'What on earth am I doing here?' moment.

I'd almost pulled out of the job three weeks ago, when news of the Tabriz riots filtered through. I nearly missed the item – it took up only an inch or two of column space on an inside page in the *Guardian*. Street riots involving students and other demonstrators, it said, ending up with six dead, 125 injured, and tanks brought in to restore order. But I hung on until I went to the final project briefing in London last week, feeling more than a little wobbly about the whole thing. I brought up the riots with Oliver, the cheerful admin officer for the British Council, the main funder for the project, and he assured me the unrest in Tabriz was not much more than a little local difficulty.

'And when they shout "Death to . . ." they don't really mean "Death to . . .", they mean more "Down with . . ." so it's not so drastic. It's more of a subtle semantic difference.'

He seemed to be treating the chants as an interesting cross-cultural linguistic problem, rather than as a contributory factor to a horrific event.

'All part of the Middle Eastern experience,' he said breezily.

As he'd said this, I faded back into a memory of Farzad telling me how the Iranians hated being referred to as Middle Easterners. It wasn't the geographical reference as such, it was because it lumped them in with all the surrounding Arab states, and they were adamant that they were not Arabs.

When I tuned in again to Oliver, he was still sounding breezy. 'Of course, you need to take the necessary safety precautions, but there's nothing to be unduly worried about.'

It sounded very much to me as though he was hedging his bets. *Yes, it's safe, as far as we can tell, but if it proves not to be, it's your responsibility to look after yourself.*

Our conversation didn't exactly put my mind at rest.

There'd been trouble in Tehran, too, over the past few weeks, although I saw no sign of it yesterday, travelling into the city from the airport. Everything looked pretty normal to me, if you could call bumper-to-bumper traffic, mad driving and horrendous fumes normal. And everything looked so much more bland and modern than I'd envisaged. Concrete office blocks, wide boulevards, flashy advertising hoardings for Coke. A bit disappointing.

I saw a few women walking around wearing full chadors wrapped over their heads and round their bodies, while a few others wore pretty coloured scarves covering just their hair, but most were bare-headed in Western dress, modest skirt lengths or trousers and boots, and warm coats against the chill of early spring. I was glad I'd decided to travel in my parka.

The *Guardian* article had said that in the recent unrest four women had been threatened with acid attacks for being 'unveiled'. I looked the term up, wondering if it meant a veil across the face, which I'd never heard of for Iranian women. As I understand it, it doesn't. The veil refers to the hejab, a more substantial scarf than a headscarf, that usually covers head, neck and shoulders, but I didn't see any on the streets of Tehran.

As I stared back at myself in the hotel mirror, I wondered, not for the first time since my conversation with Oliver, if Iran was the right move. But, then, maybe any move was the right move. I knew I couldn't face another year on my own in Oxford, just getting through.

'Well, you're here now,' I said to my reflection, so whether it was the right move or not is somewhat academic.

The noise of the landing gear clunking into place jolts me back from the hotel mirror to the view from the porthole. We've descended into a collar of round-topped, reddish mountains, still tipped with the remnants of winter snow, brightened by the mid-afternoon sun. I'm not good at landings, and this one, closed in at the foot of the ring of mountains, made me tight-chested with claustrophobia. I looked away from the view and closed my eyes. I didn't breathe easily until we taxied to a halt and I was walking towards the dingy terminal building.

The official at security took his time, flicking from my passport to my face then back again. I tried a smile. No smile back. I dropped my eyes. After what seemed an age, he signalled my way through with a slow lift of his index finger.

Farzad was waiting for me in the arrivals hall. I waved and quickened my step. 'Farzad! It's so good to see you!' His face was drawn and his eyes bloodshot. He and Firuzeh had always looked fresh-faced in Oxford, younger than their twenty-five years.

'Good to see you, too, Anna. Welcome to Tabriz,' he said, with a brief smile, but no touching, not even a handshake. He took my case. 'Please follow me to the car.' His manner was as stiffly correct as a chauffeur's.

'Would you put your hood up, please?' I wondered if his cool manner was due to shyness. After all, it had been over a year since we'd seen each other.

'My hood?'

'It's different here. This is Tabriz, not Tehran. And your blond hair makes you even more conspicuous.' He gestured round the hall. 'It's best not to draw too much attention to yourself.' His tone was softer this time, almost apologetic, and the smile was warmer.

I hadn't noticed till then that I was the only Western woman passenger. There weren't many women around in arrivals at all, and there was much more in the way of scarves and veils than there had been in Tehran. A few youngish women with their heads covered in bright-coloured scarves stood with a couple of teenagers in ordinary woolly hats. Two much older women, with men I took to be their husbands, were in the full chador, loosely wrapped round their upper bodies then over their heads, their faces left uncovered, but with all their hair tucked out of sight. Two other women around my age, who seemed to be airport staff, were bare-headed.

Farzad pointed towards the glass exit doors. 'This way.'

I followed him, getting myself into a tangle trying to sort out the strap of my overnight bag and putting up my parka hood at the same time.

*

The conversation in the car was a struggle, at least from my side. Catch-up questions, like how was Firuzeh, how was his work going, what had he been up to since he'd got back from Oxford, were all met with short replies, not rude, just quietly off-putting.

I tried again. 'Doesn't seem like six months or so ago, since we were all together in Oxford, does it?' I looked across at him and smiled.

He kept his eyes on the road. 'It seems like a lifetime.' He glanced at me. 'I'm sorry, that came out wrong. It's just that so much has happened since Oxford.'

'I read about the riots. It sounded bad.'

'It was.'

I could see the tension in his face, his jaw set tight. He wasn't any more forthcoming, so I decided to leave it. He'd either tell me more in his own time or he wouldn't. It was obviously still raw, and it felt intrusive to ask him for details.

I looked out of the window. The traffic was chaotic, cars jammed engine to boot, something I'd have to get used to in Iran, obviously. They were mostly taxis, the same make I'd noticed in Tehran, a sort of boxy shape, a bit like my next-door neighbour's old Hillman back in Oxford. We seemed to be driving down a wide avenue, with shops either side strung with bright bare lights outside and full of bustling crowds. I wondered if this was where the riots had been. It seemed OK, but I was too tired to look closely. I could feel my eyes drooping as the car began to slow and Farzad pulled over to the side of the street.

He'd stopped at the end of what looked like a narrow lane. 'The house is down this *kucheh*, through an archway,' he said. 'I'm afraid we have to walk the rest of the way.'

He carried my suitcase, keeping slightly ahead, leading the way. I worked out that '*kucheh*' must mean some sort of alley. We passed a few small shops, still open, with single bare light-bulbs over the counters inside. Then there were just high brick walls, inset at irregular intervals with greyish wooden doors, tombstone-like with their ogival tops.

I could see the archway about halfway down.

'It's like the Hertford Bridge in Oxford,' I said, a little too brightly. It wasn't at all like the Hertford, it was just a covered walkway in crumbling ochre brick, but I was desperate to break the silence. He nodded but didn't reply. We got closer to it and I could make out a small window set in its apex. We came through to the other side of the archway, and the walls had moved inwards, narrowing the *kucheh* even more. After a few more steps, Farzad stopped suddenly outside an old wooden door, ogival-topped like the others, set into an arched recess. He jabbed at a plastic doorbell, dirty white against the weathered wood. It had hardly stopped ringing before Firuzeh was there. She made up for Farzad's coolness – hugs and kisses and cries of 'Welcome, welcome!' followed by her sunburst of a smile.

'Come in,' she said, taking my arm and steering me through the doorway into a small courtyard and across a plain tiled space. There was another door, slightly ajar, modern in style this time, painted green, set into the side of a two-storey house.

Alleyways leading ever further in, walls within walls, doors within doors. The feeling of claustrophobia I'd experienced on the plane came back.

Farzad remained outside the old wall door, watching us across the courtyard.

Firuzeh glanced back. 'Are you coming in?' she asked him, sounding tentative. 'I've made chicken.'

'I have things to do. I'll call back, maybe later in the week.' He was staring intently down the *kucheh* as he spoke. He turned to me and, raising his voice slightly, said, 'Welcome, again, Anna. It really is good to see you.' I couldn't see if he was smiling or not. He sounded tired, and there was something mechanical in the way he spoke, as if it were no more than social politeness.

He walked away, back towards the archway.

*

I've got the best room in the house. Looks out onto a small courtyard, lit by a dim wall light.

'A fountain plays there in the summer,' Firuzeh told me, as she showed me the view. 'Water splashes down onto that small dish, trickles over the lip and falls into a pool. Tiny birds fly in to drink, from time to time. It's so soothing in the heat.'

But now it was silent. Cold marble, waiting for the summer to bring it back to life.

The bed was exotic – a dark wooden frame, with an unusual carved wooden headboard. I was expecting a simple wooden or metal frame, and a thin mattress, or even a rug and a mattress on the floor. There was a plain gold-coloured quilt, and thrown across that, a blue silk coverlet with embroidered birds along the border. Firuzeh's choice, I should think.

'My uncle loaned the bed to me. I think he got it from one of his contacts in the bazaar. It's from India. I thought you might like it.'

'It's beautiful. You've gone to so much trouble.'

She hugged me again. 'I'm so pleased you came. I want you to feel comfortable here – you looked after us so well in Oxford.' I thought I heard a break in her voice.

She stayed just long enough to help me settle in and for us to catch up over the meal, a normal chat about my journey, and about the house, not like the awkwardness with Farzad. It was her uncle's place, and Firuzeh managed it for him.

'You'll be safe here,' she said. 'Kucheh Mulla is on the edge of the Armenian quarter, and we always let it to visiting lecturers at the university. The neighbours are used to seeing foreign faces and are very helpful, should you need anything. There's only one other person in the house at the moment, and that's Damian,' she said. 'You'll like him. Everyone likes Damian, and it's good to have a man in the house with you. He's away tonight, but he'll be back tomorrow.'

The conversation dwindled, and she said she ought to go, let me get some sleep.

'I'm so pleased you're here, Anna,' she said, as she left. 'I'll come back later in the week and bring Farzad with me, when he's not so busy.'

Neither of us had mentioned his muted mood.

In my room, I sat down on the bed, suddenly weary again. I noticed the battered book on my bedside table – the catalogue of the *Shahnameh* exhibition. I picked it up, remembering that first morning after Firuzeh and Farzad had moved in with me. It was more dog-eared now, and a page came loose as I held it. Oxford seemed far away and unreal. Not that Tabriz seemed real.

And suddenly, from nowhere, I felt a great longing for my father, to speak to him, to hear his voice, to read a letter from him, anything that brought him close to me. I needed his steady way of looking at things. What would he say to me if he was on the end of the phone? Probably something like *Sounds like quite an adventure you've set out on, sweetheart, one to treasure. Just remember to keep yourself safe.* Imagining his voice brought tears to my eyes, even though I could rationalise it and know it was just because I was in a strange place and felt travel-worn. I hadn't yet got my bearings. But it still left me feeling low.

I climbed into bed and snuggled under the quilt, waiting for sleep and thinking it would never come. But I must have drifted off into a half-awake half-dreaming state – seeing myself walking from the wide avenue to the narrow *kucheh*, then under the archway, the walls closing in, then through a door, then another door, the way in front of me narrowing inwards, disappearing.

I woke up completely then, feeling such a sense of unease, of dislocation. As if I'd left something familiar and safe behind and walked into something else – I didn't know what, but it didn't feel good.

*

14 March

A certain amount of molestation

Met Julia Greenwood at the Council for a short briefing. Slim, verging on scrawny, sharp-faced, dark red hair scraped back into a ponytail and held in place by two tortoiseshell combs. She's perfected the mannerism of peering at you over her John Lennons, eyebrows raised.

I think it's meant to be intimidating. It works. She's a good foil to the head of administration, whom I met briefly on the way in. A gentle man, much preoccupied, it turns out, with his sick wife, who really needs to be back in London for an operation. Getting the necessary exit documents is proving to be a slow process. In the meantime, Julia is very much unofficially in charge.

We went through the usual pleasantries – how was the journey? Hotel in Tehran quiet enough? Kucheh Mulla OK?

'I believe you knew Firuzeh back in Oxford?'

'She was my lodger last year. Firuzeh and her cousin.'

'Ah, yes, Farzad. The doctor.'

She's well up on my contacts, I thought.

'We like to know the background to any connections our people might have to the local Tabrizis,' she said, as if she'd read my mind.

She fished about in her in-tray and came up with a typed sheet. 'You might like to read this. The American Consulate here in Tabriz produced it for its visitors and very kindly said we could use a copy of it for ours.'

She handed it over to me. 'Sensible stuff. And even more relevant, after the riots we've had recently.' She got up and headed for the door. 'I'll just go and rustle up some tea.'

The American coat of arms was at the top of the typed sheet, in monochrome.

American Consulate: A Guide for New Visitors

Please Note: Given recent unfortunate events, we suggest that the following advice is read carefully and adhered to at all times. Thank you.

Modesty Code

It is not comfortable for women to shop in the bazaar during certain seasons of religious activity. At all times, they must expect and be prepared to deal with a certain amount of molestation. Conservative clothing should be worn at all times.

Julia came back with a tray – two bone-china cups of tea, and a plate with two Oreos. 'There you go. Lipton's teabags, I'm afraid, best we can do – but the biscuits are yummy.'

She sat down. 'Everything clear, I hope?' She nodded at the leaflet in my hand.

'Be prepared for molestation?'

'Rather an exaggeration. But you have to be careful wherever you are – the *kucheh*s are a good case in point. They're so narrow that you'll sometimes get a man on a bicycle grabbing your boob as he passes by. Harmless enough, it's no more than a little pat usually. Best not to react. Don't shout back, not worth the hassle.'

She paused. 'What else? Let's see, never get in a taxi in the front, you might get your thigh felt, and, if you're ever on a bus – I don't advise that, by the way, but some of the American women seem to think it's all part of experiencing the real Iran, travelling on the same kind of transport the locals use – you're quite likely to find a man push up against you from behind, and it's not because it's overcrowded, which it probably is, it's because he *can* do it, so he does.'

'Bit like the London Underground, then.'

She raised one eyebrow over the right rim of the John Lennons.

'The action might be similar, but as far as the Iranian men are concerned, if you're out on your own and put yourself in close proximity to males, you're asking for it, and it's your responsibility if you get "molested".'

'And the bazaar?'

'Never go there without a man. Not for personal safety as such, although we're much more aware of that now. It's just the custom here for women to be accompanied. But the *bazaaris* are usually very polite. Many of them have sons studying overseas in the US or the UK and seem to be genuinely interested in chatting. You'd be safe enough, but given recent events, it's best not to take silly risks.'

'It's a little depressing.'

She sighed and nibbled the edge of her Oreo. 'Sign of the times, unfortunately. I've been in Iran five years, three years in Tehran, which was great, and two years here, which is . . . interesting. Most of the Iranians I've met in both places are lovely people, charming, helpful, respectful. But Tabriz is very conservative compared to Tehran, so you do have to be a bit more circumspect. And it's only lately things have got more . . . shall we say, tight, in terms of how we need to behave.'

'I suppose it could be worse. At least we're not obliged to wear a headscarf.'

'Indeed not. But that's taken a turn for the worse over the past few weeks for all Iranian women. In the recent Tehran riots, bareheaded women were threatened with acid if they didn't wear the chador.' I looked suitably shocked, and didn't mention I already knew that. I think she enjoyed shocking newbies.

She unlocked the desk top drawer, fished out a file and passed over a single sheet to me. 'It's the security procedure at the university when you go up there. You need to check in at the Faculty Office so they know you're on campus. Then you're required to go to your classroom, or in your case, your research room, and stay there for the allotted time, even if there are no students. And don't be surprised if you see someone looking in at you through the window in the door – that'll be security. It might be the local police, it might be SAVAK, it depends. There's a lot more around of both these days. Just ignore them. Then you need to check out when you go, so they know you've left.'

She put the file back into the drawer and locked it. 'There won't be any students there this week – there haven't been many since the riots, to be truthful – but this week is the weekend before Nowruz, the Persian New Year, which is on Tuesday, next week, so there definitely won't be any. I wouldn't bother going up to the university at all until after Nowruz. Take some time to settle in, get your bearings.'

She began to tidy her desk, obviously a signal I should go. 'Come back and see me if you need to check anything out. I sometimes pop into Kucheh Mulla, so I'll probably see you there.'

As I made my way home, I went over what we'd talked about. Molestation is such an ugly word. It was depressing to think that whatever the circumstances, if it happened to me it would always be my responsibility.

I walked slowly down the *kucheh*, taking in the strangeness of it for the first time. I'd been too tired and preoccupied with Farzad yesterday to take it all in. There was a timelessness about it – the narrow streets looked as though they'd been there for centuries. I passed under the archway, which seemed even more decrepit in the harsh daylight, although the little window was surprisingly clean. I wondered if anyone ever went into the space across the alleyway and looked down on the heads of those passing under their feet.

When I came out the other side, I was startled as one of the old wooden doors in the wall across the way from me scraped open a foot or so, although no one appeared. I was able to snatch a glimpse inside. A small bare-branched tree stood in the centre of a courtyard, which was beautifully tiled in a simple mosaic of earthy colours. A cat was sitting in the far corner, a grey and white moggy, basking in a triangle of the late-afternoon sun, cleaning behind its ears with a lazy rhythm. Whatever the reason for the door opening, it was shut again quickly and the cat was gone. But it had been enough to lift my mood. It was such a surprise to see something so homely behind the *kucheh* walls.

*

I got back to the house after meeting Julia to find a broad-shouldered Iranian in the kitchen, standing over the cooker, checking a pan of rice steaming gently in a pool of golden melted butter. He was talking to a slim, pale-skinned guy sitting at the kitchen table, drinking a glass of wine. They both smiled as I came in.

'Nicely timed. You must be Anna. I'm Damian,' the thin guy said. 'The cook here is Arash. There's plenty for three.'

We ate at the kitchen table with forks and fingers. Arash levered out the crusted caramelised rice from the bottom of the pan as one whole piece, and divided it into three, serving it with a side dish of sour cherries.

'I could get used to this,' I said. 'It's delicious.' Eating with them reminded me of nights in with Firuzeh and Farzad, and beans on toast.

'We cheated with the cherries,' Damian said. 'They're bottled, and we get them from the Iranian Air Force base outside Tabriz. There's an American contingent of technicians there, who get all sorts shipped in from home. The source of many a guilty treat – bacon, peanut butter, Oreos.'

'I've already sampled the Oreos with Julia.'

There was a lull in the conversation after we'd finished the rice, so we moved over to the floor cushions, Damian bringing the wine bottle and two more glasses.

We chatted about Oxford and Berkeley, and how we'd all ended up in Tabriz. I did my usual 'Just lucky, I guess' avoidance routine, and talked about Firuzeh and Farzad and our '*Shahnameh* summer' and about how Iran had intrigued me.

It was easy to see why Damian was there, the way he looked

at Arash. They're good together – Damian, nervous energy sparking like he's plugged straight into a socket, Arash thoughtful and outwardly calm. I can see how they fit.

I waxed lyrical about my room with its exotic headboard and silk coverlet. Damian said I should come up and see his skylight sometime. It was such a relief to let off steam, be a bit silly, even. I hadn't realised how wound up I was. The session with Julia had left me unsettled. After reading the Americans' advice on the dress code, I found it depressing, the notion that we should expect to have to deal with a certain amount of molestation. And Julia's response to that hadn't made things any better. As luck would have it, the longer skirts and looser tops I'd brought would pass the 'conservatively dressed' modesty test, but it felt like an imposition and it grated.

Then my rational side took over. It wasn't too much of a concession to make: it was a case of different country, different attitudes. But the politics behind the wearing of the veil for Iranian women truly disturbed me. To be threatened with acid if they didn't cover their heads in some way – I couldn't imagine how that threat must feel, and it didn't fit with my impression of the Iranian men I'd met while I was teaching in Oxford. I should talk to Firuzeh about that: she'd have a sensible female Iranian take on the subtleties of it all.

As if he'd tuned into my thinking, Damian said, 'I guess you've been given the Julia treatment then.' He grinned. 'The dress code, the "keeping your head down at all times for your own safety", the "Don't annoy the security guards at the university"?'

'All of the above.' I tried a poor imitation of Julia's no-nonsense manner: '"It's safe enough, but you need to take precautions." That's fast becoming my mantra of the month.'

'I guess the personal safety issue is important, though,' Damian said, his tone less flippant now. 'Things have changed so much since the February riots.'

'I'll make some tea,' said Arash, getting up and heading to the kitchen.

Damian frowned. 'Fuck – that just slipped out. It still gets to him, what happened. It's his home town, after all.' He got up. 'Won't be a sec. I'll just help him carry the tea in.'

He was heading across to the kitchen, when the doorbell rang, so he veered off downstairs. There were muffled voices and the sound of footsteps coming up and Damian came back in, followed by another Iranian, carrying a holdall and what looked like a camera bag. Arash set down the tray of tea and went over to him, a stream of Persian flowing between them as they hugged. Damian stood back, giving them space, then went and sat on the floor cushions against the wall.

Arash turned to me, beaming. 'Anna, this is my brother, Reza. He's just in from Tehran.'

You could tell they were brothers. Reza was a leaner version, thinner face, hair just as dark but not quite as curly.

'Anna, you finally got here. These two have been wondering if you'd actually make it.' There was a familiarity in his tone, as if he knew all about me. He smiled and sat down on the floor cushion next to me, opposite Damian.

Arash came back from the kitchen with another glass of tea for Reza and sat next to Damian.

'When did you get in?' Arash looked distinctly awkward as he spoke to his brother across the table. The way the three of them were sitting, he could only look directly at one of them at a time, either across to Reza, so that Damian was excluded, or turning sideways to talk to Damian, so that Reza was excluded. He seemed acutely aware of the limitations and ended up wriggling left and right. I wondered why it mattered.

'I arrived yesterday, slept on a friend's floor last night. I wondered if I could use your place again for the next few days. I need to develop some photos.' He pointed to his bag.

'My brother is an amateur photographer, when he's not supposedly earning a living as a lecturer in psychology,' Arash said to me, by way of explanation.

'What kind of photos?' I turned to him, aware that we were quite close to each other side by side on the cushions.

'Street scenes, mostly.'

'That covers a lot. Any particular theme – street vendors, passers-by, different kinds of traffic, that sort of thing?'

'Wherever there's trouble,' Damian chipped in.

Reza ignored him. 'Whatever catches my eye. So, I believe you're here to do research?'

Neat change of subject, I thought. 'I hope so. It's all a bit up in the air at the moment.'

He nodded. 'I'm surprised they sent you out after what's happened. In fact, I'm surprised you got a visa in. Most people at the moment are trying to get a visa out.'

'They said in London the riots were a little local difficulty.'

'Over a hundred dead, several hundreds wounded. Doesn't sound little to me. And it's definitely not just local.' His voice tightened and he shook his head.

'A hundred dead? The *Guardian* said six dead, a hundred and twenty-five wounded.'

Arash said quietly, 'You'll find each side has its own set of numbers, its own version of what went on, either to play it down or make it sound worse than it was. That's the way it goes here.'

'Looks like I came at the wrong time, as far as work is concerned.'

'Not sure there's a right time, any more,' said Damian.

Reza looked as though he was going to say something, but changed his mind.

Damian yawned ostentatiously and slowly got up off the cushions, using Arash's shoulder to steady himself. 'I think I'll go up and read for a while.' He nodded at me. 'We'll meet up sometime, if you like, Anna, and I'll fill you in on the Tabriz campus.' He bent down slightly and touched Arash's shoulder again. 'See you later.' He nodded at Reza, managing a small smile, then walked out of the room.

I took that as my cue and got up to go too.

'We'll catch up tomorrow,' Arash said. 'There's a get-together here on Thursday. The day after is St Patrick's Day, and as that's a Friday, it's a non-work day, so people can stay over if they want to, then go home after the curfew is lifted.'

'I might see you Thursday, then,' Reza said to me, smiling, and making it sound like a statement of intent, not a question.

As I got ready for bed, I wondered what the story was between Reza and Damian. Obviously past history of some sort. I didn't know quite what to make of Reza. I could imagine he'd be more interested in close-ups than long shots in his street scenes. He'd want to see what secrets his subjects had, and how you might tell what they were, by focusing on their hands, or a small detail of their face, or the way they held their heads or bodies. Sitting next to him, I was very aware of his physicality and felt he sensed that.

There was an edge to him. It made him interesting, I had to admit that.

15 March

The default position

Went up to the university with Damian. We caught a taxi at the end of the *kucheh*. The university is about five miles away, maybe a little more, but it can take twenty minutes depending on the traffic. Impressive site set against the background of the red mountains I saw when I'd flown in. Damian took me to the English faculty office but the professor in charge of the research project I was due to meet had not come in. He'd been delayed in Tehran. There were no medical students either. Julia was right. They just hadn't turned up.

The textbooks I'm supposed to be evaluating also haven't arrived. The office administrator, a rather fussy little man, tells me he knows nothing about them. They may well be stuck in Tehran, if they're even in the country.

No students. No textbooks. No project.

What am I doing here?

I went back to Julia at the Council.

'Oh dear,' she said, 'I had a feeling this might happen. Things change so much so quickly here. It's been very unpredictable since before December.'

'If there's no project, there's no job for me.' I was trying not to sound annoyed.

'I did think it was a little ambitious to be getting a research project up and running.' She adjusted her John Lennons, sliding them a little up the bridge of her nose, but not so far up she couldn't give me the raised-eyebrow treatment over the top.

'What am I supposed to do?'

'Do what everyone else is doing – sit it out, wait for a few months, see if it all blows over. You'll still get paid.'

'I don't do "sitting it out" very well.'

'You learn to do it here, I'm afraid. It's the default position.'

'I don't understand why they'd send me here, if they knew. It doesn't make sense.'

'Ah, well,' she said. 'If it doesn't make sense, it must be Iranian.' She smiled at her own joke, then said chirpily, 'Have you got time for tea?'

I went back to Kucheh Mulla and got into bed. It was only four in the afternoon, but the travelling, the sleepless overnighter in Tehran, the difficulties with the project, were all catching up with me, which wasn't helping my mood. I lay there thinking about what Julia had said. She was infuriating. But maybe she was right. What was the point of getting worked up about something that was totally out of my control?

16 March

Caravanserai

Midnight. I've left them to it. I picked my way through a sea of bodies, seven all told, curled up on the floor as near to the stove as they can get, and managed to reach my room. Thought I'd write about the evening while it's fresh in my mind.

I've got my bearings now. Kucheh Mulla is near enough to the centre of the city to be convenient for the main shops, but it's hidden away so it's quiet. There's been a curfew on since the riots, from 9 p.m. at the moment, so people began to drift in from around seven o'clock. I've never lived under curfew before, I'm not sure I'll get used to it.

All kinds of people turned up. They brought nuts and nougat and French pastries from the shops on Pahlavi Avenue. They all had sleeping bags too, or blankets, as they couldn't go home until the curfew's lifted in the morning. Some of the people are from the university, and a couple of Italians here are from the new oil refinery, where they're training computer technicians. A gentle New Zealander teaching English at the British Council has brought his wife, who is a Baha'i. There's a French guy, Bruce the Breton, with longish golden hair tucked back behind his ears, who says he's passing through, but he's not sure where to. He carries his fiddle with him wherever he goes – you can see its outline under his coat where he hides it when he's outside, apparently, in case someone is tempted to steal it.

A couple of Americans, one a Vietnam veteran called Arnie, the other a cool hippie type from Kent State University called Chris, who is extraordinarily good-looking in a dark-haired, blue-eyed Ukrainian ancestry sort of way. He reminds me of a blue-point Siamese cat, aware of how beautiful he is, and always standing at the edge of the crowd, appraising everyone else and allowing you to admire him. Turns out he's a great guitar player and sings Dylan songs, but doesn't try to be Dylan, which is a blessing, as only Dylan can sound like Dylan. The aloofness crumbles when he gets going.

The Vietnam vet, Arnie, is 'not too tightly wrapped', as Chris the cat, who has a poetic turn of phrase, would say. He's an amiable soul, quiet, and drifts off to his own private place sometimes, when everyone seems to know to leave him be. Chris keeps an eye on him. I think Chris dodged the Vietnam draft, so maybe feels duty-bound to look after Arnie, although Arnie doesn't strike me as someone who would bear a grudge – it would take too much energy.

Julia popped in but didn't stay long. She had let her hair down loose: it's thick and unruly and she's proud of it. She made a beeline for Arnie, who seemed pleased to see her – he took her John Lennons off her nose and stroked her cheek. They make an odd couple, strait-laced Julia and not too tightly wrapped Arnie, but there is a gentle ease between them.

Damian supplied the vodka and wine, the latter courtesy yet again of the Americans on the air base. Bruce the Breton brought 'passports' of hash, so-called, I learn, as the evening progresses, because they're passport-size blocks. I've never seen anything like them before but, then, I was never into hash. Bruce the Breton didn't smoke it: he ate a small piece, which amazed me, I didn't know you could eat it, and he soon got under way, lost in space and playing wild Breton fiddle music.

Chris sang 'Simple Twist Of Fate', and we joined in, somewhat raggedly, with the simple-twist-of-fate bit. There were other songs with choruses, and we joined in with those too, but it was a quiet sort of singsong, not raucous. They aren't a raucous crowd, and it wasn't that kind of party. They just seemed content to sit and talk or listen to the music, or close their eyes and float off. They seemed to need to soothe themselves. I mentioned this to Damian at one point in the evening. He says everyone has lived on their nerves since the riots and they're emotionally exhausted. It was only a month ago, and martial law was lifted three weeks ago, when the main military left. But it's thrown everyone's plans up in the air – they need to stay for the end of contract bonuses, but it's getting harder to do the jobs they are out here to do. People are trying to get back to some sort of normality, except they don't quite know what normal looks like any more.

So, that seems to be the Kucheh Mulla crowd. I've never

been part of this type of group before, this collection of one-offs. It was there at Oxford but I just never got into it. I think perhaps at Oxford they worked too hard at it – an Oxford eccentric was the thing to be. This crowd don't even know they are eccentric.

Charlie wasn't eccentric. He was safe and kind and ordinary. Maybe he was too safe, too kind. I should have been more adventurous. I'm beginning to wonder if it was because I'd had to be sensible too soon – if your mother dies when you're young, and there are no aunts around or grandmothers or other females you can turn to, you grow up quickly, have to be sensible too soon. *You seem to be a sensible young woman.* The number of times I've had that said to me, and people mean it as a compliment. I was so busy being sensible I missed out on the time to be frivolous. I gravitated towards Charlie because he liked sensible women, wasn't into the frivolous type, so I didn't need to change. I could carry on being sensible. Maybe we settled for each other because we were both scared of having to change. At least, I settled for Charlie, I realise that now.

Oh dear. I think this might be the vodka talking.

Just before I came to bed, I said this to Damian about the Kucheh Mulla crowd being a collection of one-offs, and that I wouldn't mind being a one-off too. He laughed. He said that Arash says the house on Kucheh Mulla is a caravanserai, a battered caravanserai we've all wandered into. None of us is doing what we should be doing – the riots and student strikes have put paid to that – so we're all resting here in the Kucheh Mulla caravanserai, trying to work out what might happen next.

I've just realised. Reza didn't show up. He probably stayed over at Arash's. Spending an evening with Westerners getting drunk or stoned and singing Bob Dylan songs probably doesn't appeal to someone like him. And he only said he might come.

8 March

Firuzeh and Farzad came round. The first thing Farzad did was apologise for his bad mood last week. He was holding a bowl of beautiful deep blue hyacinths, which he said his aunt had grown, and as he spoke, his voice quiet, his eyes sincere, he offered them to me with both hands. 'I am truly sorry, Anna. It was unforgivable.'

'They're for Nowruz,' Firuzeh said. 'We always have hyacinths at Nowruz.'

Farzad's hands were trembling. I was so shocked to see it that I patted his arm gently. 'I'm pleased you were there to meet me, rather than a Council person, someone I didn't know. And so glad you were my guide for my first trip down a *kucheh*.' I smiled.

He managed a weak smile and excused himself, saying he must go to the bathroom.

Firuzeh turned to me. 'He's been very down since the riots. He was called out to one of the smaller hospitals in the back-streets off the town centre – it was where the demonstrators took some of the injured. They didn't want to take them to the main hospital because they said SAVAK would be there, waiting to see who the injured were so they could arrest them later.' She shook her head. 'He saw some terrible things.'

Farzad came back into the room. He looked exhausted. His eyes had such sadness in them.

'I'll make some tea for us,' I said. 'I'm getting quite good at Tabrizi tea.' Strange how I'd slipped back into cheery landlady mode.

'If you'll give me permission to use your kitchen,' Firuzeh said, 'I'll make the tea. You stay and talk to Farzad.'

As she went into the kitchen, he raised his eyes skyward in a she-couldn't-be-more-obvious-could-she gesture, and we both smiled. For a fleeting moment, I saw the old Farzad, who took pleasure in annoying her with his anti-Shah and anti-government remarks.

He asked me how the university work was going. I said it wasn't, there were no students. He said it had been like that for ages and was likely to get worse.

'So what are you specialising in?' I asked him. I didn't want to pre-empt it by asking if he'd managed to get into heart surgery, in case it hadn't worked out for him.

'I'm working in trauma injuries,' he said. He began to rub the back of the fingers of his left hand with the thumb of his right.

I nodded. 'My father did a lot of that out in Zambia. Accidents and explosions in the copper mines and the like. Pretty dreadful stuff.'

'I've learned a lot about gunshot wounds,' he said. 'What these high-velocity bullets can do to the human body . . .' He trailed off.

Firuzeh came back with the tea.

We stuttered on. Firuzeh checked that Damian had let me know about the naphtha man and the shop he delivers to in the *kucheh*, and where the bakery is. She told me to make sure I was there early, his first batch is sold out by 7 a.m., and to ask for *barbari*, which has a crisp crust but is lovely and light inside. All this delivered in a slightly breathless way, always mindful of Farzad, who was sitting listening, but listless.

More silence.

'Julia at the Council was explaining the dress code to me,' I said. 'I'm not sure how strict it is — I've seen a lot of women wearing headscarves, and a few with full chadors, but not everyone.'

'It doesn't really apply to visitors like you,' she said, 'but if you want to be on the safe side, if you're in the bazaar for example, just put your hood up. Now it's getting warmer, a light silk scarf would do, but you shouldn't feel you have to. No one will say anything to you.'

'I thought the Shah was anti-veil,' I said.

'He is. He says it's going back to medieval ways.'

Farzad sits impassive. He would have jumped in with another anti-Shah comment back in Oxford, I thought. Now he seems totally switched off.

'It's complicated,' says Firuzeh. 'Some women have found their religion again, and are sincere in their need to wear the headscarf, or the hejab, or the full chador. Others are using it as a political statement, an anti-Shah statement. They're saying that the Shah tries to force them not to wear it so that's exactly why they do.'

'They say that in the Tabrizi riots, women were dragged out of cars and beaten up for not wearing the chador.'

'We've heard rumours like that too, but no one seems to know anyone it actually happened to,' said Firuzeh, 'but there definitely was a problem at the Parvin girls' school.'

I wondered whether to ask her if she had taken to using a hejab, but decided not to, she might be offended. I didn't see any evidence of one when I answered the door to them.

After that they didn't stay long. Farzad seemed to have become quite distant and I could see Firuzeh was agitated about him.

I saw them downstairs to the front door, and watched them go out into the *kucheh*. Firuzeh didn't have anything on her head. The sunlight caught her hennaed hair, picking up the highlights. It reminded me of our summer evenings near the clematis arch, and Farzad reciting Ferdowsi, larger than life.

Poor Farzad. He seemed lost. Not broken exactly, but a deeply saddened man, withdrawn into himself. Maybe the old Farzad was still in there somewhere, carping at the Shah, the government, the rich hangers-on, the corruption. But he had obviously been forced to confront what it meant to be out on the streets and demand change, and face soldiers and tanks, and had been traumatised by what he saw. He's had to deal not with the heroics, but with the horrors of urban conflict. The broken limbs, the cracked skulls, the high-velocity bullet wounds reducing internal organs to mush. It seems he came face to face with all that and found it too real. I don't mean too real for him as a doctor – I'm sure he slipped into automatic to cope with the medical demands – but the reality must have been such a shock for someone like him who, up to that point, had thought maybe confrontation, violent if necessary, was the only way to achieve the change he wanted.

I felt unsettled after they'd gone, and as Arash and Damian weren't due back until curfew, I decided to walk into town on my own. It was the first time I'd done this so it was quite an adventure. I wasn't sure Julia would approve, but the main shopping area on Pahlavi is very open, no dark corners, and there are always plenty of people about, usually including some Western women. I'd be perfectly safe from a 'certain amount of molestation', I thought, hearing Julia's clipped tones in my head as I set off for the bright lights.

I made straight for the French patisserie, already my favourite place on Pahlavi. Apparently, it had been damaged in the riots, but apart from scorch marks, mainly from the fire next door, it was up and running as normal. I love their window display. It's only small, but stylishly crafted to show off all the goodies to their best advantage. Chocolate eclairs, placed like the spokes of a wheel on a white fluted high plate. *Macarons*, in strawberry pink, sandwiched together with white cream and arranged like a tower of tiny lipsticked smiles. Slices of opera cake, offset on a slim turquoise platter, so you can see the alternate layers of perfect coffee cake, chocolate ganache and buttercream.

'I've got a great photo of that,' a voice said behind me. Reza stood there, smiling.

'I just love it. The whole show is a work of art.' I was really pleased to see someone I knew. I was beginning to feel as though I hadn't really connected with anyone since I'd been here, outside Kucheh Mulla.

'Do you fancy a tea party?' He raised an eyebrow. 'We could buy stuff, take it back to Arash's – it's not far from here.'

'I've not actually been to Arash's yet.'

'Well, now's your chance.'

So we went in and chose a sample of almost everything that was in the window. The assistant placed each item with great care into a pink cardboard box and tied it up with narrow pink ribbon. We could have been in one of the upmarket cake shops on the High, back in Oxford, I thought, and found that strangely comforting.

Reza called into a shop further down and bought a gift box of pistachios, arranged in the petal shapes of a Tabrizi rose, five slightly open-shelled nuts clustered upright in the centre, and a red-ribbon bow set diagonally across the corner of the cellophane top. When we got to Arash's place, we spread everything on the low table. Reza opened the *bokhari* to let a bit of heat into the room, and went to get wine from the kitchen.

'Very much an alternative early Nowruz feast, thank God,' he said. 'I can't stand all that traditional stuff.'

He was very much an alternative kind of guy, I decided.

Arash's house was small, but quiet and very him. Books, lots of books, and two comfy chairs to read them in, with an old-fashioned standard lamp between them. I could just imagine him and Damian sitting there, noses in their poetry collections.

We sat opposite each other, and divided each of the treats into halves. He poured the wine, leaned across and fed me half of the eclair. I divided the *macaron* smile into two and fed him his half. It was all very silly. But after the sadness with Farzad, it was just what I needed. I told him a little about Farzad, without giving too much away.

He nodded. 'It was a bad couple of days, such a shock to be caught up in something like that. I heard Farzad was great – he kept going through the night at the local hospital. They came in droves, with anything from a bump on the head to devastating gunshot wounds.'

'Was he with the demonstrators?'

'No, I don't think so, but I wouldn't know. I'm just going on what I heard.'

'Whatever he saw while he was treating people,' I said, 'it's disturbed him terribly.'

'That can happen in a riot. There are those who will stand and fight for the cause, whatever they throw at you. But afterwards it hits you, what you saw, what you did. And you either say: Yes, we have to do this or we won't change things, or you say: No, I can't do this, if it means killing and injuring people, even if they're prepared to do that to me.'

He paused. 'I think that's what might have happened to Farzad. The violence sickened him. He couldn't take it, even though he was just a witness. Being witness to the things men do to each other is almost worse than being involved in the action. Maybe he couldn't rationalise what he was seeing. Many like him have taken a step back – they've said they're not supporting the Shah, but they can't do what it might take to get rid of him, so they'll just wait and see how it goes.'

He looked at me. 'This is getting too serious. Let's change the subject.' He got up and stretched out his hand. 'Let's go up on the roof, get some air.'

There was a good view over the rooftops to the centre of the city, and the American Consulate was quite close. It was very much a local area where Tabrizis lived, although it was less than half a mile away from Kucheh Mulla. I'd noticed in the street that there were far more women in headscarves, and a few in full chador, than I'd seen around our house. I was surprised that the short distance made such a difference.

I noticed he had a camera tripod base set up near the wall that served as a parapet. 'Is that for your cityscapes?'

'Not exactly.'

'Sunrises? Sunsets?' I didn't take him for a landscape enthusiast.

He hesitated. 'I'll show you later.'

There was a chill on the air – the temperature drops quickly here – so we went down to the living area. He disappeared, then came back with a box file. He opened it and sorted through a

few photos. 'I told you I'd got a shot of the patisserie window.'
He passed it to me.

It was almost an exact copy of the display we'd been looking at earlier, except that the shot was framed by a jagged opening of glass, like you'd see in a cartoon to convey that someone had just thrown a brick through a window. Maybe they had, although there was no brick to be seen. There was plenty of glass lying around, though, all over the cakes and biscuits. My eye was drawn to the chocolate eclairs. This time, they'd been displayed herringbone style on a slim platter on a high stand. They looked like a miniature flotilla, berthed next to each other at a jetty. The one in the middle glinted with a shard of window glass, a perfectly shaped triangle, which had landed in the strip of chocolate icing on top of the finger of choux pastry, transforming it into a tiny longboat under full sail.

'Mayhem going on all around me, shops in flames, tyres burning, sirens, people screaming – and this just caught my eye. It actually made me smile in the middle of all that chaos. What does that say about me?' He shook his head.

'It has a touch of the surreal about it. It's a one-off. You'd never see that again,' I said.

Then it dawned on me. 'You were there?' I hadn't heard the others mention it.

'Only by accident. I came up the night before, fully intending to come on to your place after I'd dropped my equipment off at Arash's, but I was a bit late getting into Tabriz. I didn't want to get caught out in the curfew with cameras, so I went straight to Arash's – it was quicker. Then in the morning, I got up to go into town, just to have a look. I stuck around for the first hour or so, until they started to do serious damage to the banks and the government buildings. When the police arrived in force I ran back to Arash's.'

'Did you get any photos of the actual riot?'

'A few.' He sounded hesitant. 'I took some that were . . . disturbing.' He shrugged. 'I'm not quite the intrepid photographer

I thought I was. I have friends down in Tehran who take great photos – they manage to capture the gritty urban conflict, people screaming at each other, running away down side streets, setting fire to shop fronts. Wounded people sometimes, people in distress.' He took a sip of wine. 'I just don't have what it takes to focus on people who are suffering, then press the desensitising button in my head to tamp down my feelings while I take the shot. And that's what you have to do to get the kind of images that make people react, make them angry, maybe make them want to change things.'

He looked as if he was weighing something up. 'I'm probably like Farzad. I've learned a lot about myself in the past year. In my case, I've discovered I'm better at just photographing something that intrigues me personally about what I see on the street, and leave the high-impact stuff to others.'

He sounded hesitant, as if he was wondering whether to go on, then clearly decided he would. 'It's still aspects of urban conflict, or protest. I've spent a lot of time on the streets, observing, and I've become interested in how people use the streets and buildings as an integral part of their protest, to post up messages and slogans. How they use the walls, the urban trees, and all the other street paraphernalia we usually ignore as we walk past. And the way people use the streets sometimes to make a point about where they stand as individuals, within a group, to challenge the perceptions of others.'

He fished around in his box file again. 'Like this one.' He handed it to me. 'I'd be interested in your reaction to it.'

It was a colour photo, but your eye went immediately to the figure of a young woman, probably a student, dressed head to foot in black. Shapeless black woollen top, black calf-length skirt, thick black stockings and black flat shoes. She was wearing a black headscarf, wrapped tightly around her head so that no hair was visible, but the material was long enough to fall round her shoulders so that her neck was hidden, too. She was standing in the middle of a group of other young women, all dressed in fashionable, colourful clothes, modest in length and fit, but all bareheaded and chatting to each other.

She was turned slightly towards a brightly dressed woman next to her, in conversation, but neither was smiling. The photo was taken three-quarter profile, so it was possible to see the face of the woman in black. It had a certain youthful beauty, the black oval frame of the headscarf enhancing her pale unblemished skin. There was no trace of make-up. Her expression was not hostile exactly, but definitely defiant.

'So, what do you think when you see her for the first time?'

I placed the photo on the table and studied it for a while, thinking about the discussion I'd had previously with Firuzeh about the veil and the chador.

'I think she knows how different she looks but, like you say, she seems determined to make a point. Which, of course, she does, by being there, dressed in black among her fellow students. So I guess I'd be wondering if, by dressing like that, she's expressing deeply held orthodox religious views. Or is she just anti-Shah? Firuzeh says that wearing the headscarf or the hejab can now be seen as an anti-Shah, anti-Westernisation gesture, but not necessarily an expression of religious orthodoxy.'

'Right. When I took that, I was sure she was making the point that she was orthodox, and that she was willing to stand out in a crowd for her beliefs.'

'She certainly looks pro-orthodoxy. But not necessarily anti-Shah. You can't tell that from the photo.'

'Exactly. I can take a photo for many reasons, but you lay your own thinking and experience on it to interpret it.' He looked serious as he said that. 'That's something else I've become interested in – people's perception of photos, the psychology of photography, if you like. What the photographer was intending before he took it, what he sees when he looks at it, but then how others interpret it, and why they interpret it in the way they do.'

He fell silent, as if he'd suddenly become aware he was revealing a part of himself he rarely shared with others. Then he looked at his watch.

'It's getting near curfew,' he said, smiling at me as he put the photo back in his file. 'Come on, I'll walk you home.'

I realised later he hadn't told me what the camera on the roof was for.

*

Kupfermühle, 1 March
Interesting, what Anna had said about the photo of the woman in black and what Reza might use it for. And what he'd said about his reason for taking photos, which was pretty much the same as he'd said to me back in Berkeley, when we were sitting outside the Bear's Lair and I'd asked him about his happy snaps.

Met up with Jesper today. He's back in Hamburg. Wanted to chat about the house handover in April so I went to see him. It felt good to be back in a big city again. I hadn't realised how introverted I'd become, burying myself away for the whole winter. Jesper said he needed the house by the middle of April, which gives me six weeks to sort something out.

It felt like a much-needed kick up the backside. I've been mooching about here, slowly coming out of hibernation, but not putting my mind to the rather pressing question of where I go next.

The snow seems to have gone for good. It can come back sometimes for one last late blast, but Frau Jensen reckons it won't this year. We were up with the Whoopers yesterday. The yearling is doing well, and there seems to be a sense of purpose about the three of them, almost friskiness, although no self-respecting Whooper would allow itself to look frisky. They're getting ready for the big fly-away-home. It's a little early for them yet: they need to time it right – if they leave too early, they'll get back to their breeding grounds and find them still frozen. If they get there too late, the best spots will be gone. I envy them their routine, the certainty of their lives, as they must see it, looking out through their dark knowing eyes.

'I'll miss them,' I say to Frau Jensen.

'No, you won't. You won't be here,' she says, matter-of-factly.

When I get back to the house, I have a tidy-up and a clean-out. Just in case Jesper decides to visit me to check on the house and discovers what a slob I am. I make myself some lunch, and plan the next month. I feel a flutter of panic. I've slipped with the writing. It's getting towards the endgame now and I don't want to face it. But it feels like this is my last chance. I need to shift this weight, this sense of unfinished business.

There's nothing in my Tabriz journal from 23 February until August. There's nothing in Anna's until August either. We all drifted through the early summer, hoping things wouldn't get any worse. I'll start with her journal. I didn't see a lot of her, she spent a lot of time with Reza. Which was fine by me. At least he wasn't hanging around Kucheh Mulla as much.

*

Anna

6 August

The Summer of Not Being Sensible

I am thirty today. This time a year ago I was in the British Museum, mesmerised by Rostam, Rakhsh and the lion and listening later to Farzad describing the calligraphy of Ferdowsi's words on the page. *Each leaf is a word. His poetry becomes the leaves in the trees.*

I'm not sure how I feel about being thirty. I'm not sure how I feel about anything at the moment. It's been over five months since I wrote anything in my journal. A lot has happened to

234

me personally, but I haven't felt like writing it down until now. There's so much confusion, distrust, uncertainty here, in Tabriz, in Iran as a whole, it's felt like I've just had to live with it, not record it, or try to analyse it, just find a way through.

My research project has never got off the ground. The university was closed for most of the summer term, and even when it was open it closed quickly again, as students were using it as a base to support the workers' strikes in Tabriz. So, I can't do my job, but the British Embassy in Tehran won't send anyone home – neither will the American Embassy, come to that. They think it sends out the wrong message to the world, and to the opposition to the Shah here in Iran. The West is still supporting him, and has to be seen to be doing that. So we must keep our heads down and wait till it blows over, to quote Julia, who has taken to saying these things deadpan, allowing you the option to decide whether she really believes what she's being told to say.

I've found bits of work to justify my salary. I've done some private teaching at the Council, mainly young students waiting to go overseas for their studies. And I do some secondary translation work at the University Medical School. The researchers have good English – most were educated in the UK, Europe or the US, in the first tranche of overseas students in the sixties, and they came back, unlike their present counterparts studying abroad. They do the initial translation into English, and I polish it up for them.

Farzad is preparing a paper for publication in American medical journals, about treating wounds inflicted with high-velocity weapons. The professor in the cardiac department is preparing a paper on the efficacy of certain tests administered before heart surgery. Yet another has prepared a paper on introducing a medical model for treating patients in remote villages in Iran, based on the 'barefoot doctors' programme of Chairman Mao's China. It recommends village health workers, with basic training, to administer primary care. I especially enjoyed working on this: it reminded me of my father and his health-care-in-the-rural-villages programme. When I thought of him this time, it was with fondness rather than sadness. That feels like progress.

While the university has been closed, it seems to me that many professors have spent their time in writing academic papers for prestigious journals, which might help them with job applications for posts overseas. No one ever says that, of course. But there have been so many sudden decisions to take a holiday with the whole family and not return. And a contact of Reza's at one of the international banks said there has been a record amount of 'flight capital' transferred to the US and Europe.

So, I've kept busy, teaching and working on the medical papers with the doctors. The rest of my time I've spent with Reza, when he's been here in Tabriz. It was inevitable we would get together. I knew it from that first night. We went to bed for the first time during the long weekend at the end of the Nowruz break in March. Julia had advised me to stay indoors in case there was trouble. I didn't feel too apprehensive – I'd been in Tabriz less than three weeks but had got used to the permanent tension. I had to. It was part of the air you breathed.

On the Thursday, I'd ignored Julia's instructions, as Reza had taken me out to the Christian Armenian cemetery on the edge of Tabriz to see the grave of an American, Howard Baskerville, a missionary teacher from Nebraska. He'd ended up in Tabriz, in 1907, teaching at the American Memorial School, a Presbyterian mission school, and got caught up in the Constitutional Revolution in 1909.

'For the whole of this century Iran has been going through one major political conflict after another,' said Reza. 'Revolutions, internal coups, externally organised coups – you name it, we've tried it.'

Baskerville died at the head of a group of young student soldiers, fighting with the Iranians, helping them defend Tabriz against the Qajar royalist troops, who were fighting for the Shah. He was only twenty-four.

'Ironic, when you remember how some of our protesters think now about Americans and America,' said Reza, as we stared down at the simple grave, surprisingly well tended, in the cemetery corner. 'He's still considered to be a real Iranian patriot.'

That was what I liked about being with Reza, he took me to surprising places, showed me things I would never have seen if I hadn't been with him. Some places weren't pleasant – he once took me to the village of Quri-Chai, the northern slums of Tabriz: a sorry, overcrowded place of mud-built houses and indescribable poverty, no running water, no electricity. Reza said there was little in the way of school for the innumerable children out on the streets, and it was teeming with young men, mostly from peasant families who'd had to abandon their land, so their sons had to come to Tabriz, seeking work.

'They were unemployed at home, and now they're unemployed here, or working for poor wages, mainly because of the failure of the Shah's rural reforms in his so-called "White Revolution",' said Reza, a note of bitterness in his voice.

We didn't stop long. I didn't even get out of the car – I said it felt too voyeuristic. I thought he'd be scornful, yet another Westerner, a weak woman to boot, who couldn't face the reality behind the fantasy of the Shah's Iran. To my surprise, he reached out and squeezed my hand, as if he understood.

We got back from Baskerville's grave on the Thursday afternoon. Arash was with Damian at Kucheh Mulla, and I ended up with Reza in Arash's place. We ate cold chicken and drank Shiraz wine and went up on the rooftop with glasses of cardamom chocolate.

It was no big seduction on his part. More a shared need to be with someone who makes you feel good about yourself, makes you feel whole, while everything around you is fracturing. Julia had been right: the following day there was trouble in the centre of Tabriz after Friday prayers when a few banks and cinemas had their windows smashed. We stayed in bed.

He had his own room in Arash's place when he came to stay. It became our room, our place to go: 'One little room can be made an everywhere,' he said to me once, after sex in the afternoon. It was often in the afternoon, we had to work our visits around curfew.

Had he used the 'little room' line with some other woman? Probably. Maybe several women. Did it matter? Not at all. I can think of worse ways to spend an afternoon than making love and having John Donne misquoted in my ear.

Was it love? Emphatically not. But it was tenderness and need and often fun.

And I loved his little room. It was at the back of the house and looked down on an almond tree. He took me to the bazaar, with Damian as my Western chaperone, as per Julia's instructions, and introduced me to Ervand, who seemed very impressed I was an Oxford graduate and told me about his daughter who was studying medicine in London. We trooped to the fabric *raasteh* together, the three of us, and I bought coverlets with an Indian paisley design, for Reza's room, and treated myself to a length of beautiful ocean blue silk, which I used as a summer sarong to float around Arash's house. I had never had a man trace the curves of my body through silk before.

He was surprisingly considerate in bed. I say surprising, because the edge I'd identified the first night I met him in Kucheh Mulla was definitely there, sometimes. There were also no-go areas with him, in terms of what he would talk about, and an occasional aloofness. I wondered if he'd be as reserved in bed. But he wasn't. He enjoyed sex, the intimacy of it, the physicality of it, and I enjoyed sex with him. And he made great salads. Watermelon salad after sex on a hot July afternoon. One of my better memories of Tabriz to take away with me.

Occasionally I took a risk and stayed overnight. Five o'clock, with the heat of the day fading a little, we'd go up on the roof, get out the *toshak* mattress and set it on the metal frame, like most Iranians do on summer nights, and lounge around, eating and drinking wine. I'd be wearing the silk sarong, he'd lie in his shorts on the bed, or naked – that was another thing about him: he was totally at ease with his body and he made me totally at ease with mine. Until Reza, I'd always covered up after sex. The feeling of warm night air on a rooftop and someone stroking my naked body, me taking my turn to stroke his, felt like the most natural thing in the world. That was when we talked most, those summer nights on the roof. 'If you had to leave Iran, where would you go?' I asked him once.

He didn't hesitate. 'Paris.'

'Why Paris?'

'It's the most beautiful city in the world. And you can breathe free, there.'

'If you could move about more in Iran, if there weren't these restrictions and precautions we have to take now, where would you like to go? What would you like to see?'

I didn't hesitate either. 'Persepolis.'

'Why?'

'It's probably due to my classics mistress at school. She was an archaeologist by training, and had done her PhD on identifying the various tribute-givers on the Apadana frieze. She would talk for hours about it and make it come alive. So I've always had this hankering to see it. No chance now, though, with things as they are.'

'It'll still be there when all the trouble here dies down. The country's lasted two and a half thousand years, it'll last a while longer.' He turned to me and caressed my face. 'I promise I'll take you there some day. Come back when we've all sorted ourselves out.'

I'd smiled at him and gave what I hoped was a 'maybe' shrug of my shoulders.

*

The American

It was through Reza that I got to see the American in action.

Nobody in the Kucheh Mulla caravanserai liked the American. Julia, in particular, didn't like the American. Primarily because he stopped the British, and the expat community in general, using the swimming pool at the American Consulate during the summer. It's a huge, almost Olympic-sized pool, well looked after, and apparently a perk much sought-after among the British community in Tabriz.

Then the American came in 1977, and decided it would be a much better use of the pool to open it and the consulate grounds to the local Iranian community in the neighbourhood. The grounds are fantastic, around thirteen acres of beautifully kept gardens, and an almond orchard. There's also a softball field, tennis court, volleyball court, and space to kick a football about.

So why not open it up to the people? They live literally on the other side of the wall and have nowhere to play football, and football, English-style, was in the news this summer. Iran was in the World Cup for the first time this June, in Argentina – something to be proud of in the midst of all the turmoil. So, inviting young men of the neighbourhood in to kick a football about was a stroke of diplomatic genius, Reza thought.

The American decreed that the consulate grounds would open on three to four days in the summer, for use by the local people. Coaching was organised for various sports, and access to the pool was granted with a pass. Women in chadors or headscarves sat and watched their children have swimming lessons, or practising football.

But no British, not automatically, anyway. They might be able to get a pass, but only by personal recommendation. Reza got us all in, though, by virtue of Arash and him having worked at the consulate before the American's arrival, taking part-time jobs when they were students, and Arash also having done some library work there. The four of us did our 'alibi couples' routine,

Damian and I as boyfriend and girlfriend, Arash and Reza, brothers.

He's an enigma, the American. Speaks fluent Persian and Turkish, and has worked in less developed areas of Iran, in the Peace Corps.

'It's not always a good thing to speak Persian too well in Iran,' said Reza. 'It's a mixed blessing – it breaks the ice, yes, but it can make Iranians uneasy if they think you understand every word they say. You can listen in on their private conversations. In this SAVAK paranoid world, that's a definite disadvantage.'

But it works both ways. The American has a reputation for entertaining the great and the good of Tabriz, the likes of the Governor, the Mayor, the Chief of Police, the local business men, even the head of SAVAK, as well as the Russians helping maintain the railway to Jolfa. So the American gets to know what's going on at all levels and across nationalities.

'Doubtless he passes it onwards and upwards in the American Embassy,' says Reza.

'No different from the British, I should imagine.'

'No, but they don't work the local crowd quite like the American does.'

'It has its downside for him,' said Reza. 'If he gives you free rein to wander around the Consulate and its grounds as a guest, that's a good way of getting to know the lie of the land, finding out where everything is: exits, entrances, weak spots. Could come in handy if America ever becomes more of an enemy than a friend, and you want to know your way in. And that's not an entirely fanciful notion, is it?'

Nevertheless, I rather admire the American. I only saw him once from a distance, at the edge of the almond orchard, surveying the scene round the pool. Stocky, dark, pugnacious. There's a touch of the renegade about him. I wonder how he goes down with his Tehran Embassy bosses. They probably haven't a clue what he's up to – like our lot. Tabriz isn't top of their must-visit places either. Far too real for them, I should imagine. Doesn't have quite the cultural cachet of Isfahan or Shiraz.

We took advantage of his open-house policy, though, and it was one of the best places to spend an afternoon in the summer.

So, God bless the American, I say.

*

The Runner

There was an unfathomable side to Reza. An aspect of him that made me uneasy. One night in early April, I found out what the camera on the stand was for. He suggested we go up onto the rooftop, for some air, before it became too cold. It was one of those moody skies, shy stars and a cool moon obscured off and on by strands of clingy cloud. He had the camera set up, pointing across the low rooftops in the direction of the city.

'So it's moonscapes you're interested in,' I said.

He put his finger to his lips. 'Just wait,' he whispered.

At first I thought it was a dog. One of those streamlined breeds, lean body and long floppy ears blowing back as it scurried across the roof opposite. But dogs on roofs would be a rare sight in Tabriz – dogs in any part of a house for that matter. It was not much more than a moving shadow in the starlight, but then it crossed a space between the skylight frame and a giant Ali Baba planter. Then it straightened and stayed upright on its hind legs. At that moment, the moon slid out from behind a cloud and the figure was outlined clearly against the sky. I could see it was a boy, tall enough to be in his early teens, but it was impossible to tell in the dark and at that distance.

The floppy ears were the ear flaps of his *ushanka*, the Russian military-style round hat some of the Tabrizis wear in the colder weather. He dropped down again near the roof edge. In the silence, I heard a slight scraping noise and watched him as he squatted, then lifted up a short board, which must have been lying propped against the parapet. Carefully, he laid it across the gap between the rooftop he was on and the one next to him – a distance of about six feet. He wriggled the board a little, making sure it would stay firm. Then he stood quite still for a moment, as if gathering himself, crouched again, not so low this time, and scuttled across the improvised bridge.

He stood up, and stretched his head upwards, as if he were addressing the stars and the moon. That was when Reza took the photo. The boy bent down and pulled the board across. Then he was off again, until he got to the far edge where there must have been another board to help him across onto another roof. I thought of the people in the houses he was using and wondered how many made sure the bridges were back in the right place for the next night-time run. He disappeared from view.

Reza lit a cigarette. 'That's our young runner,' he said. 'Thursday, eight p.m. Regular as clockwork.'

I was struck by the grudging admiration in his voice.

Later, as we huddled next to the *bokhari* and warmed up with vodka, he told me more about the rooftop run. It was one of the ways in Tehran that they made sure Ayatollah Khomeini's cassette tapes got to the mosques for Friday prayers, so they could be played to the people. The tapes came in from Iraq, brought back by Shi'a pilgrims, and from other places in the Middle East. It wouldn't really matter if the sound quality was bad once they got to the mosque, because it was hearing Khomeini's voice that roused the crowds. Sometimes the tapes were copied and sold in the bazaars. They were cheaper, Reza said, than a few eggs in Tehran now, with food prices being so high.

'The idea of it!' he said. 'His voice brought home from exile! And he uses the language of the people – simple, powerful words. So much more immediate, as if he's with them right there in the mosque. And reaching those who can't read too

243

– sheer genius!' He shook his head. 'I didn't think that method of distributing the Ayatollah's words had reached Tabriz, but it obviously has. It's probably going on in all the big cities.'

'How did you know about tonight?'

'The usual. A rumour that the rooftop opposite had become a tape route.'

'If you got to know, then maybe others, who aren't so positive about it, do too.'

'That's a risk all the runners take. They obviously think it's worth it.'

Later, when we were in bed, I couldn't get the thought out of my mind of the boy taking such risks. The fear, the courage, the devotion.

I asked Reza if he felt the same way.

'Of course I admire his courage, who wouldn't?' He hesitated, then said slowly, 'But if I'm honest, what I mostly felt was a thrill of anticipation about the picture I took. I'm not sure it will be technically good, but I'm hoping there'll be something moonlit, atmospheric, a sense of danger. Maybe a good picture conveying the risk of the work he does is the best compliment I can pay him.'

I went back to Kucheh Mulla the following morning, feeling a bit low. No one was in, and I sat in the kitchen, sipping tea, thinking about the photo I'd seen Reza take. I leaned back in the chair and closed my eyes. The image of the boy came to me, silhouetted against the sky, looking up, probably offering Allah a little prayer of thanks that he'd got across the gap safely.

Then I thought about Reza, more interested in the technicalities of the image he'd taken than the boy himself. That's the part of him I don't particularly like.

But, despite that, our being together worked. I think the reason for this was the acceptance from the beginning that it was a bounded relationship, limited on both sides as to what we wanted from each other. Mutually bounded, not just one of us saying so and the other agreeing but not meaning it. We weren't going anywhere other than where we were now. He was leaving in August to go back to Europe. Who knew where I'd be this time next year? I saw him as a kind of experiment. See how far being with someone like him might take me. And as for what he thought about me – he once said I was an intriguing woman. I'd never been called 'intriguing' before. Maybe he said that to other women too – maybe it was part of his John Donne 'little room' toolkit. Charlie would never have thought of me as intriguing. But, then, I never thought of him as intriguing, either.

So, a few reservations, but no real regrets about Reza. 1977 might have been the summer of the *Shahnameh*, but 1978 has turned out to be the summer of not being sensible, and it was just what I needed.

He left for London last week. He'd return in December, he said. He didn't promise to keep in touch. Neither did I. I'm back permanently in Kucheh Mulla. No more silk sarongs. No more watermelon salads. I felt lonely after he'd gone. But I didn't feel bereft.

Love . . . makes a little room an anywhere – that's the correct Donne quote.

Trust Reza to leave out love.

*

Damian

Kupfermühle, 10 March

Well, well, well. Who would have thought it? We knew Anna and Reza had got it together, but they were very discreet and I was totally unaware of the intensity or the undercurrents. And she certainly got around Tabriz far more than I did. So many unanswered questions about Reza, though, despite her observations.

I'd had no idea about the runners in Tabriz or the tapes and how they were distributed. Anna kept quiet about what Reza had shown her, but looking back, that kind of activity must have been a key factor in Khomeini's success. It was only much later, in mid-October, that Arash and I got to know a little more about it because Ervand told Arash during one of their Tabrizi tea chats.

Khomeini had been forced to leave Iraq in October 1978, and ended up in exile in a Paris suburb. As it happened, the enforced move couldn't have worked out better for him because he now had access to the world's media, which he hadn't had in Iraq. And it meant he could produce more tapes more frequently, then have them smuggled in by his supporters from any point in Europe. And now, according to the rumour Ervand had heard, he had another means of distribution. Khomeini actually phoned some of his speeches directly down the line from Paris to Tehran, and they were recorded straight from the telephone. The tapes were sold openly in the bazaar, if you knew where to go, and there was a huge increase in the numbers after his move to Paris. It didn't matter how wonky they were, the power of his voice was the most important factor.

'He's more of a problem operating from Paris than he ever was in Iraq,' said Arash.

Anna was there when he said that, but she never told us about the runner. Loyalty to Reza, I suppose. Clearly we had rather different summer experiences. While she was trying out a summer of not being sensible, with rooftop sex and runners on roofs and watermelon salads, Arash and I were struggling with the emotional fallout of everything that was happening around us.

My journal picked up again as summer turned to autumn. It didn't amount to much, little more than a list of dates and events with just a few details, but they're burned into my memory and I've tried to flesh them out here. A series of strikes and rumours and awful events in August and early September left us almost numb with apprehension for what might happen next. I could barely manage to get through it, day to day, never mind try to write about and analyse it along the way. The truth was that my main worry wasn't what was happening out there all over Iran. My main worry was Arash. He was deteriorating emotionally, sinking slowly into depression, and I didn't know what to do about it.

*

Damian

Tabriz, 18 August
The mice have roared

The 40/40 has gone on throughout the spring and summer. I asked back in February: who would be next in the 40/40 pattern? Well, it turned out to be the city of Yazd, in particular, with twenty-eight dead, it was said. But there have been individual acts of violence since then too, all over the country, adding to the sense of a society unravelling.

The first week in May, in Tabriz, during one of the weeks the university was actually open, one of our English language students disappeared. The classroom he was last seen in, the morning after he disappeared, had a wide streak of blood tracking straight down the wall, from shoulder height to the floor, where he had slid down most probably. To be precise, he didn't disappear, he was disappeared. By SAVAK, it was rumoured.

Later that week, police stormed the home of Ayatollah Shariatmadari in Qom – always the action returns to Qom – and shot dead two of his theology students. In his own home.

That was what outraged people. He then warned there would be no peace in the country unless the Shah agreed to Muslim demands for the formation of a constitutional government.

'So now,' said Arash, 'Shariatmadari, the most moderate,

peaceful cleric of them all, has finally lost his patience and joined the clamour for change. And what he says in Qom will be taken up and shouted from the rooftops here in Tabriz. And round we go again.'

He shook his head in despair.

He was right. There has been a change in the city – the sullenness, the deep anger, has always been there since the riots, you can feel it, but now you can hear it too, in the steady drumbeat of small but insistent acts of insurrection. And this time, here in Tabriz at least, it isn't the middle-class intellectuals, the writers, the poets, the journalists, the academics, the lawyers, it isn't the students, it's not even the clergy, although all those groups are still at it. This time the factory workers here in Tabriz have taken a stand.

The action has centred on the machine-tool workers in the factory on the edge of the city. They went on strike in April, all 2,700 of them. The sheer numbers involved showed this was different. This was no little local dispute, this was a strike with a general political message for others. It wasn't just about an increase in wages either. In 1976, the Shah had warned his workers that they were not working hard enough. He said, in his usual infantilising tone: 'We shall take those who do not work by the tails and throw them out like mice.'

Now the mice have roared. They are not only demanding an increase in wages to cope with the spiralling cost of living, they are making political demands too. They demand that the government must stop forcing workers to attend government rallies (a dig at the pro-government rally they were forced to attend earlier in April, after the Tabriz riots, when they were 'persuaded' to wave suitably pro-government placards); it must release all political prisoners and allow exiles to return, especially Khomeini; and it must expel all SAVAK agents from factories, universities and other institutions.

Tabriz is one of the first places in the country where the workers have realised the power they have and have tried to use it. The April strike was crushed. But they went on strike again in June, then in August, only ten days ago. It feels different, what these workers have achieved, as though the political struggle now has one more group nipping at the heels of the government, and it is a group that has much to say and is here to stay.

Meanwhile the 40/40 is still going on. In June it was back to Qom, but there was a large demonstration here in Tabriz too, as another forty days' mourning for the two murdered Shariatmadari students came to an end. There's been a steady increase of rallies, riots, strikes, bombs, needless deaths, and imposition of martial law in parts of the country or threats of it in others. Relentless, as though the whole country is spinning out of control.

As for us, here in Kucheh Mulla, Reza has gone back to London; Anna is back and spends much of her time in her room, playing Bach; Arash is grimly obsessed with what's happening and horrified by it in equal measure. He's taken to going to the bazaar more often to talk with Ervand. Sometimes I go with him, sometimes I don't, he doesn't always ask me.

22 August

We got news of a horrible incident that took place in Abadan three days ago. It's hard to believe: 450 people burned to death in the Rex cinema in the town. The audience were all locked inside, so it was a deliberate act. They say SAVAK is to blame. There have been riots there. 'Death to the Shah' was heard on the streets.

Abadan is in south west Iran in the oil fields region. Anything that happens there is like something happening to the life blood of the country, and cranks up the violence yet again.

So many rumours and counter-rumours. When there's a hole where the truth should be, rumour wriggles through, closely followed by counter-rumour. Even when some version of the truth appears, rumour coils itself around it, pulling it out of shape, so that in the end you just don't know what to believe.

Which, of course, suits the perpetrators of the outrage very well: the focus isn't on them but on the source and reliability of the rumour. Eventually, the rumour settles that the Rex cinema fire was the work of SAVAK. Anti-government protesters prefer to believe that and for everyone else to believe it too.

'The sad thing is,' said Arash, 'it's the sort of thing people think SAVAK would be capable of doing, it has such a savage reputation, so even if it didn't do it, they would always believe it did.'

That's the other effect of rumour. You spread it around, repeat it often enough, and it doesn't just fill a vacuum until the truth comes along, it becomes the truth.

Tuesday, 5 September

We were at the bazaar today, visiting Ervand. We'd heard on the radio that there'd been a huge demonstration yesterday in Tehran to coincide with the celebration of Eid, the end of Ramadan. Needless to say, Ervand had already heard about it from the mosque, and told the tale with far more detail than you'd find in any newspaper.

'A large crowd set off from the northern hills in Tehran to the centre of the city. It's an eight-mile march, and as they went along, they gathered more demonstrators, some holding banners with Khomeini's face on them, and all chanting, "Khomeini is our leader," and "Why do government troops kill our people?"'

'Khomeini!' said Arash. 'It's always Khomeini, these days,' and he shook his head, as he tends to do now, whenever he hears Khomeini's name.

'On the way,' Ervand continued, 'the crowd surrounded a truck full of soldiers, and shouted at them that "Brothers don't shoot brothers!" and an army officer shouted back that, yes, they were brothers, but he had to do his duty.'

Ervand paused as he got to this point, then said slowly, 'And the crowd threw flowers into the truck.' He looked at us, eyebrows raised, as if he couldn't believe what he had just said, waiting for our reactions.

My jaw dropped, and Arash said, 'Flowers? Khomeini supporters? I don't believe it!'

Ervand must have been well rewarded by the effect he'd had on us, though he didn't show it, and carried on, complete with more hard-to-verify details that were already doing the rounds, and adding to a tale that would probably grow even more with the telling.

'They went on their way. Passers-by offered them water and fruit, and the crowd swelled with all kinds, not only the religious groups. People came out of their offices, and joined housewives and older men and women, all exchanging flowers. They say that by the time they got to the city centre, there were almost two hundred thousand marchers.'

Finishing with a flourish, he said, 'Today's paper is calling it a march for peace, because it wasn't just the mullahs and the Khomeini supporters who joined in. It was the ordinary people as well.'

That evening, we sat about on the floor cushions, drinking wine, and told Anna what we'd heard. We were both in lighter spirits. The notion of a peace march and handing flowers to the troops took the edge off the tragedy of the Rex cinema incident.

'It's the first time we've heard the word "peace" linked to the demonstrations, so that's a good sign,' Anna agreed. 'But then again, it's the government paper making it out to be a peace march, isn't it? Trying to put a positive gloss on it, rather than focusing on the obvious support for Khomeini.'

A note of cynicism is creeping into Anna's comments. Reza's influence, no doubt.

Thursday, 7 September
Phone call from Julia early this morning. There was trouble in Tehran again yesterday. A group described as terrorists opened fire on a police barracks, killing an officer. The government

announced an immediate ban on any more marches. Then another group of terrorists tossed a pipe bomb under a bus taking British Aerospace workers home. No one was injured but it was worrying as it was aimed at personnel of a British company. There is a deliberate ratcheting up of tension.

'Take the usual precautions,' Julia said. 'This sort of thing might spread.'

'So much for the march for peace,' Arash said. Anna nodded. I felt deflated.

Then, later this afternoon, another phone call from Julia, with news of another massive demonstration today. The embassy in Tehran was saying there were tens of thousands on the streets. This time, the mood was defiant. The government had banned rallies, so they had organised a rally to protest against the government's banning of rallies.

It was mainly Khomeini supporters and, chillingly, the men were dressed in white, a sign that they were willing to die and become martyrs for their cause, while the women marched separately, in black chadors, as a sign of embracing their religion, and of defying the Shah's expressed preference for women not to wear the veil or chador. All of them chanting '*Marg bar Shah!*' – 'Death to the Shah' – and demanding an Islamic republic.

'So it sounds as if it could turn quite ugly,' Julia said. 'You must definitely stay away from the bazaar tomorrow, if you were thinking of going down there. Friday prayers might get a bit hectic here in Tabriz as well.'

So far, there have been two street demonstrations in three days in Tehran, organised by Khomeini supporters, the first sending their message with flowers, the second with death chants and references to martyrdom and religious fervour.

'The flowers didn't last long, did they?' said Arash.

Flowers one day, death chants the next. How mercurial this country has become.

8 September. Friday morning

About 8 a.m. there's a telephone call from Julia. I dread hearing the ring these days.

I answered, a bit groggy – I hadn't slept well. It'll be the usual warning, I thought, as she said 'Good morning' in her brisk way.

'They've declared martial law in Tehran this morning. Came over the radio at six a.m. The army have been broadcasting it over loudspeakers throughout the night, apparently.'

'Why have they done that?'

'In response to the demonstration yesterday, I expect. Anyway, it might get tricky through the day. They're imposing it in several other cities and Tabriz may be one. Best to keep a low profile, just in case it all takes off here.'

'We've been doing that all week.'

'Well, keep doing it.'

The situation must be getting serious if she's ringing round all the British nationals who work for the Council each time she gets a special alert from the embassy in Tehran.

The three of us lazed about for the rest of the day. We were all feeling restless. We hadn't been out since Tuesday, and it had rained off and on so we couldn't even get some fresh air on the roof when we wanted to. Arash tried to work on his translations, but he's finding it difficult to concentrate, these days.

Anna made herself scarce, keeping to her room, still playing Bach. The Brandenburgs, mainly. I'd always thought of them as music that rolls along with a lilt and a swing, a sense of order, all's right with the world, and you bowl along with it. But my Oxford don had a penchant for the Brandenburgs, so we listened to them a lot. He said some music critic or other had suggested there were more deliberate hints of disorder in them than met the ear. The more I listened, the more I decided he might be right. In the Fourth, for example, you hear the violin flying along, in supreme command, then suddenly it's overtaken by two simple, jolly recorders, the country yokels of the orchestral hierarchy. It's the world tipped on its head, if only for a moment – it's mice chasing cats, as the critic said. But it doesn't last long, this upended world, this challenge to the accepted order. Cats end up chasing mice again, when the violin regains its orchestral superiority over the recorders, and they all settle down in a harmonious amble to the end.

I wonder if that's what Anna hears in the Brandenburgs, and finds it soothing, this sense of a world momentarily turned upside down, then regaining its equilibrium. Then again, maybe she just hears its cheerfulness and that's more than enough.

That's the way my mind is going at the moment – drifting off into flights of fancy about things that really aren't important. But it's better than coping with reality.

Friday evening

A late phone call from Julia. 'Big trouble in Tehran. Don't go out tomorrow. Have you got that? Under no circumstances are you to go out.'

She sounded even more clipped than usual, with a note of anxiety in her voice I'd not heard before.

'What kind of trouble, exactly?'

'Can't say too much on the phone. But it's serious enough to make sure you're extra vigilant. And that goes for anyone else who may be in the house.'

She sometimes adds that reference to 'anyone else'. It's code for *'I know you've got your boyfriend there with you. I hope you know what you're doing. Just remember it's not up to us to keep him safe. That's your problem.'*

'I'll let you know if there are any further developments,' she said, the anxiety replaced by a note of 'one more ticked off the list'.

'It'll be another demonstration, like yesterday, organised by the Khomeini lot,' Arash said. 'Probably in defiance of martial law. I hope there's none of that here.'

Saturday, 9 September

Where to start? It's all so hard to take in. They're calling yesterday 'Black Friday'.

The death toll is disputed: it's too soon for definitive numbers yet. Scores killed, according to Julia's latest phone call. So far, what we're hearing is that thousands of demonstrators marched in Tehran to protest the imposition of martial law. They reached an intersection called Jaleh Square, in the centre of the city. There, they clashed with government troops, who opened fire.

The rumours are flying fast and free again. Soldiers used machine guns to fire into the crowd indiscriminately, mowing down scores of people. Women and children were among the dead. This is the worst incident so far. The country is holding its breath to see if something similar breaks out anywhere else. If it does, this could be the start of a countrywide insurrection.

Tuesday, 12 September

More rumours today. Depending on which newspaper you can get your hands on, or which side you believe, the number of dead is appalling. The foreign papers have a high death count, quoted by journalists who were in Tehran or are in touch with the opposition. Two to three thousand dead, and reports that hundreds of bodies were carted off to unmarked mass graves in the cemetery. The government says between 95 and 250 are dead.

The rumour that has particularly incensed the people is that the Shah's personal helicopter was spotted hovering over the scene, an allegation as yet unproven. But by Friday evening, hundreds of fires were raging through the city, and the hospitals were overwhelmed.

The three of us sat about this evening, not knowing what to do with ourselves. Then Anna surprises Arash and me when she says, 'The Shah has lost the *farr*,' and then explains what it is. She surprises us again when she potters off to her room and comes back with a copy of the *Shahnameh*. 'I brought it with me, it was a gift last year from Firuzeh and Farzad,' she says, 'what better time to read it than now?' and she reads us the passage describing the time when Jamshid ruled for six hundred years. The king who did many great things, but then became filled with vanity and turned away from God, forgetting the gratitude he owed him:

> '. . . I recognise no lord but myself. It was through me that skills appeared on the earth and no throne however famed has ever beheld a monarch like me . . . Sunshine, sleep and repose all come through me and even your clothing and what enters your mouths originate from me. Power, crown and kingship are my prerogative. It is because of me that you have minds and souls in your bodies, and now you are aware that all this was accomplished by me, it is your duty to entitle me Creator of the World . . .'
>   . . . But as soon as Jamshid said these things, God took away the farr from him . . . the farr departed from him and the world became full of discord. Men deserted his court and no one desiring repute would remain in his service, for when pride combines with power of action, it brings ruin in its train and converts good fortune into bad . . . Jamshid's destiny was overcast with gloom and his world-illuminating splendour disappeared.

I closed my eyes as she was reading, and found myself thinking of Massoud, back in Berkeley. *The Emperor of Oil, the Shadow of God, and the significance of the farr.*

She finished the passage and closed the book. 'I never quite understood the power of the *farr* when I first read this back in Oxford. I just loved the way the story unfolded of a king who ruled for six hundred years and did many great things, then became undone when the power went to his head.'

She smiled a little wistfully. 'Reza took all of the romance out of it for me. I read that bit to him once, and he said he'd never believed in all that stuff about shahs and their God-given the right to rule, but even if he did, he said, this shah had lost the *farr* long ago.'

'And he was right,' said Arash, his voice flat, his face drawn. 'My brother was right about a lot of things.'

He is growing more taciturn, and there is nothing I can do to reach him. Still, I have to keep trying.

14 September

The Papakh Hat

Yesterday began much like any other of the last few days. The six o'clock convoy rumbled down the boulevard, heading from the barracks to the city centre. It was half a mile away, but the throaty growl of a trio of Chieftain tanks was always loud enough to wake me up each morning. I rolled over and tried to squeeze another half-hour. A second convoy, probably lorries driven at high revs, judging by the more raucous sound, rattled the skylight, waking me up for good. Strange how you adapt to the abnormal, using military vehicles as an alarm clock.

The door edged open and Arash appeared in his grey Berkeley sweats, backing in with coffee mugs. He'd been up since five. Best time to write, he always used to say. But, these days, he pottered mostly, getting the stove going, washing dishes.

I started where I left off at three in the morning. 'Have you changed your mind?'

'Not really.' He sat down on the bed and tried to stroke my cheek.

I turned my head away and he dropped his hand onto my shoulder. I turned back. 'Let me get you out, please.' The whine in my voice made me feel sick.

'How many more times, Damian?' He reached to stroke my face again and this time I let him, breathing in the scent of lemons. He once said, 'You either drink Tabrizi tea through a lump of sugar at the back of your teeth, and end up with no teeth, or you don't drink it at all.' So he drinks lemon tea instead, and that's another of his morning routines I've got used to: Arash slicing lemons.

I put my hand over his. 'People we know have disappeared. Or been disappeared. They'll come for you next.' This was the tack I'd decided to take, using the example of the student in the English faculty who'd left behind a blood slick, or some of the academics who'd gone on holiday and not come back.

He drew away from me slightly and sighed. 'I'm a part-time librarian, and a sometimes poet. I'm not involved in politics. I'm not important enough to anyone. So who will come for me, exactly?'

'Take your pick. SAVAK. One of the left-wing groups. The Patriotic Muslim Students. It's not safe. You're not safe.'

He stood up. 'I have to go to work. I'm late.'

I wanted to say, *What work? And late for what, exactly?* but didn't. The university was still closed, the library with it. The fear of martial law and curfew after Black Friday dampened any hope of getting a new university year up and running. But Arash still had that nightmare about the books being burned.

I couldn't stop myself. 'For Christ's sake, Arash, they're only books!'

He looked at me, an expression of pure pity on his face, as if I'd sold my soul to the devil.

He walked towards the door, turned and looked back at me, his head on one side in that birdy way he has. 'I'll see you later. We'll talk.' His smile was achingly sad.

Waves of misery rolled through me as he went out.

He'll never leave Tabriz. I know this. This insurgency, this insurrection, whatever it is, has been growing bigger every day, in a ragged sort of way, though no one is acknowledging it. After Black Friday, it feels unstoppable. Whatever he says, Arash is a target whoever ends up in power. If it all fizzles out, and I know it's unlikely now, but if it does, and the Shah and SAVAK are still in operation, they'll take him in: they'll know about us and they'll want to use that to see what we know. Mirza in Tehran, Massoud in Berkeley, even Reza, they may already have tabs on all of them because of their connection with me. It's the way it gets you, this place, paranoia.

Or, if the Marxist insurgents take over, they could also come for him. His year in Berkeley, his connections with the American Consulate: they'll say he's been too pro-America all this time and they'll want to punish him for it.

But it's the hard-line Islamists I fear most. The 'Patriotic Muslim Students' and their cleric associates are the worst. The Khomeini supporters. They'll point the finger, say he's 'Western-stricken' too, but they'll come for him mainly because of our relationship, because we're together. That's what they'll most despise about him. Somewhere, he'll be on someone's list as one of their abominations.

My hand searched his side of the bed. There was too much empty space. I lay on my back, staring through the skylight at the snow-heavy clouds.

*

'Damian.' His voice cut in from far away.

I opened my eyes to a square of iron-grey Tabrizi sky.

'Damian,' he said again, softly. He was standing in the doorway, his face drained of colour.

'What are you doing back so soon?' I felt my chest tighten. I had a sudden memory blip of the day he came back to Chilton Street with the news about Mirza.

'I found this.' His voice sounded reedy.

He wasn't really standing, more slumped against the door jamb, clutching some sort of hat. I jumped out of bed, went over to him and put my arm around him. We managed to stumble across to the kitchen and I sat him down, but he wouldn't let me take the hat from him.

He'd found a dead body on some derelict land near the

boulevard. Everyone tries to avoid that area, mainly because a pack of feral dogs usually hangs out there, but also because there's a rumour that it's where SAVAK used to dump the occasional body, when they'd finished their interrogations at the prison. It's near enough to the city centre to make sure that bodies would be found, SAVAK wanted that, but far enough away from SAVAK headquarters at the prison that no one could say for sure that they'd had a hand in it. Since the sacking of the SAVAK boss in Tabriz after the February riots, they've kept a lower profile, but nobody believes they've really changed their ways. It's more like they're just biding their time.

But this morning there were no signs of the feral dogs, and Arash made a spur-of-the-moment decision to take a shortcut. He'd got about halfway when he spotted the body lying next to a rusted oil drum.

'I thought he was sleeping,' he said, 'but his head didn't look right. It was lying too flat on the ground.' He hunched over, clutching the hat on his knees. 'He'd been dumped there. They'd tossed his hat near his feet. I realised he was dead. I didn't know what to do. No one else was around, but I had this really strong sense of being watched. So I snatched the hat and ran.'

I reached across, and this time he let me take the hat from him. It was a *papakh*. Another memory flitted in, this time of the tall young man leading the Tabrizi students in the February riots, wearing his country woollen *papakh* on the back of his head. But this *papakh* was astrakhan wool. Expensive. I edged it round on the pads of my fingers, staring at the scrollwork patterns made by the dark, tight curls of a young lamb's fleece. Most of the whorls of wool were clogged, smeared brown. I forced down the bile in my throat and placed the hat on the kitchen table.

'Maybe someone will recognise it. Maybe we can find out who he was,' Arash said. He stumbled to the sink and he threw up.

Both of us were shaky for the rest of the day.

Anna came in later from the Council where she'd been doing some coaching, and I told her what had happened. She was horrified, even more so when she saw the hat on the kitchen table. She suggested we move it to the little table in the corner of the kitchen and put a tea cloth over it.

I heated barley soup for us all, but we just dabbled in our bowls and spooned a few beans around. For once, we didn't have any music on and the only sound was the pop-popping of the stove. We stretched out on the floor cushions, our backs against the wall, Anna dozing, Arash and I both trying to read.

I had my Arberry translations, but the words danced around on the page and I gave up. Arash had his notebook and a small battered book I'd not seen before, with what looked like a hoopoe on the leather cover, its distinctive crest tooled in gold. He kept taking his glasses off, massaging the bridge of his nose with his thumb and forefinger, then putting them back on.

I reached across and stroked his fingers. 'Can't you concentrate either?' He shook his head. 'I haven't seen that book before. What are you working on?' It hurt me a little that he didn't really talk to me any more about what he was doing. *Rumi and the Dance of the Dervish* had turned out to be the last time we'd worked with each other.

'Din Attar, *Conference of the Birds*. It's an English translation of the poem, but in prose, from 1924. I found it in the bazaar. It's full of charm and idiosyncrasies. It's strange to read it as prose rather than poetry, and I find I have to take it slowly. I've only just started it.'

He looked down at the page. 'I was reading it just for pleasure. Until today.'

'Read it to us, then.' I knew reading aloud calmed him. 'I could do with soothing.'

Anna opened one eye and nodded. 'Go on, Arash. It's ages since you read to us.'

His voice was a bit wavery at first, but sounded stronger as he went on. '*Once, in the dim old days, all the birds of the world assembled in solemn conclave, to consider a momentous question . . .*'

The thirty birds of Persia and their journey through the valleys of Bewilderment and Stupefaction. The Hoopoe and the Huma and the Nightingale. And all the tiny birds full of fear with tears in their eyes. All in search of the truth, in search of the mysterious *Simorgh*. And they eventually discover the *Simorgh*, only to realise they are gazing upon themselves.

A perfect pun, of course, as *si* means thirty in Persian, *morgh* means birds. My prof would be ecstatic.

He read for about ten minutes. There was a long silence after he'd finished.

'Thanks, Arash,' Anna said. 'That's really lifted my spirits. I love the image of the hoopoe as the wisest of birds, leading all the others on their journey. When I was little, my father would tell me stories of the hoopoe. It was always seen as a faithful friend in African folklore.' She got up, came over to him and gave his shoulder a pat. 'I'd quite forgotten that good memory of my father.' Then she said goodnight and went off to bed.

I thought it best to say nothing, he seemed deep in his own thoughts, so I got up and took the tea glasses into the kitchen.

The *papakh* lurked in the corner, hidden under the tea cloth. I couldn't bear to look at it. I wished I could have shown it more respect, I knew it had been worn until today by someone who was now dead, and who'd been tossed away in the open, like so much rubbish. I found it obscene.

Arash had already gone to bed when I went back in to tidy the cushions, and I followed him up. Neither of us slept.

*

The convoy went past at six as usual, but unlike yesterday, we were both in bed, awake. Arash got up, saying he was going in to work, he needed to keep things normal. I resisted picking up on 'normal' – my anxiety would make it come out wrong. At least take a taxi, I said. No, he said, he needed to walk, but he promised to keep to the main route. I got up with him and he seemed content for once to sit and let me fuss about, slicing lemons for his tea, making coffee for me. The *papakh* was on the corner table where we'd left it, with the tea cloth over it. He uncovered it, but didn't pick it up.

'When I get back,' he said, 'we'll go to the bazaar – see Ervand. He might know something. Someone might be missing him.' He left, his shoulders stooped, his head down.

Anna came into the kitchen and took a step back, as she saw the *papakh* uncovered in the corner. 'What are you going to do with it?' she said, pulling a face.

I drank my coffee, stared at the hat, came to a decision. I'd take it to Ervand myself, find out what I could. It would please Arash. I put the hat into a plastic bag, then hid it in my shoulder satchel under some Rumi books. I felt a pulse of excitement on doing this, then a skitter of nerves. If I was stopped, I'd no idea how I'd explain the *papakh* under the poetry.

Ervand was surprised to see me – it was the first time I'd visited him without Arash – but he gave me a warm handshake and guided me through a beaded curtain into the small office at the back. It was warmer here, he said.

I'd not been in the back before. It occurred to me he might not like to be seen in the *raasteh* with a Westerner, given the current climate. But then again, he was right – it was warmer and cosier in the back, so maybe I was being too sensitive. There was an Aladdin paraffin heater in the corner, two small tub chairs and a brass table. We chatted about this and that, he asked after Reza and told me to tell him to visit him. The lanky lad soon appeared with tea and sweets, then disappeared again to tend the stall.

After a suitable time spent on the pleasantries, I rummaged

in my shoulder satchel and brought out the plastic bag. 'I have something to show you, something Arash found yesterday.' I passed it over the brass table and watched him as he peered inside. His face was impassive. I told him the story of Arash finding the body and asked if he'd heard anything.

He was clearly shocked. 'Is Arash OK?'

'A bit shaken.'

He gave me a long look. He didn't mention the hat in the bag. Instead he told me about his sister's children, twin girls aged seven, and a son, aged five. Last week, they were playing in the courtyard of their house with the next-door neighbour's children. They played the circle game of the Chain Weaver Uncle, who weaves chains of friendship for children. He and his brother, Ervand said, used to play the very same game when they were little.

In this game, they sing the song about the day the Chain Weaver Uncle does not come to see them. The children are worried about him, so they bring him presents and clasp each other's hands to make their own chain as a present for him. The children in Ervand's courtyard joined hands and chose his nephew to go into the centre of the circle. They all danced round him, singing this song. The next day, the neighbour's children came round again to play, but said their father heard them singing and told them they shouldn't be singing songs about making chains and they shouldn't be making themselves into chains and putting chains around people. People should be free. They should not sing songs like that again. And, their father said they must remember: 'The walls have mice and the mice have ears.'

Ervand told me this story, shaking his head in a kids-will-be-kids sort of way, his fingers tapping the bag with the *papakh* hat in it. Then he gave the bag back to me.

Even in the bazaar, it seems, even in our great beehive of gossip, fear has struck everyone selectively dumb.

I got home, put the *papakh* hat back on the table and poured a vodka.

When Arash came home, I told him about going to see Ervand,

and his story about the Chain Weaver Uncle. He said that was kind of me. He'd been thinking he couldn't really face the bazaar. Said it was typical of Ervand to speak in riddles, but he thought it meant we shouldn't take the matter any further. That wouldn't be difficult, he said. He'd thought of nothing but the body all day, but he didn't dare go back to the wasteland to check if it was still there. He put the hat into the plastic bag. Said he'd take it to his house tomorrow. No point leaving it here. Anna will be pleased, I said. He was tired, he said, he'd have an early night. I went too. We were both awake again through the night, but didn't talk to each other.

Friday, 15 September

It's the official end of summer this weekend. People should be out and about, although we Westerners are now more wary of being out around the time of Friday prayers and afterwards. But no one was around today. Julia rang this lunchtime to tell us that, earlier this morning, three men in military uniform had opened fire on an army unit in Tabriz. The rumour is that one civilian, six soldiers and two of the gunmen were killed. The gunmen were terrorists.

'No more solo trips to the library, Arash,' I said, my voice sounding surprisingly firm. 'We've got terrorists on street corners in Tabriz now, picking people off.'

He nodded. He looked absolutely defeated.

I felt an actual lurch in my heart – it hurt so much to see him suffering. He was sitting on the floor cushions, his back against the wall, and he closed his eyes, as if he wanted to shut the world out. Maybe shut me out.

I went across to him, sat down beside him and took his hand.

'It's been a hell of a week.' I spoke to him quietly. 'Hard to make sense of what's happening.'

'Killing each other. It's not the way. I want change too, the country's in a mess, but going out on the streets and killing each other won't achieve anything. I grew up in this city, Damian, it's my home, and bit by bit it's being destroyed from within by its own people. It fills me full of dread.'

'You're exhausted. Come on, let's go for a rest.'

I took his hand and led him upstairs. We lay on the bed, hands clasped, watching a troubled Tabrizi cloudscape struggle across the sky.

I turned to him and stroked his face. 'It'll be all right, my love. We'll see it through together.'

A single tear escaped from the corner of his eye.

'We're living on the lip of oblivion,' he whispered.

And all I could do was hold him close to my body, like a lute.

Part Three

Strange Times, My Dear

Damian

Kupfermühle, 12 March

I remember the rest of that September, after Black Friday, and all of October 1978, as being a vicious circle of ever-increasing threat. Demonstrations and mass defiance by various groups on the streets, leading to government repression. More public defiance, followed by a change in tack by the government, with attempts to placate some sectors by relaxing censorship, promising elections, releasing prisoners. More demonstrations and strikes across all sectors – from blue-collar workers to professional and administrative personnel.

I remember Anna making a list of those who went on strike: workers in hospitals, radio and television, banks, power plants, telecoms, postal service, public transport, steel industries, universities, schools and civil service. Even the newspaper employees took strike action, followed by the printers. And, most important of all, the one sector we all thought would bring down the whole country if it ever went on strike – the oil industry. It began to flex its muscles in late September when ten thousand came out on strike. But the really significant move came on 31 October. The National Iranian Oil Company saw thirty-seven thousand employees walk out over wages and political demands, which brought the oil industry to a virtual standstill. The next day, Iran Air, another Iranian flagship business, followed suit.

By the end of September, Anna was saying it would be easier to list who wasn't on strike.

I remember mostly the relentlessness of the tension. The ratcheting up, sometimes daily, of more demonstrations, then more tightening of the screws by the government. Students tried to topple a statue of the Shah. Troops fired on the students. Students took to the streets demonstrating against the actions of the troops. More troops were stationed on the streets. Students moved on, finding something else to demonstrate about or destroy.

Round and round we go, as Arash would say.

I've made it sound as though I was totally wrapped up in the politics of the place.

I wasn't. I was only interested in what was going on in so far as it affected me directly. Or, rather, affected myself and Arash. I couldn't have cared less about what was happening to the country. All I wanted to do was to help Arash through the worst of it. Keep him safe. Get him out, if it came to it. But he wouldn't be helped. He became more withdrawn and morose.

I would take myself away into a quiet corner, noting things down, trying to process what was happening, thinking it would help me distance myself from events in some way. The violence and chaos had become very real after the February riots in Tabriz – they'd taken place only half a mile from us – you couldn't ignore them. But the horror of Black Friday in September was of a different magnitude altogether. To think of troops machine-gunning men, women and children, and in such numbers, whatever the casualty totals turned out to be – that was chilling. It felt to me as though the violence had gone to a new level. Not only that, the protests and demonstrations had reached a point of no return. There was an inevitability about the upheaval and chaos to come.

I found it almost impossible to write about in detail. Living through it, and being able to describe it and understand what was going on, were very different things. Most times I could barely bring myself to write the date, and a bare outline of what I thought had happened – and that was the other problem: communications were so bad by then, you were never sure of what had really happened anyway, and rumour took over once more. Like Reza, I began to preface so much of what I wrote with 'Rumour said that . . .'

Julia had a direct line to the embassy in Tehran, of course, and relayed information to us, so that helped, but she was always brief. She told us strictly what we needed to know in order to avoid trouble, and never gave much detail. Looking back, I guess she'd been told not to panic us more than necessary or we'd be demanding to go home, like the Americans had already started to do.

Anna seemed to have had the same problem as me with her memoir. She abandoned it, except for a few entries, scattered over the months. She'd not been the same after Reza left. I think she liked him more than she would admit to herself.

So, all I have are our scrambled thoughts, our scribbled jottings and our occasionally more detailed comments. There are gaps. There are half-memories or shadows of memories, or images on the edge of my remembering that I just can't retrieve. It lacks factual detail, or what detail there is may not be accurate. But as I've written it here, I think it gives a level of insight into the state of our minds, which were distracted, and the state of our hearts, which were slowly breaking.

So, I've woven our accounts together, the threads are uneven, but it's the best I can do. Arash would probably call it a *Sufi Weave*, or something equally delicate. It doesn't feel delicate to me. It feels desperate.

*

Damian

Tabriz, 5 November

Is Good

Winter in Tabriz came suddenly yesterday, when the first hard snow fell. It was my turn to pick up the mail and the vodka so I was wearing the poacher's coat. It was Anna's down-padded parka, inconspicuous brown with an oversized fur-trimmed hood so she could keep her head covered. I always borrow it for the vodka run – the inside pocket is just the right size for two bottles, which are risky to be caught with now they've started burning down the liquor stores. I checked the pocket, made sure Anna's woolly mittens were there, then stepped outside. The snow boys had already cleared the roofs and shovelled a path down the middle of the *kucheh*. Piles of dirty slush lay refreezing against the walls, leaving just enough room to walk single file. No problem this morning, there was only me around.

Right or left? Ali the Baker, or Ali the Vodka?

Right takes me through the archway to Ali the Baker, then on to the boulevard and straight to the British Council. Left takes me further into the labyrinth, to Ali the Vodka, then out at the back of the Council, avoiding the boulevard altogether. Not strictly a labyrinth, Arash insists, there's more than one entrance, but the result is the same – I always get pleasurably lost.

Go right, I decided, bread first, swift visit to the Council, then back for the vodka.

The small ogival window set into the top of the arch was shuttered. I used to like that window, the shape of it, the strength of it, the poplar frame, grey and splitting. Now, whenever I looked up, I saw it as a good spot for watching the comings and goings in the *kucheh* and not be seen.

Ali the Baker and his son were lifting the next batch of *barbari* bread on large paddles into the clay oven, then slapping the dough onto the sides. The son ignored me. Ali served me and, as usual, practised his English. 'Is good, Mr Damian, is good.' His face reminded me of a Dürer woodcut, the lines breaking up briefly as he smiled.

'Is good,' I said – not sure whether he meant 'is good' because it's been relatively quiet so he can open and sell his bread, or the current civil protest is good, or even the Shah is good. Or maybe he just meant the bread is good. I bent the oval *barbari* to fit into my shoulder satchel and slung the bag across my chest so I could breathe in the smell of warm sesame seed.

Out onto the boulevard. Cars were travelling both ways in the middle to avoid the compacted snow at the sides of the road. Not much traffic. A few Datsun pickups loaded with thin sacks of vegetables, but mainly it was grey Paycan taxis, not enough of them on the road any more to jam up the flow. No one out on the streets now unless they have to be. A couple of people passed me coming from the opposite direction, their heads down as they picked their way through the snow. No one looked me in the face. If you look at people, you're obliged to speak. If you speak, you don't know who's listening. So no one looks at anyone any more. We've all learned to glide round each other's space, like we're using sonar.

I felt the vibration under my feet before I heard them. From the direction of the barracks, a convoy appeared: three huge camouflaged tanks. They tagged onto the string of Paycans. The cars edged to the side, bumping over snow piles, wheels mounting the path. The tanks didn't slow down, and once they'd rumbled past, both streams of traffic dodgemed each other back to the middle.

The warm bread smell from my bag was masked by the fumes of burning diesel.

At the Council, there was no mail. It's got less frequent. They say the hold-up is in Tehran. I headed out towards the side entrance, creeping past Julia's office, when, of course, out she popped.

'Damian!' She peered at me over her wire rims.

'Julia.'

'How goes it?'

The mixture of diplomat-bland and campus bonhomie doesn't usually bother me, but the tanks must have rattled me more than I knew. I took the bait.

'How goes it? It does not go good, Julia. It definitely does not go good.'

'How so?'

'How so? Let me see,' I said. 'How about the charade of turning up for work?'

She blinked.

'Getting ourselves there, checking in, finding no students, having SAVAK peer at us through a little window in the door, then checking out, coming home, facing the whole thing again the next time we're forced to go up there.' I was warming to the theme now. 'If the ambassador wasn't so shit scared of admitting the Shah was on his way out, we could all pack up and go home. Does that tell you "how so"?'

'Damian, you really shouldn't talk about the ambassador like that.' She put her hand on my arm and slid into that low-voiced I'm-making-a-very-serious-point-here tone of hers. 'We must keep going, Damian . . . we must fly the flag.' She went into her office, turning back and muttering, 'Fly the flag,' but she was frowning again. Making Julia frown was strangely satisfying.

I headed off into the labyrinth, aiming straight for Ali the Vodka, then home. No point taking my time wandering now, the mood had gone. Fly the fucking flag.

Ali the Vodka sells mostly groceries. In the back, there are plastic barrels of yoghurt and honey from the mountains, sold by the bowlful. And Stoli hidden in sacks of lentils. It's strictly business with Ali. Vodka passes one way, rials the other. No smile, no English practice. I put the bottles into the poacher's pocket, covering their necks and shoulders with Anna's mittens so they didn't clink.

At home, I buried a vodka bottle in a plastic bucket full of snow, fixed to the kitchen windowsill outside, and waited for Anna and Arash to get back.

*

Anna and I were sitting on the floor cushions, me on the first vodka of the new bottle, when we had a phone call from Julia. The British Embassy in Tehran had been set on fire. We were to stay indoors until further notice.

It was 5 November. The irony.

'Nowhere to fly the fucking flag from now,' I said, topping up my glass.

Arash brought a tray in from the kitchen. 'We're safe enough here,' he said, passing Anna a glass of tea. 'Kucheh Mulla is very safe.' He mouthed at me to put some music on.

Anna looked pale and her hands shook a little as she held the glass to her lips.

6 November

Morning. Julia rang. The whole of the Shah's civilian cabinet resigned yesterday. The Shah has installed a military government, under General Azhari. The general's first actions were to impose national martial law, curfew and newspaper censorship.

'Stay in, or if you have to go out, take the necessary precautions,' said Julia, briskly. 'The curfew is from nine p.m. until five a.m. There may be electricity cuts from eight thirty p.m. so it would be sensible for you to aim to be inside by eight.'

Evening. The Shah gave a speech to the nation this afternoon, on TV and radio.

'The revolution of the Iranian people cannot fail to have my support as the monarch of Iran and as an Iranian . . . I heard the revolutionary message of you the people, the Iranian nation. I am the guardian of the constitutional monarchy which is a God-given gift. A gift entrusted to the Shah by the people . . .'.

'Strange it should be the Shah who first mentions the word "revolution",' Arash said.

10 November

We heard via Ervand that the government has arrested some of its own former officials and other businessmen on charges of corruption, including former Prime Minister Hoveida, who had left office last year, after twelve years, just before I arrived in Tabriz. Also arrested was the head of SAVAK, General Nasiri.

'Ervand thinks they're rounding up a few scapegoats,' Arash said, 'but Nasiri is no scapegoat. He would have been in charge when they took Mirza.'

A hard look I'd never seen before came across his face. I found myself thinking of Baraheni and the 'Shadow of God' poems, and shuddered.

*

Anna

20 November

Bach and the Chelow Kabab

'That's new.' I jinked my head towards the university gate as we walked up the boulevard.

A tank was parked to the side of it. It must have appeared overnight because the news of tanks parked in particular places spreads like wildfire. It was probably sent there in anticipation of the holy month of Muharram, which begins on a Saturday this year, 2 December.

The tank's gun was pointed in our direction, but tilted upwards into the sky. The fresh snowfall blurred the lines of its turret and barrel, softening it into a mound of vanilla ice cream with a long-handled spoon stuck in it. But it was still a tank.

An armed guard slouched against the side entrance gate, looking bored. He took his time over a last drag on a cigarette, then ground the stub into the concrete with the toe of his boot. Damian and I slowed down a few yards in front of him, and turned to each other for what we hoped looked like a friendly chat.

Damian patted my arm. 'No point going any further,' he said, smiling at me as though he'd cracked a joke. 'That tank could mean they're expecting trouble. Time to go.'

We turned and walked back down the boulevard, the trees on either side of us dripping snow in the brief midday thaw.

'I don't think we'll be coming back here to check in any more,' I said. 'Even Julia can't expect us to negotiate with tanks.'

Damian seemed not to hear. 'I can't stop thinking about the prof,' he said. 'Poor old sod. Trying to carry on like nothing was happening. Just like Arash still does.' He sounded weary.

We walked on, Damian lost in thought, me remembering last week, and the day we went with the prof to the Club. I know Damian had grown fond of him. They'd done a joint reading of Hafez at the Council back in October, and the prof had charmed the socks off everyone. Damian introduced us, and it turned out we had mutual acquaintances at Wadham. I wondered if I should mention Princess Ashraf's visit, but thought better of it. I didn't want to spoil the evening with politics.

He'd invited us to lunch in the professors' dining room, unofficially known as the Club, because it saw itself as exclusive and was where visitors were taken. It served the same food as everywhere else but the ambience was more refined, with piped music – the diners could bring their own cassettes to play over the system. It had stayed open sporadically, even though there were few diners left. I guess it was jobs for the cooks in the kitchens.

The prof was determined we should celebrate Christmas, even though it was more than six weeks away. 'You can still get a half-decent meal at the Club, and goodness knows when it will be open again,' he said. 'We'll just have to squeeze in between strikes and the demonstrations and the martial law and whatever else.' He tried to sound jovial, but it rang hollow. He headed for the top table, usually reserved for professors and their important visitors, but now anyone could sit there. A few of the other seats at the end were occupied, all men, I noticed: women had virtually disappeared off the campus in the past few weeks. A picture window ran the length of the eating area, so we could see out onto the terrace, with its frozen fountain and a rough-cut copy of a Persepolis frieze, done in concrete, stretching down the side wall.

There was also an addition to the view. An armoured car was parked on the path at the side of the terrace, a driver sitting in the front, his cap pulled down over his eyes.

'Cheers!' said the prof, in his best Oxford accent, clinking his orange juice against mine and Damian's.

'And thanks for the Bach.' I raised my glass to him.

He'd found out from Damian that I liked the Brandenburgs, so he'd organised them for the piped music. The First Concerto set off, the hunting horns calling to each other in little trills and motifs, as we'd arrived back from self-service with our *chelow kabab*. It was *chelow kabab* at the university most days, wherever you were eating, plain rice and spiced lamb, although the lamb had become scarcer over the past weeks.

The man came tearing onto the terrace just as I took my first forkful. Two others raced after him, slowing down when they realised he had no way out. They weren't in uniform but they had that SAVAK sureness about them, almost casual as they watched him panic.

He ran up to the window, bouncing against it like a daddy-long-legs. He was young and he was terrified.

'Isn't that —?' Damian broke off as the prof put his finger to his lips, shaking his head.

The two men plucked the man away from the window and threw him to the ground. One pinned him down with a boot across his shoulder blades, the other hammered the back of his legs with his baton until his body squirmed down into the snow. Then they dragged him towards the car, leaving a trail of blood-spotted zigzags behind. They threw him into the back and got in with him. The driver had watched all this and already had the engine running. The car sped off towards the back entrance of the campus.

It was like watching a clip from an Eisenstein film, a soundless violent snow scene outside, while inside the buzz of conversation slowly ebbed away and the hunting horn ended the first movement of the Brandenburg in triumph. A moment of total silence, then the Menuetto echoed round, its silken, ordered music assuring us that all was well.

I could feel Damian trembling. The prof leaned over and patted my hand. I didn't know if it was his hand or mine that was ice cold. 'Go home,' he said.

'They won't let us,' I said dully. I was thinking 'home' as in the UK. 'The embassy says we have to stay and ride it out.'

'I mean go home now. Get off the campus.'

We learned later that there were big demonstrations, some starting from the campus and heading into town, in solidarity with other marches in other cities, against the martial law and the curfew.

Damian went back to the university a couple of days later to check in. It was closed again, probably for good this time.

The prof disappeared the day after our lunch. He'd decamped to Tehran for 'a few weeks' research', taking his family with him. Iran Air had just returned to work from their strike, so it was easier to get to Tehran before they went on strike again, then for the prof and his family to make their way out of the country. He must have taken his chances. Rumour said he was in Paris.

'So it wasn't about Christmas, it was about him saying goodbye,' Damian said, when he heard about the prof's 'holiday'. He looked so crestfallen.

Maziar was the student Damian had recognised who'd been beaten by the SAVAK men. He was one of the prof's protégés, a promising poet. We learned later that he'd disappeared too. But no one knew where they'd taken him.

I stopped and looked back at the university gates. The guard had taken up his position again, propping up the archway.

'People we know are starting to disappear.' It was the first time I'd said it out loud. Damian didn't answer, just quickened his pace, and I had to run to catch him up.

Friday, 24 November

Doorways

Damian went to Tehran this weekend. He didn't tell Arash what he was up to, other than that he needed to check his Irish passport and meet up with an English poet the prof had been in contact with to discuss his translations. But he told me he wanted to go round the embassies to see if any study visas were still going for Arash. I wasn't to say anything. That's how some Iranians are getting out, arranging study trips. It's a farce, everyone says so, but if you know the right people, or pay enough, they turn a blind eye. I'm not sure Damian knows the right people. But he has an Irish passport as well as a British one – comes in handy, he says, and hopes it might influence the Americans or the French.

Arash dropped him off at the airport on Friday morning in Ervand's truck, then came back. He said we could go to Kandovan and see the troglodyte village – we might not be able to get through if we left it much later, what with the weather and the political situation. Damian was going to be away until Monday, and Arash was restless – they'd not been apart since Damian came to Tabriz.

Arash said he felt it was too much of a risk for him to stay over to keep me company. 'It might damage your reputation,' he said. 'The neighbours might talk, a single Iranian man with a Western woman in a house known to be for Western foreigners only.' He can be so proper sometimes – I find it quite endearing. So the plan was to spend the day out together, then both be in our own separate houses at night. I'd be safe enough on my own. The neighbours down the *kucheh* would keep an eye on me, I gave their two daughters extra English lessons at the Council, from time to time. It was their house where I'd seen the cat on my second day here.

We drove through the outskirts of Tabriz, leaving the last of the scrappy buildings behind, and began to pass men herding flat-tailed sheep. The men scowled at us and flapped their sticks, making the animals stumble to the sides of the road, bleating and complaining. But it made me smile, the ordinariness of shepherds and their sheep negotiating traffic.

I gradually noticed my breathing had changed. It seemed to be slower. I must have been breathing short and shallow in Tabriz, as if I didn't want to take in what was going on around me. Slower, longer breaths made me light-headed.

We took the Osku Chai valley route, on a zigzag road with steep, rocky sides. About halfway there, we rounded a bend and the land gradually flattened out. To the side of me there was a horizon. Not much of a horizon, but to see one at all took me by surprise. A hummocky strip, pimpled with the odd rock poking through gritty snow, rolled to meet the smoother, blue-washed snow in the foothills of the mountains. But there was such a sense of space, of the landscape stretching on and away, that I found myself wondering when I had last stretched – physically stretched – my arms, my back, my body, upwards and outwards.

I suddenly felt heavy. Drained.

'Do you think we could stop for moment?' I said.

'Sure,' said Arash. He looked at me. 'It'll be good to get some fresh air.'

We stopped on a slight rise where we could look down at the Osku river.

On the sides of the slope, poplar trees rose through the snow, thin-stemmed, their bare branches feathered upwards against the ice-blue sky. Down by the water, some women were doing their washing, a splash of colour in their bright chadors, red and blue patterned, not the usual Tabrizi black.

We stood and watched them for a while, Arash taking photos. Their hands flashed yellow as they dipped and wrung out the clothes. I couldn't work out what the yellow was, then realised it was their washing-up gloves, giving a little modern protection against the cold.

A few donkeys were drinking downstream. The women took off their gloves to load the clothes into woven baskets slung across the donkeys' backs, and began to make their way slowly up the winding path, hanging on to the baskets as the path got steeper. From time to time, the woman leading them stopped, shouting down to the stragglers at the back, then she'd look ahead, get her bearings again and trudge on, strong and steady.

I looked up at the sky. When had I last got my bearings? When had I last looked up, really looked up, above the narrow walls of the *kuchehs*? Shown my face to the sky?

And I admitted to myself for the first time that although I was OK when I was in the house in Kucheh Mulla with Damian and Arash, I was beginning to feel scared in Tabriz. My world has become small and limited. My days consist of walking to the British Council for work and then coming home. The university is closed now, so Farzad and the others come to the Council to talk about their translations. I've not wandered into town on my own since Black Friday. In the evenings, I've tended to stay in my room after we've eaten, reading or listening to music. I can't enjoy the Brandenburgs anymore, it reminds me of the student bashing himself against the Club window and zigzags of blood in the snow. And I miss Reza, more than I care to admit.

I'm not just scared. I've allowed myself to be intimidated. I've got into the habit of wearing shapeless clothes, of pulling my hood as far forward as it will go so it flops over my eyes, of walking with my shoulders hunched, head down, hands in my pockets. It's as though I'm trying to make my body invisible. It feels like I've diminished, not just emotionally, but physically.

I stood there, watching the women struggling up the river path, turning all this over in my mind. And for the first time in months, I thought of my father. What he might say to me to help me through. He'd faded from the front of my memory during the summer, but he was suddenly back again. I could feel his presence. Then, just as suddenly, he disappeared.

I began to choke up. Arash put his arm round me. 'Breathe,' he said. 'Just breathe.'

I took in great gulps of air, the cold needling my nose. I turned into his shoulder and began to weep. 'I'm sorry,' I said, 'it must be getting out of Tabriz . . . I hadn't realised . . .'

There was a moment, standing there with my head against Arash's shoulder, when I could have wept and wept.

The woman leading the others up the slope shouted at us. She'd reached the top of the path with her donkey and had seen us. Must have thought we were kissing. I hadn't a clue what she was shouting, but it was enough for me to break away from Arash. He waved to her. She didn't wave back. The rest of them slowly reached the top and headed off down the road.

The idea of the woman maybe thinking we were lovers and chastising us from a distance made us both smile and broke the tension within me. I began to feel slightly better.

'Are you OK? You still want to go on?' Arash said.

'Yes.' We got back into the car and followed the women.

The landscape began to change again. Along the roadside, tall conical rocks appeared, standing like sentinels, some pitted with small natural holes, others with holes large enough for people to walk through. We rounded the bend and there was Kandovan, with Mount Sahand in the distance. The whole village had the look of a giant termite colony growing organically out of the volcanic rock. But the rock cones were the roofs of houses and the holes were doors and windows.

We were the only visitors. Arash parked the car at the bottom of the houses and we clambered up steps hewn out of the rock until we got to a cave with a slatted wooden door set into it and a porch above made of a flat stone slab, covered with grass. Arash called and a young man came out. He grinned at Arash and ignored me, although I caught him looking at me from the corner of his eye. He was a friend of Ervand's, and he showed us round, Arash translating for me. He was proud of the village – the houses were cool in summer and warm in winter, he said, and they faced south to the best of the sun. Most of them were two storeys, animals on the bottom floor, families on the top.

We wandered around taking photos. No one took much notice.

There was a sense of quiet permanency about the place. It had been there for hundreds of years and always would be, whatever happened round it. If the people there now had to leave, someone else would take their place and live in the rocks, make themselves at one with the landscape. My father would have loved this place. *One to treasure.* Thinking this soothed me in a strange sort of way.

Late afternoon, we headed back to Tabriz. Not many people about. As we passed the bank near the centre of town, Arash slowed down and waited for the car behind to pass, then reversed back up the street.

'Look at that!' He pointed to the bank entrance.

A man was putting the finishing touches to the top layer of a wall of breeze blocks cemented into the doorway. It took me a while to adjust to what I was seeing.

'They've blocked up the entrance to the bank,' I said, as much to myself as to Arash.

'It won't stop them if they decide to burn it down,' said Arash. 'It didn't last time.'

I took a photo quickly – you never knew who would be watching.

*

Monday, 27 November

Damian got back this afternoon. He looked wretched. No luck with the study-visa idea. They've closed the visa sections in all of the embassies for everyone except their own nationals. He told Arash he'd sorted out his passport and met the English poet, who was sad to hear about the prof, but said he was leaving too, as soon as he could get a flight.

Arash nodded, but didn't offer any comments about people leaving. He'd picked up the photos of Kandovan from Ali the Vodka. It still amazes me, the way life seems to go on as normal here – bread still gets baked, the local Pepsi delivery man still comes to the shops with crates balanced on his handlebars, and Ali the Vodka still manages a two-day development service on snapshots. Arash gave him the film on Saturday morning and got the prints back today, in a well-used yellow Kodak wallet. Better service than a Boots 'Speedy Special'.

We make a point of having little tea ceremonies now, when we have letters or photos to share. We buy honeycomb from Ali's and treats from the Pahlavi patisserie, then make tea, sit round the table, and share what we've got.

This time there were no patisserie treats but there was honeycomb from Kandovan, bought from the man who'd guided us round. Arash had been particularly pleased with it because it was brood honeycomb, the best he reckoned. It was a rich brown, not the usual golden honey colour. 'The baby bees go through it, so it's the last to be harvested. It's laden with pollen and keeps through the winter. Good for sore throats.'

Damian had warmed some flatbread and spread the honeycomb on it, biting into it and making exaggerated yum-yum-yum noises.

Arash took a piece of crumbled honeycomb from the plate and popped it into his mouth. 'That is *sooo* good,' he said.

I tried a piece too. Nutty and sweet at the same time, followed by a slight waxy taste.

Arash saw me frowning. 'You've hit the wax?' he said. 'You get used to it. Or you can spit it out.'

'I'll try to get used to it,' I said.

Damian picked at a small crumb of it on the plate, and pointed to a photo of me. 'You look like you're in one of those "intrepid explorer" spreads that *National Geographic* do.'

Arash had taken it while I was standing outside the small wooden door built into the house in the rock. The door is half-size, probably leading to a byre for the animals. It's set low down and the top is level with my waist. I look like a giant. I'm muffled up to my nose with a long scarf and down to my eyes with my parka hood pulled over.

The two photos of the Kandovan cave door and the bank with the bricked-up doorway lay side by side on the table. The bank looked like a bizarre reverse of the cave house. The concrete door filling the entrance was framed by wood either side, where they'd nailed rough planks across the windows, while the wooden door of the Kandovan house was framed in rock.

'That was a good day,' said Arash.

'Yes,' I said, but I was thinking back to when we'd stopped on the road to Kandovan to watch the women washing by the river, and how miserable I'd felt, when my father came back, then left me.

Later that evening, we all went up on the roof to look at the moon. There had been a rumour circulating that an old lady in Qom had been visited by an apparition, who told her that Ayatollah Khomeini's face would be visible on the next full moon, which was tonight. But it would be visible only to believers.

'Tehran was buzzing with it,' Damian said. 'All sorts of people you wouldn't think would believe in it – even some of the English poet's friends, who are lecturers, and the like.'

We stared for ages, feeling foolish to be going along with it – at least I was. The moon was obligingly large and full, against a star-dusted sky, but I couldn't see anything other than the face you can always see, which someone once told me was formed by dark splotches of lunar lava.

'I see no Ayatollah!' said Damian, making a telescope with his curled fingers and looking through them, aware that Arash wasn't joining in with our moon-gazing. 'But, then, I'm not a believer.'

'How could people be so gullible?' Arash sounded exasperated.

The next morning, he came home from a visit to Ervand to say the bazaar was buzzing with the rumour that the old lady's prophecy had been made up by the government, to ridicule Islam and make its followers appear backward-looking and riddled with superstition.

*

Tuesday, 28 November
Reza is back. Arrived 8 a.m. this morning. Unannounced. He was supposed to be coming next week, according to Arash. I didn't think he'd come back at all. We haven't been in touch all the time he's been away. Arash was in tears to see him. Even Damian cracked a smile. Whatever else Reza is, you immediately feel less insecure when he is around. He's a fixer. He can get things done and knows so many people.

He took me aside in the kitchen. He had a little present for me, he said. 'Do you remember up on the roof when I asked you where you would like to go in Iran, if you could?'

How could I forget, I thought. A sultry summer night, sex, and the only time he hinted there could be a future for us. But I played it cool. 'Do you mean when I said Persepolis?'

'Correct. Persepolis.' He hesitated, then grinned and said, 'Do you still want to go?'

It's incredible! He's managed to get us a flight – Iran Air will probably go back on strike again quite soon, so it's now or never. He has contacts who work for the airline, so he's wangled tickets for us to fly to Shiraz. I can't believe it. In the midst of all this chaos and gloom, we're going on a short cultural break! And by 'we' I mean all of us, Damian and Arash too.

I reminded him about the holy month of Muharram coming up, starting this Saturday, and the difficult security situation that will create. 'We'd have to be back home by Friday, at the latest, and I'd prefer to be back Thursday. I don't think we should be out round Friday prayers, especially this week. So how can we manage it?'

'It'll be a quick visit,' he said, 'just there and back to Shiraz in two days. Fly down lunchtime today, be there by the early evening and stay over. I've booked the hotel in Shiraz. Spend tomorrow at Persepolis, stay over in Shiraz, fly back early on Thursday.'

For the Shiraz hotel, we are once again assuming the mantle of the 'alibi four', as Reza calls it. Damian and I are the Western boyfriend and girlfriend, single rooms of course.

Like we did to get into the American Consulate grounds last summer.

Was it really only six months ago that we were there, the 'alibi four', watching people splashing around in the pool, Reza and I sitting as close to each other as we dared, knowing we had a long lazy day and night ahead of us? But it's so different between us now. I wasn't aware I still had a relationship with him. It was supposed to be bounded, finishing with the summer. Not sure I want to open all that up again. It would be so easy to spoil the memory. But then again, it is Persepolis.

Wednesday, 29 November

Persepolis Blue

I ran my hand over a line of carved Cappadocians, their stone flesh warmed by the brittle November sun. Arash was behind me, scribbling in his notebook. Damian was following him, clicking away, determined to photograph everything. Reza was

288

ahead of me and turned round, his face in three-quarter profile, looking like he could have stepped down from the Apadana frieze.

He smiled at me, then went back to refocusing his Nikon.

We were the only people on the whole site. I had this sudden pinch-me moment. Here I was, at Persepolis. This time two Novembers ago, I'd found it difficult even to get out of bed and face another dreary day in Oxford.

'You seem dazed,' Reza said, waiting for me to catch him up.

'This place . . . it makes my head spin.' My finger traced the fold of a Persian's fluted crown, at least 2,500 years old. 'I came out to Iran thinking I'd find Persia. But all I've found is Iran, till now.' Dust motes disturbed by my touch floated in the sunlight.

'Don't let it fool you too much.' Reza leaned casually against the Cappadocians while he adjusted his lens again. 'All of this lot had to pay tribute to an emperor, just like our present shah demands, remember. This one just happened to be Darius.'

Damian and Arash caught us up. Arash nudged his glasses up his nose and peered closely at the frieze to examine a lock of curled hair delicately chiselled behind the ear of an Assyrian. He started scribbling again.

I heard a click from Reza. Then he replaced the lens cap and put the camera into his bag. 'Come on,' he said to Arash. 'Let's show these two how our Shah of Shahs got the rich and famous to pay homage.' He set off towards the western edge of the site.

*

'Behold Tent City.' Reza gestured towards the area in front of us. 'This is where the Shah held his 1971 celebrations. Two thousand five hundred years of monarchy in the Persian Empire, dating from Cyrus the Great, and deliberately linked to the thirty years' anniversary of the Shah's Peacock Throne.'

I'd been expecting something like Firuzeh's *Shahnameh* miniature – medieval fantasy tents with scalloped edging and fluttering pennants. All I could see, spread out below, were clusters of carousel-shaped structures, metal ribbed and rusting, stretched out within the outline of a five-point star, and connected with crumbling concrete walkways.

'That's it? That's Tent City?' I said.

'The whole thing was an illusion.' Reza swept his arm over the site like a ringmaster. 'They're prefabs – steel skeletons. Shah-style prefabs, mind you – kitted out with gold-plated taps, marble floors, Persian rugs. And, a thoughtful detail, given the kind of guests who'd be staying, the windows in the tents were bulletproof. They draped the outsides in blue and gold fabric so they looked like tents. And, of course, they laid on a casino, and a nine-hole golf course with grass imported from France, in case the great and the good got bored.'

'Sounds as vulgar as anything Darius ever did to show off his power,' I said.

'That was the point, the Shah showing off his power.' Reza nodded. 'To start off the proceedings, he gave a speech, linking himself to Cyrus the Great: "Sleep easily, Cyrus, for we are awake, and we will always be awake."' He paused for a moment. 'Big mistake, that, likening himself to Cyrus and saying he was awake – it left him open to ridicule, especially now it's obvious he's anything but awake to the problems he's facing and what his people really think of him.'

He set off again, exaggerating his air of incredulity, sending up his own commentary.

'Can you believe it? A hundred million dollars' worth of pure Hollywood – some say three hundred million. Who knows? It out-DeMilled Cecil B. De Mille. A banquet, then a *son et lumière,* and a fireworks show – when, incidentally, the lights failed and everyone thought it was a terrorist attack. That must have been fun to see, some of the world's richest and most influential panicking and fleeing for cover. Next day, the guests were treated to an interminable pageant, supposedly representing Iran's history since 500 BC. Oxen pulling imitation battlements, camels, horses, chariots, ships in full sail on motorised trailers, all passed by. Thousands of his actual army came next, in over-the-top ancient costumes and huge false beards – they'd been ordered to grow their own beards, but they weren't long or thick enough. They were meant to be tribute bearers off the Apadana frieze – what would your classics mistress have thought of that, Anna?'

He was in full flow now, always at his acerbic best with the Shah in his sights.

'The French made a packet. Jansen designed the "tents", Maxim's supplied all the food, Lanvin designed the court uniforms. What was it they said about the French, Arash?'

'They supplied the champagne, the chefs and the chiffon.' Arash laughed, but then grew serious again. 'They all played the game,' he said. 'The French, the British, the Americans, they all came to pay false homage, then went home with their oil and arms contracts.'

It was strange to hear Arash talking politics, as if he'd suddenly put on a shirt that wasn't his colour. I noticed the surprised look on Damian's face.

'I bet no one back in 1971 thought it would end up like it is now,' I said.

Arash shook his head. 'Cyrus. Darius. The Shah. All emperors think they're invincible.'

A bird, big enough to be a buzzard, circled high above, its eye probably on some small creature scuttling among the prefabs below.

'What will you do if the Shah falls?' As soon as I said it, I wished I could stuff the words back.

Arash moved closer to Damian and rested a hand on his shoulder. 'All this – from Darius to Tent City – it's what we were . . . it's what we are.' He shrugged. 'It's Persia and it's Iran.

If the Shah goes, we'll have to work out what comes next. I can't help to do that if I leave, can I?'

Damian looked away.

Arash stroked Damian's neck and smiled at me. 'This corner feels a bit too much like Iran. Let's make our way back.'

The bird had lost interest and flapped off in the direction of Shiraz.

As we picked our way through the ruins of Xerxes' Palace, Reza and I fell behind Arash and Damian. He took my hand in his and kissed the palm. It was a long, slow kiss. Then he left me and walked on past the other two, heading for the Apadana portico. It was the last kiss. I knew it. I felt it.

Arash stopped and took a photo of Damian squinting into the sun, gazing up at a capital of addorsed griffins, their heads outlined like bookends against the backdrop of the sky – a sky of lapis lazuli, shading down through palest blues to smudgy white merging into the horizon.

'Persepolis blue,' Arash said. 'That's what we should call a sky like this.'

We stopped for lunch. Reza and I lay on a huge stone slab while Arash and Damian perched on the crumbling remains of two bell-shaped column bases. Arash passed chicken and cucumber salad to us. Reza lifted himself onto his elbow and helped himself to a chunk of flatbread.

I had this sensation of being outside myself, floating above the four of us, a buzzard's-eye view. Living figures on a moving frieze, surrounded by ancient columns with mythical capitals and princes frozen in stone. I thought: I want to keep this moment just like it is. I want to suspend it in my memory and remember this time and place and these men for the rest of my life.

When Reza had finished eating, he lay spread-eagled on the slab, looking up at the sky. I lay back on the slab too, and closed my eyes, the image of us all imprinted on my eyelids. I must have dozed off. When I opened my eyes again, Damian and

Arash were on the other side of the site and Reza was gone. I wandered across with Damian's camera, but he didn't want it. They weren't saying much, just leaning close into each other, Damian with his hand in the small of Arash's back, both gazing out over the plain of Marv Dasht. Way in the distance, blue smoke curled into a bluer sky.

I left them to themselves, and passed the time taking close-ups of the lion and bull panel on the Apadana. The sculptor had caught the split second after the lion had grabbed the bull's flank – the foot bones and the tendons in the front paws carved at full stretch, pulling back on the hooked-in claws, the tension in the jaws bearing down to anchor teeth into the bull's back-bone. And the bull whipping round as he felt the weight and the pain, his arched neck echoing the line of the lion's dipping head. I was transfixed by the violent beauty of it. Over 2,500 years ago, someone else must have stood here and probably felt the same.

'That should make a great photo.' I'd been concentrating so hard on the panel I hadn't heard Reza come up behind me. He fingered the stone ribbed fur of the lion's mane, murmuring something about lions and the power of kings. We drifted back to our ancient slab among the columns, but this time he didn't take my hand.

Arash poured the last of the wine into our plastic cups, and we all sat there, lost in our thoughts. A shrill screech in the distance cut into the quiet. I wondered if the buzzard had sneaked back and caught its prey among the ruins. Damian got up and started to stow away the remains of the food. Arash and I gathered up everything else and stuffed it into plastic bags. Reza packed his camera.

The heat had gone from the sun and I shivered. The Apadana columns cast long shadows, the griffins facing east and west, etched as blurry outlines in the dust of the palace floor.

*

Damian

Tabriz, 30 November

We got back late today. Reza stayed in Tehran, saying he'd be up in Tabriz towards the end of December. Not sure what went on between Anna and him, but she's been quiet ever since. Maybe Persepolis gave us both more than we bargained for, I'm still trying to process what Arash did, telling everyone that he was staying in Iran. I knew he hadn't changed his mind since the day he'd found the *papakh* hat – he'd tell me so whenever we had one of our I-could-get-you-out conversations, but to announce it like that in front of the others sounded so final. It was as if he felt he needed to do that to make it real, not just for me or them, perhaps, but for himself. I always knew he wouldn't leave. I guess my decision now is whether to stay with him or not. I'm not sure I can, or even if he'd want me to.

1 December

Julia rang early this morning to remind us that tomorrow was the first day of Muharram. Knew we'd been away. How did she find out? Said we should have told her, for the sake of security. I said I would, next time. She snorted.

'There's unlikely to be a next time, Damian, the way things are going. Anyway, usual instructions – it's Friday, so stay in.'

We lazed about, catching up with washing clothes after our trip and tidying the house. Arash cooked his caramelised rice again and found the last jar of sour cherries. We had a brief *do you remember when?* moment, of the day we first met Anna and she shared our meal with us, but it was all a little forced.

2 December

Julia rang just after 8 p.m. More trouble in Tehran, yesterday and today. Thousands marching in the streets to protest against the curfew. There'd been a small demonstration in Tabriz, too, but we'd stayed local, shopping in the *kucheh*, and had heard nothing.

We went up on the roof, to see if we could hear anything untoward coming across from the city centre, but it was quiet enough. The lights went off at 8.30 p.m., the official reason for the nightly electricity cuts being that it would save power, but the rumour was it was to clear the streets of troublemakers before curfew at 9 p.m. It had the opposite effect, of course, as most of the leaflets and slogans on walls appeared under cover of darkness in that last half-hour.

We were about to make our way down from the roof when we heard what sounded like a low murmur that grew steadily louder into a chant. It came drifting across from the city, echoing up the *kucheh*, first from the left, then from the right, point and counterpoint. Other voices joined in nearer to us on the other side of the archway near Ali the Baker's.

It was hypnotic. And it was unsettling. A three-beat rhythm to the chant. I looked across at Arash. The last time we'd heard chanting like that was back in February, when we were on the roof watching Tabriz go up in smoke.

'*Marg bar Shah! Marg bar Shah! Marg bar Shah!*'

'Death to the Shah!' said Anna, a crooked smile on her face. 'Back in London, they said you shouldn't take it literally, that it really means "the Shah must go". It's a question of semantics, that's what they said.'

I looked at Arash again. I knew we were both thinking the same thing. It had got way past a question of semantics.

We went downstairs, leaving the chants behind. They seemed to be getting even louder. We didn't say much to each other. Anna said goodnight and went straight to her room. We wandered up to bed shortly after.

I went downstairs about two in the morning to get a drink. I checked on Anna. There was a light on under her bedroom door, so I knocked softly, and she called, 'Come in.'

I poked my head round the door. 'You OK?'

'Not really.'

I went over and sat on the bed.

She sat up and rested against the pillow. 'That chanting. I can't get it out of my head.'

'It'll be OK. It's all part of Muharram. It's the chanting season. Once we get past Ashura on the eleventh, it'll all die down again.'

'"You will be safe in Kucheh Mulla." I remember Firuzeh saying that to me on my first night here,' she said. 'But up on the roof, I didn't feel safe at all.' She rested her hands on the coverlet and began to pick at the embroidered birds on the border. I noticed a few had already been unravelled.

'We're as safe here as anywhere,' I said. 'And if it gets worse, they'll get us out.'

It was the first time I'd said that out loud, that we would be 'got out'. I felt a brief flow of relief, because it was true. We were someone else's responsibility, and we would be looked after. Then the relief tightened again into a ball of panic in my chest, as I remembered that, of course, 'we' meant Anna and me, no one else. That wasn't a matter of semantics either.

3 December

A spot of light relief. The doorbell rang this morning and Arash went to answer it. He called me down after a few seconds or so. Two young girls, one about thirteen, the other a couple of years younger, were standing there, both wearing headscarves, the older one holding a large bowl of thick soup. For us, they said, for Muharram. They were from the neighbours down the *kucheh*. Anna coached them at the Council, but we'd never spoken to the girls, other than to say hello, when we'd seen them in the *kucheh* as they'd come home from school. I thanked them in Persian, which sent them off into giggles.

When we got back up the stairs, Arash burst out laughing.

'It's tradition, during Muharram, to give out charity food to poorer people,' he said.

Gheymeh soup, Arash called it, and it was delicious. Yellow split peas, small cubes of lamb, onion, dried lime and a few saffron potatoes on top. I'd always thought our neighbours probably considered us rich Westerners, flashing our cash around. Maybe they imagined us poor in spiritual wealth.

Arnie and Chris came round later. They are leaving tomorrow. Arnie's contract at the air base is over, and Chris is fed up of hanging around waiting to teach at the university with no students turning up. Besides which, they're getting twitchy about the rise in anti-American feeling here in Tabriz. Graffiti has appeared on the American Consulate wall – 'Yankee go home'. It's pretty tame, compared to some of the stuff appearing in Tehran, they say, but still. It keeps being wiped off, but reappears overnight.

And Arnie has had threatening phone calls. Possibly from someone on the base.

'Who knows? Who cares? Time to ship out,' he said, then changed the subject. 'What about you and Anna?'

I shrugged my shoulders. 'We've been told by our consulate in Tehran to stay put.'

'You don't want to be last off the roof, like in 'Nam, man,' said Arnie. He then helpfully described how we could make a booby trap – a bowl of petrol kept at the top of the stairs and a box of matches to hand: if anyone breaks in, chuck the petrol over them, followed by a match. 'That should slow the fuckers down.'

I nodded, as if I appreciated his thoughtfulness, but the idea of deliberately setting another human being on fire made me feel sick. I have a feeling Arnie might have learned the effectiveness of that trick first hand.

They brought us up to date with some of the other Caravanserai crowd. Bruce the Breton had left a couple of weeks ago, without telling anyone, then sent his Iranian girlfriend a letter from Paris. The New Zealander managed to get his Baha'i wife out and he's going next week, all being well. No one has seen the Italians from the oil refinery since July.

Chris left us a couple of packets of Oreos and some real American coffee.

Anna missed them because she'd gone round to the Council to see Julia. She'd asked her about leaving. 'See how it goes over Ashura,' Julia said. 'It might all calm down, once we get past that.'

Ashura

'*Ashura*' means the number ten in Arabic, so it's the tenth day of the month of Muharram, which is the first month in the Muslim calendar, one of the holiest days for Shi'a Muslims. This year, Muharram began on 2 December, so Ashura is on the eleventh. Always a day of heightened emotion and mourning, as it commemorates the death of the Shi'a third Imam, Hussein, the Prophet Muhammad's grandson, at the battle of Karbala in AD 680. He was killed by the Sunni Muslim Caliph, Yazid, whom Hussein had considered corrupt.

Arash had explained all that to me late last December, while we were standing on a rooftop, bundled up in our coats against the freezing weather, looking down on a wide backstreet just off the Tabriz city centre. I'd been in the country less than three months, and he'd taken me to a safe place to watch a procession of mourners down below. Some were shirtless, beating their bare chests with the palms of their hands, all chanting to the rhythm of the beat, in a state of trance-like fervour.

There are said to be flagellation rituals too, with finely wrought metal chains, fashioned like miniature cat-o'-nine-tails flailed across shoulders and backs. Arash said that this is not as common a practice as it once was, and our particular procession didn't have any of those, for which I was grateful. The idea of flagellation, whatever the religion, was anathema to me.

Hussein is seen as a Shi'a martyr, and his fate at the battle of Karbala as a symbol of good fighting evil, of a brave minority, the Shi'a Muslims, taking on an established Muslim elite, made up of Sunnis, with a corrupt leader. The Sunnis see the battle as a victory but the killing of Muhammad's grandson as a tragedy. The incident is viewed as the beginning of the establishment of the Shi'a Muslims as an alternative branch of Islam to the Sunnis.

The rumour is that this year Khomeini deliberately harnessed the symbolism of Ashura for his own political ends. He encouraged his supporters to see themselves in the role of 'the good' Shi'a Muslims fighting 'the evil' elite of the Shah and his government.

10 December – day before Ashura
An estimated half a million people marched along Shah Reza Avenue in Tehran, mainly peacefully, towards the Shahyad Tower, the huge marble monument to the Shah, holding up pictures of Khomeini and chanting: 'We want Islamic government under Khomeini.'

11 December – Ashura
A million people, it was estimated, almost a quarter of Tehran's total population, massed in the centre of the city. The chants were aggressive and anti-American, to say the least. 'We will kill Iran's dictator!' and 'Death to the American Establishment!'

'No question of semantics, there,' said Arash.

Looks like the rumour about Khomeini harnessing the symbolism of Ashura is true. He certainly seems to wield great power, considering he's so far away in France. There's also been big trouble in Isfahan. Possibly fifty dead.

And worst of all, for the Shah at least, his elite guards, his Immortals, stationed in a building near to the royal palace, were attacked by two of their own men, a corporal and a sergeant, who sprayed their officers with bullets, killing twelve and wounding many others.

There have also been reports of desertions from the army in other places. Even in Tabriz, it's rumoured that a number of soldiers put down their arms and waved to the crowds.

We knew nothing of any of these events on the tenth and eleventh: we'd stayed put since the eighth, under instructions from Julia. She relayed the details to us, as usual, by phoning us two days later.

13 December

Anna answered the phone. She looked apprehensive as she listened. When Julia had finished, we heard Anna say, keeping her voice carefully neutral, 'It doesn't look as though it's going to calm down, then, Julia, does it?'

Ashura was another turning point for the worse. Even the Council couldn't pretend any more that it was all going to be all right. They still weren't sure what to call it. An insurrection? A coup? They couldn't bring themselves to call it a revolution, or if they did, they were only saying it among themselves.

Whatever it was, Julia, super-cool as ever, went into emergency mode. There was to be a code, to let us know what we were to do. Code Level One was the highest: we should prepare for immediate evacuation. Level Two: evacuation highly probable at some point in the near future. We were already at Level Three: stay indoors and await further instructions. We could use the local *kucheh* shops today, to stock up for a week, then that was it. We should make sure we had a bag ready, so best pack it now, with just the essentials, hand luggage only.

If the need should arise, we would be taken into the Council building for protection, then flown to Tehran as soon as possible, and out of Iran to somewhere safe, via whatever flights were available. And, of course, the Council was only responsible for British citizens, no foreign nationals, whatever the relationship.

'It suddenly feels very real,' I said to Anna. 'We could be shipped out at half an hour's notice.'

The thought of that made me feel sick with worry. Not for me. For Arash.

*

Anna

14 December

Too Western and far too Queen Farah

Firuzeh and Farzad came round today. When I heard the bell I went down to let them in. Farzad was standing slightly behind Firuzeh but I hardly noticed him, I was so taken aback to see Firuzeh: she was clothed from top to toe in black. Black trousers, black knee-length coat, and a full black headscarf, her hair completely covered, except for a couple of strands peeking out, her neck hidden by the crossed scarf ends. She must have noticed my surprise, but didn't comment. I gestured for them to come in, but Farzad apologised, saying he was on duty at the hospital, he'd just come during his lunch break to escort Firuzeh to the house. He'd be back again about 3 p.m. His face was drained of colour and he had dark rings under his eyes. He smiled weakly, and with a slight nod, he was gone.

As soon as we got upstairs, Firuzeh took off the headscarf, folded it neatly, then stuffed it into her large shoulder bag and dropped it next to the desk chair.

'Thank goodness for that.' Her tone was one of exasperation. Then she took off the dark wool coat, laid it over the corner of the desk and sat down in the chair. I took the other chair so we were sitting sideways on to each other, her face close up. I could see how tired and drawn she looked. She was wearing a beautiful bronze silk shirt, which brought out the colour of her hair. It was now back to true black, striking and luxuriant as usual, but not a hint of henna. She saw me noticing that too.

'False colour no longer acceptable,' she said, sounding

contemptuous. 'Too Western, and far too Queen Farah, along with make-up and bright clothes, at least while you're outside.' She sighed. 'The Islamist militants in the demos up in Tehran are shouting "Cover your hair or get your head whacked," at the women. And they are threatening to throw acid. It's only a matter of time before they start that in Tabriz.' She shrugged her shoulders. 'So, it's best to do what they say . . .' She paused. '. . . for the time being.'

'You mean wearing the hejab is no longer about defying the Shah's instructions not to wear it?' I said.

'A lot of women still say it is. But I think they're in for a shock if the Shah goes, and the militant Islamists are still around. They're going to find it a whole lot more difficult to take the headscarf off than they did to put it on. And who knows? It might not stop at the headscarf, it could be the whole chador they're going to be intimidated into wearing. And it won't stop there. All the forward-looking changes made for women, under the Shah, that's what the Islamist militants will go after next.' She shook her head in despair.

'Not all the Islamists are militants and reactionaries, though, surely?'

'Maybe not all, but the militants are the ones pushing themselves and their ideas forward.'

'Perhaps they won't last long, once things have calmed down.' It sounded utterly weak and unconvincing, and I must have looked so uncomfortable saying it, because Firuzeh burst out laughing. But it was tight and brittle, not her usual warm laugh at all.

'Dear Anna,' she said, 'for ever trying to see the other side, just like you were in Oxford when Farzad and I would quarrel.' Suddenly her eyes filled with tears. 'But there isn't another side, not this time. They don't allow you to see any side but theirs.' She rested her head in her hands and began to cry softly.

'I'm sorry to see you so upset.' I wondered whether to pat her shoulder, but I didn't, it felt that the right thing to do was to stay put, and allow her a little space. I was aware of the *bokhari* sputtering away gently in the corner, as if in sympathy with her distress.

After a short while, she bent down and fished in her bag for her hanky. 'It's me who should be sorry. I didn't mean for you to see me like this.'

'Everything is such a mess,' I said. 'It must be so worrying for you and your family.'

There was a silence, and she gave me the look I've come to see as typically Iranian, where they're assessing how much they can trust you, how much they can say. Reza used it a lot with me.

'Yes,' she said, 'it is a mess. We are all tired.' She hesitated again, then said, 'We have decided to take a short trip away. Myself and my cousin.'

'That's a good idea,' I said, non-committally, taking my cue from her direct look at me as she'd said it. 'And it will do Farzad good too. He looks as though he's been working too hard.'

There was another silence. 'I'm going with my other cousin, Shirin. Besides, Farzad says he's too busy and can't find the time to leave the hospital. Shirin has a special visa to leave because she needs urgent medical treatment in California. And I can accompany her. We have relatives who moved there last year, so we will be staying with them.'

I nodded. 'That sounds good. When are you thinking of leaving?'

'Next week, if all goes well. My father knows someone in the visa section and it has all been fixed for us. We have tickets for a flight. They are like gold, as there are so many Americans leaving the country, but my father was willing to pay whatever the going rate was to get us out – I mean to make sure that we could go.'

I nodded to show I'd understood. Bribes for visas, and money out to relatives already at the other end were becoming the usual additional costs to be factored into 'short trips away'.

'Let's have some tea,' I said. 'Come into the kitchen and talk to me while I make it.'

While I was getting stuff out of the cupboards, I told her about the young girls in the *kucheh* who had come round at the beginning of Ashura with the big bowl of *gheymeh* for us, their less fortunate neighbours. She laughed, a genuine open laugh, like the old Firuzeh, and it was good to see her face light up with that beautiful smile of hers, one more time.

We sat and drank the tea, and we shared the last of the Oreos Chris had left.

After she'd nibbled half of hers, she said, 'I really wanted to tell you about the house . . . the practicalities.' She paused, evidently deciding how to put what she was going to say next. 'Because the situation is a little unpredictable at the moment, I wondered if you know how long you will be staying here.'

'Not really. There's nothing from the Council about our leaving yet, although they're not as firm on that as they were a month ago. It's only a matter of time, I should think.'

She looked as though she was struggling to say something and I suddenly understood what the problem was.

'Don't worry about the rent.' I made it sound as though I'd just thought of mentioning it myself. 'The Council will honour any payments outstanding when we leave.'

She visibly relaxed. 'It was more just making sure that if and when you do go, you might be in a hurry, and I'd be really grateful if you could make sure that you lock up and leave the house keys on the hook on the inside of the *kucheh* door, please. You can push the *kucheh* door key back through the gap at the bottom.'

'Of course, no problem, thanks for reminding me,' I said.

Embarrassment about discussing money had been avoided.

The bell rang exactly on three, and we went out into the living area again. I held her bag as she put on her coat and wound the headscarf around her hair, then crossed the two ends at her neck, until she stood there, head to foot in black, again.

She looked at me looking at her. Then she deliberately pulled out a couple of strands of hair from under the headscarf so they rested on her forehead. 'It makes me feel better, having a bit of my hair exposed. It's one way of showing my opposition to being forced to cover it all,' she said, and there was real anger in her eyes.

We got to the top of the stairs, where she stopped and turned to me. 'Thank you, Anna, for taking us into your home, last year.' She hugged me. 'I'll never forget those summer evenings in your beautiful garden in Oxford.'

I hugged her back. 'And I'll never forget the day we saw the *Shahnameh* manuscript in the British Museum, and Farzad saying Ferdowsi's words were the leaves on the trees.' And it was my turn to choke up. 'You have my address,' I said. 'Keep in touch. Wherever you are.'

Farzad was waiting at the door, hands in pockets, stamping his feet to keep warm. There'd been a light fall of snow. I didn't know whether I'd see him again either – he would know Firuzeh had sorted out the rent, so there would be no real reason for him to come round again on his own. I held out my hand to him and was surprised how upset I felt about saying goodbye to him.

'Take care of yourself, Farzad. Don't get ill – Tabriz needs its good doctors.' He surprised me by clasping both his hands around mine. I thought how different it felt from the briefest of greetings he'd given me when he'd picked me up at the airport back in March. We said our goodbyes as though it wouldn't be long before we met up again, and then I saw them to the door in the wall, and watched them pick their way down the *kucheh*, Farzad, tall and already slightly stooped, and Firuzeh, a neat figure in black, stark against the snow. They reached the archway, and disappeared under it, merging into the shadows.

*

Damian

16 December

This last couple of days, we've slept in our sweats with our hoods up, and thick socks, because the house has gone cold. The paraffin man has either run out of fuel, or couldn't get through with his deliveries, or the strikes have meant there's none in circulation, at least not for the ordinary folk of Kucheh Mulla. So we've stayed in the house, or scuttled along the *kucheh* to see if any fuel has arrived. This morning, Ali the Vodka had some, and we paid three times the usual price for it, but were almost delirious with joy when we lit the *bokhari* again and sat round warming our hands on our tea glasses.

We have no idea what is going on in the city. Sometimes, we've heard shouting and chanting and the odd siren, but no one in the *kucheh* can tell us what's been happening. They are as fearful as we are. Today, Arash took a risk and went to the bazaar to see Ervand, and came back saying everything is normal, or what now passes for normal. The shops in the city are open, and people are walking about in the streets. That's the way it is. Things change in an instant from the surreal to the ordinary, only the ordinary doesn't feel ordinary any more: it feels like a temporary respite before the next big upheaval.

But through it all, the sun shines, the snow falls, the snow boys clear the rooftops as usual. The Tabrizi moon still comes out at night and edges everything with silver glitter.

18 December

Tanks rolled past from the barracks as usual at six. Half an hour later, they rolled back.

7 a.m. – phone call from Julia. Some of the soldiers had refused to obey orders to point the tanks at the people. They joined anti-Shah demonstrations in the city centre. On no

account were we to go out, not even into the *kucheh*. We were on alert Level Two until further notice. Evacuation to the Council highly probable.

After I'd told Arash what she'd said, he put his arm around my shoulders and pulled me close to him. 'You'll be OK, Damian, don't worry. It will all work out OK.'

You'll be OK. Not *we'll* be OK.

How can I leave him? I don't know how much more I can take.

*

20 December

Reza arrived. He looked as drawn and anxious as we did. 'Tehran was a nightmare,' was all he'd say to Arash. 'I'm glad I'm back here with you all.'

I'd never heard him sound vulnerable before. He went across to Anna and hugged her. It was the first time I'd seen her smile in days.

Later, he regained a little of his spirit. 'The Shah has retreated to his Niavaran palace with his Immortals, but it will take more than his personal guards to save him now. "The tortoise has put his head back in," they are saying on the streets.'

He slept on the living-area floor on the cushions, next to the *bokhari*. But he'd graduated to Anna's bedroom by the morning. I took her a cup of coffee and there he was. But he was still on the floor, on the cushions, not in her bed.

*

We've locked ourselves away. What else could we do? Julia has told us to do that anyway, but deep down, I think Anna and I feel the same. Helpless. Hopeless. Powerless. What's going on here isn't my fight. What the country has become isn't my worry. I can get out, walk away. But Arash is my worry. I'd stay to fight for him, to save him. But what can I do, if he doesn't want to be saved? How am I going to walk away from him?

Neither of us sleeps well any more.

We have taken to lying on our backs in bed, taking in the Tabrizi sky in all its moods.

I sometimes think of Berkeley, when we first got together, and the thrill of lying next to each other, skin to skin. But these nights, with our Berkeley sweats doubling up as pyjamas against the midwinter cold, there are two layers between us. Three, if you count the sadness.

*

22 December

It is Yalda tonight, the Winter Solstice, and we've decided to celebrate it. We didn't bother last year. Arash and Reza have gone shopping in the *kucheh* for special food, if it can be found. Anna and I have given the place a sprucing up. It will be our first and last Yalda in Iran, but we try not to think about that.

*

Arash started the celebrations by bringing in a bag of presents. 'For tonight at least, we can enjoy a pleasant moment in a truly awful month.' He set down the bag in the middle of us on the floor. We'd moved the cushions nearer to the *bokhari*.

'I thought I'd get Yalda, Christmas, your New Year and our next Nowruz over in one,' he said.

He passed Anna a gift wrapped in a square of amethyst silk. It was a small marquetry box, patterned in a green and gold traditional geometric Persian design.

'It's lovely,' she said, turning it round in her fingers.

'Open it,' Arash said. Inside, was a thin Armenian silver-work bracelet, and dangling from it, an exquisitely fashioned hoopoe, with its feathered crown in delicate filigree.

'I thought it might remind you of Iran and your father,' Arash said.

Reza's present looked chunky, wrapped in plain brown paper. An antique photo album, leather, creased and scarred. Arash said it had a history behind it, according to Ervand, who had got it from the antiquarian book dealer in the bazaar, as per Arash's instructions.

'I've put in some of the Persepolis photos – Ali got them developed double quick. They are only happy snaps,' Arash said, smiling at his brother. 'I leave the serious stuff up to you.'

They hugged each other.

And mine was book-shaped. Arash's own copy of Masani's translation of Din Attar's *Conference of the Birds*. Close up, the little hoopoe is charming, with her tiny individual wing feathers, her long hooked beak and her crown, this time all picked out in gold, set off by the green Morocco leather. He has written a quote from Hafez on the inside cover.

I read it and looked across at him, my heart tightening. He gave me a slight nod.

He went over to the cassette recorder and put on some music, then he and Reza brought in the Yalda food and Reza poured the wine. And the longest night began.

*

Kupfermühle, 18 March 1984
So I'm back where I started. Yalda 1978. The eve of the Winter Solstice. The week following Yalda has always been a bit of a blur.

I remember reading the note, *Back at 10. Lemons in fridge*, and feeling mildly annoyed with him. Why didn't he say where he was going? Why couldn't I go with him?

I wondered if he'd gone down to the bazaar to see Ervand. If so, why didn't he take me with him? I was the first up, and

I sat there, the mild annoyance slowly turning into anxiety. It was past midday. *Back at ten.* He'd been gone at least three hours.

Reza came through to make coffee for him and Anna. He stopped dead when he saw my face. I handed him the note.

'He'll have gone to the house, maybe. I'll go round and have a look. We'll pick up fresh bread on the way back.' He didn't seem too worried. He came back about half an hour later, looking a little shaken. 'He's not there. But there's a big demonstration in the city, usual thing, anti-Shah. Maybe he's with Ervand in the bazaar and is waiting for it to end.'

I remember Julia calling and telling us about the demonstration and to stay indoors.

I remember Reza saying he'd go and stay at the house, in case the crowds settled down. Then he could check with Ervand, and wait in case Arash got back to his house.

I remember him coming back alone at around six, his face that peculiar blanched olive colour I'd last seen on Arash back in Berkeley when he'd got the bad news about Mirza.

I was all for going out on my own to look for him, but Reza and Anna said it was too risky in the dark. 'We don't want the two of you getting trapped somewhere in town, and having to wait until it's clear before you can make your way home. That's what will have happened to Arash,' Anna said.

I remember the three of us sitting up all night, drinking the last of the American coffee.

In the morning, at first light, Reza went round to the house again, then on to the bazaar and came back. Ervand hadn't seen Arash since he'd called in last week to pick up the photo album. He would put the word out among his relatives in the bazaar and around the city centre. Don't worry, they'd find him.

*

I couldn't stand it: I had to get out and look for him. I didn't care if there were more demonstrators again that day and they got hold of me. I had to do something.

It was like the fucking Via Dolorosa. I had this idea that Arash had got it into his head once again to check on the books. As far as I knew, he'd not done that since mid-September, but maybe he'd got the urge again, with all the fresh unrest. I took a taxi to the university gate, which is always closed, told the driver to wait, and walked round the outside of the campus until I was level with the library in the grounds, but it was dark and locked up.

I got the taxi driver to drop me off at the bazaar, where I saw Ervand, but he hadn't any news since yesterday. His face was impassive, but there was anxiety in his eyes too.

I walked to Arash's house. Reza was there and invited me in for a hot drink, but I said no, I'd keep moving. I made my way to the American Consulate. There was a new guy on the front desk. They used to have Iranian civilian assistants on duty there, way back before the American, but this guy had a military air about him. They must have increased security since the heightened demonstrations all over the country. He was busy sorting documents into two boxes, one labelled 'incinerator'. He was polite but cool. I played the Irish card, told him my mother was from Galway. It gained me a smile, but little else.

He was tall and thin with sad eyes. I told him Arash had once worked at the consulate and now he was the university librarian, but he'd not come home for a couple of days. Did they know anything, by any chance?

He didn't stop what he was doing but gave me a patient look. People were disappearing all the time, he said. Didn't matter what side you were on. The Shah's people were getting out while they could. The Islamists, the Marxists and God knew what other rival factions were already out of control and starting to settle old scores among themselves before one of them took over.

He isn't on any side, I said. He never takes sides. The man stopped sorting the papers for a moment and looked at me with those sad eyes. *Well now, sir, that's the most dangerous place to be. Who's going to protect him, then?* And he went back to filling the boxes.

I didn't say much to Anna when I got back. Didn't tell her about the guy at the American Consulate. Just said there was no news. We sat in the kitchen, it had become our bolthole. We didn't use the floor cushions any more, there was no point trying to relax.

Anna fidgeted away, keeping busy. I ran my finger along the gold outline of the hoopoe in the green leather of the Din Attar, and tried to read the poem, but I kept going back to what Arash had written in the front:

> *The long-drawn tyranny of grief shall pass,*
> *Parting shall end in meeting . . .*
> *Hafez*

Did he know he was going to have to leave me? Or was the Hafez quote because he thought it inevitable that I would have to leave him, and he was trying to tell me it would be OK, that we'd be together at some point? I clung to what I thought was the sense of that last line: in order to meet someone again, you have to part first.

*

There is one last entry from Anna's memoir I need to slot in here. I was so wrapped up in my own misery, I didn't give her a thought over those last days in Kucheh Mulla. Reading what she's written makes me feel sad about that.

*

Anna

27 December

Silk Thread

It's been four days now since Arash disappeared. Damian's been out looking for him, even after curfew, but he hasn't turned up at the university library, hasn't been to the American Consulate, hasn't been home to his own place. Reza is staying there on the off-chance he'll turn up there, and also because I've told him I need to keep a distance between us. I'll be leaving, he'll be staying. Persepolis was our end point. It was perfect. I don't want to spoil it.

Damian came back late tonight, grey-faced. We sat up in the kitchen till two, not saying much. No point going to bed, we wouldn't sleep. I started to sort out the cupboards. We needed to leave the house clean and neat for Firuzeh's family.

I started on the fridge. There wasn't much in it, we've been living out of tins these past few days, or on fresh yoghurt when either of us risked going out into the *kucheh* to buy it. At the back, I found a saucer of sliced lemons, the flesh dry and opaque, the rind brown and beginning to curl. They must be the ones Arash left ready the morning after Yalda. I felt a sudden lurch of pain in my chest. I put the lemons into the bin. Didn't show them to Damian.

He spent the time working through the Din Attar translation Arash gave him on the eve of Yalda. He kept stopping at certain pages, smoothing them with the tips of his fingers, then flicking back to the first page where the inscription is. I wanted to reach across to him, to say something comforting, but I knew it wouldn't do any good. After I'd put everything away, I got things out again to make tea. We drank it in silence, said goodnight to each other and wandered off to our rooms.

The hoopoe on the border of the coverlet has started to unravel. I've been picking at it.

The length of loose silk thread has got longer, leaving a trail of tiny holes in the cloth.

One more pull and it will lose the rest of its crown.

*

Damian

Kupfermühle, 19 March

Arash and the scent of lemons on his hands in the morning. The memory ambushes my senses sometimes. It is always short and razor sharp: the zing of the lemons mingling with the softness of his touch on my cheek. It usually cuts in when I've just woken up, thick-headed from drink or sleeplessness or tormented dreaming. I lie there, in some empty space, in some empty room, wherever that happens to be, and the realisation is as devastating as it was the first time it came to me: Arash is not with me and will never be with me again.

The next day, 28 December, I was planning to go out again, but the Code Level One came through from Julia. All the British had to be in one place, in case we had to move fast. It was too dangerous for us to make our own way to the Council: a car would pick us up at the end of the *kucheh*, said Julia. *You need to take precautions.*

I remember a small smile from Anna when I passed this on.

We'd already packed. Anna folded the length of blue silk she'd bought all that time ago in the bazaar, and tucked it down the side of her bag, together with her copy of the *Shanameh*. I packed Arash's *Rumi and the Dervish* translation, my Arberry collection of Rumi, Din Attar's *Conference of the Birds*, my diary jottings, and not much else.

I remember Anna standing outside the *Kucheh* house door, and pulling the parka hood up over her head as far as it would go until it flopped onto her forehead. Then she wrapped the scarf round her face and we set off down Kucheh Mulla for the last time, picking our way through the snow. Our footsteps squelched as we walked through the slush under the archway. Ali the Baker had his shutters down. No bread today. Is not good. The Council car was waiting at the end of the *kucheh*. Neither of us looked back.

The first flight Julia could get for us wasn't until 3 January. She'd done well to get that – we'd heard it was chaos at the airport, Americans leaving in droves, with their pets. Cats in baskets, rabbits in makeshift hutches. Iranians were also trying to get out. Sometimes it was a case of splitting the family, mother and one child or possibly two, father with the rest, on separate flights. Heartbreaking. They were often treated roughly by the airport staff, I noticed, when we eventually got there, I guess for deserting the sinking ship. Or maybe it was just envy because they had the money and the contacts to get out. I'm sure there were millions who would have liked to do the same but were trapped because they didn't have the wherewithal for bribes to ensure seats at already inflated ticket prices.

We had five full days in the Council building and weren't allowed to leave the grounds. Reza rang us every day and somehow got through on Julia's private line. No luck with any information about Arash. He had just vanished. On the third day, New Year's Eve, Reza came to the main gates. There was a guard on duty, and after mentioning Julia's name, he was allowed in after the man had phoned through and checked with her. She went down to show him into the Council building, through the kitchens. Strictly against the rules, but whatever he'd said to her during the daily phone calls, it had worked: she'd taken a shine to him. We met up with him in a small office next to hers.

He said he'd keep looking for Arash, but thought he'd be better off in Tehran. He had all sorts of contacts there, journalists, people in government, who might be able to help him with official information, or might have more helpful contacts here in Tabriz. He wanted to speak to Anna alone so I left them to it. She went back to her room in tears. Later she told me she thought she'd never see him again. He'd given her the photo album Arash had given him, thought it would be safer if she took it. 'It's so precious to me,' he'd said. 'Keep it safe for me in Oxford. I'll come and collect it from you one day. I'll bring Arash with me.'

*

I remember having trouble sleeping while I was in the Council building. I would catnap during the day, then jolt awake again. Then I didn't sleep at all at night. I took to going up on the roof to watch the sunrise. It was always freezing, but I wanted the sharpness of the cold numbing my face.

I remember looking over the stone balustrade and seeing a tank parked outside the gate. A British Chieftain. If I looked to my right, I could see across the roofs to the Armenian quarter. The house on Kucheh Mulla was hidden near there somewhere, through the archway. Our battered caravanserai. Somewhere to rest up, Arash said, while we worked out what happened next. Empty now, save for the odd ghost or two.

I remember standing there and realising it was New Year's Day, 1979. The date and what it represented meant nothing to me. It was shaping up to be a cruelly beautiful morning. The snow clouds had gone. The sun was up. Pale gold through Persepolis blue.

I remember going onto the roof the next morning, to find a startled army corporal manning a machine gun facing down the avenue leading to the Council gates. I gave him my cup of tea and went back down to my room. The next day, we were on the plane out.

I don't want to remember any more. I need to sleep.

*

20 March

I was woken up mid-morning by hammering on the back door. I'd finished off a bottle of schnapps by teatime yesterday so the banging only just penetrated through the fog. I ignored it at first, but it kept on, so I hauled myself up, pulled on my jeans and T-shirt and struggled downstairs. I opened the door and a look of relief passed across Frau Jensen's face, quickly followed by a frown of concern as she saw the state I was in. I could sense it was all she could do to stop herself stepping forward to give me a big hug.

'You are OK? I came twice this morning but the curtains were drawn. I thought you might be ill.'

'No,' I said. 'A little too much schnapps.'

She nodded. 'I was feeling a bit low. I was just up at the lake. The Whoopers have gone. I know it's the right time for them to leave, but it made me sad. I thought you might cheer me up and come round for coffee, later.' She smiled at me, her eyebrows raised, all innocence.

The problem is, she doesn't do innocence very well. I knew she was feeding me a line. If there is anyone who is unsentimental about nature and her beloved swans, it's Frau Jensen. Last year, she said she was always pleased to see them go: it was good to think of them going home and starting their cycle all over again. It was the way of things.

But I went along with it. 'Glad to. Can't have you feeling down. Maybe around four? That would give me time to clean up. And I need a shower and a shave.' She nodded, as if to say *You certainly do*. It was kind of her to worry about me, but not want me to know it. I'll miss her when I move on.

I'd finished writing yesterday by lunchtime and was paralytic by 6 p.m. I couldn't write any more. The pain of remembering those last few days in Iran was physical, and seemed as strong as it had been that New Year's Day on the Council roof.

The idea of leaving Tabriz, not knowing what had happened to Arash, had left me in a blind panic. I didn't think I could do it, and the day before we were due to go, I seriously considered escaping from the Council and taking my chances. I'd live wild in the *kucheh*s, or throw myself on Ervand's mercy, and hide out in the bazaar, even team up with Reza in Tehran. If I didn't last long, so what? But Anna pulled me through. Gently but firmly pointed out that I could probably do more when I got home to start enquiries about Arash, and that there would be Iranians already over in the UK with good contacts I could use. It would be too chaotic here to do anything. So I gave up the idea of going rogue.

Julia got us out. One thing I came to admire about her, she was good in a crisis. Her three years in Tehran paid off. She knew enough Iranians in influential positions in various airlines, who were still there, parents of children who had wanted to study overseas. Way back, she'd organised extra English tuition for them and they had passed the external English exams run by the Council, which were essential to gain study places over-seas. So she called in a few favours, and eventually got us tickets out to Istanbul on a Swissair flight. From there we waited a day, then flew on to London.

I went back to Oxford with Anna and stayed with her for a few days, just to get my head into some sort of shape. I told my parents a little white lie, that I needed to debrief my professor at Oxford about my work in Tabriz, and that I'd be up to see them as soon as possible. They were just relieved to know I was safe.

We got back to the worst winter for years, and found the country staggering through the political upheavals of the famous Winter of Discontent. There was a lorry drivers' strike on in full flow, so petrol was scarce. None of it touched me. Anna reckoned we were so used to political mayhem, this little lot seemed like chicken feed. I went home to Manchester to see my parents, then escaped as soon as I decently could and came back to Oxford the second week in January to stay with Anna.

Wadham College got the Iranian papers, often a couple of days late, but that was better than Tabriz sometimes. I'd often think of Reza in the early days, bringing the *Kayhan* and the *Kayhan International*, the good old *KH*, and the Western papers when he could, to keep us up to date.

The Shah left Iran on 16 January 1979. It was rumoured he was desperately ill with cancer. Wadham had the *Kayhan* news-paper two days later. The front page headline was spectacular. It was written in bold Persian letters, in a massive 84-point font. It looked like a miniature work of art. The message was simple and devastating:

Shah Raft! – 'The Shah Has Left!'

One of the Wadham Iranian postgrads pointed out the subtle insult in the headline by the choice of the verb form 'to leave'. In the past, journalists would be obliged to use the plural form of the verb with a singular noun, when writing about the Shah, as it suggests utmost respect. But this time, they chose the singular form of the verb to go with the singular form of the noun 'shah'. Suddenly he was anybody. The ultimate insult to the Shahanshah.

'I think that means they are pretty certain he's not coming back,' said the postgrad.

*

Anna and I huddled together, throughout the rest of January, in mutual misery. Then she received an invitation to visit from her distant relatives in America and decided to take them up on it. I could stay and look after her house.

I took to wandering into Wadham. Besides the newspapers, the Iranian students there also got snippets of news from various sources about what was happening at home. I was obsessive by day, finding out everything I could lay my hands on about the situation in Iran, then drinking myself stupid every night. I made contact with the Iranian community in London, but there were so many conflicting stories about what was happening that they were no better off than I was for reliable information. The only thing that was certain was that it was chaotic. And out of chaos came more chaos. And worse.

*

Who could have known Iran would end up like it has? The first three months of 1979 were a sign of things to come: it deteriorated very quickly indeed over the next two years, and now it's beyond belief.

1 **February 1979: Ayatollah Khomeini returns to Iran.** An American journalist on his plane back from France asks him: 'What do you feel in returning to Iran?'
Khomeini answers: 'I feel nothing.'

14 **February 1979: executions.** On the rooftop of a girls' school in Tehran, four of the Shah's top generals are executed by firing squad. Among them is General Nasiri, head of SAVAK. Nasiri, who answered directly to the Shah. Nasiri, the top man. And only two men down from him in the SAVAK hierarchy is the stuff of my nightmares: Dr Azudi.

8–11 **March 1979: women's rights.** Women in their thousands demonstrate, demanding the right to work and to have the choice not to wear the hejab. The demonstrators are attacked and assaulted by men wielding clubs and knives. At first, women win the right not to have to wear the hejab to work, although they are 'advised' to do so. In the meantime, an ordinary headscarf for work was permissible. (But in the summer of 1980, the hejab becomes compulsory for women who work in government offices, and by 1983, it is compulsory in all public spaces.)

1 **April 1979:** Iran is officially declared an Islamic Republic.

4 **November 1979:** American hostages are taken at the American Embassy in Tehran. Said to be in retaliation for President

Carter allowing the Shah temporary entry into the USA for cancer surgery. The American from Tabriz is among the hostages. Iran accuses the American from Tabriz, among others, of being CIA, and describes the American Embassy as 'a nest of spies'.

8 May 1980: Farrokhroo Parsa, the first woman Minister of Education in the Shah's government, becomes the first woman to be executed by firing squad in the Islamic Republic.

Mahnaz Afkami, the first woman as Minister for Women's Affairs in the Shah's government is sentenced to death in absentia, on charges of 'corruption on earth' and 'warring with God'. She was at the United Nations in New York when she heard the news and has never gone back to Iran. Anna was back in Oxford then, in between taking a job in Italy, and was moved to tears by this news. She remembers Firuzeh being so proud of the two women, and mentioning their names during a spat with Farzad, in her kitchen.

27 July 1980: the Shah of Iran dies of cancer in Egypt. He and Queen Farah had spent the eighteen months since his exile wandering the world, from Egypt to Morocco to the Bahamas, then Mexico, and on to the USA for a short stay for the Shah's cancer surgery, then Panama and finally back to Egypt.

22 September 1980: Iraq bombs Iran, including Tabriz Air Base. The Iran-Iraq war begins. After some time, Iran introduces a special fighting strategy: new conscripts, some boys as young as thirteen, are sent in front of their own attacking troops towards their enemies, willing to die as martyrs for the Islamic Republic. They call them 'the human wave'.

I remember Ervand's lanky lad in the bazaar, and my heart sank as I realised he would be of conscript age when the war began. It has been waging for over three years now, with no end in sight.

20 January 1981: American hostages released. The Iranians still maintain that the American from Tabriz was CIA. He and the American government consistently deny this.

21 June 1981: Soltanpur executed by firing squad, ostensibly for the strange charge of a currency-exchange fraud. But he was also charged with sympathising with anti-regime guerrillas, and with 'waging war on God and the Prophet'. He'd been outspoken, as ever he was, but this time about the Islamic Republic.

Soltanpur, who'd electrified us at the Ten Nights at the Goethe, his voice ringing out loud and fierce: *On this shore of fear . . . I will not stay silent . . . I chose defiance.*

His execution sent me spiralling down. When I read of it, I thought of the prof at Berkeley and his Shamlu as *engagé* lecture. That was where it had all started with Arash. Shamlu and his cockroaches. Shamlu has also spoken again and, like Soltanpur, he has spoken about the Islamic Republic. He returned to Iran in 1979, ending his self-inflicted exile from the Shah's regime. But after witnessing the ways of the Islamic Republic, with its summary executions, public floggings and stonings, all in accordance with its interpretation of Islamic practice, Shamlu has now spoken though his poetry.

I can imagine the prof, giving his latest lecture at Berkeley, Arash sitting three rows ahead of me, the light playing on his blue-black hair. The prof chalks up the title:

'In This Blind Alley'. Turning to us he says: 'This poem is Shamlu's reflection on the policing and persecution of openly expressed human love.' Then he writes up the lines:

> *They smell your mouth*
> *lest you may have said: I love you . . .*
> *Strange times, my dear.*

Then he asks: 'Any ideas on who "they" might be?'

*

In the end, I couldn't stand it, this violent, vengeful new Iran, and the thought that Arash had vanished within it. It was all too much for me. I took off from Oxford and my daily obsessive visits to Wadham. I couldn't cope. I've spent the five years since I left Tabriz not coping.

And here I am.

I have a couple of items to deal with, before I can clear out the study and clear the memories out of sight, if not out of mind. I open the less bulky envelope of the two remaining ones from Anna's parcel. It has *Reza 1980 Paris postmark* scrawled on the front in her handwriting. It contains newspaper cuttings of photographs from various photo-journal magazines, all covering Iran in the last months of 1978, then into early 1979, when Khomeini came back. They are by various Iranian photographers who have since become famous for their work there. The cuttings are dated and referenced in Persian, in Reza's handwriting:

9 November 1978 *Stern* magazine. A picture of the Shah, head and shoulders, in full dress uniform, reminiscent of his 'Emperor of Oil' pose, but this time haggard and haunted, also disfigured by a graphic of a mighty jagged crack superimposed across his face, splitting him in two. *The Shah at the End* is the caption.

20 November 1978 *Time* magazine. The photo that went round the world, showing a crowd of young men on a Tehran street, burning the portrait of the Shah. The flames lick round his face. There is elation, a touch of madness and pure relief on the men's faces.

April 1979 *Photo* magazine. A grim scene, which makes me feel sick. The four generals, who were executed on the school roof, have been photographed in the morgue, a young man posing near them with a hefty semi-automatic weapon. The generals are all lying half out of the morgue cabinets, semi-naked, their skin discoloured, although this might just be due to the black-and-white grain of the photo. Their lower bodies are each covered with a small grubby towel. Nasiri, the SAVAK general, is on the bottom row. His chest hair is thick and dark.

I think again of Dr Azudi. Did he meet the same fate? I remember my last question to him: *What will you do, Dr A? There will come a time when one day, you will be stripped naked, maybe literally, maybe metaphorically. You will be standing there degraded and dehumanised, and it will slowly dawn on you that you are, in fact, no different from the prisoner you have been torturing. The same degradation and dehumanisation you inflicted on your victims, you inflicted on yourself by doing what you did.*

Is it at this point, Dr Azudi, that you realise there is no 'you' and 'them', that you share the state of being human, you share a common humanity? Only, you lost yours long ago.

I don't spend any more time with Dr Azudi. I move on to the last bulky package. It's Arash's photo album, his Yalda gift to Reza. There is a note in an envelope tucked behind the front cover, for me from Anna.

Damian, I thought you could look after this for me. I wouldn't like it to get damaged on my far eastern travels where things go mouldy so quickly, and I didn't want it to lie around the house or in storage. It feels right for it to be with you. We all loved Arash in our different ways, but you loved him as he needed to be loved.

All the photos of Persepolis are there. The rest of the album was full of nondescript shots of Tabriz, boring houses, flowers, etc. But tucked in behind them were some quite different photos which I found by accident, although Reza obviously wanted me to find them. They are intriguing photos, some indication of what he was up to, maybe when he wasn't with us in Tabriz. He'd developed them, to 'happy-snap' size,

*as he would say, and hidden them behind the real happy snaps
and the boring ones. So I inadvertently took them out of the
country for him in my luggage. It was as well I didn't know
I was smuggling photos: I'm sure my nerves would have given
me away. But it was so chaotic at the airport – do you
remember? The staff weren't interested in searching anyone's
luggage, they just wanted us all gone as quickly as possible,
and I was only too pleased to oblige them.*

*Keep the album safe, Damian. It's part of Arash. Part of
all our lives that last winter.*

The Persepolis snaps are first. There's me, staring up at the
griffins on the columns, and Reza flat out on his stone slab, like
some ritual sacrifice. I remember Arash taking those. The rest
are colour photos Reza must have taken and had developed while
he was in Tehran before coming up for Yalda. There's Arash,
almost nose to nose with an Assyrian, trying to note down the
details of his beard, and two of Anna, one of her smoothing her
hand over a Cappadocian on the Apadana frieze, the other of
her leaning in to photograph a detail of the lion and the bull, her
hair almost white-blond in the winter sun. And there's one we
had no idea he'd taken, a back shot of Arash and me, the two
of us looking out over the plain, my hand in the middle of Arash's
back, our profiles framed by an infinite sky of Persepolis blue.

Over the next pages, there's the smuggled series of shots Reza
must have taken, with headings of what they are scrawled on
the back. They are, grainy, moody, mostly black and white, all
of them capturing the essence of a moment in time. They aren't
dated, but are obviously from 1978 and the winter in Tabriz.

The runner. A boy standing on a roof, looking as though he's
howling at the moon.

Defiance. A young woman clothed head to foot in black, wearing
the full chador, stark in the midst of other young women,
brightly dressed, a determined expression on her face.

Graffiti. Whole sequences of photos of graffiti on walls. I recognise one wall as the American Consulate in Tabriz: 'Yankee Go Home', and 'Down with America', in English. Other graffiti in Persian script: 'Death to the Shah!' and 'Long live Khomeini!' daubed on the university wall near Arash's library office. Written versions of the chants drummed out in street demonstrations and from rooftops during curfew.

Leaflets. Photos of leaflets tucked under wipers on windscreens, pasted on telephone booths, buses, walls, windows, lamp posts, trees. Photos of tree trunks with traces of thick gum and the tattered remnants of leaflets, then the same tree with a fresh leaflet pasted over the same spot, presumably to show the tussle between those putting up the leaflets and those tearing them down. Leaflets flapping in shop doorways, blowing in the wind, screwed up in corners.

Walls as newspapers. A detailed sequence of photos of wall spaces, probably different university buildings, I can't tell which. Handwritten instructions of meetings, directions. Notes from one person to another, and replies, all with code names. A corner dedicated to pictures of students, mainly men but a few women too, who had disappeared, or rather, had been disappeared. Heartbreaking questions printed with such care: *have you seen my brother? my son? my daughter? my sister?* Posters of political prisoners surrounded by bloody handprints. I caught my breath seeing those.

Walls as galleries. Khomeini is everywhere. Spray-painted stencil images, emphasising those beetle-black eyebrows; portraits with his iconic frown and turban, staring out from the very fabric of the walls. Poster-sized pictures of hero dissidents – and among them is Golesorkhi, and I am back in Berkeley and Arash, distraught, as he explains 'the problem with rose'.

Stacks of pop-music cassette tapes in a music shop, and on a stall in the bazaar. I had to think for a moment about the significance of something so ordinary, then remembered how

Ervand had told Arash about Khomeini recording his speeches straight down the line from Paris to Tehran, and how the cassettes were sold in music shops and the bazaar, a Khomeini tape slipped in with an ordinary music purchase. I had a sudden memory of Reza saying: 'When they heard Khomeini's voice in the mosque, no matter how bad the recording, it must have felt like they were hearing straight from God's right-hand man. Or even God Himself.'
Street corners as conduits for news. Newspaper booths with copies of *Time* and *Newsweek* and their startling photos of Khomeini on the front covers.

So that was what Reza was doing with his photography. No sinister intention in reporting on SAVAK agents – at least, not in Iran. And no graphic photo-journalism of human suffering. Like he'd told Anna when he'd shown her the woman in black, he'd left the images of the violence of urban conflict to others – the visceral photography showing dead bodies of demonstrators on the streets, bodies in morgues, the injured, or the Shah supporters, men and women beaten up and left for dead, the burned bodies, the mourners prostrate over graves in the cemeteries, the mothers clutching photos of husbands, sons and daughters who had been disappeared. He obviously admired it – that was why he'd kept the cuttings – and I could imagine him being proud that Iranian photographers were up there with the best in the world.

But for him, it was the street itself that was important, the way the people used it as their weapon, their only weapon, perhaps. He began chronicling David against Goliath, an uneven contest, ordinary people set against a phenomenal military firepower in an urban conflict, and armed only with words, the street as the main battleground on which to use them.

He set about documenting how people got in touch and kept in touch with each other, how they spread the news, the information, the instructions for the revolution, through leaflets, banners, placards, slogans, posters, even the written versions of chants heard as the crowds marched. How people in the city utilised the main thing it had to offer as a weapon of communication: the street itself. The walls, trees, cars, buses, buildings, windows, scaffolding, lamp posts, street corners and alleyways.

The people's words written on the people's streets, chanted on their streets, and Khomeini's voice heard on cassette tapes distributed on their streets and over their rooftops – that was Reza's revolution.

I place Anna's memoir, her marquetry box and the envelopes with the Tabriz leaflets and the cuttings inside in an old day-rucksack of mine, but leave out the album. I put my own journal in there too, with Baraheni's *God's Shadow*. It still unnerves me. It did its job back in Berkeley, it changed my way of thinking, but I have no wish to be reminded of it. I take Gertrude Bell's *Hafiz* and the album upstairs and put them on top of the small bookcase next to the bed.

So, Anna has left her memories with me and is moving on. All the Kucheh Mulla Tabrizis have moved on. Firuzeh is still in touch with Anna. She has settled well in Los Angeles, and has set up an English translations bureau for the Iranian business community. She is enjoying the freedom, misses her family but has no intention of going back while the present regime is in power. Her uncle sold the house in Kucheh Mulla at a knock-down price, apparently: the situation was so volatile in Iran he wanted to be rid of it before it became a liability. Farzad has moved to Tehran and is training doctors in the treatment of trauma injuries. He's spent some time in field hospitals near the war fronts with Iraq, and has had his paper published in a respected medical journal in the US.

And Reza? I'm not sure where Reza is, although he's obviously been in touch now and then with Anna. He's sent her postcards over the past three years, and the envelopes she's passed on to me, but all with no full return address. His last known address is Toronto, but that was a year ago. He had wanted to stay in Iran to keep looking for Arash, but was warned to leave quickly, in the late autumn of 1980, just after the war with Iraq began. The warning came from a powerful friend, the one Reza had mentioned to me back in the Bear's Lair in Berkeley, the friend studying architecture in London who went with him to Paris to see the new Pompidou Centre. He was quietly climbing his way up the secular ladder of the Islamic Republic's government, and managed to sort out Reza's exit visa, for old times' sake.

He escaped overland, by bus to Istanbul from Tehran, and eventually caught a flight to Paris. His ultimate aim, apparently, was to get to Toronto, as there is a sizeable Iranian community there. He might have made contact with them when he flew there from seeing Arash and me in Berkeley. That whole trip might have been about setting up possible destination points as a refugee from Iran, for himself and Arash, if it were ever needed, as much as it was about sussing me out. You never knew with Reza.

Anna realised long ago he didn't want to keep in touch, at least not as a two-way process. I think he kept moving with no ties so he didn't have to think. Like me. Racked with guilt, probably. It takes one to know one. But the more I've thought about his street photos, the more I've remembered this complicated and conflicted man, and the fierce love he had for his brother, the more I think I might see him again. The photo album was the last precious gift he ever had from Arash. Surely he will be back for it when he feels he can face it. I find this notion strangely comforting. We both loved Arash. Could either of us have done more to help him? To force him to get out? To stop him disappearing? To stop him being disappeared?

Round and round we go.

*

I take a quick walk up to the lake to clear my head before I go round to Frau Jensen. She won't mind me being late: she'll be pleased she got me out of bed.

It feels like a different stretch of water. Tender green grasses along the margins, insects skimming over busy surfaces. You can hear the newness. The mallards are still there. A clutch of eggs will be hidden somewhere, the nest built from soft leaves and down plucked from the female's breast. The male usually leaves after the clutch has hatched. Off to find the other males, to moult and indulge himself with unattached females. None of the bonding for life that swans are known for.

I'm glad I didn't see the Whoopers go. I'm not good at saying goodbye at the best of times and this isn't the best of times. It's calming to see the lake. I doubt I'll come again. As I walk back towards the village, I think about the past three months and how I've been writing about the last winter in Tabriz. I've been overwhelmed by memories, but there is so much still missing, distorted, unexplainable. Over and over, I've asked myself the same questions I started with. Did anyone take Arash? Did he know them? Or did he walk out deliberately into the demonstration? Was that why he gave us all presents, to remember him by? It was all so planned, the present-giving. Or were they just his way of doing what he said he was doing, making Yalda special? And what about Reza? Taking photographs was risky, it could be misinterpreted – you could get arrested. Had he been spotted on the streets, so they actually meant to take Reza and got the wrong brother by mistake?

And, as always, the last thought that still keeps coming back to me, the one I know will haunt me for ever is: if they did take Arash deliberately, did they take him because of me?

Even if I could throw all that aside, which I can't, I'm left with a story that is being told thousands of times over. People are disappeared all over the world: it is the way of conflicts. Those left behind are forever tormented by their anxieties, their guilt, their what-ifs.

I'm luckier than some. This winter has been tough, tougher than I ever imagined, but at least I've been able to write down the story. I've been able to say to myself for the first time: *The time of the Winter Solstice, on 23 December 1978, Arash was disappeared.* And I've been able to set down some of what happened leading up to that.

I'm not sure what I've achieved by it all – it's too soon to tell. I've realised that you can't grieve for the disappeared like you can for those you are certain are dead. But you can learn to live with terrible irreplaceable loss. You have to learn to accept the not-knowing.

You have to learn to allow them to be dead. To allow them to let you go.

To allow them to *arise and soar, from the snares of the world set free.*

Hafez. It was always Hafez for us.

Author's Note

This novel is a work of fiction, set against the background of events from the summer of 1977, to January 1979, leading up to the Iranian revolution. The four main characters, Damian and Arash, and Anna and Reza, are affected by the atmosphere of censorship, repression and persecution of writers, poets, journalists, and by the activities of SAVAK, the state secret police.

I thought the reader might be interested in some of the specific sources which both inspired and informed the story. Two scholarly articles, by Professor Ahmed Karimi-Hakkak, provided key information: *Protest and Perish: A History of the Writers' Association of Iran,* Iranian Studies, Vol. 18 (1983); and *Poetry against Piety: The Literary Response to the Iranian Revolution,* World Literature Today, Vol. 60 (1986). A third, by Professor Leonardo Alishan, focuses on Ahmad Shamlu, one of Iranian's most revered contemporary poets who features prominently in the novel: *Ahmad Shamlu: The Rebel Poet in Search of an Audience,* Iranian Studies, Vol. 18 (1985). (Grateful thanks to Professor Ali Gheissari, University of San Diego, Editor in Chief, Iranian Studies, for permission to quote from the above article by the late Professor Alishan.)

Small Media, Big Revolution (1994), by Annabelle Sreberny-Mohammadi and Ali Mohammadi is a fascinating description of how 'small media', in the 1970s age of the Xerox machine and audio cassette tapes, came into its own in promoting the revolution on the streets and in the mosques.

Newspaper archives provided contemporaneous versions of events and included the Iranian papers: *Kayhan,* and *Kayhan*

International (English version), and *Ettela'at;* and Western newspapers and magazines: the *Guardian; Time;* the *New York Times,* and the *Washington Post* – particularly Bill Branigin's coverage of the 'Black Friday massacre' in Jaleh Square, September, 1978: *'Iranian Troops Fire on Crowds: Scores Killed,* September 9, 1978.

Interviews with Michael Metrinko, accessed online at the Foundation for Iranian Studies, Program of Oral History of Iran,1998-99, informed my characterisation of 'The American'.

Numerous other books provided insight into the period, including: Prof. Ali M Mansari: *Modern Iran Since 1921* (2003); Andrew Scott Cooper: *The Fall of Heaven* (2016), especially useful for the references to the journalistic coverage of events; *Shah of Shahs,* by Ryszard Kapuściński (1985); Michael Axelworthy, *Revolutionary Iran:* (2013); *Persepolis,* by Marjane Satrapi (2006); and *Persian Painting* by Sheila R. Canby (1993), which features an illustration of *Rostam and the Lion,* the *Shanameh* miniature in the British Museum, referenced in the novel. *Germany Calling* by Mary Kenny (2003) and *HAW-HAW* by Nigel Farndale (2005) provided background information on William Joyce.

A note on the poetry translations. Where possible, I've tried to use English translations produced before 1979, of Persian poets, such as those of Nicholson, and Arberry, for Rumi; Masani for Din Attar; Gertrude Bell for Hafez; Levy for Ferdowsi's *Shahnameh*. There are a few exceptions to this – many thanks to Dick Davis for allowing me to use his 2012 translation of Hafez's description: 'cypress slim', as the inspiration for Arash's version of 'cypress slender'. I also used Coleman Bank's 1995 translation of *Where are we?* (Rumi).

Please see *Permissions* for more details on poetry references.

Shamlu's poems: *Song of the Man of Light Who Walked Into Shadow* (1970), and *Song of the Greatest Wish* (1977), are quoted in Professor Alishan's article above. The poem: *In this Blind Alley* (1979), is quoted in Professor Karimi-Hakkak's article,

Poetry against Piety. C.M. Bowra, *Poetry and Politics* 1966 was also useful for its discussion on the nature of political poetry.

Iran produced some wonderful photographers and photojournalists who covered aspects of the revolution. In particular, there was: Abbas (Abbas Attar); Reza Deghati; Kaveh Golestan and his wife Hengameh Golestan (who took remarkable photos in March 1979, of women on the streets during the demonstrations against the compulsory wearing of the hejab); and the lesser known Akbar Nazemi who took striking images of revolution on the streets. David Burnett's photographic representation of aspects of the revolution in its earliest days, in his book: *44 Days: Iran and the Remaking of the World,* was a major inspiration for my writing.

I also drew on my own patchy notes, photographs and fragmented memories of my time during that last winter in Tabriz in 1978.

Finally, Mark Brazil's enchanting and informative book: *The Whooper Swan* (2003), was my 'go to' book to help soothe myself after writing some of the more harrowing passages in the novel.

Poetry Permissions and Sources

Persian poetry: **Reza Baraheni:** *God's Shadow: Prison Poems,* 1976, by kind permission of the Indiana University Press. **Din Attar:** *Conference of the Birds,* Masani, R.P. (trans), Oxford University Press, 1924. **Ferdowsi:** *Shanameh: The Persian Book of Kings,* p.132, Dick Davis, (trans), 2016, by kind permission of Mage Publishers. *Shah-nama: The Epic of the Kings,* Reuben Levy, (trans), 1967, by kind permission of Taylor and Francis (Books) Ltd.

Hafez: Gertrude Bell, (trans), *The Divan of Hafiz,* ghazal nos. 31 and 43, Heinemann, 1928 edition; Dick Davis, (trans), *Faces of Love: Hafez and the Poets of Shiraz,* 2012, by kind permission of Mage Publishers. **Rumi:** A.J. Arberry, (trans), *Mystical Poems of Rumi, First Selection, Poems 1-200,* no.24, University of Chicago Press, 1968. Coleman Barks, (trans) *Rumi, Selected Poems,* 'Where are we?', pp.15-16, by kind permission of Penguin Books, 1999. **Sa'di:** The quote on Yalda on p.4 is from the *Bustan of Sa'di.* There are several versions in English of this particular quotation. The one chosen here was referred to in the Iran Heritage Foundation's Annual Report for 2015. G.M. Wickens's English translation of the *Bustan* is the standard translation: *Morals Pointed and Tales Adorned,* Toronto, 1974.

Shamlu: *Song of the Man of Light Who Walked Into Shadow,* (from *Blossoming in the Mist,* 1970), and *Song of the Greatest Wish,* (from *Dagger in the Dish,* 1977), are quoted in *Ahmad Shamlu, The Rebel in Search of an Audience,* Leonardo Alishan, pp.375-422, Iranian Studies, 1985. *In This Blind Alley* (1979), is quoted in *Poetry against Piety: The Literary Response to the*

Iranian Revolution, Ahmad Karimi-Hakkak, World Literature Today, pp. 251-256, 1986.

Soltanpur: *On this Shore of Fear* was first publically performed at the Ten Nights *(Dah Shab)* Poetry Readings at the Goethe Institute, Tehran, in October 1977.

Non Persian Poetry: Uwe Kolbe: *Wir Leben mit Rissen,* ('We Live with Cracks'), from *Hineingeboren,* ('Born into it'), Aufbau-Verlag Berlin und Weimar, 1980. **Walt Whitman,** *I Sing the Body Electric* (from *Leaves of Grass,* 1855).

Acknowledgements

I owe a great deal to the late Professor Ciaran Carson, at the Seamus Heaney Centre for Poetry, Queen's Belfast, who first encouraged me to write about Tabriz, the revolution, and Iranian poets. He is much missed. Professor Ian Sansom, my mentor at the Centre, also read early drafts of what was once just an idea for a novel, and supported me throughout the early writing. Sinead Morrissey, Malachi O'Docherty, Tim Loane, Chris Agee, all lent their support in various ways on earlier drafts. Special thanks to Maureen Boyle, Jean Bleakney and Damian Smyth, who kept me going with sympathetic e-mails, when I was almost derailed after a bad accident. Damian was also key in supporting my work in a professional capacity, and spent some of his valuable time on the manuscript.

I was greatly helped in the research for the novel by personal communication with the following: the poets, Dick Davis, and Uwe Kolbe; photojournalist/journalist David Burnett; Bill Branigin of the *Washington Post;* Geoff Hill, of Belfast, for sharing his impressions of Tabriz and life there under the Islamic Republic; Tom Dalzell (tom@quirkyberkeley.com) for his personal knowledge of the Berkeley campus in the 1970s; and David Brazil, for his permission to quote directly from his book on whooper swans.

Personal communication also helped with the academic research into the work of contemporary Iranian poets. Dominic Parviz Brookshaw, of Wadham College Oxford, and Professor Ali Gheissari, University of San Diego, both made me aware of contemporaneous articles on poets writing in the 1960s-80s pre- and post-revolution era.

Bill Hamilton my agent, has always been there when needed, with advice and encouragement. Francine Toon, my editor at Hodder and Stoughton, has been hugely personally supportive throughout a tricky eighteen months, and professionally astute with her advice on the final work on the novel.

My family, including David, my brother, and my in laws, Liz and Dougie, in Belfast, and more recently, Maggie in California, have helped me to be mindful of what really matters during this unsettling year.

My husband, Ken, has always been there, with love and patience. Strange times, my dear, but we got through in the end!

I am also grateful for the financial assistance I received during the writing of the novel from the Arts Council, Northern Ireland, for an Artists' Career Enhancement Scheme Award, and from the Society of Authors, for an Authors' Foundation Award.